Includes Bonus Story of
Along Unfamiliar Paths
by Amy Rognlie

Logan's Lady

TRACIE
PETERSON

BARBOUR BOOKS
An Imprint of Barbour Publishing, Inc.

Logan's Lady ©1997 by Barbour Publishing, Inc.
Along Unfamiliar Paths ©1998 by Barbour Publishing, Inc.

Print ISBN 978-1-63409-653-9

eBook Editions:
Adobe Digital Edition (.epub) 978-1-60742-574-8
Kindle and MobiPocket Edition (.prc) 978-1-60742-575-5

All scripture quotations are taken from the King James Version of
the Bible.

This book is a work of fiction. Names, characters, places, and
incidents are either products of the author's imagination or used
fictitiously. Any similarity to actual people, organizations, and/or
events is purely coincidental.

Published by Barbour Books, an imprint of Barbour Publishing, Inc.,
P.O. Box 719, Uhrichsville, OH 44683, www.barbourbooks.com

*Our mission is to publish and distribute inspirational products offering
exceptional value and biblical encouragement to the masses.*

ecpa Member of the
Evangelical Christian
Publishers Association

Printed in the United States of America.

Logan's Lady

Dedication

To Rebecca Germany, one of my favorite editors.
Your friendship means a great deal to me and I
thank God upon my every remembrance of you.

Chapter 1

A melia grimaced as she heard her father and Sir Jeffery Chamberlain break into yet another discussion on the implementation of fertilizer to boost agricultural yields. *It was this dreadful country that did it,* she thought. *America! A country filled with barbaric men, ill-mannered women, and positively rotten children.*

Shifting uncomfortably in the seat of their stage, Amelia wished fervently that if there were a God, He would reach down and smite the lot of them in order that she might be allowed to return home to England. But of course that wasn't going to happen because Amelia had firmly decided for herself that there was no God.

"I say, Chamberlain," her father stated with a marginal note of enthusiasm. "I believe we're slowing down."

"Yes, quite right," the younger man responded and peered out the window. "We've made an excellent way thanks to our time spent on the railroad. American railroads are quite the thing. Good money here, what?"

"Indeed, the stagecoaches are just as abominable as those back home, but I believe their railway system to be quite superior," came the reply and the conversation erupted into a spirited discussion of the American rail system. Amelia sighed, adjusted her lace collar and waited for the announcement that they had arrived in some small, forsaken Colorado town.

She hadn't wanted to come on this trip to America. America had been the furthest thing from her mind, in fact, but her father was insistent and clearly closed the matter to discussion. Amelia's sisters Penelope and Margaret were just as loath to travel, but they were quite interested in Sir Jeffery Chamberlain.

Amelia held a small wish that she could share their enthusiasm. After all, he was to become her husband. At least that was the plan as her father saw it, but Amelia had no intention of marrying the pompous man. Jeffery Chamberlain was a long-time crony of her father's. He wasted his days doing as little as possible, furthering his already-sound reputation of being a spoiled dandy. He had been knighted, but only because his mother held a tender place in the queen's heart. And he owned vast estates with wondrous woods that beckoned the visitor to take a turn about, but those were his only redeeming qualities as far as Amelia was concerned.

Her father viewed him in a different light, however. Sir Jeffery Chamberlain was rich and popular with Queen Victoria's court. He had a sound education and a quick wit that had managed to keep him out of trouble on more than one occasion, and he was worth an enormous sum of money, which not only could keep his own lands well-kept but also would surely flow over to his future father-in-law, Lord Reginald Amhurst, the sixth earl of Donneswick—should that need arise.

Staring hard at the man, Amelia noted all of his flaws. His nose was too long, his forehead too shiny. He had perfect white teeth, which seemed to be constantly bared for all the world behind unflattering smiles and his beady eyes were placed too close together. Added to this, the man was an unmitigated bore.

Amelia shook her head uncomfortably and tried, against the rocking and bouncing of the stage, to look at the magazine she'd bought in Cheyenne. Flipping through pages of ladies' fashions, Amelia tried to rationalize her thoughts. *I cannot blame Father for setting out to arrange a marriage. It is done all the time in my circle of friends. Why, I don't even remember the last time one of my companions managed to marry for love, and not because the union was of financial benefit to one family or the other.* Some of her friends had grown to genuinely love their intended mates. Others had not. Her dear friend and confidant, Sarah Greene, had managed to find herself engaged to a charming man of wit and gentlemanly breeding and had quickly lost her heart. But that was not to be the case for Amelia. She could not find it in her heart to love Sir Jeffery, as he insisted they call him, nor did she think love would grow there for this man.

Amidst a roar of *whoa's* and a cloud of dust, Amelia realized that they had come to a stop. Ignoring her father's window description of the town, Amelia tucked the magazine into her bag. Immediately Penelope and Margaret began fussing and going on about the wilds of America.

"I suppose we might very well be scalped by Indians," Penelope said with a fearful expression. She allowed Sir Jeffery to assist her from the stage before adding, "We're so very glad to have your company, Sir Jeffery." She oozed congeniality and interlaced her arm with his. At seventeen she was more than a little bit aware of the power a young woman's simpering could have over the male gender.

"It is my pleasure, Miss Penelope," he assured her.

Margaret, a year Penelope's junior, secured her place on the opposite arm of Sir Jeffery as soon as her father had helped her from the stage. "Yes, it would be quite frightful to have come all this way into the heart of the American wilderness with only Father and Mattersley to offer protection. Why, whatever would three women and two old men do should the heathens truly choose to attack us?" Mattersley, the other "old man" she referred to, was the earl's man-servant and constant companion.

Amelia watched all this through the open door of the stage. She rolled her eyes and sighed. *Indeed, what would Sir Jeffery, pompous dandy that he was, do in such a situation? Bore the poor Indians to death with questions of what fertilizer they were using on the Colorado plains?* She couldn't abide the simpering of her sisters and chose instead to remain in her seat on the stage until her father beckoned her forward.

"Amelia, allow me to help you down. Why, you've scarcely said two words since we left Cheyenne. You aren't ill, are you? Taken with vapors, what?"

Amelia's pale blue eyes met those of her father's. "No, Father, I'm not at all indisposed. I simply have had my mind consumed with a variety of subjects."

Sir Jeffery untangled himself from Amelia's sisters and came to offer his hand. "May I accompany you to the hotel, Lady Amhurst?" he questioned with a slight bow. Amelia noticed her father's frown as if he could read the curt reply she was thinking. Containing her thoughts with absolute ladylike control, she nodded. "Of course. Thank you," she murmured, putting her gloved fingers into Jeffery's palm.

"I have arranged for us to have rooms at a boardinghouse here in Greeley," the earl began. "It's a temperance colony so there will be no wine with dinner, nor any after-dinner brandy, I'm afraid." Amelia, knowing her father's distaste for alcohol, realized that he said the latter for Jeffery's sake.

"Ah, the barbarians." Jeffery sighed and Amelia knew he meant it. To Jeffery, any measure of discomfort represented a less-than-acceptable social standing. And for Jeffery to be without his brandy was definitely a discomfort.

For a reason beyond her understanding, Amelia was put out at Jeffery's attitude. Not because of the alcohol—although she herself couldn't abide the stuff—no, it was more than simple issues of food and drink. Jeffery's entire demeanor put her at odds. Maybe it was just that she wanted to conflict with his ideals. Maybe it was the fact that she was completely disgusted with his companionship and still hadn't been able to get it across to either her father or Jeffrey that she had no desire to marry.

Glancing upward, Amelia instantly felt the noon sun bear down on her. Grimacing, she opened her white parasol and lifted it overhead to ward off the harsh rays.

"Oh Father," Penelope began to whine, "it's ever so hot here. Must we stand about as though we were hired help?" She looked for all the world as though she might faint dead away at any moment.

They were all quite used to Penelope and Margaret's displays of weakness, and for several moments no one said anything. Finally the earl motioned for his loyal valet, Mattersley, and gave him several coins. "See if you can't arrange for our things to be brought up." The man, close in age to his employer, gave a regal bow and set out on his mission. "There," the earl said, turning to the party, "I'd say that settled itself rather nicely. Let's make our way up, what?"

"Indeed," Jeffrey answered as though his was the only opinion to be had. "This harsh American sun is quite hard on fair English skin." He said the words looking at Amelia, but she had the distinct impression they were given more in consideration of his own situation than of hers.

The dry, dusty streets of Greeley did nothing to encourage the entourage. The boardinghouse was a far cry from the regal estate they'd left behind in England It wasn't even as nice as the furnishings they'd acquired in New York City or Chicago. In fact, Amelia knew it was by far the worst accommodations they'd know yet, and her opinion of America slipped even lower. Why, even when they'd toured India, they'd resided on lovely estates.

From the moment they walked into the questionable place, arguments ensued and miseries were heightened. The owners of the atrocious little house actually expected Amelia and her sisters to share one bed. The very thought of it caused Penelope to cry and Margaret to fan herself feverishly as though she might actually faint from the very suggestion.

"I believe we'd arranged to have all five of your rooms," the earl protested, combating a roving horde of black flies.

"Kain't hep it a bit, mister," the slovenly dressed proprietor announced. "I hed a man come in last night what needed a place to stay."

"This is Reginald Amhurst, the sixth earl of Donneswick," Chamberlain interjected angrily. "Lord Amhurst to you."

The proprietor looked over the rim of his dirty spectacles. "Ferenors, eh? We gets 'em all kinds here. You sound to be them thar British gents. I guess the missus said you was comin'."

Amelia grew tired with the exchange and glanced around the room to where a crude painting hung at the base of the stairs. She studied it intently, wishing she could forget the heat. The picture fascinated her from afar, as it seemed to almost move with life. Stepping closer, Amelia found it half covered with pesky black flies.It was only then that she really noticed most everything suffered from such a fate.

"Excuse me," a stranger's voice sounded over her head. "This isn't an art gallery. Besides, I don't think old Farley's painting is all that interesting."

Amelia was so lost in thought that she hadn't realized she was blocking the stairway. She looked up with a surprised expression and found herself noticing the broad, muscular frame that accompanied the voice. The mustached mouth seemed to twitch a bit as though it might break into a laugh.

Without so much as a smile, Amelia backed away. "My pardon,

sir." Her voice was haughty and her look froze the man in his place. She still found it disconcerting to be openly addressed by men without a proper introduction. Childhood teachings were hard to lay aside, even for a holiday to America.

With a grin, he gave a broad sweep. "You are quite pardoned, ma'am."

Amelia raised her handkerchief and turned away to keep from muttering something most unladylike. *Rude. That's what all Americans are.*

"Hey thar, Logan," the boardinghouse proprietor called as the man passed to the front door.

"Afternoon, Ted."

Amelia tried to watch the scene without letting the man called Logan see she was at all interested in the conversation.

"Logan, didn't ya tell me you was gonna be leadin' a group of ferenors up the mountains?"

"I did."

"Well, I think this here party be yer folks."

Logan eyed the group suspiciously as though he'd just been told that they were responsible for having robbed the local bank.

"You're Earl Donneswick?" Logan questioned Amelia's father.

"I am, indeed," Lord Amhurst replied, before Jeffery could speak. Amelia turned to watch the introduction. "This is Sir Jeffery Chamberlain, my man Mattersley, and my daughters."

Logan let his gaze travel around the room to each of the women before settling on Amelia. He smiled slightly when his blatant stare caused her to blush, then turned his attention to the matter at hand.

"I'm Logan Reed, your guide to Estes Park."

"Mr. Reed, we are quite anxious to be started on our journey. Can you advise us as to when we might expect to begin? The heat is positively wilting our ladies." Jeffery commented before the earl could do the same.

Logan looked again at the women. "Are you proposing to take your womenfolk along?"

"Indeed we are," the earl replied.

Amelia watched as Logan cast a skeptical glace at her. "There are places where we'll scarcely have a trail to follow. Packing into the Rockies isn't a Sunday school picnic."

"My daughters have climbed in the Alps, my good man. I assure you they are quite up to the challenge."

Logan's smile broadened. "If you say so. I just wouldn't want the ladies to get hurt." His gaze returned to Amelia, who stuck her chin in the air defiantly and turned toward the fly-covered window.

"Lady Amhurst and her sisters are quite capable," Jeffery interjected irritably.

"Lady Amhurst? I thought you said your name was Donneswick."

The earl smiled tolerantly. "I am Reginald Amhurst, the sixth earl of Donneswick, I am called Lord Amhurst, but it is common when I travel abroad to have my title mistaken for my name. My daughters, of course, are called by the family name of Amhurst. A bit confusing for you Yanks, but nevertheless, easy enough to remember."

"With that matter resolved," Chamberlain stated in a cool, even voice, "when can we expect to begin? You surely can't expect us to remain in this poor excuse for a town for much longer."

"Whoa, now. Just hold on for a minute," Logan said raising his hand. Amelia glanced back over her shoulder, fascinated in spite of herself at the way Logan Reed seemed to naturally take charge. "We've got some ground rules to cover first and I don't think standing around the front door of Ted's is the place for it. Ted, can we use the dining room?"

"Sure enuf, Logan. Ya go right ahead." Ted seemed to be happy to rid himself of the commotion. "Ya want I should have the missus bring somethin' to drink?"

He addressed Logan, but it was Lord Amhurst who answered. "Yes, please have tea and cakes sent 'round."

Ted stared at the man for a moment, then turned to Logan. "It's okay, Ted. Why don't you bring whatever's at hand." This the man understood and nodded agreement before taking himself off to the kitchen.

The party stared collectively at Logan, barely tolerating his breach of etiquette, but Amelia was certain that for Mr. Logan Reed, breaching etiquette was probably a daily routine.

"Come on this way," Logan ordered and led the way without even waiting to hear an approval from the earl or Jeffrey. The entourage followed, murmuring among themselves as to the character and manners of the tall man.

"Everybody might as well sit down," Logan said, giving his well-worn hat a toss to the sideboard.

Amelia watched in complete amazement. At home, in England, her father would never have been addressed in such a manner. At home he commanded respect and held a position of complete authority. Here in America, however, he was just a man and it didn't matter in the least that he was titled.

While Amelia stood in motionless study, Logan pulled out a chair and offered it to her. Her blue eyes met the rich warmth of his green ones. She studied his face for a moment longer, noting the trimmed mustache and square, but newly shaven jaw.

"Thank you," she murmured and slipped into her chair without taking her gaze from his face.

"Now, we need to discuss this matter in some detail," Logan announced. He stood at the head of the table looking as though he were some famed orator about to impart great knowledge upon the masses.

"Mr. Reed," Amelia's father interrupted. "I have an understanding with the owner of several cabins in the Estes Park valley. He assured me that he would send a guide to bring our party to Estes. Furthermore, there is to be another family accompanying us: Lord and Lady Gambett and their two daughters."

Logan nodded. "I know about the Gambetts and was headed up to speak to them when you arrived. According to Ted, they're staying on the other end of town at Widow Compton's place. I suppose they're planning to bring their womenfolk along as well?"

"Indeed, they are. What, may I ask, is the difficulty here?"

Logan ran a hand through his brown hair and sighed. "The problem is this: I wasn't expecting to have to pack women into the mountains. No one mentioned women at all, in fact. I was told I'd be taking a hunting party to Estes. A hunting party seemed to lend itself to the idea of men."

Amelia suppressed a laugh and received the stunned glances of her traveling companions.

"You have something to say here, Miss. . ." Logan paused as if trying to remember which name she was to be addressed by.

"I am Lady Amhurst. Lady Amelia Amhurst. And while we're to discuss this trip, then yes, I suppose I do have a few things to say." She ignored the frown on her father's face and the "darling, please be silent" glare of Jeffery. "In England, women quite often ride to the hunt. We enjoy sporting as much as our menfolk. Furthermore, I assure you, we are quite capable of handling a gun, a mount, and any other hardship that might present itself on the trip."

"I'm glad to hear that you are so capable, Lady Amhurst. You won't be offended then when I state my rules. We will begin at sunrise. That doesn't mean we'll get up at sunrise, have a leisurely tea, and be on the road by nine. It means things packed, on your horse, ready to ride at sunrise. We'll head into Longmont first, which will give you a last chance at a night's rest in beds before a week of sleeping on the ground. If you're short on supplies you can pick them up there."

No one said a word and even Amelia decided against protesting, at least until she'd heard the full speech.

Logan continued. "It gets cold at night. We'll eventually be 7,000 feet up and the air will be thinner. Every morning you'll find hoarfrost on the ground so staying dry and warm will be your biggest priority. Each of you will pack at least three blankets and a canteen. Again, if you don't have them, pick them up here in Greeley or get them in Longmont. If you don't have them, you don't go. Also, there will be no sidesaddles available. You women will be required to ride astride, so dress accordingly. Oh, and everyone wears a good, sturdy pair of boots. This is important both for riding and for walking if your horse should go lame."

"Mr. Reed!" Lord Amhurst began to protest. "You cannot expect my daughters to ride astride these American horses. First of all it is most unacceptable and second, it—"

"If they don't ride astride, they don't go," Logan replied flatly. "Having them riding sidesaddle is more danger than I'm willing to take on. If you want them to come out of this alive, they need to have every possible chance at staying that way."

"Perhaps, Amhurst," Jeffery addressed him less formally, "we could arrange to employ another guide."

Logan laughed and crossed his arms against his chest. "I challenge you to find one. I'm one of only two in the area who will even bother with you people."

"And what, pray tell, is that supposed to mean?" Amelia interjected.

Logan met her eyes. "It means, I resent European tourists and rich socialites who come to take the air in my mountains. They don't care for the real beauty at hand and they never stay longer than it takes to abuse what they will before going off to boast of their conquests. I made a promise, however, to pack you folks into Estes, but you," he pointed a finger at each of the women, "are completely unsuited for the challenge. There are far too many things to consider when it comes to women. Your physical constitution is weaker, not to mention that by nature being a woman lends itself to certain other types of physical complications and private needs."

"See here! You have no right to talk that way in front of these ladies," Chamberlain protested.

"That is exactly the kind of coddling I'm talking about. It has no place on a mountain ridge. I am not trying to make this unpleasant, but we must establish some rules here in order to keep you folks from dying on the way." Logan's voice lowered to a near whisper. "I won't have their blood on my hands, just because they are too proud and arrogant to take direction from someone who's had more experience." He said "they," but his steely gaze was firmly fixed on Amelia.

"What other rules would you have us abide by, Mr. Reed?" the earl finally asked.

"No alcohol of any kind. No shooting animals on the way to Estes. No stopping for tea four times a day and no special treatment of anyone in the party. If you can't cut it, you go back." Logan took a deep breath. "Finally, my word is law. I know this land and what it's capable of. When I tell you that something needs to be done a certain way, I expect it to be done without question. Even if it pertains to something that shocks your genteel constitutions. I'm not a hard man to get along with," he said pausing again, "but I find the institutions of nobility a bit trying. If I should call you by something other than by your privileged titles, I'll expect you to overlook it. During a rock slide it could be difficult to remember if I'm to address you by earl, lady, or your majesty. My main objective is to get your party to Estes in as close to one piece as possible. That's all."

"I suppose we can live with these rules of yours," Lord Amhurst replied. "Ladies, can you manage?" Penelope and Margaret looked to Amelia and back to their father before nodding their heads.

"Well, Amelia?" her father questioned and all eyes turned to her.

Facing Logan with a confident glare, she replied, "I can certainly meet any challenge that Mr. Reed is capable of delivering."

Logan laughed. "Well, I'm capable of delivering quite a bit, believe me."

Chapter 2

Amelia spent the remainder of the afternoon listening to her sisters alternate between their praises of Sir Jeffery and their concerns about the trip.

"You are such a bore, Amelia," Penelope said with little concern for the harshness of her tone. "Why, Jeffery has simply devoted himself to you on this trip and you've done nothing but act as though you could not care less."

"I *couldn't* care less," Amelia assured her sister.

"But the man is to be your husband. Father arranged this entire trip just to bring you two closer. I think it was rather sporting of Jeffery to endure the open way you stared at that Reed fellow."

Amelia gasped. "I did not stare at Mr. Reed!"

"You did," Margaret confirmed. "I saw you."

Amelia shook her head. "I can't be bothered with you two twittering ninnies. Besides, I never said I approved of Father's arrangement for Sir Jeffery to become my husband. I have no intentions of getting closer to the man and certainly none of marrying him."

"I think Sir Jeffery is wonderful. You're just being mean and spiteful," Penelope stated with a stamp of her foot. A little cloud of dust rose from the floor along with several flies.

"If you think he's so wonderful, Penelope, why don't you marry him?" Amelia snapped. The heat was making her grumpy and her sister's interrogation was making her angry.

"I'd love to marry him," Margaret said in a daft and dreamy way that Amelia thought epitomized the typically addle-brained girl.

"I shall speak to Father about it immediately," Amelia said sarcastically. "Perhaps he will see the sense in it." *If only he would.*

Margaret stared after her with open mouth, while Penelope took the whole thing with an air of indifference. "You know it doesn't matter what you want, Amelia. Father must marry you off before you turn twenty-one this autumn, or lose mother's money. Her fortune means a great deal to him. Surely you wouldn't begrudge your own father his mainstay."

Amelia looked at her younger sisters for a moment. As fair-haired as she, yet more finely featured and petite, Amelia had no doubt that they saw her as some sort of ogre who though only of herself. Their mother's fortune, a trust set in place by their grandmother, was specifically held for the purpose that none of her daughters need feel pressured to marry for money. The money would, in fact, pass to each daughter on her twenty-first birthday, if she were still unmarried. If the girls married before that time, the money reverted to the family coffers and could be used by their father, for the benefit of all he saw fit. Amelia knew it was this that drove her father forward to see her married to Sir Jeffery.

"I have no desire for Father to concern himself with his financial well-being. However, there are things that matter deeply to me, and Jeffery Chamberlain is not one of them." With that Amelia left the room, taking up her parasol. By the time she'd reached the bottom step she'd decided that a walk to consider the rest of Greeley was in order.

Parasol high, Amelia passed from the house in a soft, almost-silent swishing of her pale pink afternoon dress. She was nearly to the corner of the boardinghouse when she caught the sound of voices and immediately recognized one of them to be Logan Reed's.

"You sure asked for it this time, Logan. Hauling those prissy misses all the way over the mountain to Estes ain't gonna be an easy ride," an unidentified man was stating.

"No, it won't," Logan said, sounding very disturbed. "Women are always trouble. I guess next time Evans sends me over, I'll be sure and ask who all is supposed to come back with me."

"It might save you some grief at that. Still," the man said with a pause, "they sure are purty girls. They look as fine as old Bart's spittoon after a Sunday shining."

Amelia paled at the comparison, while Logan laughed. How she wished she could face him and tell him just what she thought of Americans and their spittoons. It seemed every man in this wretched country had taken up that particularly nasty habit of chewing and spitting. *No doubt Mr. Reed will be no exception.*

19

"I don't think I'd compliment any of them in exactly those words, Ross. These are refined British women." Amelia straightened her shoulders a bit and thought perhaps she'd misjudged Logan Reed. Logan's next few words, however, completely destroyed any further doubt. "They are the most uppity creatures God ever put on the face of the earth. They have a queen for a monarch and it makes them feel mighty important."

Amelia seethed. *How dare he even mention the queen. He isn't fit to…* The thought faded as Logan continued.

"The Brits are the hardest of all to work with. The Swedes come and they're just a bunch of land-loving, life-loving primitives. The Germans are much the same and always bring a lot of life to a party. But the Brits think everything goes from their mouth to God's ear. They are rude and insensitive to other people and expect to stop on a ledge two feet wide, or any other dangerous or unseemly place, if it dares to be time for tea. In fact, I'd wager good money that before I even get this party packed halfway through the foothills, one of those 'purty' women, as you call them, will expect to have tea and biscuits on a silver tray."

At this, Amelia could take no more. She whipped around the corner in a fury. Angered beyond reason and filled with rage, she took her stand. "How dare you insult my family and friends in such a manner. I have never been so enraged in all of my twenty years!" She barely paused to take a breath. "I have traveled all across Europe and India and never in my life have I met more rude and insensitive people than here in America. If you want to see difficulty and stubbornness, Mr. Reed, I'm certain you have no further to go than the mirror in your room." At this she stormed off, feeling quite vindicated.

∞

Logan stared after her with a mocking grin on his lips. He'd known full well she was eavesdropping and intended to take her to task for it quite solidly. The man beside him, uncomfortable with the display of temper, quickly excused himself and ran with long strides toward the busier part of town. When Logan began to chuckle out loud, Amelia turned back indignantly.

"Whatever are you snickering about?" Amelia questioned, her cheeks flushed from the sun and the encounter. Apparently remembering her parasol, she raised it to shield her skin.

"I'm amused," Logan said in a snooty tone, mocking her.

"I see nothing at all funny here. You have insulted good people, Mr. Reed. Gentlefolk, from the lineage of nobility, with more grace and manners than you could ever hope to attain. People, I might add, who are paying you a handsome wage to do a job."

She was breathing heavily. Beads of perspiration were forming on her brow. Her blue eyes were framed by long blond lashes that curled away from her eyes like rays of sunshine through a storm cloud. She reminded Logan of a china doll with her bulk of blond hair piled high on her head, complete with fashionable hat. Logan thought he'd never seen a more beautiful woman, but he still desired to put her in her place once and for all.

"And does your family consider eavesdropping to be one of those gracious manners of which you speak so highly?" he questioned, taking long easy strides to where she stood. Amelia recoiled as though she had been slapped.

"I see you find my words disconcerting," Logan said, his face now serious. Amelia, speechless, only returned his blatant stare. "People with manners, miss," he paused, then shook his head. "No, make that Lady Amhurst. Anyway, people of true refinement have no need to advertise it or crow it from the rooftops. They show it in action. And they need not make others feel less important by using flashy titles and snobbery. I don't believe eavesdropping would be considered a substantial way to prove one's merit in any society."

Amelia found her tongue at last. "I never intended to eavesdrop, Mr. Reed," she said emphasizing the title. "I was simply taking in a bit of air, a very little bit I might add. Is it my fault that your voice carries above the sounds of normal activity?"

Logan laughed. "I could excuse a simple wandering-in, but you stood there a full five minutes before making your presence known. I said what I said knowing full well you were there. I wanted to see just how much you would take before jumping me."

Amelia's expression tightened. "You couldn't possibly have known

I was there. I had just come from the front of the house and I was making no noise."

Logan's amusement was obviously stated in his eyes. He stepped back to the house, pulling Amelia with him. Leaving Amelia to stand in stunned silence at his bold touch, he went around the corner. "What do you see, Lady Amhurst?"

Amelia looked to the corner of the house. "I see nothing. Whatever are you talking about?"

"Look again. You're going to have to have a sharper sense of the obvious if you're to survive in the wilds of Colorado."

From around the corner Logan waited a long moment before deciding he wasn't being quite fair. He reached up and adjusted his hat, hoping his shadow's movement on the ground would catch her eye.

"Very well, Mr. Reed." Amelia sounded humbled. "I see your point, but it could have just as easily been one of my sisters. You couldn't possibly have known it was me and not one of them."

Logan looked around the corner with a self-satisfied expression on his face. "You're a little more robust, shall we say, than your sisters." His gaze trailed the length of her body before coming again to rest on her face.

Amelia turned scarlet and for a moment Logan wondered if she might give him a good whack with the parasol she was twisting in her hands. She did nothing, said nothing, but returned his stare with such umbrage that Logan was very nearly taken aback.

"Good day, Mr. Reed. I no longer wish to listen to anything you have to say," Amelia said and turned to leave, but Logan reached out to halt her.

She fixed him with a stony stare that would have crumbled a less stalwart foe.

"Unhand me, sir!"

"You sure run hot and cold, lady." Logan's voice was husky and his eyes were narrowed ever so slightly. "But either way, one thing you'd better learn quickly—and I'm not saying this to put you off again," he said, pausing to tighten his grip in open defiance of her demand, "listening to me may very well save your life."

"When you say something that seems lifesaving," she murmured, "I will listen with the utmost regard." She pulled her arm away and gathered her skirts in hand. "Good day, Mr. Reed."

Logan watched her walk away in her facade of fire and ice. She was unlike any women he'd ever met in his life—and he'd certainly met many a fine lady in his day. She was strong and self-assured and Logan knew that if the entire party perished in the face of their mountain challenge, Amelia would survive and probably thrive.

He liked her, he decided. He liked her a great deal. For all her snooty ways and uppity suggestions, she was growing more interesting by the minute and Logan intended to take advantage of the long summer months to come in which he'd be a part of her Estes Park stay.

Logan stood in a kind of stupor for a few more minutes, until the voice of Lord Amhurst sounded from behind him.

"Mr. Reed," he began, "I should like to inquire as to our accommodations. The proprietor here tells me that you have taken one of the rooms intended for our use. I would like to have it back."

"Sorry," Logan said without feeling the least bit apologetic. "I'm gonna need a good night's rest if I'm to lead you all to Longmont. It isn't anything personal and I'm sorry Ted parceled out your evening comforts, but I need the room."

The earl looked taken back for a moment, apparently unaccustomed to his requests being refused, but nodded as he acquiesced to the circumstances.

Logan took off before the man could say another word. He could have given up the room easily, but his pride made him rigid. "Oh Lord," he whispered, "I should have been kinder. When I settle down a bit, I'll go back to the Earl of Donneswick and give him the room." Logan rounded the corner of the house and found Penelope, Margaret, and Chamberlain sitting beneath the community shade tree. It was the only shade tree on this side of town. He couldn't help but wonder where Amelia had gone, then chided himself for even thinking of her. There'd be time enough on the trip, not to mention when they reached Estes, to learn more about her. He could take his time, he reasoned, remembering that Evans had told him the party would stay until first snow.

Whistling a tune, Logan made his way past Amelia's simpering sisters, tipped his hat ever so slightly, and headed for the livery. *Lady Amelia Amhurst,* he thought with a sudden revelation. "There's no reason she can't be my lady," Logan stated aloud to no one in particular. "No reason at all."

Chapter 3

The following day brought the hunting party together. Lord and Lady Gambett arrived with their whiny daughters, Henrietta and Josephine. Both of the girls were long-time companions of Penelope and Margaret, and their reunion was one of excited giggles and squeals of delight. Amelia stood beneath the shade of the community tree and waited for the party to move out to Longmont. She studied the landscape around her and decided she was very glad not to live in this dusty community of flies and harsh prairie winds. To the west she noted the Rocky Mountains and though they were beautiful, she would have happily passed up the chance to further explore them—if her father would have given her the option to return home.

Lady Gambett fussed over her daughters like a mother hen, voicing her concern quite loudly that they should have to wear such a monstrous apparatus as what the store clerk had called a "lady's mountain dress." The outfit appeared for all intents and purposes to be no different from any other riding habit. A long serviceable skirt of blue serge fell to the boot tops of each young lady, while underneath, a fuller, billowing version of a petticoat allowed the freedom to ride astride.

Amelia knew her own attire to be quite comfortable and didn't really mind the idea of trading in her dainty sidesaddle for the fuller and more masculine McClellan cavalry saddle. She'd heard Lady Bird speak of these at one of her lectures on the Rockies and just remembering the older woman made Amelia smile. Lady Isabella Bird was a remarkable woman. Traveling all over the world to the wildest reaches was nothing to this adventuresome lady. She had come to the Rockies only two years earlier on her way back from the Sandwich Islands. By sheer grit and force of will, Lady Bird had placed herself in the hands of strangers and eventually into the hands of no one at all when she took a rugged Indian pony and traveled throughout the Rocky Mountains all alone. Amelia admired that kind of gumption. She'd never dreamed of doing something so incredible herself, but she thought Lady Bird's accounts of the solitude sounded refreshing. Watching the stars fade into the dawn, Amelia wondered to herself what it might be like to lay out on a mountaintop, under the stars and trees, with no other human being around for miles and miles.

"You look pretty tolerable when you smile like that," Logan's voice sounded in her ear.

Startled, Amelia instantly drew back and lost the joy of her self-reflection. "Haven't you better things to do, Mr. Reed? As I recall, we were to be on our way by now. What seems to be keeping us?"

Logan smiled. "Loose shoe on one of the horses. Should have it fixed in a quick minute."

Amelia hoped this would end their conversation, but it didn't.

"You gonna ride in that?" Logan asked seriously, pointing to her wind-blown navy blue skirt, which blew just high enough to reveal matching bloomers beneath.

Amelia felt her face grown hot. "I assure you I will be quite able to ride. This outfit is especially designed to allow a woman to ride astride. Just as you demanded."

"Good. I don't want any of you dainty ladies to be pitched over the side."

Amelia jutted her chin out defiantly and said nothing. Logan Reed was clearly the most incorrigible man she'd ever met in her life and she wasn't about to let him get the best of her.

"Logan!" A man hollered and waved from where the others were gathered. "Horse is ready."

"Well, Lady Amhurst, I believe we are about to get underway," Logan said with a low sweeping bow.

❧

Amelia was hot and dirty and very unhappy when the party at last rode into Longmont, Colorado. The day had not been a pleasant one for Amelia. Her sisters had squabbled almost half the way about who was going to wear the blue-veiled straw riding bonnet. Penelope had latched on to it in Greeley, but Margaret had soon learned the benefits of her sister's veil and insisted she trade her. Margaret had protested that as the youngest, at sixteen, she was also the more delicate of the trio. Josephine, Margaret's bosom companion, heartily agreed. Pushing up tiny round spectacles, Josephine was only coming to realize the protection her glasses offered from the dust. While the others were delicately blotting their eyes with lace handkerchiefs, Josephine's eyes had remained a little more sheltered.

This argument over the bonnet, along with Logan's sneering grins and her father's constant manipulation to see her and Jeffery riding together, made Amelia want to run screaming in the direction of the nearest railroad station. But of course, convention denied her the possibility of such display.

Glancing around at the small town of Longmont, Amelia was amused to see the townsfolk apparently could not even decide on the town's spelling. Some signs read LONGMOUNT, while others gave the title LONGMONT. The name St. Vrain seemed to be quite popular. There was the St. Vrain Café, the St. Vrain Saloon, and the St. Vrain Hotel, which looked to her to be an oasis in the desert. Brilliantly white against the sun's light, the two story hotel beckoned the weary travelers forward and Amelia couldn't wait to sink into a hot bath.

Upon alighting from her horse, it was instantly apparent that Longmont suffered the same plague of black flies that had held Greeley under siege. The flies instantly clung to her riding habit and bonnet, leaving Amelia felling as though her skin were crawling. The Gambett girls and her sisters were already whining about the intolerable conditions and although Amelia whole-heartedly agreed with their analysis that this town was completely forgotten by any kind of superior being, she refused to raise her voice in complaint.

"I assure you, ladies," Logan said with a hint of amusement in his tired voice, "this place is neither forsaken by God, nor condemned. The people here are friendly and helpful, if you treat them with respect. There's a well-stocked hardware store down Main Street, and if you ladies wish to purchase another veiled bonnet, you can try the mercantile just over there."

The words were meant to embarrass her sisters, but as far as Amelia could tell, neither Penelope nor Margaret were aware of Logan's intent.

"Remember, this is one of those trips where you'll have to do for yourself," Logan said, motioning to the pack mules. "You might just as well get used to the fact here and now. No one is going to care for you, or handle your things, but you. You'll be responsible for your bags and any personal items you choose to bring on this trip. Although, for the sake of your horses, the mules, and even yourselves, I suggest you greatly limit what you bring along."

Jeffery immediately appeared at Amelia's side. "Never fear, Lady Amhurst, I am your faithful servant. You find a comfortable place to rest and I will retrieve your things."

Amelia watched Logan's lips curl into a self-satisfied smile. Obviously he had pegged her for one of those who would choose to be waited on hand and foot. What further irritated her was that if Logan had not been there, she would have taken Chamberlain up on his offer.

"Never mind that," she said firmly. "I can manage, just as Mr. Reed has made clear I must." She pulled down her bedroll and bags without another glance at Logan.

"Surely there is no reason you cannot accept my help," Jeffery spoke from her side. He reached out to take hold of her bedroll. "I mean to say, you are a gentlewoman—a lady. It is hardly something Mr. Reed would understand, but certainly it does not escape my breeding to intercede on your behalf."

Amelia wearied of his nonsensical speech. She glared up at Jeffery harshly and pulled her bags away from his hands. "I am of sturdy stock, I assure you. I have climbed in the Alps without assistance from you." She couldn't help remembering the bevy of servants who had assisted her. "I have also barged the Nile, lived through an Indian monsoon, and endured the tedium of life at court. I surely can carry baggage into a hotel for myself." The chin went a notch higher in the air and Amelia fixed her gaze on Logan's amused expression. "Perhaps Mr. Reed needs assistance with *his* things."

Jeffery looked from Amelia's stern expression to Logan's near-laughing one. Appearing confused, he neither offered his assistance to Logan, nor did he protest when Amelia went off in the direction of the hotel, bags in hand.

The St. Vrain Hotel was no cooler inside than it had been outside.

If anything it was even more stifling because there was no breeze and the flies were thicker here than in the streets. She turned at the front desk to await her father and struggled to contain a smile when he and Mattersley appeared, each with his own bags, and her sisters struggling dramatically behind them.

"Oh Papa," Margaret moaned loudly, "you simply cannot expect me to carry all of this!" The earl rolled his eyes, bringing a broad smile from Amelia. The clerk at the desk also seemed amused, but said nothing. Amelia was thankful Logan Reed was still outside with the horses.

Jeffery strode in, trying hard to look completely at ease with his new task. He put his things down in one corner and announced he would go with Mr. Reed to stable the horses. Amelia was stunned by this. So far as she knew, Jeffery had done nothing more than hand his horse over for stabling since his privileged childhood. How she would love to watch him in the livery with Mr. Reed!

Amelia gave it no more thought, however, as the clerk led them upstairs to their rooms. She would share a room with her sisters again, but this time there were two beds. One was a rustic-looking, double-sized bed. It looked roughly hewn from pine, yet a colorful handmade quilt made it appear beautiful. The other, a single bed, looked to be even more crudely assembled. It, too, was covered with a multicolored quilt, and to the exhausted Amelia, looked quite satisfactory. Other than the beds, the room was rather empty. There was a single night table with a bowl and pitcher of water and a tiny closet that was hardly big enough to hang a single dress within.

"Oh, such misery!" Penelope exclaimed and Margaret quickly agreed.

"How could Papa make us stay in a horrible place like this?" Margaret added.

"I think it will seem a great deal more appealing after you've spent two or three nights on the trail," Amelia said, plopping down on the single bed. She tossed her things to the floor and stretched out on top of the quilt, still dressed in her dusty clothes.

The bed isn't half bad, Amelia thought. *It beats being on the back of that temperamental mount Mr. Reed had insisted she ride.* Twice the beast had tried to take his own lead and leave the processional, but Amelia, seasoned rider that she was, gave the gelding beneath her a firm understanding that she was to decide the way, not he. No doubt Mr. Reed had intentionally given her the spirited horse. *He probably hoped to find me sprawled out on the prairie ground,* she mused. *I guess I showed him that I can handle my own affairs.* It was the last conscious thought Amelia had for some time.

∞

She had no idea how long she'd laid upon the bed. Her sisters had begun arguing about who would sleep on the right side of the bed and who would go to search out another veiled bonnet. The noise was something she was used to—it was the silence that seemed to awaken her. Staring at the ceiling for a moment, Amelia tried to remember where she was and what she was to do next. She had no time for further contemplation, however, when a knock sounded at her door.

"Yes?" she questioned, barely cracking the door open.

A young woman wearing a starched white apron stood before her bearing a towel and bar of soap. "We've a bath ready for you, Lady Amhurst."

No announcement could have met with her approval more. Amelia opened the door wide and grimaced at the stiffness that was already setting into her bones. It had been awhile since she'd been riding, what with the boat ride to America and the constant use of trains and stages thereafter.

"Thank you. Will you direct me?"

The woman, hardly old enough to be called that, motioned Amelia to the room at the end of the hall. "I can get you settled in and take your clothes to have the dust beaten out. I'll bring you something else to wear if you tell me what you want."

Amelia stepped into the room and thought the steaming tub of water too good to be true. She immediately began unfastening the buttons of her half jacket. "You are very kind to arrange all of this for me. I must say the service here is quite good."

"Oh, it's my job," the girl replied. "'Sides, Logan told me you'd probably want to clean up and he gave me an extra coin to make sure you were taken care of personally."

Amelia's fingers ceased at their task. "I beg your pardon? Mr. Reed paid for this bath?"

"Yes ma'am."

Amelia hesitated, looked at the tub and considered her pride in the matter. The steaming water beckoned her and her tired limbs pleaded for the refreshment. She could always settle things with Logan Reed later.

"Very well." She slipped out of the jacket and unbuttoned her skirt. "If you'll bring me my black skirt and a clean shirtwaist, I'll wash out these other things." She would show Mr. Reed just how self-sufficient she could be.

"Oh no, ma'am. I can take care of everything for you. My mother does the laundry and she can have these things ready by morning. Pressed fresh and smelling sweet. You'll see."

Amelia reluctantly gave in. "Very well." She sent the girl off with her riding clothes, keeping only her camisole and bloomers. These she washed out by hand and hung to dry before stepping into the tub. With the window open to allow the breeze, the items would dry by the time she finished with the bath. That was one of the nice things about the drier air of Colorado. Things took forever to dry back home in England. The dampness was nearly always with them and it was better to press clothes dry with an iron than wait for them to dry on their own. But here the air was crisp and dry and even in the heat of the day it was completely tolerable compared to what she'd endured when they visited a very humid New Orleans.

Sinking into the hot water, Amelia sighed aloud. How good it felt! Her dry skin seemed to literally drink in the offered moisture. Lathering the soap down one arm and then the other, Amelia wanted to cry with relief. The bath was pure pleasure and she felt like the spoiled aristocrat Logan Reed thought her to be. After washing thoroughly, she eased back on the rim of the tub and let the water come up to her neck, soothing and easing all the pain in her shoulders. It mattered very little that Logan Reed had arranged this luxury. At that moment, the only thing that mattered was the comfort at hand.

When the knock on the door sounded, Amelia realized she'd

dozed off again. The water was tepid now and her muscles were no longer sore and tense.

"It's me, Lady Amhurst," the voice of the young woman called. "I've brought your clothes."

"Come ahead," Amelia called, stepping from the tub to wrap the rough towel around her body.

The girl appeared bringing not only the requested shirt and shirtwaist but also Amelia's comb and brush. "I thought you might be needin' these, too. I can help with your hair, if you like."

Amelia smiled. What a friendly little thing. She'd make a good chambermaid if she were a little less familiar. But that was the way of these Americans and Amelia found herself growing more accepting of it as the days wore on. To be friendly and openly honest was not a thing one could count on in the finer classes of people. Women of high society were taught to keep their opinions to themselves, and in fact were encouraged to have no opinion at all. From the moment she was born, Amelia was strictly lectured that her father, and later her husband, would clearly do her thinking for her. Amelia had other ideas, however, and often she came off appearing smug and superior in her attitude. People misjudged her confidence and believed her to think herself better than her peers. But it wasn't true.

Logan Reed came to mind. He, too, had misjudged her and her kind. Americans seemed more than happy to lend their opinion to a situation. Even this young woman gave her opinion at every turn. But, where Logan had made her feel quite the snob, this young woman made her feel like royalty. Then a thought crossed her mind and she frowned. "Did Mr. Reed pay for you to assist me with my hair as well?"

"Oh no, ma'am. I was just thinking you might want some help what with it coming down in back and all. I can't do it up fancy like you had it, but I can help pin it up."

Amelia nodded. "Yes, I'd like that very much." The girl turned away while Amelia stepped into her underthings. There were a little damp and this seemed to make them cooler. Light was fading outside and Amelia knew it must nearly be dinnertime. These Americans had the barbaric custom of eating a full meal not long after the time when she was more accustomed to tea and cakes. Supper at home was always an affair to dress for and always served late into the evening—sometimes even after nine. *Alas, yet another American custom to adapt to.*

The girl instructed Amelia to sit on a stool while she combed out the thick, waist-length tresses. Amelia prided herself on her hair. It was a light, golden blond that most all of her peers envied. To be both blond-headed and blue-eyed in her society, was to be the picture of perfection. Added to this was her, *how did Mr. Reed say it?* robust figure. Amelia smiled to herself. Many a glance had come to her by gentlemen too well-bred to say what Logan Reed had issued without the slightest embarrassment. She was robust, or voluptuous as her dear friend Sarah would say. When corseted tightly, she had a perfect hourglass figure, well near perfect. Maybe time ran a little heavier on the top half than the bottom.

"There, how's that?"

Amelia took the offered mirror and smiled. The young woman had done a fine job of replicating her earlier coiffure. "It's exactly right, Miss…"

"Oh, just call me Emma."

"Well, thank you very much, Emma." Amelia got to her feet and allowed Emma to help her dress. "Are the others going to bathe?"

"Oh, the menfolk went down to the steambath at the barbershop. The other womenfolk didn't seem to take kindly to my trying to offer up help, so I pretty much left them alone."

Amelia nodded and smiled. She could well imagine her sisters' snobbery keeping them from accepting the assistance of this young woman. And no doubt, Lady Gambett and her pouty brood had taken themselves off to a private washbasin. With a final pat to her hair, Amelia gathered up her things and followed Emma from the room. "You should see my father, Lord Amhurst, for the cost of this bath and my clothing being cleaned. Mr. Reed is no more than a hunting guide to our party and certainly has no call to be arranging my affairs."

Emma smiled. "Oh, that's just Logan's way. He's friendly like that."

"Well, I assure you that I am not in the habit of allowing strangers, especially men, to be friendly like that with me. Please see my father with the bill."

∞

Supper that evening was a surprisingly pleasant fare of roasted chicken, sage dressing, a veritable banquet of vegetables—mostly canned, but very tasty, and peach cobbler. Amelia had to admit it was more than she'd expected and only the thick swarm of hovering black flies kept her from completely enjoying her evening. That and Logan Reed's rude appraisal of her throughout the meal. He seemed to watch her as though she might steal the silver at any given moment. Amelia grew increasingly uncomfortable under his scrutiny until she actually found herself listening to Sir Jeffery's soliloquy on the founding of the London Medical School for Women and the absurdity of anyone believing women would make acceptable physicians.

"Why the very thought of exposing the gentler sex to such grotes-queries is quite abominable," Jeffery stated as though that would be the collective reasoning of the entire party.

Normally Amelia would have commented loud and clear on such outdated thoughts, but with Logan apparently anticipating such a scene, she chose instead to finish her meal and quietly excuse herself. This was accomplished without much ado, mainly because Lady Gambett opened the matter and excused herself first, pleading an intolerable headache.

Amelia soon followed suit and very nearly spilled over a water glass when she got to her feet. Her hands were shaking as she righted the glass. Looking up, she found Logan smiling. She had to get away from him quickly or make a complete fool of herself, of this she was certain.

Unfortunately, she was barely out the front door when Jeffery popped up at her side.

"Ah, Sir Jeffery," she said stiffly.

"Good evening, Lady Amhurst," he said, pausing with a smile, "Amelia."

She stiffened even more. Eyeing him with complete contempt,

she said nothing. There was no need. She'd often heard it said that with a single look she could freeze the heart right out of a man and Jeffery Chamberlain was certainly no match for her.

"Forgive me, Lady Amhurst," he said bowing low before her. "I sought only to escort you to wherever it is you might be going. The familiarity is born only out of my fondness for you and your good father's desire that we wed."

Amelia nodded. "You may be assured that those desires reside with my father alone. Good evening." She hurried away before Jeffery could respond. She hadn't the strength to discuss the matter further.

The evening had grown quite chilly and Amelia was instantly sorry she'd not stopped to retrieve a shawl. She was grateful for the short-waisted jacket she'd donned for dinner and quickly did up the remaining two buttons to insure as much warmth as possible. After two blocks, however, she was more than happy to head back to the hotel and remain within its thin walls until morning sent them ever upward.

Upward.

She glanced to the now-blacked silhouettes of the mountain range before her. The shadows seemed foreboding, as if some great hulking monster waited to devour her. Shuddering from the thought, she walked back to the St. Vrain Hotel and considered it no more.

Chapter 4

It was the wind that woke Amelia in the morning. The great wailing gusts bore down from the mountains causing the very timbers around her to shake and tremble. Was it a storm? She contemplated this for a moment, hoping that if it were, it would rain and drown out each and every pesky fly in Longmont. All through the night, her sleep had been disturbed by the constant assault of flies at her face, in her hair, and at her ears. It was enough to make her consider agreeing to marry Jeffery if her father would pledge to return immediately to England.

A light rapping sounded upon her door. Amelia pulled the blanket tight around her shoulders and went to answer it.

"Yes?" she called, stumbling in the dark.

"It's me, Emma."

Amelia opened the door with a sleepy nod. "Are we about to blow away?"

Emma laughed softly and pushed past Amelia to light the lamp on her night table. "Oh no, ma'am. The wind blows like this from time to time. It'll probably be done by breakfast. Mr. Reed sent me to wake you and the other ladies. Said to tell you it was an hour before dawn and you'd know exactly what that meant."

Amelia frowned. "Yes, indeed. Thank you, Emma."

"Will you be needin' help with your hair and getting dressed?"

"No, thank you anyway. Mr. Reed made it quite clear that simplicity is the means for success on this excursion. I intend only to braid my hair and pin it tight. From the sound of the wind, I suppose I should pin it very tight." Emma giggled and Amelia smiled in spite of herself. *Perhaps some of these Americans aren't so bad.*

"Lady Gambett was near to tears last night because Logan told her that she and those youngun's of hers needed to get rid of their corsets before they rode another ten feet."

It was Amelia's turn to giggle. Something she'd not done in years. "Surely you jest."

"Jest?" Emma looked puzzled.

"Joke. I merely implied that you were surely joking."

"Oh no! He said it. I heard him."

"Well, I've never been one to abide gossip," Amelia began rather soberly, "but I can well imagine the look in Lady Gambett's face when he mentioned the unmentionable items."

"She plumb turned red and called for her smelling salts."

"Yes, she would."

Glancing to where Penelope and Margaret continued to slumber soundly, Emma questioned, "Will you need me to wake your sisters?"

Amelia glanced at the bed. "No, it would take more than your light touch. I'll see to them." Emma smiled and took her leave.

"Wake up, sleepyheads," Amelia said, pulling the quilt to the foot of the bed. Penelope shrieked a protest and pulled it back up, while Margaret stared up in disbelief.

"I believe you're becoming as ill-mannered as these Americans," she said to Amelia.

"It's still dark outside," Penelope added, snuggling down. "Mr. Reed said we start at dawn."

"Mr. Reed said we leave at dawn," she reminded them. "I for one intend to have enough time to dress properly and eat before climbing back on that ill-tempered horse."

Margaret whined. "We are too tired to bother with eating. Just go away, Amelia."

"Have it your way," Amelia said with a shrug. And with that she left her sisters to worry about themselves, and hurried to dress for the day. Pulling on black cotton stockings, pantaloons, and camisole, Amelia smiled privately, knowing that she was quite glad for the excuse to be rid of her corset. She packed the corset away, all the while feeling quite smug. She wasn't about to give Logan Reed a chance to speak so forwardly to her about things that didn't concern him. Pulling on her riding outfit, now clean and pressed, she secured her toiletries in her saddlebags and hurried to meet the others at breakfast.

Much to her embarrassment she arrived to find herself alone with Logan. The rest of her party was slow to rise and even slower to ready themselvesfor the day ahead. Logan nodded approvingly at her and called for the meal to be served. He bowed ever so slightly and held out a chair for Amelia.

"We must wait for the others, Mr. Reed," she said, taking the offered seat.

"I'm afraid we can't," Logan announced. "You forget I'm experienced at this. Most folks refuse to take me seriously until they miss at least one breakfast. Ahhh, here's Emma." The young girl entered bringing a mound of biscuits—complete with hovering flies—and a platter of fried sausages swimming in grease and heavily peppered. It was only after taking one of the offered links that Amelia realized it wasn't pepper at all, but still more flies.

Frowning at the food on her plate, it was as if Logan read her mind when he said, "Just try to think of 'em as extra meat."

Amelia almost smiled, but refused to. "Maybe I'll just eat a biscuit."

"You'd best eat up and eat well. The mountain air will make you feel starved and after all the hard work you'll be doing, you'll wish you'd had more than biscuits."

"Hard work?"

Logan waited to speak until Emma brought two more platters, one with eggs, another with fried potatoes, and a bowl with thick white gravy. He thanked the girl and turned to Amelia. "Shall we say grace?"

"I hardly think so, Mr. Reed. To whom should we offer thanks, except to those whose hands have provided and prepared the food?"

For the first time since she'd met the smug, self-confident Logan Reed, he stared at her speechless and dumbstruck. *Good,* she thought. *Let him consider that matter for a time and leave me to eat in silence.* She put eggs on her plate and added a heavy amount of cream to the horrible black coffee Emma had poured into her cup. She longed to plead with the girl for tea, but wouldn't think of allowing Mr. Reed to see her in a weakened moment.

"Do you mean to tell me," Logan began, "that you don't believe in God?"

Amelia didn't even look up. "Indeed, that is precisely what I mean to say."

"How can a person who seems to be of at least average intelligence—" at this Amelia's head snapped up and Logan chuckled and continued, "I thought that might get your attention. How can you look around you or wake up in the morning to breathe the air of a new day and believe there is no God?"

Amelia scowled at the black flies hovering around her fork. "Should there have been a God, surely He would not have allowed such imperfect creatures to mar His universe."

"You don't believe in God because flies are sharing your breakfast table?" Logan's expression was one of complete confusion. He hadn't even started to eat his own food.

"Mr. Reed, I believe this trip will go a great deal better for both of us if you will merely mind your own business and leave me to do the same. I fail to see where my disbelief in a supreme being is of any concern to you, and therefore, I see no reason to discuss the matter further."

Logan hesitated for a moment, bowed his head to what Amelia presumed were his prayers of grace, and ate in silence for several minutes. For some reason, even though it was exactly what Amelia had hoped for, she felt uncomfortable and found herself wishing he would say something even if it was to insult her.

When he continued in silence, she played at eating the breakfast. She'd hoped the wind would send the flies further down the prairie, but it only seemed to have driven them indoors for shelter. As the gales died down outside, she could only hope they'd seek new territory.

"I guess I see it as my business to concern myself with the eternal souls of mankind," Logan said without warning. "See the Bible, that's the Word of God. . ."

"I know what the Bible is perceived to be, Mr. Reed. I wasn't born without a brain, simply without the need for an all-interfering, all-powerful being."

Logan seemed to shake this off before continuing. His green eyes seemed to darken. "The Bible says we are to concern ourselves with our fellow man and spread the good news."

She put her fork down and matched his look of determination.

"And pray tell, Mr. Reed, what would that good news be? Spread it quickly and leave me to my meal." Amelia knew she was being unreasonably harsh, but she tired of religious rhetoric and nonsensical sermons. She'd long given up the farce of accompanying her sisters and father to church, knowing that they no more held the idea of worshipping as a holy matter than did she.

"The good news is that folks like you and I don't have to burn in the pits of hell for all eternity, because Jesus Christ, God's only Son, came to live and die for our sins. He rose again, to show that death cannot hold the Christian from eternal life."

Amelia picked up her thick white mug and sipped the steaming contents. The coffee scalded her all the way down, but she'd just as soon admit to the pain as to admit Logan's words were having any affect on her whatsoever. *The pits of hell, indeed,* she thought.

She tried to compose herself before picking her fork up again. "I believe religion to be man's way of comforting himself in the face of death. Mankind can simply not bear to imagine that there is only so much time allotted to each person so mankind has created religion to support the idea of there being something more. The Hindu believe we are reincarnated. *Incarnate* is from the Latin *incarnates*, meaning 'made flesh.' So they believe much as you Christians do that they will rise up to live again."

∞

"I know what reincarnation means, and I am even familiar with the Hindu religion. But you're completely wrong when you say they believe as Christians do. They don't hold faith in what Jesus did to save us. They don't believe in the need for salvation through Him in order to have that eternal life."

Amelia shrugged. "To each religion and culture comes a theory that will comfort them the most. In light of that, Mr. Reed, and considering the hundreds of different religions in the world, even the varied philosophies within your own Christian faith, how can you possibly ascertain that you and you alone have the one true faith?"

"Are you saying that there is no need for faith *and* that there is no such thing as God?" Logan countered.

"I am a woman of intellect and reason, Mr. Reed. Intellectually and reasonably, I assure you that faith and religion have no physical basis for belief."

"Faith in God is just that, Lady Amhurst. Faith." Logan slammed down his coffee mug. "I am a man of intellect and reason, but it only makes it that much clearer to me that there is a need for God and something more than the contrivances of mankind."

Amelia looked at him for a moment. *Yes, I could believe this barbaric American might have some understanding of books and philosophies. But he is still of that mindset that uses religion as a crutch to ease his conscience and concerns.* Before Amelia could comment further, Logan got to his feet and stuffed two more biscuits into the pocket of his brown flannel shirt. Amelia appraised him silently as he thanked Emma for a great meal and pulled on his drifters coat.

"We leave in ten minutes. I'll bring the horses around to the front." He stalked out of the room like a man with a great deal on his mind, leaving Amelia feeling as though she'd had a bit of a comeuppance, but for the life of her she couldn't quite figure out just how he'd done it.

Emma cleared Logan's plate and mug from the table and returned to find Amelia staring silently at the void left by their guide.

"I hate to be a busybody, Lady Amhurst," Emma began, "but your family ain't a bit concerned about Mr. Reed's timetable and I can tell you from experience, Logan won't wait."

This brought Amelia's attention instantly. "I'll tend to them. Are there more of these biscuits?"

"Yes ma'am."

"Good. Please pack whatever of this breakfast you can for us and we'll take it along. As I recall, Mr. Reed said there would be a good six miles of prairie to cross to the canyon."

"I can wrap the biscuits and sausage into a cloth, but the rest of this won't pack very good."

Amelia blotted her lips with a coarse napkin and got to her feet. "Do what you can, Emma, and I'll retrieve my wayward family."

Ten minutes later, Amelia had managed to see her family to the front of the hotel. Penelope and Margaret were whining, still struggling to do something with their hair. Upon Amelia's threat to shear them both, they grew instantly silent. Lady Gambett cried softly into a lace-edged handkerchief and bemoaned the fact that her nerves would never stand the jostling on horseback. Her daughters were awkward and consciously concerned about their lack of corseting, and Amelia had to laugh when she overheard Margaret tell Josephine that Mr. Reed was no doubt some kind of devious man who would do them all in once they were far enough away from the protection of town. A part of Amelia was beginning to understand Logan Reed's misgivings about her people.

Logan repacked the mules with the baggage and items brought to him by the party, but Amelia noticed he was unusually tight-lipped. Light was just streaking the eastern skies when he hauled up onto the back of his horse and instructed them to do the same.

Amelia allowed Jeffery to help her onto her horse and winced noticeably when the softer parts of her body protested from the abuse the trek had inflicted the day before. She said nothing, noting Logan's smirk of recognition, but her sisters and the Gambetts were well into moans and protests of discomfort. Logan ignored them all, however, and urged his horse and the mules forward.

∞

It wasn't yet ten o'clock when Logan first heard Amelia's sisters suggesting they stop. He couldn't help but cast a smug look of satisfaction toward Amelia when Penelope suggested they should imbibe in a time of tea and cakes.

He watched Amelia's face grow flush with embarrassment, but she said nothing, choosing instead to let her mount lag behind the others until she was nearly bringing up the rear of the party. Chuckling to himself, Logan led them on another two hours before finally drawing his horse to a stop.

Dismounting, he called over his shoulder, "We'll take lunch here." It was as if the entire party sighed in unison.

Logan quickly set up everything they would need. He drew cold water from the mountain river that they'd followed through the canyon, then dug around in the saddlebags to produce jerked beef and additional biscuits.

"You surely don't mean this to be our luncheon fare," Jeffery Chamberlain complained in complete disgust.

The earl looked down his nose at the pitiful offering. "Yes, Mr. Reed, surely there is something better than this."

Logan pushed his hat back on his head. "We'll have a hot meal for dinner this evening. If we're to push ahead and reach our first camping point before dark, we'll only have time to rest here about ten, maybe fifteen minutes. It'll give the horses a well-deserved break and allow them to water up. The higher we go the more water you'll need to drink. Remember that and you won't find yourself succumbing to *sorche*."

"I beg your pardon?" Lord Amhurst questioned.

"Mountain sickness," Reed stated flatly. "The air is much thinner up here, but since you've traipsed all over the Alps, you should already know all about that. You need to take it slower and allow yourselves time to get used to the altitude. Otherwise, you'll be losing what little lunch you get and dealing with eye-splitting headaches that won't let you go for weeks. It's one more reason I insisted the ladies dismiss the idea of corsets." Shudders and gasps of indignant shock echoed from the now-gathered Gambett and Amhurst women. With the exception of Amelia. She stood to one side admiring a collection of wildflowers, but Logan knew she was listening by the amused expression on her face.

Logan continued, trying hard to ignore the graceful blond as she moved about the riverbank studying the ground. "As inappropriate as you might think my addressing the subject of women's undergarments might be, it is a matter of life and death. Up here beauty is counted in the scenery, not the flesh. The air is thinner and you need more of it to account for what you're used to breathing down below. Losing those corsets just might save your life. I wouldn't even suggest putting them back on after we arrive in Estes. The altitude there is even higher than it is here and I'd sure hate to have to run around all day picking up women in dead faints. Now I've wasted enough time. Eat or don't, the choice is yours. I'll water the horses and mules while you decide." He started to walk away then turned back. "I hate to approach another delicate subject, but should you take yourself off into the trees for privacy, keep your eyes open. I'd also hate to have to deal with an agitated mother bear just because you startled her while she was feeding her cubs."

With that said, he walked away grumbling to himself. These prim and proper Brits were more trouble to deal with than they were worth. This was the last time he'd ever act as a guide for anyone of English nobility.

He tethered his horse at the riverbank and pretended to adjust the saddle while he watched Amelia picking flowers and studying them with an almost scientific eye. From time to time, she drew out a small book and pressed one of these samples between the pages before moving on to the next point of interest. He found himself admiring the way she lithely climbed over the rocks and couldn't help but notice her lack of fear as she neared the rushing river for a closer look.

As she held a leaf up to catch the sunlight, Logan was reminded of her atheistic views. *How could anyone behold the beauty of this canyon and question the existence of God?* It was one thing not to want to deal with God, or even question whether He truly cared to deal with mankind, but to openly declare there to be no God—that was something he couldn't even fathom. Even the Indians he'd dealt with believed in God. Maybe they didn't believe the same way he did, but they didn't question that someone or something greater than man held the universe in order and sustained life.

Logan tried not to stare at Amelia, but he found himself rather helpless to ignore her. The other women were huddled together relaying their misfortunes, hoping for better times ahead and assuring each other that such torture could be endured for the sake of their menfolk. The men were gingerly sampling the lunch fare and after deciding it was better than nothing, they managed to eat a good portion before convincing the women to partake.

Logan wondered if Amelia would partake, but then he saw her draw a biscuit from the deep pocket of her skirt and nibble at it absentmindedly as she bent to pick up a piece of granite. *She is an industrious woman,* he thought, watching her turn the stone in her hand. Who else could have gotten that sour-faced brood of travelers together in such a short time? Who else, too, would have thought to get Emma to pack food for them to take, rather than whine and beg him to allow them a bit more time for breakfast?

As if sensing his gaze upon her, Amelia looked up and met his stare. Neither one did anything for a moment and when Amelia returned her attention to the rock, Logan tried to focus on the mules. His stomach did a bit of a flip-flop and he smiled in spite of himself at the affect this woman was having on him. Stealing a sidelong glance, he watched her cup water from the river's edge and drink. *Yes, Lady Amhurst is quite a woman.*

∽

"We'll be leaving in a few minutes," Logan announced to the weary band. "Take care of your needs before that." He walked to where Amelia sat quietly contemplating the scenery. "It's impressive, don't you think?" he asked, wondering if she'd take offense.

"Yes, it is," she admitted.

"Those are cottonwood trees," he said pointing out tall green-leaved trees. "Those with the lighter bark are aspen." He reached down and picked up a leaf. "This is an aspen leaf." Amelia seemed interested enough and so he continued. "I noticed you were saving flowers and if you need any help in identifying them later, I'd be happy to be of service. I'm pretty knowledgeable about the vegetation and wildlife in these parts." He tried to sound nonchalant for fear he'd frighten her away or anger her.

"I especially like those blue flowers," Amelia replied.

"Those are columbine. ''Tis said that absence conquers love; But Oh, believe it not! I've tried, alas! its power to prove, But thou art not forgot.' A fellow named F. W. Thomas wrote that. It's from a poem called 'The Columbine.'"

"How interesting." She said nothing more for a moment, then added, "What of those white ones with the short hairy stems?"

"Pasqueflowers. So named because they usually start flowering around Easter time. Comes from the Latin word *pascha* or the Hebrew *pesah* meaning 'a passing over', thus the Jewish feast of Passover and the Christian celebration of Easter, the death and resurrection of Christ." He really hadn't intended it as a mocking to Amelia's earlier lessons on *incarnate*, but even as the words left his mouth, he knew that was what they'd sound like.

Amelia stiffened, picked up her things and walked back to the horse without another word. Logan wanted to kick himself for breaking the brief civil respite from the tension between them. *Sometimes, Reed,* he thought, *you can sure put your foot in your mouth.*

Chapter 5

Amelia tried not to remember the way Logan Reed had stared at her. Or how green his eyes were. Or how his mustache twitched whenever he was trying not to smile. She found herself unwillingly drawn to him and the very thought disturbed her to the bone. He was refreshingly different from English gentlemen and far better mannered than she'd given him credit for. His gruff exterior was mostly show, she'd decided while watching him help Lady Gambett onto her horse. He had tipped his hat and said something that had caused Lady Gambett to actually smile. Keeping these thoughts to herself, Amelia concentrated on the scenery around her.

"You are particularly quiet," Jeffery spoke, riding up alongside her. It was one of those rare places along the path that allowed for riders to go two abreast.

"I'm considering the countryside," she replied rather tightly.

"Ah, yes. America and her rough-hewn beauty."

Amelia frowned. "And what, pray tell, is that supposed to mean?"

Jeffery smiled tolerantly. "Simply that I'll be happy to return home to England. I'll be even happier when you reconcile yourself to our union and allow me to properly court you."

"I do not wish to discuss the matter."

"I know that very well, but I also know it is your father's intentions that we do so."

He lifted his face to catch a bit of the sun's warmth and Amelia was reminded of a turkey stretching his neck. *Perhaps he might let out a gobble at any moment.* She chuckled in spite of her resolve to be firm.

Jeffery lowered his head and stared at her soberly. "Have I somehow amused you?"

Amelia shook her head. "No, not really. I'm just a bit giddy from the thin air. I'm sure you will understand if I wish to save my breath and discontinue our conversation." She urged her horse ahead and was relieved when Jeffery chose to leave her alone.

Their stop for the evening came early. The sun was just disappearing behind the snow-capped peaks in front of them when Lord Amhurst's pocket watch read 3:35. Amelia slid down from the horse and stretched in a rather unladylike display. Margaret gasped and Penelope laughed, while the Gambett women were too intent on their own miseries to notice. Amelia shrugged off her sisters' questioning stares and began pulling her bedroll free from behind the saddle.

"Get your horses cared for first," Logan called out. "Take down your things and I'll come around and take care of the saddles and staking the animals out."

Moans arose from the crowd and Amelia wasn't sure but what even Mattersley was echoing the sentiment of the group. The older man looked quite worn and Amelia felt concern for him. He would die before leaving her father's side, and thus, he accompanied them whenever they traveled. But this time the trip was so much rougher. Amelia wondered if he would be able to meet the demands of the American wilderness.

"You did good today," Logan said, taking the reins of her mount. "If you think you're up to it, I could use some help putting up the tents and getting dinner started."

Amelia nodded and for some reason she felt honored that he'd asked for her assistance. While Logan removed saddles, Amelia went to Mattersley and helped him remove his bedroll. She didn't know why she acted in such a manner but felt amply rewarded when Mattersley gave her a brief, rare smile. She took his mount and led it to where Logan was staking out Lady Gambett's mount.

"I see you're getting into the spirit of things," Logan said, quickly uncinching the horse.

"I'm worried about Mattersley. He doesn't seem to be adapting well to the altitude." Amelia looked beyond the horses to where Mattersley was trying to assist her father. "He won't be parted from my father," she added, as though Logan had asked her why the old man was along. "He is completely devoted to him."

"I can't imagine what it'd be like to have someone devoted to you like that," Logan replied softly.

Amelia locked into his eyes and found him completely serious. "Me either," she murmured. He made her feel suddenly very vulnerable, even lonely.

Logan's green eyes seemed to break through the thinly placed wall of English aristocracy, to gaze inside to where Amelia knew her empty heart beat a little faster. Could he really see through her and find the void within that kept her so distant and uncomfortable?

"My mother was devoted to my pa that way," he added in a barely audible voice.

Amelia nodded. "Mine, too. When she died I think a part of him died as well. There is a great deal of pain in realizing that you've lost something forever."

"It doesn't have to be forever," Logan said, refusing to break his stare.

Amelia licked her dry lips nervously. "No?"

"No. That's one of the nice things about God and it isn't just a theory to give you comfort when somebody dies. If you and your loved ones belong to Him, then you will see them again."

Amelia swallowed hard. For the first time in many years, in fact since her mother's death, she felt an aching urge to cry for her loss. "My mother believed that way," she murmured.

Logan's face brightened. "Then half the problem is solved. She's in heaven just waiting for you to figure out that she knew what she was talking about. You can see her again."

Amelia's sorrow faded into prideful scorn. "My mother is entombed in the family mausoleum and I have no desire to see her again." She walked away quickly, feeling Logan's gaze on her. *How dare he intrude into my life like that? How dare he trespass in the privacy of my soul?*

⌒⌒

"Come on," Logan said several minutes later. He tossed a small mallet at Amelia's feet and motioned for her to follow him.

Picking up the mallet, Amelia did as she was told. She wasn't surprised when she found Logan quite serious about her helping him assemble tents. He laid out the canvas structures and showed her where to drive the stakes into the ground. Pounding the wooden stakes caused her teeth to rattle, but Amelia found herself attacking the job with a fury.

Logan secured the tent poles and pulled the structure tight. To Amelia's surprise and pleasure, an instant shelter was born. Two more structures went up without a single mishap, or word spoken between them. Amelia was panting by the time they'd finished, but she didn't care.

Logan had sent the others to gather wood, but their production was minimal at best. When he and Amelia had finished with the tents, he then instructed the weary entourage to take their things into the tents. "The ladies will have two tents and the men can use the other. It'll be a close fit, but by morning you'll be glad to rug up with the other occupants."

No one said a word.

Amelia took her things to the tent and started to unroll her bedding. "Leave it rolled," Logan instructed from behind her.

"I beg your pardon?" She pushed back an errant strand of hair and straightened up.

"Unrolled, it will draw moisture or critters. Wait until you're ready to sleep."

Amelia nodded. "Very well. What would you like me to do now?"

"We're going to get dinner going. Hungry?"

She smiled weakly. "Famished." In truth, she was not only hungry but also light-headed.

"Come along, then," he said in a rather fatherly tone. "I'll show you how to make camp stew."

"Camp stew?" she said, concentrating on his words against the pulsating beat of her heart in her ears.

He grinned. "Camp stew is going to be our primary feast while en route to your summer home. It's just a fancy way of saying beans and dried beef. Sometimes I throw in a few potatoes just to break the monotony."

Amelia allowed herself to smile. "At this point it sounds like a feast."

"You can take this to the river and get some water," he said, handing her a coffee pot. "I'll unpack the pot for the beans. You'll need to fill it with water first; then bring the coffee pot back full and we'll make some coffee."

She nodded wearily and made her way to the water's edge. Her head was beginning to ache and a voice from within reminded her of Mr. Reed's warning to drink plenty of water. Scooping a handful to her lips, Amelia thought she'd never tasted anything as good. The water was cold and clear and instantly refreshed her. With each return trip Amelia forced herself to drink a little water. On her last trip she dipped her handkerchief in the icy river and wiped some of the grime away from her face. She drew in gasping breaths of chilled mountain air, trying hard to compensate for the lack of oxygen. For a moment the world seemed to spin.

Lowering her gaze, Amelia panicked at the sensation of dizziness. It seemed to come in waves, leaving her unable to focus. She took a step and stumbled. Took another and nearly fell over backward. *What's happening to me?* she worried.

"Amelia?" Logan was calling from somewhere. "You got that coffee water yet?"

The river was situated far enough away that the trees and rocks kept her from view of the camp. She opened her mouth to call out, then clamped it shut, determined not to ask Mr. Reed for help. Sliding down to sit on a small boulder, Amelia steadied the pot. *I'll feel better in a minute,* she thought. *If I just sit for a moment, everything will clear and I'll have my breath back.*

"Amelia?" Logan stood not three feet away. "Are you all right?"

Getting to her feet quickly, Amelia instantly realized her mistake. The coffee pot fell with a clatter against the rocks and Amelia felt her knees buckle.

"Whoa, there," Logan said, reaching out to catch her before she hit the ground. "I was afraid you were doing too much. You are the most prideful, stubborn woman I've ever met."

Amelia tried to push him away and stand on her own, but her head and legs refused to work together and her hands only seemed to flail at the air. "I just got up too fast," she protested.

"You just managed to get yourself overworked. You're going to lay down for the rest of the night. I'll bring you some chow when it's ready, but till then, you aren't to lift a finger." In one fluid motion he swung her up into his arms.

"I assure you, Mr. Reed—"

"Logan. My name is Logan. Just as you are Lady Amhurst, I am Logan. Understand?" he sounded gruff, but he was smiling and Amelia could only laugh. She'd brought this on herself by trying to outdo the others and keep up with any task he'd suggested.

"Well?" His eyes seemed to twinkle.

"I understand!" she declared and tried not to notice the feel of his muscular arms around her.

His expression sobered and Amelia couldn't help but notice that there was no twitching of that magnificent mustache. Sometimes, just sometimes, she wondered what it would be like to touch that mustache. *Is it coarse and prickly, or smooth and soft like the pet rabbit Margaret had played with as a child?*

He was looking at her as though trying to say something that couldn't be formed into words and for once, Amelia didn't think him so barbaric. These new considerations of a man she'd once thought hopelessly crude were disturbing to her. Her mind began to race. *What should I say to him? What should I do? I could demand he release me, but I seriously doubt that he would. And what if he did? Did she really want that?*

This is ridiculous, she chided herself. Forcing her gaze to the path, she nodded and said, "Shouldn't we get back? Maybe you could just put me down now. I'm feeling much better."

Logan gave her a little toss upward to get a better hold. She let out an audible gasp and tightly gripped her arms around Logan's neck.

"Don't!" she squealed with the abandonment of a child. Logan looked at her strangely and Amelia tried to calm her nerves. "I–I've always been afraid of falling," she offered lamely. "Please put me down."

"Nope," he said and started for camp. When he came to the edge of the clearing it was evident that everyone else was still collecting firewood. Logan stopped and asked, "Why are you afraid of falling?"

Amelia's mind went back in time. "When I was very young someone held me out over the edge of a balcony and threatened to spill me. I was absolutely terrified and engaged myself in quite a spell until Mother reprimanded me for being so loud."

∞

"No reprimand for the one doing the teasing, eh?" Logan's voice was soft and sympathetic.

"No, she knew Jeffery didn't mean anything by it." Amelia could have laughed at the stunned expression on Logan's face.

"Not Sir Jeffery?" he asked in mock horror.

"None other. I think it amused him to see me weak and helpless."

"Then he's a twit."

Amelia's grin broadened into a smile. "Yes, he is."

"Amelia! What's wrong?"

"Speaking of the twit," Logan growled low against her ear and Amelia giggled. His warm breath against her ear, not to mention the mustache, tickled. "Amelia's fine, she just overdid it a bit. I'm putting her down for a rest."

"I can take her," Jeffery said, dropping the wood he'd brought. He brushed at his coat and pulled off his gloves as he crossed the clearing.

"Well, Lady Amhurst, it's twits or barbarians. Which do you prefer?" he questioned low enough that only Amelia could hear.

Amelia felt her breath quicken at the look Logan gave her. *What is happening to me? I'm acting like a schoolgirl. This must stop*, she thought and determined to feel nothing but polite gratitude toward Mr. Logan Reed. When she looked at each man and said nothing, Logan deposited her in Jeffery's waiting arms.

"Guess your feelings are pretty clear," he said and turned to leave.

"But I didn't say a thing, Mr. Reed," Amelia said, unconcerned with Jeffery's questioning look.

Logan turned. "Oh, but you did." As he walked away he called back to Jeffery, "Put her in her tent and help her with her bedroll. I'll have some food brought to her when it's ready."

"He's an extremely rude man, what?"

Amelia watched Logan walk away. She felt in some way she

had insulted him, but surely he hadn't really expected her to choose him over Jeffery. He was only a simple American guide and Jeffery, well, Jeffery was much more than that. If only he were much more of something Amelia could find appealing.

"Put me down, Jeffery. I am very capable of walking and this familiarity is making me most uncomfortable," she demanded and Jeffery quickly complied. She knew deep in her heart that Logan would never be bullied in such a way.

"Mr. Reed said to have you lie down."

"I heard him and I'm quite capable of taking care of myself. Now shouldn't you help get the firewood? Mr. Reed also said we were to expect a cold night." Jeffery nodded and Amelia took herself to the tent, stopping only long enough to give Logan a defiant look before throwing back the flaps and secluding herself within.

"Men, like religion, are a nuisance," she muttered as she untied the strings on her bedroll.

Chapter 6

Morning came with bone-numbing cold and Amelia was instantly grateful for her sisters. Snuggling closer to Penelope, Amelia warmed and drifted back to sleep. It seemed only moments later when someone was shouting her into consciousness and a loud clanging refused to allow her to ease back into her dreams.

"Breakfast in ten minutes!" Logan was shouting. "Roll up your gear and have it ready to go before you eat. Chamberlain, you will assist in taking down the tents."

Amelia rolled over and moaned at the soreness in her legs and backside. *Surely we aren't going to ride as hard today as yesterday.* Pushing back her covers, Amelia began to shiver from the cold of the mountain morning. Could it have only been yesterday that the heat seemed so unbearable? Stretching, Amelia decided that nothing could be worse than the days she'd spent on the Colorado prairie. *At least here, the black flies seem to have thinned out. Maybe the higher altitude and cold keeps them at bay.* Amelia squared her shoulders. *Maybe things are getting better.*

But it proved to be much worse. A half-day into the ride, Amelia was fervently wishing she could be swallowed up in one of the craggy ravines that threatened to eat away the narrow path on which she rode. The horse was cantankerous, her sisters were impossible, and Mattersley looked as though he might succumb to exhaustion before they paused for the night.

When a rockslide prevented them from taking the route Logan had planned on, he reminded the party again of the altitude and the necessity of taking it easy. "We could spend the next day or two trying to clear that path or we can spend an extra day or two on an alternate road into Estes. Since none of you are used to the thinner air, I think taking the other road makes more sense."

Logan's announcement made Amelia instantly self-conscious. *Was he making fun of me because of the attack I suffered last night? Why else would he make such an exaggerated point of the altitude?*

"I do hope the other road is easier," Lady Gambett said with a questioning glace at her husband.

"I'm afraid not," Logan replied. "It climbs higher, in fact, than this one and isn't traveled nearly as often. For all I know that trail could be in just as bad of shape as this one."

"Oh dear," Lady Gambett moaned.

"But Mama," Josephine protested, pushing her small spectacles up on the bridge of her nose, "I cannot possibly breathe air any thinner than this. I will simply perish."

Logan suppressed a snort of laughter and Amelia caught his eye in the process. His expression seemed to say "See, I told you so" and Amelia couldn't bear it. She turned quickly to Lady Gambett.

"Perhaps Josephine would be better off back in Longmont," Amelia suggested.

"Oh, gracious, perhaps we all would be," Lady Gambett replied.

"But I want to go on, Mama," the plumper Henrietta whined. "I'm having a capital time of it."

"We're all going ahead." Lord Gambett spoke firmly with a tone that told his women that he would brook no more nonsense.

"Are we settled and agreed then?" Logan asked from atop his horse.

"We are, sir," Gambett replied with a harsh look of reprimand in Josephine's direction.

Amelia tried to fade into the scenery behind Margaret's robust, but lethargic, palomino. The last thing in the world she wanted to do was to have to face Logan. She was determined to avoid him at any cost. Something inside her seemed to come apart whenever he was near. It would never do to have him believing her incapable of handling her emotions and to respond with anything but cool reservation would surely give him the wrong idea.

Logan was pushing them forward again. He was a harsh taskmaster and no one dared to question his choices—except for the times when Jeffery would occasionally put in a doubtful appraisal. Logan usually quieted him with a scowl or a raised eyebrow and always it caught Amelia's attention.

But she didn't want Logan Reed to capture her attention. She tried to focus on the beauty around her. Ragged rock walls surrounded them on one side, while what seemed to be the entire world spread out in glorious splendor on the other side. The sheer drop made Amelia a bit light-headed, but the richness of the countryside was well worth the risk of traveling the narrow granite ledge. Tall pines were still in abundance, as were the quaint mountain flowers and vegetation Amelia had come to appreciate. Whenever they stopped to rest the horses she would gather a sample of each new flower and press it into her book, remembering in the back of her mind that Logan Reed would probably be the one to identify it later.

Soon enough the path widened a bit and Amelia kept close to Lady Gambett, hoping that both Jeffery and Logan would keep their distance. Her father was drawn into conversation with Lord Gambett, and Lady Gambett seemed more than happy for Amelia's company.

"The roses shouldn't be planted too deep, however," Lady Gambett was saying, and Amelia suddenly realized she hadn't a clue what the woman was talking about. "Now the roses at Havershire are some of the most beautiful in the world, but of course there are fourteen gardeners who devote themselves only to the roses."

Amelia nodded sedately and Lady Gambett continued rambling on about the possibility of creating a blue rose. Amelia's mind wandered to the rugged Logan Reed and when he allowed his horse to fall back a bit, she feared he might try to start up a conversation. Feeling her stomach do a flip and her breathing quicken, Amelia gripped the reins tighter and refused to look up.

"Are you ill, my dear?" Lady Gambett asked suddenly.

Amelia was startled by the question, but even more startled by the fact that Logan was looking right at her as if awaiting her answer. "I. . .uh. . .I'm just a bit tired." *It wasn't a lie*, she reasoned.

"Oh, I quite agree. Mr. Reed, shouldn't we have a bit of respite?" Lady Gambett inquired. "Poor Mattersley looks to be about to fall off his mount altogether."

Logan nodded and held up his hand. "We'll stop here for a spell. See to your horses first."

Amelia tried not to smile at the thought of dismounting and

stretching her weary limbs. She didn't want to give Logan a false impression and have him believe her pleasure was in him rather than his actions. Without regard to the rest of the party, Amelia urged her horse to a scraggly patch of grass and slid down without assistance. Her feet nearly buckled beneath her when her boots hit the ground. Her legs were so sore and stiff and her backside sorely abused. Rubbing the small of her back, she jumped in fear when Logan whispered her name.

"I didn't mean to scare you," he apologized, "I hope you're feeling better."

Amelia's mind raced with thoughts. She wanted desperately to keep the conversation lighthearted. "I'm quite well, thank you. Although I might say I've found a new way to extract a pound of flesh."

Logan laughed. "Ah, the dilemma of exacting a pound of flesh without spilling a drop of blood. *The Merchant of Venice*, right? I've read it several times and very much enjoyed it."

Amelia tried not to sound surprised. "You are familiar with Shakespeare?"

He put one hand to his chest and the other into the air. "'My only love sprung from my only hate! Too early seen unknown, and known too late!'" He grinned. "'Romeo and Juliet.'"

"Yes, I know," she replied, still amazed at this new revelation.

"'Hatred stirreth up strifes: but love covereth all sins.'"

Amelia tried to remember what play these words were from, but nothing came to mind. "I suppose I don't know Shakespeare quite as well as you do, Mr. Reed."

"Logan," he said softly and smiled. "And it isn't Shakespeare's works, it's the Bible. Proverbs ten, twelve to be exact."

"Oh," she said and turned to give the horse her full attention.

"I thought we'd worked out a bit of a truce between us," Logan said, refusing to leave her to herself.

"There is no need for anything to be between us," Amelia said, trying hard to keep her voice steady. *How could this one man affect my entire being?* She couldn't understand the surge of emotions, nor was she sure she wanted to.

"It's a little late to take that stand, isn't it?" Logan asked in a whisper.

Amelia reeled on her heel as though the words had been hot coals placed upon her head. "I'm sure I don't understand your meaning, Mr. Reed," she said emphasizing his name. "Now if you'll excuse me, I have other matters to consider."

"Like planting English roses?" he teased.

Her mouth dropped open only slightly before she composed her expression. "Have we lent ourselves to that most repulsive habit of eavesdropping, Mr. Reed?"

Logan laughed. "Who could help but overhear Lady Gambett and her suggestions? It hardly seemed possible to not hear the woman."

Amelia tried to suppress her smile but couldn't. Oh, but this man made her blood run hot and cold. Hot and cold. She remembered Logan stating just that analysis of her back in Greeley. Just when she was determined to be unaffected by him, he would say or do something that made the goal impossible. She started to reply when Lady Gambett began to raise her voice in whining reprimand to Henrietta.

"It would seem," Amelia said, slowly allowing her gaze to meet his, "the woman speaks for herself."

Logan chuckled. "At every possible opportunity."

Lady Gambett was soon joined by Josephine as well as Margaret and Penelope, and Amelia could only shake her head. "I'm glad they have each other."

"But who do you have?" Logan asked Amelia quite unexpectedly.

"I beg your pardon?"

"You heard me. You don't seem to have a great deal of affection for your sisters or your father. Sir Jeffery hardly seems your kind, although I have noticed he gives you a great deal of attention. You seem the odd man out, so to speak."

Amelia brushed bits of dirt from her riding jacket and fortified her reserve. "I need no one, Mr. Reed."

"No one?"

His question caused a ripple to quake through her resolve. She glanced to where the other members of the party were engaged in various degrees of conversation as they saw to their tasks. How ill-fitted they seemed in her life. She was tired of pretense and noble games, and yet it was the very life she had secured herself within. Didn't she long to return to England and the quiet of her father's estates? Didn't she yearn for a cup of tea in fine English china? Somehow the Donneswick estates seemed a foggy memory.

"Why are you here, Amelia?"

She looked up, thought to reprimand him for using her name, then decided it wasn't so bad after all. She rather liked the way it sounded on his lips. "Why?" she finally questioned, not truly expecting an answer.

"I just wondered why you and your family decided to come to America."

"Oh," she said, frowning at the thought of her father and Sir Jeffery's plans. There was no way she wanted to explain this to Logan Reed. He had already perceived her life to be one of frivolity and ornamentation. She'd nearly killed herself trying to work at his side in order to prove otherwise, but if she told him the truth it would defeat everything she'd done thus far. "We'd not yet toured the country and Lady Bird, an acquaintance of the family who compiled a book about her travels here, suggested we come immediately to Estes."

"I remember Lady Bird," Logan said softly. "She was a most unpretentious woman. A lady in true regard."

Amelia felt the challenge in Logan's words but let it go unanswered. Instead, she turned the conversation to his personal life. "You are different from most Americans, Mr. Reed. You appear to have some of the benefits of a proper upbringing. You appear educated and well-read and you have better manners than most. You can speak quite eloquently when you desire to do so, or just as easily slip into that lazy American style that one finds so evident here in the West."

Logan grinned and gave his horse a nudge. "And I thought she didn't notice me."

Amelia frowned. "How is it that you are this way?"

Logan shrugged. "I had folks who saw the importance of an education but held absolutely no regard for snobbery and uppity society ways. I went to college back east and learned a great deal, but not just in books. I learned about people."

"Is that where you also took up religion?" she questioned.

"No, not at all. I learned about God and the Bible from my mother and father first, and then from our local preacher. The things they taught me made a great deal of sense. Certainly more sense than anything the world was offering. It kept me going in the right direction."

Amelia nodded politely, but in the back of her mind she couldn't help but wonder about his statement. Most of her life she had felt herself running toward something, but it was impossible to know what that something was. Her mother had tried to encourage her to believe in God, but Amelia thought it a mindless game. Religion required you to believe in things you couldn't see or prove. Her very logical mind found it difficult to see reason in this. If God existed, couldn't He make Himself known without requiring people to give in to superstitious nonsense and outrageous stories of miraculous wonders? And if God existed, why did tragedy and injustice abound? Why did He not, instead, create a perfect world without pain or sorrow?

"I've answered your questions, now how about answering some of mine?" Logan's voice broke through her thoughts.

"Such as?" Amelia dared to ask.

"Such as, why are you really here? I have a good idea that Lady Bird has very little to do with your traveling to America."

Amelia saw her sisters move to where Jeffery stood and smiled. "My father wanted me to come, so I did. It pleased him and little else seemed to offer the same appeal."

"Is he still mourning your mother's passing?"

"I suppose in a sense, although it's been six years. They were very much a love match, which was quite rare among their friends."

"Rare? Why is that?"

Amelia smiled tolerantly. "Marriages are most generally arranged to be advantageous to the families involved. My father married beneath his social standing." She said the words without really meaning to.

"If he married for love it shouldn't have mattered. Seems like he did well enough for himself anyway," Logan replied. He nodded in the direction of her father in conversation with Mattersley. "He is an earl, after all, and surely that holds esteem in your social circles."

"Yes, but the title dies with him. He has no sons and his estates, well—" she found herself unwilling to answer Logan's soft-spoken questions. "His estates aren't very productive. My mother had a low social standing, but she brought a small fortune and land into the family, which bolstered my father's position."

"So it *was* advantageous to both families, despite her lack of standing?"

"Yes, but you don't understand. It made my father somewhat of an outcast. He's quite determined that his daughters do not make the same mistake. It's taken him years to rebuild friendships and such. People still speak badly of him if the moment presents itself in an advantageous way. Were we to marry poorly it would reflect directly on him and no doubt add to his sufferings."

"But what if you fall in love with someone your father deems beneath you?" Logan asked moving in a step. "Say you fall in love with a barbarian instead of a twit?" His raised brow implied what his words failed to say.

Amelia felt her face grow hot. *He is really asking what would happen if I fell in love with him.* His face was close enough to reach out and touch and as always that pesky mustache drew her attention. *What if?* She had to distance herself. She had to get away from his piercing green eyes and probing questions. "It could never happen, Mr. Reed," she finally said, then added with a hard stare of her own, "Never."

Chapter 7

Estes Park was like nothing Amelia had ever seen. Completely surrounded by mountains, the valley looked as though someone had placed it there to hide it away from the world. Ponderosa pine, spruce, and aspen dotted the area and Lord Amhurst was delighted to find the shrub-styled junipers whose berries were especially popular with the grouse and pheasants. She knew her father was becoming eager for the hunt. She had seen him eyeing the fowl while Jeffery had been watching the larger game.

They made their way slowly through the crisp morning air, horses panting lightly and blowing puffs of warm air out to meet the cold. To Amelia it seemed that the valley wrapped itself around them as they descended. Birds of varying kinds began their songs, and from time to time a deer or elk would cross their path, pausing to stare for a moment at the intruders before darting off into the thicket.

Gone was the oppressive prairie with its blasting winds, insufferable heat, and swarming insects. Gone were the dusty streets and spittoons. The place was a complete contrast to the prairie towns she'd seen. Even the air was different. The air here, though thinner, was also so very dry and Amelia marveled at the difference between it and that of her native land. Already her skin felt tough and coarse and she vowed to rub scented oils and lotions on herself every night until they departed. But departing was the furthest thing from her mind. What had started out as an unpleasant obligation to her was now becoming rather appealing. She found herself increasingly drawn to this strange land, and to the man who had brought them here.

She silently studied Logan's back as he rode. He was telling them bits and pieces of information about the area, but her mind wouldn't focus on the words.

What if she did fall in love with a barbarian? What if she already had?

∽

The lodge where they'd made arrangements to stay was a two-story log building surrounded by smaller log cabins. Lord Amhurst had arranged to take three cabins for his party, while Lord and Lady Gambett had decided to stay in the lodge itself. Lady Gambett had declared it necessary to see properly to the delicate constitutions of her daughters. This thought made Amelia want to laugh, but she remained stoically silent. Delicate constitutions had no place here and it would provide only one more weapon for Logan Reed to use against them. She was bound and determined to show Logan that Englishwomen could be strong and capable without need of anyone's assistance. Amelia chose to forget that Lady Bird had already proven her case to Logan Reed two years ago.

"This place looks awful," Margaret was whining as Mattersley helped to bring in their bags.

Amelia looked around the crude cabin and for once she didn't feel at all repulsed by the simplicity. It was one room with two beds, a small table with a single oil lamp, and a washstand with a pitcher and bowl of chipped blue porcelain that at one time might have been considered pretty. A stone fireplace dominated one wall. Red gingham curtains hung in the single window and several rag rugs had been strategically placed in stepping-stone fashion upon the thin plank floor.

"It's quite serviceable, Margaret," Amelia stated firmly, "so stop being such a ninny. Perhaps you'd like to sleep in a tent again."

∽

"I think this place is hideous," Penelope chimed in before Margaret could reply. "Papa was cruel to bring us here, and all because of you."

This statement came just as Logan appeared with one of several trunks containing the girls' clothes. He eyed Amelia suspiciously and placed the trunk on the floor. "I think you'll find this cabin a sight warmer than the tent and the bed more comfortable than the ground," he said before walking back out the door.

Amelia turned on her sisters with a fury. "Keep our private affairs to yourselves. I won't have the entire countryside knowing our business. Mother raised you to be ladies of quality and refinement. Ladies of that nature do not spout off about the family's personal concerns."

Margaret and Penelope were taken aback for only a moment. It mattered little to them that Logan Reed had overheard their conversation. Amelia knew that to them he was hired help, no different than Mattersley. They were quite used to a house filled with servants who overheard their conversations on a daily basis and knew better than to speak of private matters, even amongst themselves. Logan Reed was quite a different sort, however, and Amelia knew he'd feel completely within his rights to inquire about their statement at the first possible moment.

"I suggest we unpack our things and see if we can get the wrinkles out of our gowns. I'm sure you will want a bath and the chance to be rid of these riding costumes," Amelia said, taking a sure route she knew her sisters would follow.

"Oh, I do so hope to sink into a tub of hot water," Penelope moaned. At seventeen she was used to spending her days changing from one gown to another, sometimes wearing as many as six in the same day. "I'm positively sick of this mountain skirt or whatever they call it."

"I rather enjoy the freedom they afford," Amelia said. Satisfied with having distracted her sisters, she unfastened the latches on the trunk. "But I would find a bath quite favorable."

They spent the rest of the day securing their belongings and laying out their claims on the various parts of the room. By standing their trunks on end they managed to create a separate table for each of them and it was here they placed their brushes, combs, and perfumes. Helping Penelope to string a rope on which they could hang their dresses, Amelia realized they'd brought entirely too many formal gowns and not nearly enough simple outfits. Where had they thought they were traveling? It wasn't as if they'd have anyone to dress up for.

Logan came to mind and Amelia immediately vanquished his image from her thoughts. She would not concern herself with looking nice for him. Her father expected her to look the lovely English rose for Sir Jeffery. That was why the clothes were packed as they were. Her desires were immaterial compared to her father's.

∞

"Amelia has twice as many gowns as we have," Penelope complained at dinner that evening.

Lord Amhurst gave her a look of reprimand, but it was Lady Gambett who spoke. "Your sister is the eldest, and by being the eldest, she is to have certain privileges afforded her. You mustn't complain about it for once she's married and keeping house for herself, you shall be the eldest."

This placated the petite blond, but Amelia felt her face grow hot. She was grateful that Logan was nowhere to be seen.

"I suggest we make an early evening of it," the earl said with an eye to his daughters. "There is to be an early morning hunt and I'm certain you won't want to lag behind."

Margaret and Penelope began conversing immediately with Henrietta and Josephine about what they would wear and how they would arrange their hair. Amelia could only think on the fact that she would be forced to spend still another day in Logan Reed's company.

"Papa," she said without giving the matter another thought, "I'd like to rest and walk about the grounds. Please forgive me if I decline the hunt."

The earl nodded, appraising her for a moment then dismissing the matter when Lady Gambett spoke up. "I will stay behind as well. I can't possibly bear the idea of another ride."

With the matter settled, the party dispersed and went to their various beds. Amelia faded to sleep quickly, relishing the comfort of a bed and the warmth of their fire. In her dreams she kept company with a green-eyed Logan, and because it was only a dream, Amelia found herself enjoying every single moment.

Logan was glad to be home. The valley offered him familiar comfort that he had never been able to replicate elsewhere. His cabin, located just up the mountain, wasn't all that far from the lodge where he'd deposited the earl and his traveling companions. But it was far enough. It afforded him some much-needed privacy and the peace of mind to consider the matters at hand.

Kicking off his boots, Logan built a hearty fire and glanced around at his home. Three rooms comprised the first floor. The bedroom at the back of the cabin was small but served its purpose. A kitchen with a cookstove and several crude cupboards extended into the dining area, where a table and chairs stood beneath one window. This area, in turn, blended into the main room, where the fireplace mantel was lined with small tintype photos and books. A comfortable sofa, which Logan had made himself, invited company, which seldom came, and two idle chairs stood as sentinels beside a crude bookshelf. The tall shelf of books seemed out of place for the rustic cabin, but it was Logan's private library and he cherished it more than any of his other possessions. Whenever he went out from the valley to the towns nearby, he always brought back new books to add to his collection. This time he'd picked up an order in Greeley and had five new books with which to pass the time. Two were works by Jules Verne that promised to be quite entertaining. Of the remaining three, one was a study of science, one a collection of poetry, and the final book promised an exploration of Italy.

With a sigh, Logan dropped down onto the sofa and glanced upward. Shadows from the dancing fire made images against the darkened loft. The house was silent except for the occasional popping of the fire, and Logan found his mind wandering to the fair-haired Lady Amelia. He knew he'd lost his heart to her, and furthermore he was certain that she felt something for him. He wanted to chide himself for his love-at-first-sight reaction to the delicate beauty, but there was no need. His heart wouldn't have heeded the warning or reprimand. Lost in his daydreams, Logan fell asleep on the sofa. He'd see her tomorrow before the party went out on the hunt, but how would he manage the rest of the day without her at his side?

∽

Amelia hung back in her cabin until well after her family had left for the hunting expedition. She was determined to keep from facing Logan Reed and having to deal with his comments or suggestions. She couldn't understand why he bothered her so much. *It isn't as if he has any say in my life. It isn't as if he could change my life, so why give him the slightest consideration?*

Making her way to the lodge, Amelia guessed it to be nearly eight o'clock. She could smell the lingering scents of breakfast on the air and knew that Logan had been right about one thing. Mountain air gave you a decidedly larger appetite.

"Morning," a heavyset woman Amelia knew to be the owner's wife called out. "You must be Lady Amhurst. Jonas told me you were staying behind this morning." Amelia nodded and the woman continued. "I'm just making bread, but you're welcome to keep me company."

Amelia smiled. "I thought to tour around the woods nearby, but I'd be happy to sit with you for a time, Mrs. Lewis." She barely remembered her father saying the place was owned by a family named Lewis.

The woman wiped her floury hands on her apron and reached for a bowl. "Just call me Mary. Mrs. Lewis is far too formal for the likes of me and this place."

Amelia sensed a genuine openness to the woman. "You must call me Amelia," she said, surprising herself by the declaration. The mountain air and simplicity of the setting made her forget old formalities. "What is that you are doing just now?" she asked, feeling suddenly very interested.

Mary looked at her in disbelief. "Don't tell me you've never seen bread made before?"

"Never," Amelia said with a laugh. "I'm afraid I've never ventured much into the kitchen at all."

"But who does the cooking for your family?"

"Oh, we've a bevy of servants who see to our needs. Father believes that young women of noble upbringing have no place in a kitchen."

Mary laughed. "I guess I'm far from noble in upbringing. I was practically birthed in the kitchen." She kneaded the dough and sprinkled in a handful of flour. "Would you like to learn how to make bread?"

Surprised by an unfamiliar desire to do just that, Amelia responded, "I'd love to."

Mary wiped her hands again and went to a drawer where she pulled out another apron. "Put this on over your pretty dress so that it doesn't get all messy. And take off those gloves. It doesn't pay to wear Sunday best when you're working in the kitchen."

She turned back to the dough while Amelia secured the apron over what she had considered one of her dowdier gowns. The peach-and-green print was far from being her Sunday best. Amelia tucked her white kid gloves into the pocket of the apron and rolled up her sleeves like Mary's.

"I'm ready," she said confidently, anxious to embark on this new project. Lady Bird had told her that only in experiencing things first-hand could a person truly have a working knowledge of them. One might read books about crossing the ocean or riding an elephant, but until you actually participated in those activities, you were only touching the memories of another.

"Here you go," Mary said, putting a large hunk of dough in front of her. "Work it just like this." She pushed the palms of her hands deep into the mass. "Then pull it back like this." Amelia watched, catching the rhythm as Mary's massive hands worked the dough. "Now you do it." Mary tossed a bit of flour atop the bread dough and smiled.

Amelia grinned. "You make it look simple enough." But it was harder than it looked. Amelia felt the sticky dough ooze through her fingers and laughed out loud at the sensation. *Father would positively expire if he saw me like this.*

"That's it," Mary said from beside her own pile. "You can work out a great many problems while kneading bread."

"I can imagine why," Amelia replied. Already her thoughts of Logan were fading.

She worked through two more piles of dough with Mary's

lively chatter keeping her company. When all of the dough had been prepared Mary showed her how to divide the mass into loaves. Placing the last of her dough into one of the pans, Amelia wiped a stray strand of hair from her face and smiled. It was satisfying work. Twenty-two loaves lay rising before her and some of them had been formed by her own hands.

"There are so many," she commented, noting some of the dough had been placed in pans before her arrival. Already they were rising high, while still others filled the lodge with a delicious scent as they baked.

"I've been collecting bread pans for most of my life. Working this lodge takes a heap of bread for the folks who stay, as well as those who help out. I alternate the loaves so that some are always baking or rising or getting kneaded down. Bread is pretty much alike the country over, so travelers take right to it when they won't eat another thing on the table. And I sell a few loaves on the side. Menfolk around here don't always want to bake their own bread, so they come here to buy it from me." As if on cue the door opened and Logan Reed strode in.

Amelia stared at him in stunned silence, while Logan did much the same. A lazy smile spread itself under the bushy mustache, making Amelia instantly uncomfortable. "You don't mean to tell me that Lady Amhurst is taking lessons in bread baking?"

"She sure is," Mary said, before Amelia could protest the conversation. "Amelia here is a right quick learner."

"Amelia, eh?" Logan raised a questioning brow to keep company with his lopsided smile.

"Sure," Mary said, betraying a bit of German heritage in her voice. "She's a charming young woman, this one."

"That she is," he replied then turned his question on Amelia. "Why aren't you on the hunt?"

Amelia couldn't tell him that she'd purposefully avoided the hunt because of him. She tossed around several ideas and finally decided on the closest thing to the truth. "I wanted to tour about the grounds. I've had enough horsebackriding for a while."

"I see."

For a moment Amelia was certain he really did see. His expression told her that he knew very well she'd made her decision based on something entirely apart from the discomfort of the old cavalry saddle.

"Why are you here? I thought you'd be off with the others." Amelia knew that if he had doubted the reason for her decision, she had just confirmed those doubts.

Mary looked rather puzzled. "He comes for the bread. One of those menfolk I told you about." She nudged Amelia playfully. "He needs a good wife to keep him company and make his bread for him."

"Mary's right. That's probably just what I need." Logan said with a knowing look at Amelia.

"If you'll excuse me, Mary, I'm going to go clean up and take my walk. I appreciate your lessons this morning." Amelia untied the apron and put it across the back of a nearby chair, her kid gloves forgotten in the pocket.

"Come back tomorrow morning and we'll make cinnamon rolls," the heavyset woman said with a smile.

"Now there's something every good wife should know," Logan piped up. "Mary's cinnamon rolls are the best in the country. Why, I'd walk from Denver to Estes to get a pan of those."

"If time permits, I'd be happy to work with you," Amelia said and then hurried from the room.

Images of Logan Reed followed her back to the cabin, where Amelia hurriedly grabbed her journal and pencil, as well as a straw walking-out hat. Balancing the journal while tying on the bonnet, Amelia quickened her pace and determined to put as much distance as possible between her and the smug-faced Mr. Reed. Why couldn't he have just taken her party on the hunt and left her to herself? Why did he have to show up and see her wearing an apron and acting like the hired help? But she'd enjoyed her time with Mary, and she never once felt like hired help. Instead she felt. . .well, she felt useful, as though she'd actually accomplished something very important.

Making her way along a tiny path behind the cluster of cabins, Amelia tried to grasp those feelings of accomplishment and consider what they meant. Her life in England seemed trite when she thought of Mary's long hours of work. She was idle in comparison, but then again, she had been schooled in the graceful arts of being idle. She could, of course, stitch lovely tea towels and dresser scarves. She could paint fairly well and intended to sketch out some pastoral scenes from her hike and later redo them in watercolors. But none of these things were all that useful. Mary's work was relied upon by those around her. She baked their bread and kept them fed. She braided rugs and sewed clothes to ward of the mountain chill. She knew all of this because Mary had told her so in their chatty conversation. *Mary's is not an idle life of appearances. Mary's life has purpose and meaning.*

Before she realized it, Amelia was halfway up the incline that butted against the Lewis property. She turned to look back down and drew her breath in at the view. The sun gave everything the appearance of having been freshly washed. The brilliance of the colors stood out boldly against the dark green background of the snow-capped, tree-covered mountains. The rushing river on the opposite side of the property shimmered and gurgled in glorious shades of violet and blue. But it was always lighting which appealed to her painter's eyes. The light here was unlike any she'd ever seen before. It was impossible to explain, but for a moment she felt compelled to try. She sat down abruptly and took up her journal.

"There is a quality to the light which cannot be explained. It is, I suppose, due to the high mountain altitude and the thinner quality of oxygen," she spoke aloud while writing. "The colors are more vivid, yet, if possible, they are also more subtle. The lighting highlights every detail, while creating the illusion of something draped in a translucent veil. I know this doesn't make sense, yet it is most certainly so." She paused and looked down upon the tiny village. She would very much like to paint this scene, but how in the world could she ever capture the light?

Beside her were several tiny white flowers bobbing up and down in the gentle breeze. She leaned over on her elbow, mindless of her gown, and watched them for a moment. She considered the contrast of their whiteness against the green of their leaves and wondered at their name. Plucking one stem, she pressed it between the pages of her book, jotted a note of its location, and got to her feet.

The higher she climbed, the rougher the path. Finally it became quite steep and altogether impassable. It was here she decided to turn away from the path and make her own way. The little incline to her left seemed most appealing even though it was strewn with rocks. The way to her right was much too threatening with its jagged boulders and sheer drops. Hiking up her skirt, with her journal tucked under her arm, Amelia faced the challenging mountainside with a determined spirit. She was feeling quite bold and was nearly to the top when the loose gravel gave way beneath her feet and sent her tumbling backward. Sliding on her backside and rolling the rest of the way, Amelia finally landed in a heap at the foot of the incline. Six feet away stood Logan Reed with an expression on his face that seemed to contort from amusement to concern and back to amusement.

Amelia's pride and backside were sorely bruised, but she'd not admit defeat to Logan. She straightened her hat and frowned. "Are you spying on me, Mr. Reed?" she asked indignantly from where she sat.

Logan laughed. "I'd say you could use some looking after given the scene I just witnessed. But no, I didn't mean to spy. I live just over the ridge so when I saw you walking up this way, I thought I'd come and offer my services."

Amelia quickly got to her feet and brushed the gravel from her gown. Seeing her book on the ground, she retrieved it and winced at the way it hurt her to bend down. "Your services for what?" she asked, hoping Logan hadn't seen her misery as well.

"To be your hiking guide," he replied coming forward. "It would sure save on your wardrobe." He pointed to a long tear in the skirt of her gown. "Why in the world did you hike out here dressed like that?"

"I beg your pardon?"

"At least that riding skirt would have been a little more serviceable. You need to have sturdy clothes to hike these hills," he chided.

"I will hike in whatever is most comfortable to me, Mr. Reed."

"And you think corsets and muslin prints are most comfortable?"

Amelia huffed. "I don't think it is any of your concern. I'm quite capable of taking care of myself."

Logan rolled his eyes and laughed all the harder. "Yes, I can see that." He shook his head and turned to walk back to the lodge, leaving Amelia to nurse her wounded pride.

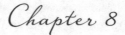

Chapter 8

Amelia spent the rest of the morning making notes in her journal and contemplating Logan Reed. As much as she tried to forget him, she couldn't help thinking of his offer to be her hiking guide. *Logan knows every flower and tree in the area. He would certainly be the most knowledgeable man around when it came to identifying the vegetation and landmarks. If I am going to put together a book on the area it seems sensible to utilize the knowledge of the most intelligent man.*

The book idea wasn't really new to her. She'd been considering it since speaking with Lady Bird long before departing for America. Lady Bird told Amelia she should do something memorable with her time abroad. *Writing a book and painting dainty watercolor flowers seems very reasonable. Falling in love with a barbaric, American guide does not.*

Closing her book with a loud snap, Amelia got to her feet. "I'm not in love," she murmured to the empty room. "I will not fall in love with Logan Reed." But even as she said the words, a part of Amelia knew that it was too late for such a declaration.

∞

At noon, she made her way to the lodge house, where the hunting party had returned to gather for a large midday meal. Amelia saw the hunt was successful, but for the first time she wondered about the business of cleaning the kill and how the skins of the animals were to be used afterward. She'd never given such matters much thought in the past. There was always someone else to do the dirty work.

"I say, Amelia, you missed quite a hunt. Sir Jeffery bagged a buck first thing out."

Amelia glanced at Jeffery and then back to her father. "How nice." She pulled out a chair and found Jeffery quickly at her side to seat her.

"It was a clean and easy shot, nothing so very spectacular," he said in false humility. "I could name a dozen animals that present a greater challenge to hunt."

"Perhaps the challenge comes in bagging a wife, what?" Lord

Amhurst heartily laughed much to Amelia's embarrassment and the stunned expressions of the others.

"Indeed true love is the hardest thing on earth to secure," Lady Gambett said in a tone that suggested a long story was forthcoming. She was fresh from a day of napping and eager to be companionable.

"Papa had a good morning as well," Penelope declared quickly and Margaret joined in so fast that both girls were talking at once. This seemed to be a cue to Josephine and Henrietta, who began a garbled rendition of the hunt for their mother's benefit.

Jeffery took a chair at Amelia's right and engaged her immediately in conversation. "I missed your company on the hunt. Do say you'll be present tomorrow."

"I'm afraid I didn't come to America to hunt. Not for animals of any kind," she stated, clearly hoping the implied meaning would not be lost on Jeffery. The sooner he understood her distaste for their proposed matrimony, the better.

"What will you do with your time?"

Amelia folded her hands in her lap. "I plan to write a book on the flowers and vegetation of Estes Park." The words came out at just the exact moment that her sisters and the Gambetts had chosen to take a collective breath. Her words seemed to echo in the silence for several moments. Stunned faces from all around the table looked up to make certain they had heard correctly.

"You plan to do what?" Margaret asked before anyone else could give voice to their thoughts.

"You heard me correctly," Amelia said, taking up a thick slice of bread she'd helped to make that morning. "The flowers here are beautiful and quite extraordinary. Nothing like what we have at home. Lady Bird told me I should use my time abroad to do something meaningful and memorable. I believe a book of this nature would certainly fit that suggestion."

The earl nodded. "If Lady Bird believes it to be of value, then I heartily agree." With Mattersley nowhere in sight, he filled his plate with potatoes and laughed when they dribbled over the rim. "Waiting on yourself takes some practice." The dinner party chuckled politely and the mood seemed to lighten considerably.

As everyone seemed intent on eating, Amelia's declaration passed from importance and escaped further discussion. With a sigh of relief, Amelia helped herself to a thick slice of ham and a hearty portion of potatoes. Jeffery would think her a glutton, but let him. She was tired of worrying about what other people thought. She found it suddenly quite enjoyable to be a bit more barbaric herself. Almost guilty for her thoughts, Amelia's head snapped up and she searched the room for Logan. She knew he wouldn't be there, but for some reason her conscience forced her to prove it.

"So how will you get about the place?" the earl was suddenly asking and all eyes turned to Amelia.

"I beg your pardon, Papa?"

"How will you travel about to gather your flowers and such? Will you have a guide?"

Amelia felt the ham stick in her throat as she tried to swallow. She took a long drink of her tea before replying. "Mr. Reed has offered to act as guide, but I told him it wasn't necessary."

"Nonsense," her father answered. "If you are to undertake this project, do it in a correct manner. There is a great deal to know about this area and you should have a guide, what?"

"I suppose you are fair in assuming that," Amelia replied. "But I hardly think Mr. Reed would be an appropriate teacher on flowers."

Mary Lewis had entered the room to deposit two large pies on the table. "Logan's an excellent teacher," she said, unmindful of her eavesdropping. "Logan led an expedition of government people out here last summer. He's got a good education—a sight more than most of the folks around these parts, anyway."

Everyone stared at Mary for a moment as though stunned by her boldness. "It seems reasonable," the earl said, nodding to Mary as if to dismiss her, "that Mr. Reed should direct you in your studies. I'll speak to him this afternoon and make certain he is reasonably recompensed for his efforts. Perhaps this evening at dinner we can finalize the arrangements."

Amelia said nothing. In truth, she had already decided to speak to Logan about helping her. She knew herself to be a prideful woman and what had once seemed like an admirable quality now made her feel even more of a snob. Lady Bird had lowered herself to even help harvest the crops of local residents. How could she resist the help of Logan Reed and possibly hope to justify herself? But just as her feelings were starting to mellow toward the man, he ruined it by joining them.

"Looks like you did pretty good for yourself, Amhurst," Logan said, taking a seat at the table.

Mary Lewis entered, bringing him a huge platter of food. "I saved this for you, Logan."

"Much thanks, Mary." He bowed his head for a moment before digging into the steaming food.

Everyone at the table looked on in silent accusation at Logan Reed. Even Mattersley would not presume to take his meals at the same table with the more noble classes. Logan Reed seemed to have no inclination that he was doing anything out of line, but when he glanced up he immediately caught the meaning of their silence. Rather than give in to their misplaced sense of propriety, however, Logan just smiled and complimented Mary on the food as she poured him a hot cup of coffee.

"Will Jonas be taking you out again tomorrow?" Logan asked as if nothing was amiss.

Amelia saw her father exchange a glance with Lord Gambett before answering. "Yes, I suppose he will. I understand you have offered to assist my daughter in gathering information for her book. I would like to discuss the terms of your employment after we finish with the meal."

Logan shook his head. "I didn't offer to be employed. I suggested to Lady Amhurst that I act as a hiking guide and she refused." He looked hard at Amelia, but there was a hint of amusement in his eyes and his mustache twitched in its usual betraying fashion.

"It seemed improper to accept your suggestion," Amelia said rather stiffly.

"Nonsense, child. The man is fully qualified to assist you," Lord Amhurst stated. "I'll make all the arrangements after dinner."

Amelia felt Logan's eyes on her and blushed from head to toe. The discomfort she felt was nothing compared to what she knew would come if she didn't leave immediately. Surprising her family, she got up rather quickly.

"I beg your forgiveness, but I must be excused." Without waiting for her father's approval, Amelia left the room.

Much to her frustration, Jeffery Chamberlain was upon her heels in a matter of seconds. "Are you ill, Amelia?" His voice oozed concern.

"I am quite well," she replied, keeping a steady pace to her walk. "I simply needed to take the air."

"I understand perfectly," he replied and took hold of her elbow as if to assist her.

Amelia jerked away and once they had rounded the front of the lodge, she turned to speak her mind. "Sir Jeffery, there are some issues we must have settled between us."

"I quite agree, but surely you wouldn't seek to speak of them here. Perhaps we can steal away to a quiet corner of the lodge," he suggested.

Amelia shook her head. "I am sure what I desire to speak of will not be in keeping with what you desire to speak of."

"But Amelia—"

"Please give me a moment," she interrupted. Amelia saw his expression of concern change to one of puzzlement. She almost felt sorry for him. Almost, but not quite.

"You must come to understand," she began, "that I have no desire to follow my father's wishes and marry you." She raised a hand to silence his protests. "Please hear me out. My father might find you a wonderful candidate for a son-in-law, but I will not marry a man I do not love. And, Sir Jeffery Chamberlain, I do not now, nor will I ever, love you."

The man's expression suggested anger and hurt, and for a moment Amelia thought to soften the blow. "However, my sisters find you quite acceptable as a prospective husband, so I would encourage you to court one of them."

At this Jeffery seemed insulted and puffed out his chest with a jerk of his chin. "I have no intentions of marrying your sisters," he said firmly. "I have an agreement with your father to acquire your hand in matrimony."

"But you have no such agreement with me, Sir Jeffery."

"It matters little. The men in our country arrange such affairs, not addlebrained women."

"Addlebrained?" Amelia was barely holding her anger in check. "You think me addlebrained?"

"When you act irresponsibly such as you are now, then yes, I do," he replied.

"I see. And what part of my actions implies being addlebrained?" she questioned. "Is it that I see no sense in joining in a marriage of convenience to a man I cannot possibly hope to love?"

"It is addlebrained and whimsical to imagine that such things as love are of weighted importance in this arrangement. Your father is seeing to the arrangement as he would any other business proposition. He is benefiting the family name, the family holdings, and the family coffers. Only a selfish and greedy young woman would see it as otherwise."

"So now I am addlebrained, whimsical, selfish, and greedy," Amelia said with haughty air. "Why in the world would you seek such a wife, Sir Chamberlain?"

Jeffery seemed to wilt a bit under her scrutiny. "I didn't mean to imply you were truly those things. But the air that you take in regards to our union would suggest you have given little consideration to the needs of others."

"So now I am inconsiderate as well!" Amelia turned on her heel and headed in the direction of her cabin.

Jeffery hurried after her. "You must understand, Amelia, these things are done for the betterment of all concerned."

She turned at this, completely unable to control her anger. "Jeffery, these things are done in order to keep my father in control of my mother's fortune. There hasn't been any consideration given to my desires or needs, and therefore I find it impossible to believe it has anything to do with my welfare or betterment."

"I can give you a good life," Jeffery replied barely keeping his temper in check. "I have several estates to where we might spend out our days and you will bring your own estate into the arrangement as well. You've a fine piece of Scottish land, or so your father tells me."

"But I have no desire to spend out my days with you. Not on

the properties you already own, nor the properties that I might bring into a marriage. Please understand, so that we might spend our days here in America as amicably as possible," she said with determined conviction, "I will not agree to marry you."

Jeffery's face contorted and to Amelia's surprise he spoke out in a manner close to rage. "You will do what you are told and it matters little what you agree to. Your father and I have important matters riding on this circumstance and that alone is what will gain consideration. You will marry me, Amelia, and furthermore," he paused with a suggestive leer on his face, "you will find it surprisingly enjoyable."

"I would sooner marry Logan Reed as to join myself in union to a boorish snob such as yourself." Silently she wished for something to throw at the smug-faced Jeffery, but instead she calmed herself and fixed him with a harsh glare. "I pray you understand, and understand well. I will never marry you and I will take whatever measures are necessary to ensure that I win out in this unpleasant situation."

She stormed off to her cabin, seething from the confrontation, but also a bit frightened by Jeffery's strange nature. She'd never seen him more out of character and it gave her cause to wonder. She knew there had always been a mischievous, almost devious side to his personality. The memory of hanging over the banister in fear of plunging to her death on the floor below affirmed Amelia's consideration. Jeffery had always leaned a bit on the cruel side of practical jokes and teasing play. Still, she couldn't imagine that he was all that dangerous. He wanted something very badly from her father and no doubt he could just as easily obtain it by marrying one of her sisters. After all, they adored him.

Reaching her cabin, Amelia reasoned away her fears. Her father's insistence that she marry Jeffery was in order to preserve the inheritance. Perhaps there was some other legal means by which Amelia could waive rights to her portion of the estate. It was worth questioning her father. If he saw the sincerity of her desire to remain single, even to the point of giving up what her mother had planned to be rightfully hers, Amelia knew she'd have no qualms about doing exactly that.

"I would sooner marry Logan Reed." The words suddenly

came back to haunt her. At first she laughed at this prospect while unfastening the back buttons of her gown. What would married life be like with the likes of Logan Reed? She could see herself in a cold cabin, kneading bread and scrubbing clothes on a washboard. She didn't even know how to cook and the thought of Logan laboring to choke down a meal prepared with her own two hands made Amelia laugh all the harder.

The gown slid down from her shoulders and fell in a heap on the floor. Absentmindedly Amelia ran her hands down her slender white arms. Laughter died in her throat as an image of Logan doing the same thing came to mind. She imagined staring deep into his green eyes and finding everything she'd ever searched for. Answers to all her questions would be revealed in his soul-searching gaze, including the truths of life that seemed to elude her. Shuddering in a sudden wake of emotion, Amelia quickly pulled on the mountain skirt.

"He means nothing to me," she murmured defensively. "Logan Reed means nothing to me."

Having dismissed himself from the dinner table on the excuse of bringing in wood for Mary, Logan had overheard most of the exchange between Jeffery and Amelia. At first he thought he might need to intercede on Amelia's behalf when Jeffery seemed to get his nose a bit out of joint, but the declaration of Amelia preferring to marry Logan over Jeffery had stopped him in his tracks.

At first he was mildly amused. He admired the young woman's spirit of defense and her ability to put the uppity Englishman in his place. He imagined with great pleasure the shock to Sir Chamberlain's noble esteem when Amelia declared her thoughts on the matter of marriage. At least it gave him a better understanding of what was going on between the members of the party. He'd felt an underlying current of tension from the first time he'd met them, especially between the trio of Lord Amhurst, Jeffery, and Amelia. Now, it was clearly understood that the earl planned to see his daughter married to Jeffery, and it was even clearer that Amelia had no desire to comply with her father's wishes. *But why?* Logan wondered. *Why would it be so important for the earl to pass his daughter off to Chamberlain?*

"*I would sooner marry Logan Reed.*" He remembered the words and felt a bit smug. He knew she'd intended it as an insult to Jeffery, but it didn't matter. For reasons beyond his understanding, Logan felt as though he'd come one step closer to making Amelia his lady.

Chapter 9

In spite of her father's desire to have Amelia seek out Logan's assistance as her hiking guide, Amelia chose instead to hike alone. She was often up before any of the others and usually found herself in the kitchen of the lodge, learning the various culinary skills that Mary performed.

"You're doing a fine job, Amelia," Mary told her.

Amelia stared down at the dough rings as they floated and sizzled in a pool of lard. "And you call these doughnuts?" she questioned, careful to turn them before they burned on one side.

"Sure. Sure. Some folks call them *oly koeks*. The menfolk love 'em though. I could fix six dozen of these a day and have them gone by noon. Once the men learn doughnuts are on the table, I can't get rid of them till they get rid of the doughnuts."

Amelia laughed. They didn't seem all that hard to make and she rather enjoyed the way they bobbed up and down in the fat. It reminded her of the life preservers on board the ship they'd sailed across the Atlantic. "I'll remember that."

"Sure, you'll make a lot of friends if you fix these for your folks back in England," Mary replied.

Amelia couldn't begin to imagine the reaction of her "folks back in England" should they see her bent over a stove, laboring to bring doughnuts to the table. "I'm afraid," she began, "that it would never be considered appropriate for me to do such a thing at home."

"No?" Mary seemed surprised. "I betcha they'd get eaten."

"Yes, I'd imagine after everyone recovered from the fits of apoplexy, they just might eat the doughnuts." She pulled the rings from the grease and sprinkled them with sugar just as Mary had shown her to do. It was while she was engrossed in this task that Logan popped his head through the open doorway.

"Ummm, I don't have to ask what you're doing today, Mary."

"Ain't me, Logan. It's Amelia. She's turning into right handy kitchen help."

Logan raised a brow of question in Amelia's direction. "I don't believe it. Let me taste one of those doughnuts." He reached out before Amelia could stop him and popped half of the ring into his mouth. His expression changed as though he were considering a very weighty question. Without breaking his stoic expression he finished the doughnut and reached for another. "I'd better try again." He ate this one in three bites instead of two and again the expression on his face remained rigidly set. "Mary, better pour me a cup of coffee. I'm going to have to try another one in order to figure out if they're as good as yours or maybe, just maybe, a tiny sight better."

Amelia flushed crimson and turned quickly to put more rings into the grease before Logan spoke again. "Now I know we'll have to keep this one around."

Mary laughed and brought him the coffee. "That's what I keep tellin' her. I don't know when I've enjoyed a summer visitor more. Most young ladies of her upbringin' are a bit more uppity. They never want to learn kitchen work, that's for sure."

Amelia tried not to feel pride in the statement. She knew full well that Logan had once considered her one of those more uppity types and rightly so. For the past few weeks even Amelia couldn't explain the change in her attitude and spirit. She found the countryside inspiring and provoking, and with each passing day she felt more and more a part of this land.

Not realizing it, she shook her head. *I'm English,* she thought and turned the doughnuts. *I cannot possibly belong to this place.* She looked up feeling a sense of guilt and found Logan's gaze fixed on her. A surge of emotion raced through her. *I cannot possibly belong to this man.*

Swallowing hard, she took a nervous glance at her pocket watch. "Oh my," she declared, brushing off imaginary bits of flour and crumbs, "I must go. I promised I'd wake Margaret by seven."

Mary nodded. "You go on now. I've had a good long rest."

"Hardly that," Amelia said and took off her apron. "I have been here three weeks and I have yet to see you rest at any time."

"I saw it once," Logan said conspiratorially, "but it was six years ago and Mary was down sick with a fever. She sat down for about ten minutes that day, but that was it."

Amelia smiled in spite of herself. "I thought so. Thanks for the lesson, Mary. I'll see you later." She hurried from the room with a smile still brightening her face.

"Don't forget," Mary reminded, "you wanted to start quilting and this afternoon will be just fine for me."

"All right. I should be free," she replied over her shoulder.

"Hey, wait up a minute," Logan called and joined her as she crossed from the lodge to the grassy cabin area.

Looking up, Amelia felt her pulse quicken. "What is it?"

"I was hoping you'd be interested in a hike with me. I thought you'd like to go on a real adventure."

Amelia's curiosity was piqued. "What did you have in mind?"

"Long's Peak."

"The mountain?"

Logan grinned. "The same. There's quite a challenging climb up to the top. If you think you're up to it, I could approach your father on the matter."

"He'd never agree to such a thing."

Logan's smile faded. "He wouldn't agree, or you don't agree?"

Amelia felt a twinge of defensiveness but ignored it. She found herself honestly wishing she could hike up Long's Peak with Logan Reed and to argue now wouldn't help her case one bit. "Without an appropriate chaperone, Logan," she said his name hoping to prove her willingness, "it would never be allowed."

Logan cheered at this. "So what does it take to have an appropriate chaperone?"

"Someone like Mary or Lady Gambett."

Logan nodded. "I guess I can understand that. I'll work on it and let you know."

Amelia saw him turn to go and found a feeling of deep dissatisfaction engulfing her. "Logan, wait."

He turned back and eyed her questioningly. "Yes?"

"I've collected quite a variety of vegetation and flower samples and I thought, well actually I hoped—" she paused seeing that she held his interest. "I was too hasty in rejecting your offer of help. My father wanted me to accept and so now I'm asking if you would assist me in identifying my samples."

"What made you change your mind?" he asked softly coming to stand only inches away. His eyes were dark and imploring and Amelia felt totally swallowed up in their depths.

"I'm not sure," Amelia said, feeling very small and very vulnerable.

Logan's lopsided grin made his entire face light up. "It doesn't matter. I'd be happy to help you. When do you want to start?"

"How would this morning work out for you? Say, after the others have gone about their business?"

"That sounds good to me. I'll meet you at the lodge."

Amelia smiled and gave a little nod. It had been a very agreeable conclusion to their conversation. She watched Logan go off in the direction of the lodge and thought her heart would burst from the happiness she felt. What was it? Why did she suddenly feel so light? For weeks she had fought against her nature and her better judgment regarding Logan Reed. Now, giving in and accepting Logan's help seemed to free rather than burden her.

She approached the cabin she'd been sharing with her sisters and grew wary at the sound of voices inside.

"Amelia is simply *awful*. She gives no consideration to family, or to poor Papa's social standing." It was Penelope, and Margaret quickly picked up the challenge.

"Amelia has never cared for anyone but Amelia. I think she's hateful and selfish. Just look at the gowns she has to choose from and you and I must suffer through with only five apiece. I'm quite beside myself."

"And all because Papa is trying to see her married to poor Jeffery. Why he doesn't even love Amelia, and she certainly doesn't love him. I overheard Papa tell him that he would give him not only a substantial dowry, but one of the Scottish estates, if only Jeffery could convince Amelia to marry him before we returned to England."

"She'll never agree to it," Margaret replied haughtily. "She doesn't care one whit what happens to the rest of us. She never bothers to consider what might make others happy. If she hurts Papa this way and ruins my season in London, I'll simply die."

Amelia listened to the bitter words of her sisters and felt more alone than she'd ever felt before. Her entire family saw her only as an obligation and a threat to their happiness. *Surely there is some way to convince them that I don't care about the money. All I really want is a chance to fall in love and settle down with the right man.* Instantly Logan Reed's image filled her mind and Amelia had to smile. She would truly scandalize her family if she suggested marriage to Mr. Reed.

The conversation inside the cabin once again drew her attention when Penelope's whining voice seemed to raise an octave in despair. "I hate her! I truly do. She's forced us to live as barbarians and traipse about this horrid country, and for what? So that she can scorn Sir Jeffery, a man in good standing with the queen herself?"

Amelia felt the bite of her sister's words. She'd never considered her siblings to be close and dear friends, but now it was apparent that even a pretense of affection was out of the question. Hot tears came unbidden to her eyes and suddenly years of pent up emotion would no longer be denied.

"Oh Mama," she whispered, wiping desperately at her cheeks, "why did you leave me without love?" Gathering up her skirt, Amelia waited to hear no more. She ran for the coverage of the pines and aspens. She ran for the solitude of the mountainous haven that she'd grown to love.

Blinded by her own tears, Amelia fought her way through the underbrush of the landscape. She felt the biting sting of the branches as they slapped at her arms and face, but the pain they delivered was mild compared to the emptiness within her heart. Panting for air, Amelia collapsed beside a fallen spruce. Surrendering to her pain, she buried her face in her hands and sobbed long and hard.

It isn't fair. It wasn't right that she should have to bear such a thing alone. Her mother had been the only person to truly care about her and now she was forever beyond her reach. A thought came to Amelia. Perhaps a spiritualist could put her in touch with her mother's spirit. Then just as quickly as the thought came, Amelia banished it. In spite of the fact that spiritualists were all the rage in Europe and America, she didn't believe in such things. Life ended at the grave—didn't it?

"I don't know what to believe in anymore," she muttered.

She was suddenly ashamed of herself and her life. She wasn't really a snob, as Logan had presumed her to be. Her upbringing had demanded certain things of her, however. She didn't have the same freedoms as women of lower classes. She wasn't allowed to frolic about and laugh in public. She wasn't allowed to speak her mind in mixed company, or to have her opinion considered with any real concern once it was spoken. Amelia found herself envying Mary and her simple but hard life here in the Rocky Mountains. The men around Mary genuinely revered and cared for her. Her husband had no reason to fear when he took a party out hunting, because everyone looked out for Mary.

I wish I could be more like her, Amelia thought, tears pouring anew from her eyes. She'd not cried this much since her mother's passing. Mother was like Mary. Amelia could still see her mother working with her flowers in the garden wearing a large straw bonnet cocked to one side to shield her from the sun, and snug, mud-stained gloves kept her hands in ladylike fashion. Amelia traced the fingers of her own hands, realizing that she'd forgotten her gloves. *Oh Mama, what am I to do?*

Looking up, Amelia was startled to find Logan sitting on a log not ten feet away. "What are you doing here?" she asked, dabbing at her eyes with the edge of her skirt.

"I saw you run up here and got worried that something was wrong. Generally, folks around here don't run like their house is on fire—unless it is." He gave her only a hint of a smile.

Amelia offered him no explanation. It was too humiliating even to remember her sister's words, much less bring them into being again by relating them to Logan.

Seeming to sense her distress, Logan leaned back and put his hands behind his head. He looked for all the world as though he'd simply come out for a quiet moment in the woods. "There's an old Ute Indian saying that starts out, 'I go to the mountain where I take myself to heal the earthly wounds that people give to me.' I guess you aren't the first person to come seeking solace, eh?"

"I'm not seeking anything," Amelia replied, feeling very vulnerable knowing that Logan had easily pegged her emotions.

"We're all seeking something, Amelia," Logan said without a hint of reprimand. "We're all looking to find things to put inside to fill up the empty places. Some people look for it in a place, others in things, some in people." His eyes pierced her soul and Amelia looked away as he continued. "Funny thing is, there's only so much you can fill up with earthly things. There's an empty place and a void inside that only God can fill and some folks never figure that out."

"You forget, Mr. Reed," she said in protected haughtiness, "I don't believe in the existence of God." The words sounded hollow even to Amelia.

Logan shrugged. "You're sitting in the middle of all this beauty and you still question the existence of God?"

"I've been among many wonders of the world, Mr. Reed. I've traveled the Alps, as well as your Rockies, and found them to be extraordinarily beautiful as well. What I did not find was God. I find no proof of an almighty being in the wonders of the earth. They are simple, scientifically explained circumstances. They are nothing more than the visual representation of the geological forces at work in this universe. It certainly doesn't prove the existence of God." She paused to look at him quite seriously. "If it did, then I would have to counter with a question of my own."

"Such as?"

"Such as, if the beauty of the earth proclaims the existence of God, then why doesn't the savagery and horrors of the world do as much to denounce His existence? This God you are so fond of quoting and believing in must not amount to much if He stands idly by to watch the suffering of His supposed creation. I've seen the beauty of the world, Mr. Reed, but so, too, have I seen many of its tragedies and injustices. I've been in places where mothers murder their children rather than watch them starve to death slowly. I've seen old people put to death because they are no longer useful to their culture. I've beheld squalor and waste just as surely as I've seen tranquility and loveliness, and none of it rises up to assure me of God's existence."

"Granted, there's a lot wrong in this world, but what about the forces of evil? Don't you think evil can work against good and interfere with God's perfect plan? When people stray from the truth, the devil has the perfect opportunity to step in and stir up all kinds of chaos."

"Then your God isn't very strong, is He?" She lifted her chin a little higher. "As I recall, the devil you believe exists is a fallen angel named Lucifer. Is not your God more powerful than a fallen angel? Don't you see, Mr. Reed, these are nothing more than stories designed to make mankind feel better about itself and the world. The poor man trudges through life believing that even though he has nothing on earth, he will have a celestial mansion when he dies. A rather convenient way of bolstering spirits and keeping one's nose to the grindstone, don't you think?"

Logan shook his head. "You're talking about something you obviously know very little about. An eternal home in heaven isn't all the repentant sinner has to look forward to."

"No?" She looked away as though studying the trees around them. "I suppose you will tell me that he can pray and have his desires magically met by a benevolent God who wants His children to live in abundance and earthly wealth."

"Not at all. God isn't in charge of some heavenly mercantile where you step in and order up whatever your little heart wants. No, Amelia, I'm talking about living in truth. Knowing that you are following the path God would have you travel, and in knowing that, you will find the satisfaction of truth, faithfulness, peace, and love."

⚭

"Oh, please," Amelia said meeting his eyes. "This is all religious rhetoric and you know it. The fact of the matter is that truth is completely in the heart and mind of the person or persons involved. I see the truth as one thing and you obviously see it as another. Do not believe I'm any less satisfied for the things I believe in, because I assure you I am not." She bit her lip and looked away. She could hardly bear to meet his expression, knowing that deep inside, the things she believed in were not the least bit satisfying.

As if reading her mind, Logan sat up and said, "I feel sorry for you, Amelia. You are afraid to consider the possibility that there is a God, because considering it might force you to reckon with yourself."

"I don't know what you mean." She got to her feet and brushed off the dirt and leaves that clung to her skirt.

Logan jumped to his feet. "That's it. It's really a matter of you being afraid."

Amelia bit at her lower lip again and looked at the ground. "I need to get back. They'll have missed me at breakfast."

Logan crossed the distance to stop her. Putting his hand out, he took hold of her arm and gently turned her back to face him. "God can fill that void inside, Amelia. He can wrap you in comfort and ease your burden. He can be all that human folks fail to be."

Amelia pushed him away. She was, for the first time in a long, long time, frightened. Not of Logan Reed, but of what he represented. "I have to go."

"In a minute," Logan said softly. "First tell me why you were crying."

Amelia shook her head. "It was nothing. Nothing of importance."

Logan reached out and before Amelia could move, he smoothed back a bit of hair from her face and stroked her cheek with his fingers. "It's important to me." His voice was barely a whisper.

Amelia stared up at him and found herself washed in the flood of compassion that seemed to emanate from his eyes. Her mouth went dry and her heart pounded so hard that she was sure Logan could hear it. She struggled with her emotions for a full minute before steadying her nerves to reply. "I don't want to be important to you."

Logan laughed. "Too late. You already are."

Amelia balled her hands into fists and struck them against her side. "Just leave me alone, Logan. I can't do this."

Logan looked at her in surprise. "Do what?"

Amelia opened her mouth as if to speak, then quickly shut it again. She had nearly said, "Love you." Now, standing here in the crisp freshness of morning, Amelia knew beyond doubt, that Logan understood exactly what she'd nearly said. "I can't do this," was all she could say.

Logan backed away. "I have an idea. Why don't you come on a hike with me tomorrow? Your family and friends will be on an overnight hunt; I heard Jonas telling Mary all about it after you left the kitchen. We could spend the whole day gathering your samples and I could spend all evening telling you what they are."

"I don't think—"

"Don't think," Logan said with such longing in his voice that Amelia couldn't ignore his plea.

"All right," she said quickly, hoping that if she agreed to his suggestion he'd leave her alone. There'd be plenty of time to back out of the invitation later. Later, when she was calmer and could think more clearly. Later, when the warmth of Logan's green eyes didn't melt the icy wall she'd built between them.

Logan's mustache twitched as it always did before his lips broke into a full smile. "I'm holding you to it."

Amelia nodded and headed back down the mountain. Two things deeply troubled her. One was Logan's words about God. The other was Logan himself.

Chapter 10

Logan had spent a restless day and night thinking of what his hike with Amelia might accomplish. He saw the desperation in her eyes. He knew she longed to understand what was missing in her life. But how could he lead her to the truth about God when she didn't believe in the validity of God? Usually, whenever he witnessed to someone, Logan knew he could rely on the scriptures to give them something solid that they could put their hands on—the written Word of God. That seemed to be important to folks. With Amelia's disbelief in God and her position that the Bible was nothing more than the collective works of men from the past, Logan felt at a loss as to how he could proceed without it. His mother and other Christians he'd known had assured him that all he needed was a faith in God and in His Word. And even now, Logan believed that was still true. But what he couldn't figure out was how to apply it all and show Amelia the way to God. Somehow, he felt, he must be failing as a Christian if this simple mission eluded him. *How can I defend my faith in God and show Amelia the truth, when it is that very truth that makes her run in the opposite direction?*

Logan took up his Bible and sat down to a self-prepared breakfast of smoked ham and scrambled eggs. He opened the book and bowed his head in prayer. "Father, there's a great deal of hurt inside Amelia Amhurst. I know You already see her and love her. I know You understand how to reach her. But I don't know how to help and I seek Your guidance and direction. I want to help her find her way home to You. Give me the right words and open her heart to Your Spirit's calling. In Jesus' name I pray, amen."

Logan opened his eyes and found comfort in the scripture before him. "The Spirit itself beareth witness with our spirit, that we are the children of God," he read aloud from the eighth chapter of Romans. A peace came over him and he smiled. God's Spirit would speak for him. It wasn't Logan Reed's inspirational words or evidence that would save Amelia; it was God's Holy Spirit. The Holy Spirit would also show her the validity of the Bible. He needn't compromise his beliefs and put the Bible aside. Neither did he need to go out of his way to defend God. God could fully take care of all the details.

He almost laughed out loud the way he'd taken it all on his own shoulders. It was typical of him to rush in and try to arrange things on his own. But now he didn't have to and God had made that quite clear. Amelia Amhurst was here for a reason. Not for her father's matrimonial desires or Chamberlain's financial benefits in joining with her. Amelia was here because God knew it was time for her to come to the truth. The Holy Spirit would bear witness to Amelia that not only was God real but also she had a way to reconcile herself with Him. With a lighter heart, Logan dug into his breakfast and prepared for the day.

∽

Logan whistled a tune as he came into the lodge through the kitchen. He found Amelia bent over a sink full of dishes and paused to consider her there. Her blond hair was braided in a simple fashion to hang down her back and the clothes she wore were more austere than usual. She no longer appeared the refined English rose, but rather looked to be the descendant of hearty pioneer stock.

"I see you dressed appropriately," he said from behind her.

∽

Amelia whirled around with soapy hands raised as though Logan had threatened a robbery. In a rather breathless voice she addressed him. "I borrowed some clothes from Mary." Gone was any trace of her agitation with him the day before.

"Good thinking." Logan felt unable to tear his gaze away from her wide blue eyes.

"She gave me some sturdy boots as well." Amelia's voice was a nervous whisper as soap suds dripped down her arms and puddled onto the wood floor.

"You gonna be much longer with those?" Logan asked, nodding toward the sink, but still refusing to release her gaze.

"No. I'm nearly finished."

"I can help," he offered.

"No. Why don't you have a cup of coffee instead? I can see to this."

Amelia was the one who finally turned away. Logan thought her cheeks looked particularly flushed, but he gave the cookstove and fireplace credit for this and took a cup. Pouring rich, black coffee, Logan nearly burned himself as his glances traveled back and forth between Amelia and the coffee.

"How'd the quilting lesson go yesterday?" he asked.

"My stitches were as big as horses," Amelia admitted, "but Mary told me not to worry about it. She said it was better to work at consistency and spacing."

"Mary should know. She does beautiful work."

"Yes, she does." Amelia finished with her task and dried her hands on her apron. "I don't suppose I'll ever do such nice work."

"You don't give yourself enough credit. Look how quick you took to making doughnuts. When you reach Mary's age you'll be every bit as good at making quilts as she is."

"I seriously doubt that," she replied and Logan thought she sounded rather sad. "You see, once we return to England, I know it will hardly be acceptable for me to sit about making quilts and frying doughnuts."

"Maybe you shouldn't go back."

The words fell between them as if a boulder had dropped into the room. Sensing Amelia's inability to speak on the matter, Logan changed the subject. "Well, I have a knapsack full of food, so if you're ready—"

Amelia nodded and untied her apron. "Let me get my coat." She hurried over to a nearby chair and pulled on a serviceable broadcloth coat. The jacket was several sizes too big, obviously another loan from Mary, but Logan thought she looked just right.

Smiling, he nodded. "You look perfect."

"Hardly that, Mr. Reed, but I am. . .well—" she glanced down at her mismatched attire and raised her face with a grin, "I am prepared."

He laughed. "Well out here that suggests perfection. A person ought to always be prepared. You never know when a storm will blow up or an early snow will keep you held up in your house. Preparation is everything."

∽

The sun was high overhead before Logan suggested they break for lunch. Amelia was secretly relieved and plopped down on the ground in the most unladylike manner. The scenery around her was hard to ignore. The rocky granite walls were imposing and gave her a powerful reminder of how little she knew of taking care of herself. *What if something happened to Logan? How would I ever return to Estes without his assistance?*

"You up to one more thing before I break out the chow?"

Amelia looked up and hoped that the weariness she felt was hidden from her expression. "I suppose so." She made a motion to get up, but before she could move Logan reached down and lifted her easily.

"You look pretty robust," he said, dropping his hold, "but you weigh next to nothing. I've had dogs that weighed more than you."

Amelia thought it was a strange sort of observation, but then remembered back in Greeley when her beauty had been compared to a polished spittoon. "And I've had horses more mannerly than you," she finally replied, "but I don't hold that against you and I pray you won't hold my weight against me."

"You pray?" he said, acting surprised.

"It's a mere expression, I assure you. Now please show me what you had in mind and then feed me before I perish."

Logan took hold of her hand and pulled her along as though they traveled in this manner all the time. He walked only a matter of ten or twelve steps, however, before drawing Amelia up to a frightening precipice.

"Oh my!" she gasped, gazing over the edge of the sheer drop. She clung to Logan's hand without giving thought to what he might think. "How beautiful," she finally added, gazing out beyond the chasm. A tiny ledge of rock stuck out some six or seven feet below them, but after that there was nothing but the seemingly endless open spaces below. Beyond them, the Rocky Mountain panorama stretched out and Amelia actually felt a lump form in her throat. There were no words for what she was feeling. Such a rush of emotions simply had no words. It was almost as if this country beckoned to her inner soul. She felt something here that she'd never known anywhere else. Not in the Alps with all of their grandeur. Not amongst the spicy, exotic streets of Egypt. Not even on her father's estate in England.

Her eyes scanned the scene and her mind raced with one pounding sensation. When her eyes settled on Logan's face, that sensation was realized in a single word. *Home. I feel,* she thought, *as though I've come home.*

For a moment she thought Logan might kiss her, and for as long a moment, she wished he would. She longed for his embrace. The warmth of his hand on hers drew her further away from thoughts of her family and England. *Is this true love? Are this man and this place to forever be a part of my destiny? Yet how could it be? How could I even imagine it possible?* She was a refined English lady—the daughter of an earl. She had been presented to Queen Victoria and had even made the acquaintances of the princesses.

Logan's voice interrupted the awe-inspired moment. "Come on, let's eat."

He pulled her back to the place where she'd rested earlier, and without ceremony, plopped himself down on the ground and began wrestling with the knapsack. Amelia was very nearly devastated. Didn't he feel it, too? Didn't he feel the compelling, overwhelming attraction to her that she felt to him?

Chiding herself for such unthinkable emotions, Amelia sat down and took the canteen Logan offered her. She drank slowly, the icy liquid quenching her thirst, but not her desire to know more. *But what is it that I want to know?* She refused to be absorbed with questions of immortality and religious nonsense, and yet there were so many questions already coming to mind.

Logan slapped a piece of ham between two thick slices of Mary's bread and handed the sandwich over to Amelia. "It's not fancy, but I promise you it will taste like the finest banquet food you've ever had."

Amelia nodded and nibbled on the edge of the crust. She was famished and yet, when Logan bowed his head in prayer, she paused in respectful silence, not really knowing why. When he finished, he pulled out a napkin and revealed two pieces of applesauce cake.

"Mary had these left over from last night and I thought they'd make a great dessert."

"Indeed they will," Amelia agreed and continued eating the sandwich.

In between bites of his own food, Logan began sharing a story about the area. "This is called Crying Rock," he explained.

"Why Crying Rock?" Amelia asked, looking around her to see if some rock formation looked like eyes with water flowing from it.

"Legend holds that an Indian warrior fell to his death from that very spot where we stood just minutes ago. He had come to settle a dispute with another warrior and in the course of the fight, he lost his life."

"How tragic. What were they fighting about?" Amelia asked, genuinely interested.

"A young woman," he said with a grin. "What else?"

Amelia jutted out her chin feeling rather defensive. "How foolish of them both."

"Not at all. You see the warrior was in love with a woman who was already pledged to marry the other man. It was arranged by her father, but her heart wasn't in it. She was in love with the other warrior."

Amelia felt the intensity of his stare and knew that he understood her plight in full. She felt more vulnerable in that moment than she'd ever felt in her life. It was almost as if her entire heart was laid bare before Logan Reed. She wished she could rise up with dignity and walk back to the lodge, but she hadn't the remotest idea how she could accomplish such a feat. Instead, she finished her sandwich and drank from the canteen before saying, "Obviously, she lost out in this situation and had to marry the man she didn't love."

Logan shook his head. "Not exactly. After the death of her true love, she was to marry the victor in five days and so she brought herself up here and sat down to a period of mourning. As legend tells it, she cried for four straight days. The people could hear her, clear down in the village below, and folks around here say at night when

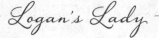

the wind blows it can still sound just like a woman crying."

"What happened after that?" Amelia asked, almost against her will.

"On the fifth day she stopped crying. She washed, dressed in her wedding clothes and offered up a final prayer in honor of her lost warrior." Logan paused and it seemed to Amelia that he'd just as soon not continue with the story.

"And?" she pressed.

"And, she threw herself off the rock and took her own life."

"Oh." It was all Amelia could say. She let her gaze go to the edge of the rock and thought of the devastated young woman who died. She could understand the woman's misery. Facing a life with Jeffery Chamberlain was akin to a type of death in and of itself. And then, for the first time, the realization that she would most likely be forced to marry Jeffery truly sunk in. The tightness in her chest made her feel suddenly hemmed in. Her father would never allow her to walk out of this arrangement. There was no way he would care for her concerns or her desires to marry for love. The matter was already settled and it would hardly be affected by Amelia's stubborn refusal.

"You okay?" Logan asked softly.

She looked back to him and realized he'd been watching her the whole time. "I'm well—" she fell silent and tried to reorganize her thoughts. "The story was fascinating and I was just thinking that perhaps a book on Indian lore would be more beneficial than one on wildflowers."

Logan seemed to consider this a moment. "Why not combine them? You could have your flowers and identification information and weave in stories of the area. After all, the summer is coming quickly to an end and you've already done a great deal of work on the area vegetation."

"Would you teach me more about the lore from this area?" she asked, swallowing down the depression that threatened to engulf her.

"Sure," he said, so nonchalant that Amelia knew he didn't understand her dilemma.

No one understands, she thought as a heavy sigh escaped her lips. *No one would ever understand.*

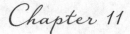

A week and a half later, Amelia watched as Mary finished packing a saddlebag with food. "Mary, are you sure that you and Jonas want to do this?" she questioned quite seriously. "I mean, Long's Peak looks to be a very serious climb."

"Oh, it's serious enough," she said with a smile. "I've made it four times before, and I figure number five ain't gonna kill me."

"You've climbed up Long's Peak four times?" Amelia questioned in disbelief.

Logan laughed at her doubtful expression. "Mary's a great old gal and she can outdo the lot of us, I'm telling you."

Mary beamed him a smile. "He only says that 'cause he knows I'll cook for him on the trail."

Amelia was amazed. Long's Peak stood some 14,700 feet high and butted itself in grand majesty against one end of Estes Park. It was once heralded as one of the noblest of the Rocky Mountains and Lady Bird had highly recommended taking the opportunity to ascend it, if time and health permitted one to do so. Amelia was still amazed that her father had taken to the idea without so much as a single objection. He and Sir Jeffery had found a guide to take them hunting outside the village area. They would be gone for over a week and during that time he was quite unconcerned with how his daughters and manservant entertained themselves. After all, he mused, they were quite well-chaperoned, everyone in the village clearly knowing what everyone else was about, and the isolation did not afford for undue notice of their activities by the outside world. Logan had immediately approached him on the subject of Amelia ascending Long's Peak, with a formal invitation to include her sisters and the Gambett family. Lady Gambett looked as though just thinking of such a thing made her faint and the girls were clearly uninterested in anything so barbaric. After a brief series of questions, in which Mary assured the earl that she would look after Amelia as if she were her own, Lord Amhurst gave his consent and went off

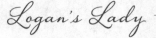

to clean his rifle. And that was that. The matter was settled almost before Amelia had known the question had been posed.

"You've got enough grub here to last three weeks," Jonas chided his wife.

"Sure, sure," his Mary answered with a knowing nod, "and you and Logan can eat three weeks worth of food in a matter of days. I intend that Amelia not starve." They all laughed at this and within the hour they were mounting their horses and heading out.

"Some folks call it 'the American Matterhorn,'" Logan told Amelia.

"I've seen the Matterhorn and this is more magnificent," she replied, rather lost in thought.

The valley was a riot of colors and sights. The rich green of the grass contrasted with wildflowers too numerous to count. But thanks to Logan, Amelia could identify almost every one of them and smiled proudly at this inner knowledge. She would have quite a collection to show off when she returned to England. For reasons beyond her understanding, the thought of leaving for England didn't seem quite as appealing as it always had before. She pushed aside this thought and concentrated instead on the grandeur of a blue mountain lake that seemed to be nestled in a bed of green pine.

The Lewises' dogs, a collie mix and a mutt of unknown parentage, ran circles around the party, barking at everything that crossed their paths, often giving chase when the subject in question looked too small to retaliate. Amelia laughed at the way they seemed to never tire of chasing the mountain ground squirrels or nipping after the heels of the mule-eared deer.

As the sun seemed to fall from the sky in an afterglow of evening colors, Amelia felt a sadness that she couldn't explain. The emptiness within her was almost more than she could bear. She thought of her mother and wondered if she were watching from some celestial home somewhere, then shook off the thought and chided herself for such imaginings. No doubt they'd been placed there by the irritating conversations of one Logan Reed. His beliefs seemed to saturate everything he said and did, and Amelia was quite disturbed by the way he lived this faith of his.

"We'd best make camp for the night," Logan called and pointed. "Over there looks to be our best choice."

Later, Amelia could see why he was so highly regarded as a competent guide. The area he'd chosen was well sheltered from the canyon winds and had an ample supply of water. Added to this were feathery pine boughs, so surprisingly soft that when Amelia lay down atop her blanketed pine mattress, she sighed in unexpected delight. Staring up at the starry sky, Amelia uncomfortably remembered Bible verses from the thirty-eighth chapter of Job. Her mother had been particularly fond of these and had often quoted them when Amelia had questioned the hows and whys of God's workings.

Where wast thou when I laid the foundations of the earth? declare, if thou hast understanding. Who hath laid the measures thereof, if thou knowest? or who hath stretched the line upon it? Whereupon are the foundations thereof fastened? or who laid the corner stone thereof; when the morning stars sang together, and all the sons of God shouted for joy?"

Her mother's explanation had always been that Amelia had no right to question God, and Amelia remembered countering that if God's position wasn't secure enough to be put to the test, then He wasn't as omnipotent and omniscient as people said. Suddenly, she felt very sorry for those words. Not because she believed in God's existence, but for the sorrow she remembered seeing in her mother's eyes. Sitting up, she hugged her knees to her chest and watched the flames of their campfire for a while.

You wouldn't be very pleased with me now, Mother, she thought. The flames danced and licked at the cold night air and when a log popped and shifted, Amelia jumped from the suddenness of it.

"I'm surprised you're still awake," Logan said from where he lay watching her.

Amelia felt suddenly very self-conscious and shrugged her shoulders. "Just thinking."

Logan leaned up on his elbow. "Care to share it?"

Amelia smiled and the reassuring sounds of Mary and Jonas's snoring made her relax a bit. "I was thinking about my mother."

"I bet you miss her a lot," Logan offered.

"Yes, I do. It seems like she's been gone forever and it's only been six years. She was sick quite awhile before she died." Then as if Logan had vocalized the question, Amelia added, "Consumption."

"And she was a Christian?"

Amelia rocked back and forth a bit and looked up to the heavens. "Yes."

"So how is it that you came to believe there was no God?"

"He never listened when I prayed," she replied flatly.

"How do you know?"

"Because my mother died."

Logan said nothing for several moments, then sat up and added a few more pieces of wood to the fire. "Did your mother ever deny you something that you wanted?"

"Of course," Amelia said, not understanding his meaning.

"So why wouldn't God be inclined to do the same?"

Logan's eyes were intense and his expression so captivating that for a moment Amelia forgot to be offended. Instead she simply asked, "To what purpose? I was fourteen years old; my youngest sister was barely ten. To what purpose does a merciful God remove mothers from children?"

"Good question. Wish I had the answer."

Amelia felt instant disappointment. She'd fully expected one of those quaint Christian answers like, "God needed another angel for heaven." Or, "God had need of your mother elsewhere." Amelia knew better. Especially since she left three grieving children and a devastated husband.

"You seem taken aback," Logan said softly. "Did you expect me to tell you the mind of God?"

Amelia couldn't help but nod. "Most other Christians would have. They have their wonderful little answers and reasons for everything, and none of it ever makes sense. To me, if there were a God, He would be more logical than that. There would be a definite order and reason to things, of course, a purpose."

"And you think that's missing in our world?" Logan questioned, seeming genuinely intrigued by the turn the conversation had taken.

But Amelia felt weary of it all. She was tired of seeking answers when she wasn't even sure what the questions were. She couldn't make sense of her life or of her mother's death, and therefore, to cast her frustration aside seemed the only way to keep from going insane.

"I think," she said very softly, "that the world has exactly the order we give it. No more. No less. If people are out of control, then so, too, the world."

"I agree."

"You do?"

Logan smiled. "Surprised?" Amelia nodded and he continued. "God gave mankind free will to choose Him or reject Him. A great many folks refuse Him and chaos and misery ensue. They seek their own way and call it wisdom when they settle in their minds how the universe has come together."

"But is your Christianity any different? Didn't you decide in your own way how the universe has come together?"

"No," Logan replied. "I decided to accept God's way was the only way and that put the rest of my questions at rest."

"But don't you ever worry that you might be wrong?" Amelia asked, knowing that she was very concerned with her own version of the truth. Perhaps that was why she felt herself in a constant state of longing. There was an emptiness inside her that refused to be filled up by the reasonings and logic of her own mind, yet she didn't know what to put in its place.

Logan stretched back on his pallet. "I guess if I'd come to God as an adult, I might have wondered if the Bible was true and if God was really God. But I became a Christian when I was still very young and it was easy to believe what my parents told me about the Bible and faith. I can see where it would be a whole heap harder for you. You have a lifetime of pride and obstacles to overcome. Accepting that the Bible is true would mean that your life would change, and some folks aren't willing to risk what that change might entail."

He fell silent and before long, Amelia noticed that his breathing had grown deep and even. Lying back down on her own pine bed, Amelia felt more lonely and isolated than she'd ever been in her life. *What if Logan is right?* her mind questioned. She quickly pushed the thought away. But as she drifted to sleep it came back in a haunting reminder that followed her even into her dreams.

The next day, Amelia awoke before it was fully light. The night had turned cold and Amelia's teeth chattered as she dragged her blankets around her shoulders and went to throw more wood on the fire like she'd seen Logan do. The dying coals quickly ignited the dry wood and soon a cheery blaze was crackling once again. It was this and not any sound made by Amelia that caused the rest of the camp to stir.

Logan was first to sit up, rubbing his eyes and yawning. Mary and Jonas murmured good mornings to each other before Mary took herself off for a bit of privacy. Jonas didn't seem inclined to talk and Logan was already pulling out things for breakfast.

While they were all occupied, Amelia took herself off a ways in order to study the sunrise in private. At first the blackness gave way to midnight blue and then as the slightest hint of lemon coloring suggested light, it gave way to a turquoise and brightened as the sun stretched over the snow-capped peaks. How beautiful! She marveled at the glory of it all.

They quickly breakfasted and were on their way by seven, the sunrise permanently fixed in Amelia's mind. They made good time, passing an area Logan called "The Lava Beds." It was here that huge boulders mingled with small ones to create a strangely desolate area. They were nearing the place where Logan said they would have to picket the horses and climb, when dark clouds moved in and rain appeared imminent.

Logan immediately went to work to find them even the smallest shelter to wait out the storm. He finally found a suitable place where they would be snug under the protective ledge of a particularly wide rock shelf. Jonas and Logan picketed the horses, while Amelia and Mary carried their things to the rock. The heavens opened up, as if cued by their having found shelter, and poured down a rain of tremendous proportion. Lightning flashed around them just as Jonas and Logan came to join the women.

C-R-A-C-K! Thunder roared, causing Amelia to nearly jump out of her skin. It seemed as if they sat atop the world and the fullest impact of the storm was to be spent on them alone.

Logan grinned and eased a little closer to Amelia. Another

flash of lightning caused Amelia to put her hands to her ears and press herself tighter to the wall. She felt terribly embarrassed by her childish display, noting that Mary and Jonas had their heads together talking as though nothing at all was amiss. She rallied herself in spirit and was determined to display more courage when a blinding strike of lightning hit directly in front of them with its deafening boom of thunder.

Amelia shrieked and threw herself at Logan in such a way that she feared she'd knocked the wind from him. Hearing him groan, she pulled back quickly but found his arm around her.

"Stay, if it makes you feel better. I promise, Mary and Jonas aren't going to care."

Amelia smiled weakly at Mary. "I've never been in a storm like this," she said, barely able to form audible words.

"Logan knows how they go," Mary replied, which seemed to offer Amelia approval for her actions.

Turning to Logan, Amelia temporarily forgot the storm around her and concentrated instead on the one in his eyes. Her heart pounded harder, while her breath felt as though it were caught around the lump in her throat. Licking her dry lips, she eased away and hugged her arms around her. *Better to find strength and comfort from within than to lose another portion of myself to this rugged mountain man.*

After a time the storm passed, but Logan judged by the skies that another would soon follow and the climb to the top of Long's Peak was postponed. As they descended back down the mountain, hoping to reach the heavy cover of pines before the next storm was upon them, Logan tried to treat the matter lightheartedly.

"We'll just try again later on," he said confidently. "Sooner or later, we're bound to get you to the top."

Amelia tried not to be disappointed. In truth, by this time her emotions were so topsy-turvy that she wasn't at all certain whether she cared if the trip was canceled or not. She rode sedately, saying very little except when addressed with a direct question. There was a great deal this trip had brought to mind and there was still the rest of the summer to think it through.

Chapter 12

From that day, the summer passed much more quickly than Amelia had expected. Not a moment went by when she wasn't painfully aware that soon the snows would threaten to close off access to the plains. Soon she would be headed back to England and her marriage to Sir Jeffery. She tried to push down her fear, but it rose up like a phoenix from the ashes of her heart, threatening to slay her in mind and soul.

Her joy came in spending her days with Logan. With her father and Jeffery absorbed in their hunting and her sisters busy with the Gambett girls, Amelia found herself free to work with Mary each morning and then with Logan. She had copied down nearly every specimen of vegetation in the area, and Logan had taught her how to identify animal tracks and to mark her position from the village using the elements around her. She thought it almost her imagination but swore her hearing had become better as she could make out sounds in the forested mountains that she'd never heard before. One day, when their water ran out, Logan had taught her how to listen for the sounds of water. Once she learned what it was that she was trying to hear, Amelia was amazed. The sounds had always been there, but she was just unaware of them. Before, the sounds in the air had come to her as a collective noise, but now she could separate the trickling of a mountain stream from the rustling of aspen leaves.

She had learned to depend more upon her other senses as well. Her sight and sense of smell were two things Logan said were absolutely necessary for staying alive. As they traipsed through the woods together he would often stop her and ask what certain smells were, and Amelia was quite proud to find that she was rapidly learning to identify each of these as well. Without realizing it, Amelia had spent the summer learning how to survive in the Rockies.

The bittersweetness of her circumstance, however, caught up with her one afternoon when her father sought her out.

"Amelia, we need to talk."

She looked up from where she was jotting down notes on a strange little bird that she had mistaken for a woodpecker.

"Just a moment, Father," she said, finishing her notes. "I've identified that pesky noise we've lived with these months. You know that pecking sound that comes at all hours of the day and night?" She didn't wait for him to reply. "It seems that this bird is a chipping sparrow and it chips away all the time. It actually feeds its young even into adulthood when they are fully capable of feeding themselves. Isn't that fascinating?" This time she put the pen down and looked up to find her father's serious expression.

"Quite," was all he would reply on the matter before taking a seat across from her. "Amelia, you have sorely neglected the one duty I gave you—which was to allow Sir Jeffery to pay you court. I say, I've never seen a more stubborn woman in all my life, unless of course it was your mother."

Amelia smiled. "A high compliment if ever there was one."

The earl shook his head. "I'm afraid it wasn't intended as one. See here, I know how you feel about being forced to marry, but the truth is I can't have the family coffers being depleted because of your foolishness. Why any reasonable solicitor would allow your grandmother to set out a trust to unmarried daughters is beyond me. Why it positively reeks of inappropriateness."

"It was Grandmama's money, after all, and she was only worried that her family might find themselves in situations of desperation and heartache. Grandmama had found it necessary to marry a man she didn't love, and all for financial reasons. She didn't want the same fate to befall her daughter or her granddaughters, yet now you propose to do just such a thing in order to keep the money for yourself." Amelia knew the anger in her heart was rapidly flooding over into her tone of voice.

"You have no right to speak to me thusly," the earl said rather stiffly. "I have to do what I feel is right for the benefit of the entire family, not just one member."

Amelia shook her head. "No, Father, I believe you are considering only one member—yourself." She slammed her book shut, mindless of smearing the still-damp ink. "I've tried to be orderly about this and I've tried not to bring you undue pain, but I must speak honestly here." She swallowed hard and thought of the conversation she'd overheard her father having with Jeffery the night before. Logan would chide her for eavesdropping, but this time it served to clarify the mystery behind her father's desperation to marry her to Jeffery.

"I know about your gambling debts," she began, "and the fact that you owe Sir Jeffery a great deal of money." The earl's eyes widened in surprise. "I'm not the simpleton you would give me credit for being. It wasn't hard to learn about this, nor was it difficult to learn that you had promised Jeffery land in Scotland, land, I might add, that has been in our family for generations and that must pass through the succession of marriage or death, rather than be sold."

"Furthermore, I know that Jeffery covets the land for his own purposes, some known to me and others I'm sure are unknown, but nevertheless he wants that land. So now we come to the inheritance my grandmother set in place, an inheritance that passed to my mother and made the prospects of marrying beneath our status not quite so distasteful."

The earl pounded his fists on the table. "Enough! You know very well that I loved your mother and she loved me. Ours was not a marriage for fortune and status and you know well how the name of Amhurst suffered for just such impropriety."

Amelia took a deep breath and sighed. "Yes, but I must ask if it wasn't worth it."

Lord Amhurst said nothing for a moment. His expression fell and he, too, sighed. "I could lie and say that if given the choice to do it all over again, I would marry another woman. But the truth is, I loved your mother very much and I would not trade our time together."

"So why are you trying to force such a thing upon me? If I were to inherit my share of the trust, do you believe I would leave you to suffer? How heartless you must think me."

"Nay, I never thought you heartless, but your share of the trust would never pay back what I owe Chamberlain. I'm sorry, Amelia." His resolve seemed to return. "You will have to marry Sir Jeffery."

Amelia felt as though a noose were being slipped around her neck. She rose with as much dignity as she could muster. "Your foolishness, not mine, has caused this situation. I find it completely unreasonable that I should be the one to pay for your mistakes. Let Jeffery marry one of my sisters. They both seem quite head-over-heels in love with the man."

Her father shook his head. "He wants the land that is to pass to you, Amelia. It is the Scottish estate that passes to the eldest that appeals to him."

"So I am to be sold off for the price of land and the sum of gambling debts?"

"Call it what you will," her father replied in a voice that suggested deep regret, "but avail yourself to Sir Jeffery in a proper courting manner and settle your mind on the fact that this marriage will take place."

∞

Later that week while dressing quietly for dinner, Amelia felt a desperation building inside that couldn't be cast away with the assurance that she'd somehow work things around to her way. Jeffery had lost little time in picking up his pursuit of Amelia and as his attentions became bolder, Amelia was forced to sequester herself to her cabin for fear of what he might do next.

Penelope and Margaret were already talking of returning home and of all the things they would do. Amelia tried to remember her own earlier desires to return to England, but they'd passed from existence and now she wanted instead to remain in Estes. It was almost humorous to her that in the three months they'd spent in America, and Estes in particular, her views about the barbaric ways of the Americans had changed. She had come to look at Mary as a mother image and she cherished the time spent under her tutelage. She'd learned to cook and bake, as well as sew practical garments and quilt. Mary had also shown her how to properly clean house and wash clothes. And when time had permitted, Amelia had even taken lessons in tending the vegetable garden and livestock.

As she pulled on her gloves for dinner she looked at her hands and realized how worn and rough they'd become. Back in England her friend Sarah would be appalled at the sight of calluses upon a lady's fingers, but Amelia wore them as badges of honor. She'd earned those calluses by working at Mary's side and she was proud of what she'd accomplished.

"Oh do hurry, Amelia," Penelope whined. "We'll never be able to sit down to dinner if you don't finish getting ready."

"I, for one, refuse to wait," Margaret said, grabbing her shawl. "Come along, sister. Amelia will bring herself when she's ready. Maybe we can corner Sir Jeffery and he'll tell us more tales of his adventures in China."

"Oh yes," Penelope said, nodding her head. "That would be grand."

They left Amelia in a rush of chatter and anticipation of the night to come. She stared after them through the open door and shook her head. If only she could feel such enthusiasm for Sir Jeffery, none of this might have ever happened. The afterglow of sunset left a haunting amber color to the sky over the mountains. The chill of autumn was approaching and with it came a longing that Amelia could not explain. If only they had never come to America she would never have laid eyes on the Rocky Mountains and never have met Logan Reed.

Logan.

Her heart ached from the very thought of his name. She was hopelessly in love with him, and yet there was nothing to be done about it. Logan was as poor as a church mouse and he could never offer to pay off her father's debts the way Jeffery could. Her father owed Jeffery over three thousand pounds, nearly seventeen thousand American dollars and even with her trust, the debt would barely be half paid. It was rapidly becoming a hopeless state of circumstances.

"Well, well," Jeffery announced from the door. "I looked about for you and found you missing."

"With good reason," Amelia said rather angrily. "I wasn't yet ready to present myself at dinner."

Jeffery leered. "I could help you. . .dress."

"As you can see, I'm quite dressed and I suggest you keep your disgusting thoughts to yourself."

She moved across the room to retrieve her shawl and heard Jeffery close the cabin door. Turning around, she found that he'd already crossed the room. He took hold of her roughly and crushed her against him in a fierce embrace.

"Stop it, Jeffery!" she declared and pushed at his chest.

Jeffery only laughed and held her fast. "You mustn't put me off. We're to be man and wife after all. A kiss of passion shared between two lovers is quite acceptable."

"But you forget. I do not love you," Amelia answered, kicking Jeffery's shin as hard as she could.

He immediately released her and Amelia scurried from the room, panting for breath and close to tears. Jeffery had so frightened her with his actions that she was quite uncertain as to what she should do next. Fleeing into the darkness behind the lodge, Amelia waited until her breathing had calmed and her heart stopped racing. *What should I do? What can I do?* Her father had made it quite clear and there was no other answer. She waited several more minutes, knowing that she was keeping everyone from their meal, then with a sigh she went to face them all. Walking slowly, as if to her own execution, Amelia entered the lodge and the dining hall without the slightest desire to be among people.

"Ah, there she is now," Lord Amhurst announced. "Amelia dear, come and join us in a toast."

Amelia looked up and found the entire party staring at her. Everyone seemed quite joyous and Jeffery stood with an expression of sheer pride on his face. They weren't apparently unhappy with her for the delay of their dinner and instead seemed extremely animated.

"What, might I ask, are we drinking a toast to?" she asked hesitantly.

The earl beamed a smile upon her. "Sir Jeffery has told us that this night you have accepted his hand in marriage." Her father raised his drink. "We are drinking to you and Sir Jeffery and a long, happy marriage."

Amelia felt the wind nearly knocked from her. She looked from her father to Jeffery and found a sneering grin on his face. His expression seemed to say, "I told you I would have my way."

"Well, do come join us," her father said, rather anxiously. "We've waited all summer for this."

Amelia found it impossible to speak. A lump formed in her throat and tears were threatening to spill from her eyes. Without concern for appearances, she turned and ran from the lodge.

Fleeing down the stairs and into the night, Amelia barely stifled a scream as she ran full speed into Logan Reed's arms. She couldn't see his face but heard his chuckle and felt a sense of comfort in just knowing he was near.

"I'm so sorry," she said, trying to disentangle her arms from his.

"I'm not. Want to tell me what you were running from?" Amelia felt the tears trickle down her cheeks and a sob escaped her throat. Logan's voice grew more concerned. "What is it, Amelia? What has happened?"

"Nothing," she said, unable to keep from crying.

He took hold of her upper arms. "You're crying, so something must be wrong."

"Just leave me alone."

His voice was low and husky. "Amelia, I care about your pain and so does God. He can help you through this, even if I can't."

She jerked away, angry at the suggestion. "If God cares so much about pain, then why does He let His children suffer? I'm going to my cabin," she declared and walked away.

Logan was quickly at her side and it wasn't until she'd opened the door to her still-lighted cabin that she could see that he was smiling.

"What? Are you going to laugh at me now?"

"Not at all. It's just that I thought you didn't believe in God."

"I don't."

"Then why did you say what you did about God letting His children suffer."

"Because you are always throwing your religion and God in my face!" she declared. "You always fall back on that and always use that to settle every issue that has ever arisen between us."

"Because He is my foundation and my mainstay. God cares about your pain, but haven't you brought it on yourself? Don't you hold any responsibility for your own actions?"

"Oh go away, Logan," she moaned in sheer misery. *Why did he have to say those things?*

With a shrug of his shoulders, Logan surprised her by turning to leave. "I'm gonna pray for you, Amelia. I know you're having a rough time of coming to terms with God, but just remember, He already knows what's in your heart and He knows the future He holds for you."

With that he was gone and Amelia closed the door to cry in earnest. *Why is this happening to me and what in the world am I to do about any of it?* Giving up on the world and conscious thought, Amelia stripped off her dinner clothes and pulled on a nightgown. Then, mindless of her sisters, she blew out the lamp and threw herself into bed to have a good long cry.

Chapter 13

Well if you ask me," Penelope began, "I think it positively scandalous the way you put Sir Jeffery off."

"No one asked you," Amelia said flatly. She busied herself with quilting and tried to ignore her sisters and the Gambett girls.

"Mother says it is outrageous for you to suppose you will get a better match than Sir Jeffery," Josephine Gambett said, pushing up her glasses. They immediately slid back down her nose.

"Yes, Mother believes you are seriously jeopardizing your family's position with the queen. After all, Sir Chamberlain's mother is a dear friend of Her Majesty," Henrietta added, not to be outdone by her sister.

Amelia felt her cheeks burn from the comeuppance of these younger girls. She thought of a hundred retorts, but bit her tongue and continued stitching.

"I think it's pure selfishness on your part," Margaret said with a little stomp of her foot. "There are other people to consider in this situation."

Amelia finally set aside her quilting and looked hard at each of the girls. "If you'll excuse me, I believe I would prefer the company of adults." With that she got up and, without any conscious plan to do so, made her way to the cabin her father shared with Mattersley. She knew he would be there cleaning his guns and in her mind she formed one last plan to plead her case.

"Father?" she said, knocking lightly upon the open door.

Mattersley shuffled across the room. His face looked pinched and his eyes were sunken. "Come in, Lady Amhurst. The earl is just now occupied with the weapons."

Amelia smiled at him. Even here in the wilds of America, Mattersley held to the strict code of English propriety. "Thank you, Mattersley." She started to walk past him then stopped and asked, "How are you feeling? You look a bit tired."

Mattersley seemed stunned by her concern. "I am well, miss."

"You should have some time off to yourself," she said, glancing to where her father sat. "Father, don't you agree?"

"Say what?" the earl questioned, looking up.

"I believe Mattersley is working too hard and some time off would serve him well."

"Oh, well yes," her father said, genuinely seeming to consider this. "A capital idea! Mattersley, you go right ahead and take the rest of the day—"

"No," Amelia interrupted, "a day will certainly not afford him much of a rest. I suggest the rest of the week. He can stay up at the lodge. I know Mary has an extra room."

"Oh." Her father seemed quite taken aback.

"There is no need for that, sir," Mattersley said in a voice that betrayed his weariness.

"My daughter is quite right," Lord Amhurst answered, seeming to see the old man for the first time. "You've been out on nearly every hunt with us and working to keep my things in order. I can surely dress myself properly enough for the rest of the week, what?"

∽

"Very good, sir," Mattersley replied and Amelia thought it almost sounded like a sigh of relief.

"Well now that this matter has been resolved," she began and took the chair beside her father, "I thought we might address another."

"Do tell?" the earl replied and continued with cleaning his shotgun.

"Father, I have come to plead with you one final time to release me from this preposterous suggestion that I marry Sir Jeffery." The earl said nothing and so Amelia continued. "I cannot marry a man I do not respect, and I hold not the slightest respect for Sir Jeffery. I also cannot bring myself to consider marrying a man I do not love."

"Such modern notions do you a grave injustice, my dear," her father replied. "My mind is set and this is my final word. You will marry Chamberlain. In fact, I've arranged for us to depart Estes in three weeks. We will travel by stage from Greeley to Denver and there you will be married."

"What! How can you suggest such a thing? Why that won't even allow for a proper wedding, much less a proper English wedding," Amelia protested.

"It is of little concern. Sir Jeffery and I discussed the matter and we both believe it to be to the benefit of both parties."

"What parties? You and Jeffery? Because I assure you it will never be to my benefit." She got to her feet, trembling from her father's declaration. "I cannot understand how my own father would sell me into such an abominable circumstance."

"And I cannot imagine that I raised a daughter to be so defiant and disobedient," the earl replied, looking at her with a stern expression of dismay. "Your mother would not be pleased in the way you've turned out. Even she would find your temperament to be unwarranted."

"Mother would understand," Amelia said softly, the anger being quickly replaced by the realization that her father could care less about her feelings. "And once, when you and she were still together, you would have understood, too."

She left the cabin and felt as though a damp, cold blanket had been thrust upon her shoulders. The weight of her father's sudden declaration was more than she'd even imagined him capable of turning out. Immediately her mind sought for some manner of refuge. *There has to be something I can do.*

She walked a ways up the mountainside and paused beside a formation of boulders and rock. Hiking up her skirt, she climbed to the top by inching her way along the crevices and handholds. Once she'd managed to achieve her goal, she sat down in complete dejection and surveyed the village below.

Three weeks was a very short time.

She sighed and thought of leaving Estes and knew that it was tearing at her in a way that she'd never prepared herself for. She would have to leave the clean, crisp mountain air and the beauty that she'd never grow tired of looking upon. *And for what? To return to the cold, damp English winters? To be the wife of that unbearably cruel bore?*

She felt a tear trickle down her cheek and rubbed it away with the back of her sleeve. She almost laughed at herself for the crude gesture. *In so many ways I've become one of them. How can I go back to England now?*

"I can't do it," she whispered. "I can't go back."

That left her with very few alternatives. She couldn't very well talk her father into letting her remain in America. Soon enough she would be twenty-one and her father would never allow that day to come without her being properly married to Sir Jeffery.

"I could run away," she murmured and the though suddenly seemed very possible. *Logan has taught me how to find my way around,* she reasoned. *I could hide out in the mountains until after my birthday and then Father would have no choice.* But her birthday was the twenty-third of November and by that time this entire area would be snow-packed and frightfully cold. There was no way she would survive.

"But I don't want to survive if I have to marry Jeffery."

With that declaration an entirely different thought came to mind. Taking her own life could not be ruled out as a possible alternative. She thought of Crying Rock and the Indian maid who'd bravely gone to her death rather than face the unbearable ordeal of marrying a man she abhorred. *I'm no different than that woman. My sorrow is certainly well-founded. To leave this place, this lovely, wonderful place would be sheer misery.* And yet, even as she thought it, Amelia knew it wasn't just the place—it was Logan. Marriage to any man other than Logan was simply unthinkable.

"But he doesn't feel the same way I do," she chided. *"He has his God and his religion and he doesn't need a woman who would fight him with intellectual words and philosophies."* No, *Logan needs a wife who would work at his side, worship at his side, raise a family at his side. Logan would expect her to believe as he did, that God not only existed but also played an intricate role in the lives of His children. And that in doing so, He gave them a Savior in Jesus Christ.*

Something her mother had once said came back to haunt her. "Only the foolish man believes there is no God, Amelia. For the Bible says, even 'the devils believe, and tremble.'"

Amelia gazed out over the valley and sighed. Logan said she had but to open her eyes to the handiwork of God to realize His existence. But how could she believe in God, much less in the need to worship

Him and follow all manner of rules and regulations laid out in the Bible? To what purpose was there such a belief as the need for eternal life? Wasn't it just that mortal man could not stand to believe that his important life ended in the grave? Wasn't the idea of immortality something mankind comforted itself with in lieu of facing the truth that once you died, that was all there was? After all, most religions she'd studied had some form of immortality for their believers. It was rather like a parting gift from a high-society soiree. Something to cherish for those who had the courage to play the party games.

"I do not need such comfort," she whispered and hugged her arms close. "When my life is done, it is done and there will be no marriage to Sir Jeffery and no longing for what I can never have."

Suddenly it seemed quite reasonable to put an end to her life. In fact, it was almost calming. If there was nothing else to concern herself with, why not stop now? She'd seen more of the world than most people. She'd enjoyed the pleasures of the privileged life and she'd once known the love of good parents and siblings. *So what if I never know the love of a man—never know the joys of motherhood?* She wiped the tears that were now pouring freely from her eyes.

"I will go to Jeffery and plead my case before him. I will tell him honestly that I have no desire to marry him and suggest to him a different course," she told the valley before her. She climbed down from the rock and smoothed her skirt. "If he refuses to give consideration to my desires, then the matter will be resolved for me."

She thought that there should be some kind of feeling of accomplishment in making such a decision, but there wasn't. She felt empty and void of life. "I am resigned to do this thing," she said as an encouragement to her broken spirit. "There is no other way."

Chapter 14

"Sir Jeffery, I wonder if I might have a moment of your time," Amelia began one evening after dinner.

He seemed to sneer down his nose at her as though her request had somehow reduced her to a beggar. "I would be honored," he said and extended his arm for her.

Amelia, seeing all faces turned to behold her action, placed her hand upon his sleeve. "I suggest a short walk, if that would meet with your approval," she said cautiously.

"But of course, Lady Amhurst. I am your servant."

Amelia said nothing more, but allowed Jeffery to lead her amicably from the lodge.

"I must say this is a pleasant surprise. Dare I hope you're coming around to my way of thinking?"

Amelia let go of him and shook her head. "No, rather I was hoping to persuade you to my way of thinking."

"How so?"

"Sir Jeffery, I have no desire to marry you. I do not love you and I never will. I cannot make it any clearer on this point." She turned to him in the dim lamp light of the porch and hoped he would understand. "I know about your hold on Father and I know about your desire for the Scottish property." She held up her hand to wave off his question. "I overheard you two discussing the matter one evening. Therefore, I know, too, that you are not marrying me because of any great love, but rather because you want a good turn of business."

"Fair enough," Jeffery replied and leaned back against the porch railing. "But your knowing the circumstance does nothing to change my decision."

"But why not? Why not be an honorable man about this and allow Father some other means by which to settle his debt?"

"I'm open to other means. If you can put the three thousand pounds in my hand, I'll call the entire wedding off."

"Truly?" she asked, feeling at once hopeful.

Jeffery sneered and laughed. "But of course you can't put that kind of money in my hands, even if you inherit, can you?"

"Perhaps not right away, but I could put over half of it in your hands."

"What? And leave yourself with no income. If you do not marry, your father is sure to exile you to that pitifully cold Scottish estate you seem so inclined to hang on to. Without funds, how do you propose to live?"

"I hope to sell my book when we return to England. Lady Bird suggested—"

"No, Amelia. I will not call off this wedding on your hopes and the suggestions of Lady Bird."

"And there is no other way to convince you?"

"None. Now stop being such a foolish child about it all. You'll have the very best of everything, I assure you. And if you're concerned about your freedom to find true love, I will even go so far as to say that as long as you are discrete about your affairs, I will be most tolerant of them."

Amelia was totally aghast. "I would never consider such a thing!"

Jeffery sighed and spoke tolerantly as though dealing with a simpleton. "It is done all the time, Amelia dear. Most of nobility take lovers because they've been forced into loveless marriages. I'm simply trying to offer you what would be an acceptable arrangement in lieu of your sacrificing to a marriage of arrangement."

Noises from the front of the lodge porch told Amelia that her sisters and their friends were making their way over to the Amhurst cabin. They were giggling and talking in breathless succession about some point or another. It probably amounted to nothing more than their ritual game of after-dinner whist. Amelia lowered her voice to avoid drawing attention to herself.

"I am appalled that you would suggest such a thing. Marriage is a sacred institution, not something to be flaunted about and infringed upon by numerous affairs."

"My dear, you are quite naive to believe such a thing. I had thought you to be more mature about these matters, especially in light of your disbelief in holy affairs. I thought you above all other women to be removed from such nonsense."

"Faithfulness has never been nonsense to my way of thinking."

"Ah, but it is your way of thinking that is keeping this matter unresolved. Your father made up his mind to accept my generous offer. It will benefit all people in one way or another. Yes, even you will benefit, Amelia, and if you would but stop to think about it, you would see that I speak the truth. You might even come to enjoy my company after a time, and furthermore, to find pleasure in my bed."

Amelia dismissed such notions with her coldest stare. She hoped Jeffery felt frozen to the bone from her look. "I believe we've said all there is to say," she stated and turned to leave. Jeffery did nothing to stop her.

"You'll soon see for yourself, Amelia." He called after her, then laughed in a way that suggested he was very much enjoying the entire matter.

Amelia hurried to her cabin, fighting back tears and angry retorts. She knew that there was little to be done but accept her fate. Suicide seemed her only answer and her heart grew even heavier as she considered how she might accomplish such a fate.

"I want to wear the green one," Penelope argued and pulled the gown from Margaret's hold. Both sisters looked up guiltily as Amelia entered the room to find them fighting over her gowns.

When Amelia remained fixed in her place, saying nothing of reprimand, Penelope took the opportunity to explain. "There is to be a dance tonight. They're clearing the lodge's main room and Mary is fixing refreshments. It won't be as nice as a fancy ball, but I'm positively dying to dance. And Mr. Reed said the local men will come and serve as partners."

Margaret lifted her nose in the air and said, "I do hope they bathe. Some of these Americans seem not to know what a benefit water and soap can be." Her attitude suggested she might be reconsidering her appearance at the dance, but just when Amelia figured her to be absent, Margaret's expression changed to one of pleading desperation. "You simply must let us borrow your dresses. You have so many pretty gowns that you've not even worn and we've only those old things." She waived to a small stack of discarded gowns.

"Do whatever you like," Amelia finally said in a voice of pure resignation. "You may have all of my dresses for all I care. I won't be needing them anymore."

"You're only saying that to make me feel bad," Penelope said, puffing out her chest indignantly. "Just because you are marrying Sir Jeffery in Denver and will receive a new trousseau, you think you can be cruel."

"Yes, you are very mean-spirited, Amelia," Margaret agreed. "I think I've never met a more hateful person. You'll have Sir Jeffery and his money and go to court and spend your days in all the finery and luxury money can buy. We'll still be trying to make a proper match."

"Yes," Penelope added with a sigh, "and hoping that our husbands will be as handsome and rich as Sir Jeffery." Both of them broke into tittering giggles before Penelope sobered and tightened her hold on the gown as though Amelia might change her mind. "So you needn't be so smug, Amelia. You may walk around with your nose in the air for all we care."

Amelia looked at them both. She was stunned by their harshness and hurt by their comments. These were her sisters and there had been a time when they were all close and happy. She remembered joyous times when they were little and she'd played happily with them in the nursery. She loved them, even if they couldn't see that. Even if time and sorrow had made them harsh, and strained their ability to be kind. She saw hints of their mother woven in their expressions. Margaret looked like their mother more than any of them, but Penelope shared a similar mouth and nose. Amelia sighed. They should be close, close as any three people could ever be. But they thought her a snob and a spiteful prideful person, and perhaps they were right. It seemed only to fuel the idea that the world would be a better place without her in it.

Not wishing to leave them with a bitter memory of her, she offered softly, "I do apologize. I fear you have misjudged me, however. It was never my intention to make you feel bad."

Margaret and Penelope looked at her in complete surprise. Amelia wondered if they had any idea of what she was about to do. They were so young and childish and probably concerned themselves only with what color would best highlight their eyes or hair. No doubt they prayed fervently that Amelia would allow Jeffery the freedom to dance with them and pay them the attention they so craved. *Will they mourn me when I am gone? Will anyone?*

"You don't care at all how we feel. All summer you've pranced around here like some sort of queen. Always you've had the best of everything and Father even allowed you to remain behind from the hunt when we had to drudge about this horrid country looking for sport!" Penelope declared.

"Yes, it's true!" Margaret exclaimed in agreement. "You had Jeffery's undivided attention and positively misused him. You have no heart, Amelia."

Amelia could no longer stand up under their criticism. She felt herself close to tears again and rather than allow them to see her cry, turned at the door to walk away. "You needn't worry about the matter anymore," she called over her shoulder. "I'll take myself to the Crying Rock and relieve you of your miseries."

Crossing the yard, Amelia looked heavenward. A huge milky moon shown down to light her way and a million stars sparkled against the blackness. Mother had told her that stars were the candlelights of angels.

"We can't always see the good things at hand, but we can trust them to be there."

Amelia sighed and rubbed her arms against the chill. "You were wrong, Mother. There is no good thing at hand for me."

She made her way up the mountain through the heavy undergrowth of the forest floor. She only vaguely knew the path to the Crying Rock and hoped she'd find the right way. Tears blinded her from seeing what little moonlight had managed to filter down through the trees. She'd never been one given to tears, but during these few months in America she'd cried enough for a lifetime. Now it seemed that her lifetime should appropriately come to an end.

Her sisters' harsh comments were still ringing in her ears and her chest felt tight and constricted with guilt and anguish. *Perhaps they're right. Perhaps I am heartless and cruel. The world would be a much better place without me.*

"God cares about your pain." Logan's words came back to mind so clearly that Amelia stopped in her place and listened for him to speak. The wind moaned through the trees and Amelia realized that it was nothing but her mind playing tricks on her. *There is no God,* she reminded herself, chiding herself for being foolish.

"Even if there were," she muttered, "He wouldn't care about me."

∽

Logan leaned against the stone wall of the fireplace and wondered if Amelia would join the evening fun. He'd watched her from afar and saw that her mind was overly burdened with matters that she refused to share. He'd prayed for her to find the answers she longed for.

Over in one corner, Lord Amhurst and Sir Jeffery were steeped in conversation and Logan couldn't help but watch them with a feeling of contempt. What kind of man forces his child to marry against her will? Especially a man who represents nothing but fearful teasing from childhood and snobbish formality in adulthood. He longed to understand better and not feel too judgmental about Amelia's father and his insistence that she wed Jeffery Chamberlain. He knew very little except for what he'd overheard and none of that gave him the full picture. He'd tried to get Amelia to talk about it, but even when he'd caught her in moments where she was less guarded about her speech, she refused to share her concerns with him.

His mind went back to the conversation he'd overheard earlier that evening between Amelia and Jeffery. He'd been coming to the lodge and rounded the back corner just in time to hear Amelia tell Chamberlain that she believed in faithfulness in marriage. Chamberlain certainly hadn't, but it didn't surprise Logan.

"Well, well, and here come some of our lovely ladies now," the earl stated loudly.

Logan looked up to find Amelia's sisters flouncing about the room in their finery. Lady Gambett and her daughters were quick to follow them into the room, but Amelia was nowhere to be found.

"I say, Penelope," Lord Amhurst began, "isn't that one of Amelia's gowns?"

Penelope whirled in the pale green silk. "Yes, Father, it is."

"You know how particular your sister is about her gowns. It will certainly miff her to find you in it."

"She knows all about it," Penelope replied.

"Yes, Father, she does. In fact, this is her gown also and she told me I could wear it," Margaret chattered. "Although it is a bit large."

Logan smiled, seeing for himself that Margaret's girlish figure couldn't quite fill out the bodice. He could imagine Amelia growing impatient with them both and throwing the gowns in their faces. Sipping a cup of coffee, Logan tried to hide his smile and keep his thoughts to himself.

In one corner, several of the boys were tuning up their fiddles and guitars to provide the evening's music, while the earl exchanged formalities with the newly arrived Lord Gambett. They talked for several minutes while the ladies gathered around Jeffery, each vying for his compliments. Some of the local men straggled in and Logan nearly laughed at the way they each paused at the door to shine their boots on the backside of the opposite leg. Never mind their jeans might show a smudge of dirt, so long as their boots looked good. Logan almost felt sorry for them, knowing that the prim and proper English roses would hardly appreciate the effort.

"We're certain to beat the snow if we leave at the end of next week instead of waiting," Logan heard Lord Gambett say.

"What do you say, Mr. Reed? Is the snow upon us?" Lord Amhurst suddenly questioned.

"It's due, that's for sure," Logan replied. "But I think you're safe from any real accumulation. We might see a dusting here and there, but it doesn't look bad just yet. Of course, with mountain weather that could all change by morning."

The musicians were ready and awaited some kind of cue that they should begin playing. The fiddle player was already drawing his bow across the strings in what Logan knew to be an American-styled call to order. He looked around the room and, still seeing no sign of Amelia, he questioned the earl about beginning the music.

"I see Lady Amhurst is still absent, but if you would like, the boys are ready to begin playing."

The earl glanced around as though Amelia's absence was news.

"I say, Penelope, where is that sister of yours? She doesn't seem to be here."

Penelope shrugged. "She left the cabin after telling us to wear whatever we wanted. She was mean-tempered and said she wouldn't be needing these gowns anymore. We presumed she said that because of her marriage to Sir Jeffery. Don't you think it was mean of her to boast that way?"

Lord Amhurst laughed, "At least she's finally coming around to our way of thinking, what?" He elbowed Jeffery and laughed.

"Indeed it would appear that way," the sneering man replied.

Logan hated his smugness and thought of his lurid suggestion that Amelia would come to enjoy his bed. Logan seethed at the thought of Amelia joining this man in marriage. He had worked all week long to figure out what he could do to resolve Amelia's situation. He couldn't understand her loyalty to a father who would be so unconcerned with her feelings, and yet he respected her honoring him with obedience. *Somehow there has to be a way to make things right for Amelia.* He though of approaching the earl and asking for Amelia's hand, but he was already certain that the man would never consider him a proper suitor, much less a proper husband.

"I congratulate you, Chamberlain, on your powers of persuasion. You must have given her a good talking to in order to convince her to marry."

"Maybe it was more than a talking to," Lady Gambett said in uncharacteristic fashion.

The girls all giggled and blushed at this. They whispered among themselves at just what such possibilities might entail, while Jeffery smiled smugly and accepted their suppositions. Logan barely held his temper and would have gladly belted the grin off Chamberlain's face had his attention not been taken in yet another startling direction.

"But did Amelia say when she might join us?" the earl asked, suddenly seeming to want to push the party forward.

"No," Penelope replied, "she said she was going off to cry on some rock. I suppose she'll be at it all night and come back with puffy red eyes."

"Then she'll be too embarrassed to come to the party," Margaret replied.

Logan felt his breath quicken and his mind repeated the words Penelope had just uttered. *"She said she was going off to cry on some rock." Did she mean Crying Rock?* He put his cup down and signaled the band to begin. He wanted no interference on exiting quickly and figured with the music as a diversion he could make his way out the back kitchen door.

He was right. Logan slipped from the room without anyone voicing so much as a "Good evening." His thoughts haunted him as he made his way to the end of the porch. He grabbed a lighted lantern as he jumped down from the steps. *She doesn't want this marriage and she knows about Crying Rock.* He mentally kicked himself for ever taking her there.

"Lord, if I've caused her to seek a way out that costs Amelia her life, I'll never forgive myself," he muttered.

Chapter 15

As if drawn there by sheer will, Amelia finally made her way to Crying Rock. She stood for a moment under the full moon and looked down at the valley below. Across the mountains the moon's reflection made it appear as though it were day. The dark, shadowy covering of pine and aspen looked like an ink smudge against the valley. The mournful sound of the wind playing in the canyons seemed to join Amelia's sobs in sympathetic chorus.

Her gown of lavender crepe de chine did little to ward off the bite of the mountain breeze. The polonaise styling with its full skirt and looped-up draping in back gave a bit of protection, but the wind seemed to pass right through the low-cut bodice and was hardly deterred by the chiffon modesty scarf that she'd tucked into it. The finery of a Paris gown meant little to her now. What good were such baubles when no one cared if you lived or died?

She stepped closer to the edge and wiped her tear-stained face. *Father will be very unhappy when he learns what I've done. All of his plans will be for naught, and yet he'll still have his money and the land will pass to Penelope.* Perhaps her sister would go willingly into marriage with Sir Jeffery. Thinking of Jeffery made her stomach hurt. He was mean and crude and just standing over the dizzying drop made her remember his cruelty to her as a child.

"This thing must be done," she said to the sky and then sank to her knees in misery. *If only there were some reason to go on with life.* She simply couldn't see herself at Jeffery's side playing the innocent wife while keeping her lovers waiting in hidden rooms. Furthermore, to imagine that Jeffery would entertain himself in such a manner bothered her pride more than she could admit. If Jeffery had at least loved her, it might have been possible to go into the marriage. But he wanted nothing more than her father's money and the manipulative power to control all that she would inherit. Amelia felt sick just imagining the arrangement.

"If God did exist—" she said softly and lifted her gaze again to the panoramic view of the mountains. She thought of Logan and all that he'd share with her about God and the Bible. She thought of his faith to believe in such matters. He was totally unwavering, even when she made what she knew was a strong argument against his beliefs, Logan wouldn't argue with her about God. And it wasn't because Amelia hadn't sought to stir up a conflict now and then. Logan would merely state what he believed to be the facts and leave Amelia to sort through it herself. She remembered one conversation that had taken place several days earlier in which she had asked Logan how he could be so certain that he was right in his beliefs.

"How can you be so certain that I'm not?" he had questioned. *"I'm willing to bet my life on my beliefs. Are you?"*

Amelia felt a chill run through her at the memory. Was she willing to bet her life on her beliefs? Her mother's faith had been the foundation for their household. Her father had even admitted that it was one of the things that had attracted him to her in the first place.

"Mother, why did you leave us?" Amelia whispered. "Why did you have to leave me with so many questions? If God loves us as you always said He did, then why did He cruelly take you from the children who needed you? Where is God's mercy in that? Where is the love?"

The rustlings of the wind in the trees below were all that came back in reply.

"All right," she said, giving in to the tremendous longing in her soul. "If You exist, God, then why do you allow such tragedy and injustice? Why, if You are such a loving Father, do You allow Your children to experience such pain?" She paused in questioning and rubbed her arms against the mountain chill. "Why do You allow *me* to hurt so much?"

"I want to believe," she said and this time the tears came. "I want to believe." She sobbed and buried her face in her hands. "But it hurts so much and I'm so afraid that You won't be any more constant than Mother was. If I believed, would You merely go away when I needed You most, just as she did?"

A verse of scripture from childhood from the last chapter of Matthew, came to memory. *"And, lo, I am with you always, even unto the end of the world."*

"But the world is filled with a variety of beliefs and religious nonsense," Amelia protested against the pulling of her spirit. "How can I know that this is real? How can I know that I am choosing the right path?"

Logan had said it was a matter of faith and in believing that the Bible was truly the Word of God. Logan had also said that God proved himself over and over, even in the little day-to-day points of life.

"God, if You are real," Amelia said, lifting her face to the starry, moonlit sky overhead, "then You must show me in such a way that I cannot miss it in my blind foolishness."

But even if God was real He wouldn't change my plight. What tiny thread of hope had begun to weave itself through her broken heart, snapped with this sudden realization. She was still facing her father's edict that she marry a man she didn't care about. She would still find herself headed back to England within the month. And she would still lose the man she loved.

Logan came to mind with such a powerful urgency that Amelia no longer fought against it. She loved him as truly as she had ever loved anyone, and in many ways, intimate and frightening ways, she loved him more than she had ever loved anyone else. Logan was like no one else in the world. He cared to share his faith with her in such a way that it wasn't merely preaching for the sake of fulfilling his obligation to God—rather it was that his heart was so full to overflowing with love for his God and Savior that he couldn't help but share it.

Then, too, Logan was perhaps the only man who had ever treated her with respect that didn't come from a sense of noble obligation. Logan spoke his mind and refused to play into her role of "Ladyship," but he also afforded her a kindness and gentleness of spirit that only her mother had ever given her. But of course, that didn't mean he loved her and love was truly all that Amelia longed for in life.

"There is no reason to live without it," she whispered. "Oh God, if You are real then give me a reason to live. Send me love. Real and true love. Please, let someone love me." She sobbed.

"I love you," Logan said from somewhere behind her. "Even more, God loves you, Amelia."

∽

The sound of his voice startled her so badly that Amelia hurried to her feet, tangling her skirt around her legs as she tried to straighten up. Caught off guard by Logan and by the gown's hold on her, Amelia lost her balance and fell to the ground. The impact caused a piece of the rocky ledge to give way and Amelia felt herself slipping from the safety of Crying Rock.

Digging her hands into the rock and dirt, she thought, *Not now. I can't die now!* But even as the thought crossed her mind, she was more than aware of her dangerous situation. With what she thought would surely be her last breath, she screamed Logan's name.

"Amelia!" he cried out from overhead. "I thought I'd lost you!"

She pressed her body against the cold, hard granite and for the first time in her life began praying earnestly. She barely heard Logan calling her name and refused to even lift her face to search for him overhead.

"Amelia, you have to listen to me," Logan said again. "Can you hear me?"

"Yes." She barely breathed the word.

As he moved overhead, bits of rock and dirt pelted down on her head causing Amelia to shriek in fear. "Don't be scared, Amelia. I'll soon have you right as rain."

She would have laughed had the predicament not been so grave. *Don't be scared?* She was long past scared. She was terrified to the point that she thought she might pass out cold and end any hope of her rescue.

"Listen to me, Amelia. I can reach your hand if you lift your arm up."

"No, I'm not moving," Amelia replied, hardly daring to breathe.

"You have to do as I say or you may well be on that ledge for whatever time you have left on earth."

She said nothing for several heartbeats and then spoke in a barely audible voice. "I can't do it, Logan."

Logan seemed not to hear her. "Look up and to your right. I'm reaching down as far as I can and I can almost touch your head. All you have to do is give me your hand. I promise I won't let you go."

"I can't do it," she repeated sternly.

"Yes you can," he told her, sounding so confident that she felt a surge of hope. "Trust me, Amelia. Have faith in me and what God can do."

Amelia felt the pounding of her heart and the fierce chill of the wind as it whipped up under her skirt from the canyon below. She wanted to believe that Logan could do what he claimed. She wanted to trust that God would honor her prayer of desperation.

Slowly, methodically, she released her grip on the rock. Her hands ached from their hold, but slowly she stretched her fingers until they were straight. She lifted her arm ever so slowly. She refused to look up, terrified that she would find the distance too far to make contact with Logan's hand. But then his hand clamped down on her wrist jarring her rigid body to her toes. Amelia had to force herself not to cry out.

"I've got you. Just don't fight me and we'll be okay," Logan called down to her. "I'm going to pull you back up on the count of three. One. Two—"

Amelia's heart was in her throat. *If I die now there will never be any hope of reconciling myself to God.*

"Three!" Logan exclaimed and Amelia found herself being hoisted back up the rock wall. She heard her crepe de chine skirt tear against the jagged edge and the loose dirt rolling off the ledge as Logan dragged her across it. In the time that it took to realize what had happed Amelia lay atop the ground with Logan panting heavily at her side.

He jumped up quickly and pulled her away from the edge to more stable ground. Wrapping his arms around her, he held her in a trembling embrace that told her how afraid he'd been. He sighed against her ear and Amelia thought it all more wondrous than she could take in. She relished the warmth of his body against hers and the powerful hold of his arms. *He loves me* she thought. If only she could stay in his arms forever.

Then, without warning, she started to giggle and then to laugh and Logan pulled away to look at her quite seriously. The thoughts flooding through her mind, however, would not let her speak a word of explanation. It was almost as though the missing joy in her life had suddenly bubbled over inside.

"Amelia, are you all right?"

She nodded and continued to laugh so hard that tears came to her eyes.

"It's shock," he said authoritatively. "Come sit down."

Shaking, Amelia allowed him to lead her to a small boulder and sat willingly when he pushed her to do so. She was still laughing, however, at the very idea that she had asked God to give her a sign so clear that she could not miss the truth! What remained comical in her mind was that God could hardly have made it any clearer, and even Amelia, in her childish refusal to believe in His presence, was ready to admit her folly.

Logan sat down beside her and pulled her gently into his arms. She looked over and found his expression so fearful that it sent her into new peals of laughter.

"I'm sorry," she alternated between gasps and giggles. "It's just so, so—" Her voice fell away in uncontrollable mirth.

"Amelia honey, you've got to calm down," Logan said softly. Her hair had come loose during her escapade up the mountain, and Logan methodically stroked it as if to calm her.

"It's just," she said, finally gaining control of her voice, "that I asked God to prove Himself to me. I asked Him for a sign that even I couldn't ignore and then He does just that, getting my full attention by dangling me over the ledge! Oh Logan, don't you see how funny it is?"

Logan nodded and smiled. "I remember you asking Him for love, too."

This did the trick in sobering her completely. "Yes, I did." She looked deep into his eyes, unable to make out their brilliant green shading in the moonlight. "I'm glad you came."

"Me, too."

With their faces only inches apart, the kiss that followed seemed more than natural. Amelia felt Logan bury his warm fingers in her hair in order to slant her head just enough to give him free access to her mouth. She was stunned by the kiss at first, and then a flaming warmth seemed to radiate out from where their lips touched. It flowed down through her body until Amelia wanted to shout aloud with joy.

"Amelia," Logan sighed her name as he pulled away from the kiss. "I love you, Amelia. Please tell me that you could love a barbarian."

She smiled. "I *do* love you, Logan Reed."

With this, he kissed her again, only this time less urgently and when he pulled away, Amelia could see that his eyes glistened. "I thought I'd lost you," he whispered.

"I couldn't see a reason to go on, but neither did I have the courage to put an end to my life," Amelia admitted.

"It doesn't take courage to kill yourself," Logan interjected. "That's the coward's way out."

"I was in such turmoil. I kept remembering the things my mother had taught me about God and the things you kept pushing in my face." At that she smiled and took hold of his hand. "Logan, you were right to keep after me. I've always known God existed, but I didn't want to admit it because if He existed in the power and glory people told me about, it also meant that He had the power to keep the bad things in my life from happening. But He didn't. He let Jeffery torture me as a child. He let my Mother die before I was ready to say good-bye to her and He left me to be forced into a marriage with a man I can't abide." She paused and searched Logan's face for condemnation. When she found only love reflected in his gaze, she continued.

"To believe in His existence meant I had to accept that He knew what was happening and that He stood by and let it happen. That seemed cruel and heartless to me. The God my mother had always told me of was merciful and loving. I couldn't accept that He would do such a thing or even allow someone else to do those things. Does that make any sense?"

"I think so," Logan replied. "But how about now? Those things haven't changed. And there are still horrible tragedies in life. Tragedies that won't just go away overnight."

"That's true," Amelia said thoughtfully, "but I suppose I must simply accept that fact. I don't imagine life will always make sense, but what does make sense to me is that if there is a way to deal with the bad times in peace and confidence, then that's what I want. I've watched you all summer and your peace and assurance have driven me nearly insane."

He laughed at this and hugged her close. "Your uppity, stubborn 'I'll do it myself' attitude has nearly driven me to drink, so I guess we're even." He ran his hand through the blond silk and smiled. "Oh, and I always wondered what you'd look like with your hair down and now I know."

"And what exactly do you know?" she asked impishly.

"That you are the most beautiful woman in the world," Logan replied. "What little of it I've seen."

"There's no place else in the world as pretty as Estes, Logan, and no place I'd rather be."

"So what are we going to do now?" he asked softly.

Amelia smiled and pulled back far enough to look into his face. "I'm ready to lay it all out before God, Logan. I'm ready to face life and march back down the mountain and do what I'm told to do." She bit at her lower lip and looked away before adding, "At least I think I am. It won't be easy to leave you."

"Leave me? Who said anything about you leaving me? I want you to marry me, Amelia."

She shook her head. "That, Logan, is impossible. There are things you don't know about that prevent my giving in to such a dream. And believe me, that is my dream. I would love to marry you and stay here in the mountains for the rest of my life. I know it deep down inside me, just as I know that I'm ready to accept Christ as my Savior." She paused, feeling suddenly shy about her declarations. "But it is not possible for us to marry."

"'With God,'" Logan said, reaching out to touch her face, "'all things are possible.' The Bible says so and I believe it with all of my heart, just as I believe you will one day be Mrs. Logan Reed."

Amelia felt the tears come anew. She looked at him there in the moonlight and tried to commit to memory every line and angle. She reached out and touched the mustache that she'd so often longed to touch and found it soft, yet coarse, against her fingers. Funny, but she'd not even noticed it when he'd kissed her.

She gazed into his eyes, seeing the longing and love reflected there for her—longing and love she held in her own heart for him. *How can I explain that I could never be his wife? How can I walk away from the only man I will ever love and marry another?*

As if sensing her thoughts, Logan took hold of her hand and kissed her fingers gently. "All things are possible with God," he repeated. "Not just some things, but all things."

"You don't understand, Logan. My father needs me to marry Jeffery. He owes him a great debt and Sir Chamberlain will brook no nonsense in collecting on the matter."

"Does he love you?" Logan asked quite seriously.

"No. I think that man's incapable of love. But he does desire my land," she said, smiling at the irony of it all. One man wanted her heart, another her land and she was stuck in the middle with her own longing and need and no one but God knew what that might mean to her.

"Do you love him?"

"Certainly not!" she declared with a look of horror.

"I love you, Amelia," he said simply. "I love you and I want to marry you, not for land or money or noble title, but because life without you would be unbearable. I think I fell in love with you the morning after our first all-day ride. You tried so hard to keep from grimacing in pain as you got on that horse the next morning and I thought to myself, 'Here's a woman with real spirit.' Then I think I loved you even more when you went bustling around camp trying so hard to work at every job I gave you. I pushed you a bit too hard, but I got my reward. It put you in my arms."

"You asked me to choose between barbarians or twits," she murmured. "And you thought I chose Jeffery."

"No, I didn't."

"But you said—" She paused, cocking her head to one side as if to better understand him.

"I said that I could see you'd made your choice. I never said you chose Sir Twit. But I could see the argument you were having with yourself over feelings that you couldn't yet come to terms with. So I gave you over to him, hoping that the misery would drive you right back to me."

"I couldn't sleep that night for the things you made me feel," she admitted.

"Me either. So you see, I'm not ready to give up and say this can't be done. I'm quite willing to fight for you and pay off your father's debt if necessary."

"You can't. It's a great deal more money than either of us could hope to raise."

"How much?" he asked flatly, with a look of disbelief on his face.

"Three thousand pounds."

"Done."

"Done?" she questioned. "Where in the world are you going to come up with three thousand pounds?"

"Well, it probably won't be pounds, but American dollars will spend just the same."

She shook her head. "Don't joke about this."

"I'm not joking."

She could see by the serious expression on his face that, indeed, he wasn't joking. "How are you going to come by that kind of money?"

"I'll take it out of the bank."

"You mean rob it?" she asked in alarm.

Logan laughed until Amelia thought he would fall off the rock on which they were sitting. "No, silly. I'll withdraw that much from my account."

"You have that much money?"

"And a good deal more," he said soberly.

"But I thought—"

"You thought because I live here in Estes and lead guided tours into the park that I was too dirt poor to go anywhere else. Isn't that right?" She nodded, feeling quite guilty for her assessment. "Well, it isn't true. I've got more money that I'll ever need thanks to a little gold mine my father and I own. The truth is, I live this way because I love it. Estes is the only place in the world I ever came to that when I first laid eyes on it, I felt like I'd come home."

"Me, too," she whispered, barely able to speak. *Did God bring me here to bring me home to Him? To Logan?* It was more than she could take in all at once. *Is this how God is making Himself real in my life? To suddenly answer all my needs in one powerful stroke?*

Logan got to his knees and pulled her down with him. "First things first," he said, pulling her closer. "You said you were ready to accept Christ as your Savior, right?" Amelia nodded, forgetting everything else for a moment. "Then that is where we start our new life together," he replied and led her in a prayer of repentance.

Chapter 16

Snow blanketed the mountaintops while a light powdery dusting covered the valley below. They had left Estes days ago and Amelia had felt an apprehension that grew into genuine fear. What if Logan couldn't convince her father to release her from the engagement to Sir Jeffery? What if Jeffery himself refused? With each step the horses took, with every descending clip of their hooves against the dirt and rocks, Amelia felt something inside her die.

She watched both men with anxious eyes, all the while praying fervently. Her father seemed mindless of her dilemma and Jeffery only appeared smug and self-satisfied with the circumstance. Logan promised that God would provide an answer and a way to see them through, but Amelia wasn't as steady in her faith as Logan and the possibility seemed completely out of reach.

Shortly before noon, Logan stopped the party to rest the horses and to Amelia's surprise he beckoned Sir Jeffery to follow him into the forest. Appearing quite annoyed with their barbaric guide, Jeffery did as he was bid, but not without a scowl of displeasure plastered across his aristocratic face. In a short while they returned to join the party and Jeffery seemed all smiles and satisfaction. Amelia was puzzled by this turn of events, but no more so than when Jeffery heralded her father and the two men began to have a feverish discussion. From time to time her father nodded and glanced in her direction, but no one summoned her or indicated a need for her presence and so Amelia remained with her horse, seeing to it that he was properly watered.

They remounted and made their way another hour or so, weaving back and forth across the St. Vrain River before emerging from the canyon to face some six miles of flat prairie land. Longmont would be at the end of the prairie ground and Amelia felt her hope giving way. Longmont represented the place where they were to take the stage to Denver and forever leave Estes, and Logan, behind them. She shuddered, fought back tears and prayed for strength to endure whatever God decided. And all the while she felt her heart nearly breaking with desire to turn around and run back to the safety of Estes.

How could she leave?

She glanced over her shoulder to the mountains. They seemed gray in the harsher light, and the chill in the air left little doubt that winter would soon be a serious business in the area. She gripped the reins tighter and ignored the single tear that slid down her cheek.

How could she leave Logan?

She watched him lead the way across the dried-out prairie and tried to imagine sitting in her damp, drafty English manor house without him. Months ago, she wouldn't have given a single shilling to extend her trip to America by even a day, and now she knew she'd gladly trade the rest of her life to be able to marry Logan and share even a few days as his wife.

"I say," the earl called out to his companions, "this place seems worse for the passing of time."

"Indeed," Lord Gambett replied, gazing about. "Not at all pleasant. It was hot and unbearable when we departed and now we find it dusty and devoid of life."

Amelia smiled at this. Months ago, she would have agreed with Lord Gambett, but now, with the training Logan had given her, Amelia observed life everywhere. Insects, animals, autumn vegetation. It was all here; it was just a matter of where you looked.

"Whoa," she heard Logan call to the party. She glanced forward to find that everyone had halted their horses on the edge of town. "I believe you all know your way from here," Logan said sternly. "Tie up your mounts in front of the hotel and take your personal belongings with you. I'll see to the horses and gear and meet you to settle up in about half an hour. I'll also bring your trunks at that time."

Everyone nodded and urged their horses forward to the hotel. Amelia saw her father and Mattersley press forward with Penelope and Margaret in tow, but she couldn't bring herself to join them. She stared, instead, at Logan astride his horse. Logan, whose face was tanned and sported a new two-day growth of beard. Logan, whose jeans accented his well-muscled legs and whose indigo-dyed, cambric shirt hugged him in a way Amelia longed to imitate. He pulled off his hat, wiped his brow and finally noticed that she was watching him. With a grin, he replaced the hat and nudged his horse her direction.

"You having trouble following directions again, Lady Amhurst?"

She felt a lump in her throat that threatened to strangle her. "No," she barely croaked out.

His mustache twitched as he broke into a broad smile. "Faith, Amelia. Have faith."

"It's stronger when I'm with you," she replied.

"Don't put your faith in me. Remember, your strength comes from God and He will help you."

She nodded. "Okay, Logan. My faith is in God." She spoke the words aloud hoping it would help her to feel more confident. "But how are we going to—"

"Don't worry about anything. Now join up with your family and I'll see you in half an hour." He winked at her before leading his horse off in the direction of the livery.

"Don't worry—have faith," she murmured and urged her mount forward. "Easier said than done."

∞

Half an hour later, Amelia was just as nervous as when she'd left Logan. Her father seemed preoccupied with some matter, while Sir Jeffery was suddenly paying far more attention to Penelope and Margaret than he'd done throughout the entire trip. When she could stand it no longer, Amelia went to the earl and demanded to know what was going on.

"Amelia, Sir Jeffery has agreed to release you from your engagement."

Her mouth dropped. Recovering her composure she asked, "He did? But what of the money?" At this Mattersley took several steps away from the earl and pretended to be preoccupied by studying the ceiling.

Her father shrugged. "He dismissed the debt as well. I have no idea what you said to him, Amelia, but there it is."

"But I don't understand."

"It would seem that you have won this round. I. . .well. . .perhaps

I was overly influenced to marry you off because of the debt." He looked at her intently. "I never meant any harm by it, Amelia. I thought you could be happy in time. I suppose now you are free to remain unmarried."

"But what of the inheritance and your concerns for the family coffers?" she asked warily.

Weariness seemed to mar his brow. "You gave your word that you'd not see us suffer and I've always known you to be a woman of truth. Having you stay on with me as your sisters marry and leave will no doubt be a comfort in my old age."

How strange, Amelia thought, wondering how she might broach the subject of Logan's proposal and her own desire to remain in America. How could she explain the change in her heart when she'd been the one to protest leaving England in the first place?

"Ah, good, you're all here," Logan said, striding into the room as though he were about to lead them all in a lecture symposium.

Lord Amhurst looked up with Mattersley doing likewise, but Penelope and Margaret remained in animated conversation with Sir Jeffery. Lord and Lady Gambett stared up wearily from their chairs, while Henrietta and Josephine looked as though they might start whining at any given moment. Amelia dared to catch Logan's gaze and when he smiled warmly at her it melted away some of the fear she felt.

"Your trunks are outside," he announced, "and the stage is due in two hours. I'd suggest you take your breaks for tea and cakes before heading to Denver. There isn't much in between here and there, and you'll be mighty sorry if you don't."

"I believe this will square our account," Lord Gambett said, extending an envelope.

Logan looked the contents over and nodded. "This is mighty generous of you, Gambett." The man seemed notably embarrassed and merely nodded before muttering something about seeing to the trunks.

"And this should account for us," Lord Amhurst announced, providing a similar envelope.

Logan tucked the envelope into his pocket without even looking.

"If you have a moment, I'd like to speak with you privately, Lord Amhurst."

"I dare say, time is short; speak your mind, Reed. We haven't even secured our tickets for the stage."

"They're reserved in your name, I assure you. Five tickets for Denver."

"Five? You mean six, don't you? Or did you reserve Sir Jeffery's separately?"

"No, I meant five." Logan looked at Amelia and held out his hand to her.

Amelia hesitated only a second before joining Logan. Even Penelope and Margaret gasped at the sight of their sister holding hands with their American guide. Mattersley was the only one to offer even the slightest look of approval and that came in the form of a tight-lipped smile.

"I've asked Amelia to marry me, and she said yes. Now I'm asking for your blessing, Lord Amhurst."

"Why I've never heard of such rubbish!" the earl exclaimed. "Amelia, what nonsense is this man speaking?"

"It isn't nonsense, Father." Amelia noted that her sisters had gathered closer, while Lady Gambett, seeing a major confrontation in the making, ushered her girls into the dining room. Jeffery stood by looking rather bored and indifferent. She smiled up at Logan and tried to calm her nerves. "It's all true. I would very much like to marry Logan Reed and since Sir Jeffery has kindly released me from our betrothal, I am hoping to have your blessing."

"Never! You are the daughter of an earl. You've been presented at court and have the potential to marry. . .well. . .to certainly marry better than an American!"

"But I love an American," Amelia protested. "I can do no better than to marry for love."

"I forbid it!"

"Father, I'm nearly twenty-one," Amelia reminded him. "I can marry without your consent, but I'd much rather have it."

"You marry this man and I'll cut off all inheritance and funding from you. You'll never be welcomed to set foot on my property again."

"Isn't that what Grandfather Amhurst told you when you decided to marry Mother?" Penelope and Margaret both gasped in unison and fanned themselves furiously as though they might faint.

The earl reddened at the collar and looked quite uncomfortable. "That was a different circumstance."

"Not so very different to my way of thinking." Amelia dropped her hold on Logan and gently touched her father's arm. "Father, don't you want me to know true love as you and Mother did?"

"And you love this man enough to lose your fortune?"

"She doesn't need a fortune," Logan interjected. "I have enough for the both of us." This drew everyone's attention. "Look, there doesn't need to be any pretense between any of us." Logan drew out two envelopes and handed them to the earl. "I won't take your money for the trip and you can give this back to Lord Gambett as well. Also, "he said reaching in for yet another envelope, "this is yours, Chamberlain. You will find fifty thousand dollars awaiting you at the bank in Denver."

"Fifty thousand?" Amelia questioned.

Logan smiled. "I had to make it worth his trouble." Jeffery said nothing but tucked the envelope into his pocket. Lord Amhurst stood staring at his own envelopes while Logan continued. "As I said, Amelia doesn't need the Donneswick fortune. She'll be well-cared for by me and she won't want for anything, unless of course, it's your blessing."

The earl looked positively torn and Amelia instantly felt sorry for her father. "I love him, Father," she said, tears glistening in her eyes. "You wanted me to marry before my twenty-first birthday and I'm finally agreeing to that."

"Yes, but—" he looked at her and suddenly all the harshness of the last year seemed to fade from his expression. He looked from Amelia to Logan and seemed to consider the idea as if for the first time. "I say, you truly wish to be married to him and live here, in America?"

"I truly do." She leaned over and kissed her father on the cheek, whispering in his ear, "Logan makes me happy, Papa. Please say yes."

He smiled and touched Amelia's cheek. "You will come for visits, won't you?"

"Of course we will," she replied. "So long as we're both welcomed."

He sighed. "Then you have my blessing, although I offer it up with some misgivings."

"Oh, thank you, Father. Thank you!" Amelia gave him an uncharacteristic public embrace before throwing herself into Logan's arms.

Logan hugged her tightly and happily obliged her when Amelia lifted her lips for a kiss.

"Ah, I say," the earl interrupted the passionate display, "but I don't suppose we could find a man of the cloth in this town, what?"

Logan broke the kiss and nodded. "Parson's waiting for us as we speak. I didn't figure you'd much want to leave her here without seeing her properly wed."

The earl very ceremoniously took out a pocket watch and popped open the cover. "Then I say we'd best be going about it. I have a stage to catch shortly, as you know."

Epilogue

I thought you said May around here would signal spring," Amelia said, rising slowly with a hand on her slightly swollen abdomen. She looked out the cabin window for the tenth time that morning and for the tenth time found nothing but snow to stare back at her.

"Hey," Logan said, coming up from behind her, "we didn't make such bad use of the winter." He wrapped his arms around her and felt the baby's hefty kick. "See, our son agrees."

"What he agrees with," Amelia said in her very formal English accent, "is that if his mother doesn't get out of this cabin soon, she's going to be stark raving mad."

"We could read together," Logan suggested. "We could get all cozied up under the covers for warmth, maybe throw in some heated rocks from the fireplace to keep our feet all toasty. . . ." His words trailed off as he nuzzled her neck.

"I believe we've read every book in the cabin, at least twice," she said, enjoying his closeness.

"We could play a game of cards. We could get all cozied up—"

"I know. I know," she interrupted. "Under the covers for warmth and throw in some heated rocks, but honestly Logan I'm going to throw one of those rocks through the window if we can't do something other than sit here and count snowflakes."

"Maybe, just maybe, if you can bear to be parted from me for a spell, I'll ride down to Mary's and see if she can come up here for a bit. Maybe you ladies could share quilting secrets."

"But I want to get out! I want to walk around and see something other than four walls and frosted windows. I may be with child, but that certainly doesn't mean I'm without feet on which to walk. Please, Logan."

Logan sighed and laid his chin atop her head. "If you promise to dress very warmly and to wear your highest boots, and do everything I say, then I suppose I could be persuaded to—"

"Oh Logan, truly?" Amelia whirled around, causing Logan's head to snap back from the absence of support. "When can we go? Can we go now?"

Logan laughed, rubbed his chin and gave Amelia a look that said it all. She liked the way he was looking at her. It was a look that suggested that she alone was responsible for his happiness and if they remained snowed in the cabin for another six months, he'd still smile in just exactly the same way. He touched her cheek with his calloused fingers and smiled. "Good things take time, Lady Amhurst."

"Mrs. Reed," she corrected. "I'm happily no longer a lady of noble standing."

He grinned roguishly. "Oh, you're a lady, all right. But you're my lady now."

She smiled and felt a surge of joy bubble up inside her. "God sure had a way of getting my attention," she said, putting her hand over his.

"The stubborn, impatient ones are always the hardest," he whispered before lowering his mouth to hers.

Amelia wrapped her arms around Logan's neck and returned his kiss with great enthusiasm. She'd found the happiness that she'd never thought possible, and come September, she was going to have a baby. Logan's baby—and she was Logan's lady, and somehow that made the long winter seem not quite so unbearable.

Tracie Peterson, bestselling, award-winning author of over ninety fiction titles and three non-fiction books, lives and writes in Belgrade, Montana. As a Christian, wife, mother, writer, editor and speaker (in that order), Tracie finds her slate quite full.

Published in magazines and Sunday school take home papers, as well as a columnist for a Christian newspaper, Tracie now focuses her attention on novels. After signing her first contract with Barbour Publishing in 1992, her novel, *A Place To Belong*, appeared in 1993 and the rest is history. She has over twenty-six titles with Heartsong Presents' book club (many of which have been repackaged) and stories in six separate anthologies from Barbour. From Bethany House Publishing, Tracie has multiple historical three-book series as well as many stand-alone contemporary women's fiction stories and two non-fiction titles. Other titles include two historical series co-written with Judith Pella, one historical series co-written with James Scott Bell, and multiple historical series co-written with Judith Miller.

Along Unfamiliar Paths

Dedication

Dedicated to the memory of my beloved sister, Sarah P. Weston, who ran with patience the race set before her and victoriously traveled the ultimate Unfamiliar Path. We'll see you again soon, Sarah!

Prologue

The clanging bells jerked him from a deep sleep seconds before the pounding on his cabin door began. Leaping from his bunk, the dark-haired sailor wrenched the door open, finding nothing but his captain's voice echoing down the hall. "She's going down! The ship is going down! This is not a drill."

The man snatched up his life jacket, pausing for one precious moment to assure himself that the locket was still there, lying warm against his chest. He felt a dark feeling of premonition, a sense that mortal danger hovered over him. Flying up to the top deck, he ripped the object from the chain that had held it close to his heart for so long. Pressing it into his captain's hand, he felt a weight lift off his shoulders.

For a moment, though, tears sprang to his eyes unbidden. *Surely now she would understand. . .* A surge of water over the deck interrupted his thoughts. Pulling himself together, he turned to the task of evacuating the ship.

He reassured each fearful passenger with a smile, ignoring the acrid smoke that stung his nostrils and the memories that wounded his heart. Lowering the last woman to the safety of the lifeboat, he caught a quick movement out of the corner of his eye. He whirled, but it was in vain. The hands of his nemesis were too swift. Staggering from the hard slash across his face, the burly sailor felt himself being shoved over the railing.

He snatched at the hands that were thrusting him downward, clinging desperately to them. "It won't matter," he gasped. "The papers are—" His hands slipped and he plunged silently toward the icy water, blinded by his own blood. The balsa wood in his life preserver struck him under the chin as he hit the water, throwing his head back with such force that he was knocked unconscious.

The frigid cold of the water brought the sailor back to consciousness at last. . .and filled him with terror. How long could he last in this icy grave?

How foolish he had been, to think he could win by his own rules. He groaned aloud as his father's angry face rose up to taunt him. And the locket. Surely it wouldn't be too late. . . *God, I can't die this way!*

His tears spilled over, bathing his frozen cheeks in momentary warmth. Did anyone even know or care that he was dying out here? He shivered violently, colder than he ever thought possible. And the thick, unnerving quiet. No sound, except his own labored breathing. Was this what it felt like to die? He would just slip quietly under the water, and no one would ever know. . .

God will know. A new wave of dread washed over him at the thought. He wasn't ready to face God.

Desperation lending strength to his numbed senses, he raised his head an inch to peer across the inky waters and into the frozen night sky, only to have his last hope fade away. The lights of the ship were gone. Gone! Like a young man's dreams of the future. Fear rose in his throat, ready to strangle him.

"God!" He cried out to the One he had so long forgotten. "Save me!"

Chapter 1

London, England
1906

Ben Thackeray leaned back in his chair with a weary sigh. Lifting his eyes to the window overlooking the wharf, he absently scanned the activity as his mind continued to mull over the problem at hand. *It just may be that I'll have to go to New York myself,* he mused. *There are just so many loose ends, so many things that could go wrong, so many buttons. . .*

Buttons? He found himself staring distractedly at the back of a woman's dress. *There must be a hundred buttons down the back of that dress,* he thought as she moved past his window. He watched a moment longer as she picked her way across the pier.

Catching a glimpse of her face, he felt his mouth go dry. He turned back to his desk, running a shaking hand through his hair. "Get back to work, old chap," he muttered out loud to himself. "It couldn't be her after all this time."

Images of a slender waist and soft lips teased his mind as he studiously bent over his papers. Giving up after a few minutes, he unfolded his long legs from under the desk. From his viewpoint, he could see halfway down the waterfront. Ah, there she was.

He watched her as she spoke to an elderly fisherman, enjoying the graceful gestures of her hands. He saw her turn to leave, her shoulders slumping. His heart leapt as she turned toward him.

You're imagining things, he told himself sternly. *It just can't be. . .*

Now staring in earnest, he tried to decide what it was about the woman that compelled him. Was it the glimpse of chestnut-colored curls. . .the curve of the jaw. . .the smooth forehead just visible under her hat. . .that was it!

He had to see her without the hat, he decided.

∞

Raine Thomas glanced at the leaden sky. *It's now or never,* she told herself firmly.

Lifting her heavy skirts an inch as she edged around the mud puddle that stood between her and the wharf, she grimaced at the muck. It reminded her of the barnyard back home.

It wasn't that she minded talking to Jacob; not at all. It was just that the waterfront was not her favorite place to be. All those men staring at her and making their crude remarks, not to mention the smell of the place. And then there was the time she had caught her heel and fallen headlong into that pile of crates. . . She felt her face burn at the remembrance.

But a promise was a promise, and that's what she had given to little Anna Peters—a promise. Not that it would matter very much since Raine would be gone soon, but still. . .

She realized she was almost running to keep up with the pace of her thoughts. Slowing her steps as well as her mind, she sighed, her mind replaying once again the meeting with the Mission's new administrator.

"I've only been here a couple of weeks, Miss Thomas," Mr. Duncan had begun in his frigid tone, "but already I can see that I do not approve of your methods for running the Mission school. They are not at all consistent with the rest of our efforts. Your informal attitude with your students encourages a laxness that I cannot condone."

Raine felt the blood rush into her face. "Mr. Duncan, I. . ."

"Please allow me to finish what I was saying, Miss Thomas."

Raine bit her tongue, feeling her world crumble around her as he finished his speech.

The rest of the painful conversation had dimmed in her memory, but the import of it had not. What it had come down to was that Mr. Duncan and his new advisory board felt strongly that a man would be more "suitable" as director of the Mission School. Raine was dismissed as of the end of the month.

But where can I go? She rubbed her hand over her forehead wearily. There was no use going over it again. Going home to Papa was out of the question, and she had already considered every other possible alternative. She drew a deep breath, wishing God would send her some kind of message, some guidance. The breath of air made her nose wrinkle; the air here by the wharf was heavy with moisture, making the ever-present odors of unwashed bodies and fresh fish almost unbearable.

I hope You're not calling me to be a fisherman, Lord. She smiled with a glimmer of her usual good humor. *I know You must have something for me. I just wish You'd show me what it is...*

Ah, there's Jacob. Raine's prayers were interrupted as she spotted the man she had been seeking. "Good morning, Jacob!" she called to the big fisherman.

"Miz Thomas," Jacob acknowledged, turning back to his nets after a brief nod in her direction.

"Your children haven't been to the Mission School in two weeks." Raine's tone was gentle, questioning. "Anna would like..."

"They're needed at home!" he growled. "Got to git back to work, Miz Thomas."

Raine sighed in aggravation as she turned to go. What would she tell Anna? She pictured the girl's sad little face. *I don't know why I even try anymore, when I'm going to be replaced in a few weeks anyway,* she thought, feeling a new wave of frustration and anger begin to flood over her. The now-familiar sick feeling in her stomach grew as she turned to go. *Lord, please give me strength...*

As she picked her way absently through the bustling wharf, she suddenly felt the weight of someone's gaze. Glancing around, she met a pair of bright blue eyes. The tall owner of the eyes took a step toward her, then turned on his heel and disappeared into the doorway where he had been standing.

Raine was not unaccustomed to admiring glances from strangers, but this was...different. *Almost as if he had wished to speak to me,* she thought. She shrugged off the odd sensation, focusing on making it to the street without catching her heel between the rotting boards of the wharf.

She breathed a sigh of relief as she reached the brick-paved street. So what was she going to do? It was already the fifteenth of the month, and she was no closer to finding somewhere else to go. *I'd sooner be a fisherman than go home,* she thought, recalling her prayer of a few minutes ago.

The Mission had been her home and employment for years

now, and she hated to think of doing anything else besides teaching. True, some women did go to work in offices now. Perhaps she could even learn how to operate that queer new invention called a typewriter. *But I don't want to leave,* she thought. She loved teaching, and besides, what would become of the children? Their small faces had been so woebegone when she announced that she would be leaving.

"Why, Miss Thomas?"

"Don't ya love us no more?"

"Where're you going to go?"

The questions had nearly broken her heart. But she did have two more weeks. During that time, she would make sure they knew she loved them. And of course Charlotte would still be there for them. She just wasn't so sure about Mr. Graysdon, the new headmaster. She hoped he wouldn't be as stiff as he seemed. She sighed again. Life could be so. . .bothersome sometimes.

Her hat pins were poking unbearably by the time she neared the Mission. Yanking them out of her hat, she almost laughed with relief as she pulled the abominable thing off. Why did such large hats have to be in style these days anyway? Feeling decidedly grumpy and still no closer to a solution, she was looking forward to a time of quiet before she had to teach her afternoon class.

A crack of thunder hurried her toward the dilapidated steps of the old brownstone building. Hearing someone approaching from behind, she hastily jammed her hat back on. *I might as well at least try to stay in Mr. Duncan's good graces while I'm still here,* she thought wryly. Mr. Duncan would be appalled to see his headmistress in public without her hat.

"Miss?"

Raine glanced back over her shoulder as she reached the top of the steps. The man from the wharf! Had he followed her here? She grasped the porch railing, turning to watch him hasten up the steps to join her. His blue eyes searching her face, he stopped directly in front of her. Close. Close enough for her to see the vein pulsing in her neck.

∞

Ben ran his fingers through his hair, feeling as if he were in a dream. It had to be her. His senses throbbed as he stood near enough to smell the lilac fragrance she wore. She was even more beautiful up close. . .

"Can I help you?" her tone was cool, interrupting his thoughts.

"Yes, I. . .ah. . ." Ben felt idiotic, but he had to know for sure. "My name is Ben Thackeray and I. . .could you take your hat off again?"

"What?"

"Please?" He tried to put his earnestness and uncertainty into his face, hoping she wouldn't deny his request. Reluctantly, she swept off her hat, cocking a questioning eyebrow at him.

There it was.

Ben sucked in his breath when he saw what he had suspected. The oddly shaped birthmark on her right temple seemed to jump out at him.

Her hand flew up of its own accord to cover the mark. She stared at him, her eyes wide. He came back to his senses then, realizing that he had frightened her. *You're such a cad,* he berated himself silently. *Couldn't you have been a little more subtle?*

"I'm sorry to appear so rude." He started to run his fingers through his sun-bleached hair, then stopped himself. He hadn't felt this nervous the first time he piloted the ship. The way she was staring at him didn't help matters any, either. He didn't like the wariness that lurked in her sage green eyes, as if he might actually harm her. She reminded him of a fawn he had startled out of its hiding spot once as he hiked through the woods.

"I'm sorry I frightened you," he apologized again. "I just had to be sure it was you. You are Raine Thomas. . . ?"

Her face turned paler, if that were possible. She stood poised as if to run, just like the little deer. He grimaced. This wasn't exactly how he had pictured this moment happening. . . Not trusting himself to try to explain further, he drew a small package from his breast pocket. He unwrapped it with care and handed her the contents, watching carefully as she took the locket and held it to her heart.

"Paul?" she whispered.

He nodded.

She stared at him, her eyes begging him to give her hope. "Is he—alive?" Her voice was a tortured whisper.

He watched her compassionately, warring with himself. He longed to tell her what she wanted to hear, but. . . "Raine—may I call you that?"

She nodded.

"Let me tell you the story, then if you have any questions, I'll try to answer them as best I can. I'll start by saying that I don't know for sure that Paul is dead."

"Go on." Her voice trembled.

"I first met Paul in 1901, and. . ."

Raine interrupted, "1901. . .that was a year after he left. . .I was nineteen."

". . .and that's when he signed on as a crewman on one of my ships," Ben said. "I own a shipping company," he explained.

Raine smiled, as though the picture of Paul on a ship, his black hair glinting in the sun, a gentle breeze blowing, had broken through her anxiety. "He always did love to be on the water," she murmured lovingly. Her gaze grew misty and faraway.

"Raine?"

"I'm sorry. I was just. . ."

He smiled gently. "It's all right. I know this has all come as a shock to you." He saw her swallow a lump in her throat, and he looked away, giving her a chance to compose herself.

"How did you happen to have the locket?" Her voice still quavered.

"Paul and I had become quite close friends. He made me swear that if he ever needed me to, I would find you and give it to you." Ben's voice was rough with emotion. "I've been looking for you for three years, Raine."

"Three years!" Tears gathered in her eyes. "You haven't seen Paul in three years?"

Ben shook his head. "I'm sorry."

"Tell me the rest, please." She closed her eyes for a moment, as though she were dreading to hear what he would say next.

"There's not much more," he said slowly, hating to kill whatever hope she had left. "We pulled out from Boston on February 22, 1903. Since we primarily ship cargo, we didn't have too many passengers, thank God. There was a slight mishap as we left the harbor, but no one paid too much attention. The voyage went smoothly for the first week. . ." Ben stopped, unwilling to relive once again the horror of that night. It had been so cold, so quick, so. . .

He felt a small hand touch his lightly. "You can tell me," she encouraged him.

He drew a deep breath. "On Monday the twenty-eighth, I had just retired for the evening. Shortly after I got to bed, the warning alarms rang. I jumped up and raised the alarm. I banged on Paul's door," he remembered. "Fire was raging in the hold, and we soon realized we weren't going to be able to save the ship. We concentrated on getting the passengers into the lifeboats. Paul gave me the locket—he must have sensed. . .something." He shook his head. "The. . .the last I saw of Paul, he was helping a woman and her baby into lifeboat number four." Ben closed his eyes in pain, then went on. "We both had life jackets on, but there was so much confusion, and everything happened so fast. . . I was helping keep control of the situation on deck, and I just never saw Paul after that." He stopped abruptly, as if drained of all emotion.

Tears had been flowing down Raine's face as he talked. He gave her a wan smile, then standing up heavily, he offered her his hand. "I'm sorry, Raine," he whispered. "Most of the crew were able to get on the lifeboats. Some of the others were rescued from the water, but no one knows what happened to Paul. His body was never recovered." His hand rested on her shoulder for a brief moment, but his blue eyes never met hers again. "I'll be at my office tomorrow if you need to ask me anything more."

He handed her a card with the address elegantly inscribed on it, then turned and walked away.

⌒

Raine stared after him a moment, then looked at the locket she still held clenched in her hand. "Where are you, Paul?" she whispered.

She stood rooted to the spot until the first cold drops of rain mingled with the warmth of her tears. Making her way slowly to her room, she ran into her friend Charlotte.

"Oh Raine! I was just looking for you. Would you mind if I borrowed. . . What's the matter?"

"I'm not exactly sure, Charlotte." Raine gazed into the concerned eyes of her best friend. "Could you teach my class for me this afternoon?"

Charlotte nodded, giving Raine's shoulders a quick squeeze. "I'll pray for you."

Raine sank down on the bed remembering the day Paul had left. She had pressed the locket she always wore into his hand, needing to give him a part of herself to take with him. . .

She felt the pain stab her heart anew, and slipped to her knees, calling out to her only strength. *Father, please help me. I love Paul so much, and I always thought one day I would find him again. I need Your peace.* She stayed on her knees, a tiny flame of hope flickering in her heart. *The man did say that he didn't know for sure that Paul is dead,* she told herself. *But then why haven't I heard from him in so many years?*

She pushed that thought out of her mind, concentrating instead on the person who had brought her the news. What was his name? Ben something or other, she recalled. Tall and golden, he was the perfect counterpart to dark-haired, compactly-built Paul. *What a pair they must have been. They had to have been close friends for Paul to entrust Ben with the locket,* she mused.

The locket! Why hadn't she opened it before now? Maybe there was a message from Paul! Almost dropping it in her haste, she finally got the small heart open. Something white fell to the floor, so minute she might have missed it had she not seen it fall. She picked it up, unfolding the tiny piece of paper with trembling fingers.

Her heart began to pound as she recognized Paul's firm handwriting. Even in her agitation, she smiled to see that he had written in code. How like him. Racking her brain to remember the ciphers she had not used in years, she experimented for several minutes. It was just a simple substitution cipher; she was sure of it. She frowned in concentration, then smiled as it suddenly came to her. She decoded all that was legible, disappointed to find that most of the message was obliterated by waterstains.

Would Mr. Thackeray know what the missing words were? Could she trust him? *Surely if Paul trusted him with the locket, I can trust him with the message,* she decided, remembering his gentle eyes.

❧

Engrossed in his work, Ben started when he realized he was not alone in the office. He caught his breath when he saw Raine standing just inside the door, smiling at him uncertainly. *How lovely she is,* he thought, taking in the eager face and demure dress. Her dark curls were piled on top of her head today in the fashionable Gibson girl style. He was glad she wasn't wearing a hat, and wondered briefly what her hair would look like flowing around her face and down her back.

"How are you, Raine?" Ben rose to offer her a seat. He caught a whiff of her perfume and forced himself to sit down behind his desk.

"Quite well, thank you," she said. "Mr. Thackeray," she began, then stopped, as though suddenly shy.

"What is it, Raine? Did you come up with some questions?" He was charmed with the way she held her chin down the tiniest bit, looking up at him.

"Yes, I. . . Did you know what was in the locket?"

He shook his head, saying nothing.

She looked at him thoughtfully. "Mr. Thackeray, how well did you know Paul?"

"He was my first mate and friend for two years." He looked into her eyes and saw the confusion there. "You can trust me, Raine," Ben said. "Paul was like a brother to me."

She stared at him for a long moment, then silently she pulled the water-stained note from her pocket and handed it to him. He stiffened as he stared at the strange writing. So, it was true all along. He wouldn't have believed it of Paul, but this proved it now, didn't it?

Raine's laughter broke into his glum thoughts. "I take it Paul didn't teach you any ciphers. I would have thought in all your time together, he would have shared his great passion with you."

She didn't seem to notice Ben's lack of response as she retrieved the note from him. "As you can see, the words near the bottom are missing. I was hoping you could help me fill in the gaps." She looked up at him appealingly. "What I have so far doesn't make much sense to me, but maybe you'll understand it: 'Am being pursued. Go to 284 H. . .Ask. . .key. I will be. . .going. . .C. . .Love, P.'"

Ben recovered himself quickly. Either Raine was an innocent party, or she played her part extremely well. He'd just play along for a while and see what happened.

"Let's see. . . Go to 284 H. . .284. . .284. . . Sounds like an address," he muttered. "Wait a minute!" Whirling around to his file cabinet, he dug through it a moment, then triumphantly pulled out a sheet of paper. "This is a list of our crewmen's home addresses," he explained. "Ah, here it is! 284 High Street! Paul lived at 284 High Street in Boston!"

Raine jumped up from her chair with a shriek of joy. "But what does the rest of the message mean?" she asked, returning his wide smile.

"I don't know, Raine," he said, sobering. "But at least you have a good start. I'll. . ."

"Mr. Thackeray, Miss Daniels is. . . Oh, excuse me." Ben's clerk backed out the door in confusion as he saw Raine.

"That's fine, Jerry. I'll be there in a moment," Ben called to the retreating clerk.

"Anyway, Raine, I'll think about the message and see if I can come up with anything else. Can you come back to the office in the morning?"

"Certainly," Raine said crisply, a hint of annoyance in her tone.

"I'll be looking forward to it, Raine Ellen." Ben's voice was soft.

After she left, he leaned back in his chair, a small smile playing about his lips. The look that had crossed Raine's face when Miss Daniels had been announced had been priceless. Nevertheless, he was loathe to face the consequences of keeping one Vida Daniels waiting, so he had unwillingly hurried Paul's lovely fiancée on her way.

Watching her out the window now as he rose to admit Miss Daniels, Ben was startled as he glimpsed a large, red-haired man standing in the shadows of the tavern next door. The man watched

Raine until she disappeared from view, then turned and stared intently at Ben's office. Apparently satisfied, he sauntered onto the busy wharf and was swallowed up in the crowd.

Something about the man seemed familiar to Ben, but he couldn't be sure. He would have given it more thought, but the insistent tapping on his office door grew unavoidable. Rolling his eyes in aggravation, he opened the door to a very red-faced Miss Daniels, narrowly missing being jabbed by the end of her parasol as she pushed past him into the room.

"Good morning, Miss Daniels," Ben said as politely as possible. "I was just coming out to greet you. Won't you have a chair?" *A chair in another country would do nicely,* he thought.

∞

Her irritation inexplicably erased by the warm smile Ben had given her as she left his office, Raine had smiled at Ben in return and then, hoping to get a glimpse of Miss Daniels, she took her time in passing through the outer office. But besides the clerk Jerry who studiously avoided looking her way, the only others present were two elderly women. Neither of them could possibly be Miss Daniels, she surmised disappointedly.

Strolling back to the Mission, she pondered what her next step should be. *Is this Your doing, Father?* she prayed. The tiny seed of desire to go to America had been planted long ago, but had never sprouted until today. *Am I to go to Boston? Please show me Your will, Lord.*

Something was tugging at the back of her mind, causing her to lose her train of thought. She glanced behind her several times, feeling as though she were being watched. Unable to catch a glimpse of anyone, she shrugged the feeling aside as she entered the Mission building. The familiar smell of ancient books, unwashed children, and stewed onions was somehow comforting, and her little room felt cool after the hot mid-morning sun. She knelt by her bed, suddenly feeling full of unexplained anticipation. Picking up her Bible, she began reading where she had left off last night. *"And I will bring the blind by a way that they knew not; I will lead them in paths that they have not known: I will make darkness light before them. . ."* The verse from Isaiah leapt out at her, filling her heart with the peace that she needed. The Bible was talking about her life, she realized. "I need You to lead me," she whispered. "I can't see where I'm going and I will be walking some unfamiliar paths. . ."

By the next morning, the tiny sprout of desire to go to America had bloomed into a magnificent flower. She had resolved one thing—she was going to Boston! The last she had heard from Paul, he had been in Boston. And now the message in the locket. She was sure it was not a coincidence.

I'll find you, Paul, she vowed. *By God's grace I'll find you.*

Convinced that Ben Thackeray could help her, Raine rehearsed her request as she dressed. Surely such a close friend of Paul's would be willing to give her a little advice, wouldn't he? Even if he wouldn't agree to help her, she'd get to Boston somehow. *I know You're leading me there, Lord.* She brushed her long, dark hair until it shone, then made a face at herself in the mirror. *Just who are you trying to impress, Raine Thomas?* She laughed out loud, her heart light. It felt so good to be happy again.

Twisting her hair into a loose chignon, she chose her favorite hat. More comfortable than the rest of the hats she owned, the small cream-colored toque was trimmed with navy velvet. It was perfect with her favorite shirtwaist suit.

She took one last peek in the mirror and closed the door firmly behind her. Her hurried descent down the stairs was anything but ladylike, so it was with some dismay that she found Mr. Duncan waiting for her at the foot of the stairway.

"Good day, Miss Thomas." He nodded politely, obviously choosing to ignore her breach of conduct. "I haven't seen much of you lately. Have you had any success in finding a new. . .ah, position?"

"I just may have, Mr. Duncan." She tried hard not to smile at the expression on his face. She always imagined he must have perpetual stomach acid or some other malady to make him frown so.

"Humph." He shook his head as she yielded to the temptation to smile. Her smile broadened as she sailed out the door.

Pushing through the door that read THACKERAY SHIPPING CO., Raine nearly ran headlong into Jerry, who seemed to be embarrassed to be caught combing the few strands of hair he had left on his head.

"Pardon me, Jerry," she apologized to the clerk. "Is Mr. Thackeray in yet this morning?"

"Not until nine." He cocked his head, reminding her of a large parrot she had seen once at the fair.

She looked at the clock. Ten minutes till nine. She sat down, then stood up, too excited to sit still. Pacing around the little office, the many drawings and photographs that cluttered the walls caught her eye. She stopped in front of a grouping of framed sketches depicting various ships. The *Ladyhawk*, the *Golden Hind*, the *Half Moon*, the *Goodspeed*, the *Constellation*. What romantic names these ships bore. Maybe Paul had sailed on one of these.

She could almost see him standing on the deck, wearing a smart blue uniform. A smile creased his face while the wind ruffled his coal black hair. . .

"Good morning, Miss Thomas."

She whirled around. "Mr. Thackeray! You startled me!"

His twinkling blue eyes held the same look as six-year-old Tim's had the day he had put a frog in her desk drawer. "Please, call me Ben. May I escort you into my office?" He pulled out a chair for Raine. "Now, tell me what that sparkle in your eye means."

"I'm going to America!"

Ben's eyebrows shot up, but he said nothing as she continued. "I've been saving my money for a long time so I could start searching for Paul. The last time I heard from him, he was in Boston, and the address in the locket just confirms that I should begin searching there," she explained logically. Her green eyes shone with determination. "If Paul is alive, I will find him."

Ben's eyes lingered on her face, his expression almost wistful. He said, "It sounds as if you've pretty much made up your mind, Raine. How do you plan on getting there?"

"Well, I. . ."

"You aren't planning to go alone?" he interrupted, suddenly remembering the man he had seen watching her earlier.

"Well, yes, I. . ."

"Do you know how dangerous New York can be, let alone the journey over there?" He was incredulous. "Besides, you'd never make it in without a sponsor."

"Ben," Raine said quietly. "I'm not afraid, and I do have a place to stay once I get there. My uncle John who lives in Boston has offered over and over to sponsor me." She hesitated, and then said, "I was hoping you could recommend a reputable ship. I've heard the horror stories. . ."

Ben nodded. He had seen some of the wretched vessels first-hand. He would never put his worst enemy aboard such a ship, if they could be called ships. He stared out the window, an idea forming slowly. "How long would it take you to get your papers in order?" he asked finally.

"I was hoping to leave within the month."

"Hmm."

She waited.

At last he said, "Yes, I think that will work out perfectly."

"I beg your pardon?"

"Simple." He grinned at her. "You can go with me as far as New York, then I'll escort you the rest of the way to. . . Where did you say you were going to stay?"

Raine shook her head. "What do you mean, go with you?" She stared at him.

"You can lower your eyebrows, Miss Thomas. I'm not suggesting anything improper." He chuckled at the blush that rose to her cheeks. "You know that we don't take many passengers on our ships." He paused until she nodded. "But I was planning to go to New York this month to take care of some business anyway. I would be glad for the pleasure of your company."

"On one of your cargo ships?" she asked, considering the plan.

"Yes." He made a face. "It's not as luxurious as a passenger ship, of course, but you would have your own cabin, and the food is decent. Oh, and there will be several other women aboard," he added, putting to rest her last fear.

She eyed him thoughtfully. Could she trust this man? It was hard to believe she was actually considering going halfway across the world, much less with a man she hardly knew. What would Papa think? And what if Ben weren't as trustworthy as he seemed? What if. . . Suddenly the peace that she had felt after her prayer the day before came flooding over her again.

"When do we leave?"

"The *Capernaum* departs in sixteen days. Can you be ready?"

"The *Capernaum*?"

A strange look dropped into Ben's eyes. "All my ships are named after Biblical cities. I'm not sure why, actually. I suppose it's a habit I picked up from my father." He cleared his throat. "Can you be ready to go by then?"

"I'll be ready. How much will I owe you?"

He looked at her blankly. "Owe me? Oh, for the passage. Let's just say it's a favor to an old friend."

Raine was overwhelmed. She had been wondering if the small amount she had managed to save over the last few years would be enough. "Thank you," she whispered, sudden tears threatening to spill over.

He stepped closer to her and said softly, "Paul was more than just a first mate, he was my friend. It's the least I can do."

She gave him a small smile, and she saw his eyes widen, his lips part—and then he took a quick step backward and said brusquely, "Now—I'm sure you have a lot of things to attend to before we depart, and I need to get busy with this paperwork." He moved back another step away from her. "I'll call on you sometime next week to make arrangements for the voyage."

Raine blinked at the abrupt change in mood, then turned to leave. "I'll be ready," she said softly. He didn't look up from his desk.

⚭

Ben rose to stand at the window as soon as the door closed behind her. He stared after her, wanting nothing more than to run after her. Even the photograph of her he had fallen in love with years ago didn't do justice to her beauty.

I could almost wish she would never find Paul. . . . He turned away sharply. *Get ahold of yourself, Thackeray,* he told himself. *Her heart will always belong to Paul.*

∞

Unaware of the turmoil she was causing Ben, Raine made her way home to the Mission with a light step. Feeling as though an enormous weight had been lifted from her shoulders, she dipped herself a glass of ice-cold water from the bucket in the kitchen, then went directly to Mr. Duncan's office. Her knock was firm.

"Come."

Raine entered the stuffy office and immediately began to recite the speech she had practiced on the way. ". . .and so, I'll be departing in approximately two weeks."

"Well, this is a surprise." He sniffed. "I suppose you've made proper arrangements for your, ah, excursion?"

She was slightly ashamed of herself for enjoying his reaction to her news. "Yes sir. I will be traveling on a reputable ship, and I already have a sponsor in America."

"Your duty to the Mission does not expire until the end of the month, Miss Thomas," Mr. Duncan reminded her. "I expect you to fulfill your obligation."

She sighed in frustration. She had thought he would be happy to be rid of her. "Mr. Graysdon has already arrived to take my place, has he not?"

"Yes, he has."

"I sincerely doubt that one extra day will be a burden on him," Raine said, hoping she sounded more polite than she felt.

"I will not tolerate impertinence, Miss Thomas," he snapped. "If you insist on leaving on the thirtieth, I will subtract two days' wages from your salary."

She gritted her teeth. Why did this man remind her so much of Papa? Sending up a silent prayer for patience, she restrained herself from dumping the glass of water down his back. Forcing her voice to stay calm, she looked him in the eye. "I'm sorry you feel that way,

Mr. Duncan, but I don't have much of a choice. I have to be on that ship when it sails."

His raised eyebrows were his only response.

She fled from his office, convinced that her tongue would get her in trouble if she lingered one more second. *That is one person I certainly won't miss,* Raine thought uncharitably as she climbed the stairs to her room, unsure if she were referring to Papa or Mr. Duncan. Her conscience pricked her. *And aren't you a sweet one today,* she thought uncomfortably.

∞

Three days later she looked up from her desk to see Ben grinning at her from the back of the classroom. Startled, she dropped her eyes back down to the tests she was grading. What was he doing here?

"All right, children. You may open your readers now. We will begin on page forty-two." She sincerely hoped she had remembered to powder her nose before class. If not, it was surely shining like one of those electric light bulbs she had heard about. "James, start reading aloud please."

She went to greet her visitor. "Ben. How nice to see you." All at once there didn't seem to be enough air to breathe.

"And you." He was silent then, leaning against the doorjamb comfortably. He studied her face like it was the morning newspaper. It made her nervous.

"Can I help you?" The same words she used the first time they met. She felt herself color.

A smile crept into his eyes and twitched at the corner of his mouth. "I just came by to see if we could have supper together this evening, say, around six o'clock? I need go over the details of the voyage with you."

"Oh yes, the voyage." He wasn't staring at her nose, was he?

"You haven't changed your mind?"

"No. I, ah. . ." Raine noticed her students had stopped reading and were gawking. "Six o'clock would be fine."

His parting smile was enough to turn the rest of her day upside down.

171

∞

"You're going to supper with the captain of the ship?" Charlotte's brown eyes were huge. "Is he the one who brought you the locket from Paul?"

"Mmm-hmm." Raine answered around a mouthful of hairpins.

"Tsk, tsk. What would Paul say?"

"There." Raine stuck the last pin in and tilted her head to see the side of her hair. "Paul wouldn't say anything. It's just a business meeting."

"Ah." Charlotte nodded. "Then why are you taking so many pains?"

Raine glared at her friend as she fastened the lacy guimpe around her neck. "Speaking of pains. . ."

Charlotte laughed. "All right, I'll leave you alone. But do I at least get to meet him?"

∞

"Ben, this is my good friend, Charlotte Denoire. Charlotte, Captain Ben Thackeray." Raine rolled her eyes as Charlotte curtsied. She noticed her friend had added a bit of extra lip rouge for the occasion.

"A pleasure, I'm sure, Miss Denoire." Ben bent over her outstretched hand for the briefest second. He turned to Raine. "Shall we?"

She smiled up at him as he took her arm, the glint of humor in his eye doing wonders for her disposition.

Big Ben was booming out the hour of seven by the time they reached the Golden Cross Hotel.

"Oh, I've always wanted to eat here." Her mouth began to water at the aromas wafting from the famous establishment.

He smiled at her. "Are you hungry?"

"As a horse."

Ben laughed out loud.

∞

El Paso County, Colorado

Tom Cox sat astride his panting mount, surveying with pride the land spread before him. He absently rubbed the scar on his left cheek as he gazed with appreciation at the majestic Rocky Mountains looming blue and mysterious in the distance. Though it appeared one could reach the cool shade of the Rockies in a matter of minutes, he knew from experience that the ride was long and dusty. Wistfully, he turned once again to the east, shielding his dark eyes from the glare of the newly-risen sun.

He owns the cattle on a thousand hills. The bit of scripture came unbidden to his mind as he gazed upon the gently rolling plains and grazing cattle that comprised the Crooked P Ranch. Frowning in annoyance at his train of thought, he urged the patient mare forward.

"Come on, Trixie. Let's go home." Slouching comfortably in the saddle, he let the horse pick her way home through the sagebrush as he reflected on the past couple of years. The young Denver City had been more progressive than he had expected it to be, but the "Queen City of the Plains" nonetheless still carried with it the unmistakable influences of the Wild West. Everywhere he looked were Stetson hats and cowboy boots; feed stores and saloons shared the street with banks and lawyer's offices.

Glad that he was going to be some distance from the city's hustle and bustle, Tom had wasted no time in obtaining a horse. Riding southward past Colorado Springs to the land he had purchased sight-unseen, he was awestruck by the wild beauty of the land, grateful that he had chosen this place to start anew. Now, three years later, the Crooked P Ranch was prospering.

Trixie picked up her pace as they passed the bunkhouse and neared the stable. Her rider dismounted with a troubled sigh. He had made a home in this untamed, yet peaceful land. His ranch was prospering, but his soul was not. There remained a chapter in his life he could not close. . .

Chapter 2

Up since 3:00 A.M., Raine was awaiting Ben's arrival, feeling much the same as she did the morning of her first day of school. The stillness of the gray, pre-dawn hours contrasted sharply with the butterflies dancing in her midsection.

As she made her way downstairs, no one else in the Mission stirred; she had said all of her good-byes yesterday. The surprise party for the children had gone so well. She knew she would never forget the joy in their eyes as they opened the tiny gifts she had managed to find for each one. Nor would she forget the arms wrapped around her neck and the shy kisses placed on her cheek. It was harder than she had thought to be leaving them, and she wasn't even gone yet! Equally hard was ignoring the tiny pricks of guilt she felt when she thought of her decision to leave without telling Papa good-bye.

After peering out the window yet again, she dropped down in the straight-backed chair in the Mission's front parlor. Her Bible was lying on top of her carpetbag. She picked it up and began to read until a soft knock on the door alerted her to Ben's arrival.

"Good morning!" His eyes studied her face, and she was sure he saw the excitement that radiated from her heart.

"Good morning to you!"

She saw his gaze drop to her mouth for the briefest instant before he said firmly, "We'd better get going." His tone was tight as he gathered her luggage and directed her out the front door.

She glanced at him as he preceded her, carrying her trunk. Had she done something wrong, for him to become so brusque all the sudden? Or perhaps he was regretting taking her along? "Ben."

He looked up from loading her baggage into the carriage.

"Are you sure you want to take me to Boston?" she ventured in a small voice.

"Of course I want you to go," he said a little too heartily. "Don't mind me. I've got a lot on my mind this morning." He didn't meet her eyes.

Raine frowned, studying his face, but her thoughts were interrupted by a voice behind her.

"Raine! I'm so glad I caught you before you left!" A sleepy-eyed Charlotte came flying down the front steps, her mousy hair still in braids.

Raine smiled at her friend. "I haven't even left yet, and you miss me so much already?"

"No. I mean, yes. Oh, you know what I mean." Charlotte reached behind her back and pressed a soft package into Raine's hand. "I'll miss you, Raine."

Tears filled Raine's eyes. "I'll miss you, too, Char. I'll pray for you."

"And I you."

They gazed at one another. "Don't forget to write to me, Charlotte."

"Maybe I'll come and join you in America sometime."

"I'll look for the day."

With a last hug, they said good-bye and Raine climbed into the carriage. Although tears still clouded her vision, Raine's anticipation grew as she caught glimpses of the waterfront through the early morning fog. Sensing Ben's reticence, she had refrained from chattering on the short drive, but now she couldn't help it.

"The *Capernaum* is so much larger than I expected," she commented, gazing at the huge ship.

"Yes, she's a hefty one," Ben replied, following Raine's gaze. "There's no telling how many storms she's weathered, but she hums along like it was her maiden voyage," he added proudly.

The lonely cries of gulls and a damp, fishy smell assailed her senses as Ben assisted her out of the carriage. There seemed to be barrels and crates everywhere, not to mention the baggage of the passengers and crew. Ben gave her his arm and they waded through what seemed to be mountains of rope to get to the gangway. *Thank goodness bustles have gone out of fashion,* she thought. *It would have been almost impossible to dodge these barrels of pickled herring while wearing one of those ridiculous things.*

"Mornin', Cap'n, miss." A bewhiskered sailor nodded to Ben

and Raine, then leaned down to grasp Raine's small trunk.

Looking up at Ben, Raine said lightly, "Shall I call you 'sir' from now on, now that I'm on your ship?"

"No," he said. "You're not a part of the crew, you're. . .a friend," he finished, his blue gaze holding her captive.

Raine stared back at him, seeing him as if for the first time. She clasped her hands together behind her back, quelling an unexpected desire to run her fingers through his golden brown hair.

"Miss."

Raine jumped. The grizzled sailor was holding her last bag, studying her with a curious expression. "Are you ready ta board?"

"Ah. . .yes. That would be fine." She turned. "I'll be seeing you later, Captain?"

"Yes, perhaps tomorrow, Miss Thomas." He hated his formal tone, but he couldn't seem to help himself. "Sully here will get you settled in and answer any questions you might have."

I'm sure Sully can answer any question I have except the question of why you act so strangely sometimes, Ben Thackeray, she thought, still shaken by the intensity of his gaze. Obediently following the patient Sully, she turned to wave to Ben, but he was gone.

∽

Settled at last in her small but adequate cabin, Raine took in a breath of cool air that was blowing in through the open porthole. The butterflies in her stomach had settled down to a slow waltz.

She opened the small package from Charlotte, shaking her head as she read the note that accompanied the hand-embroidered pillowcase set.

Dear Raine,

These are for your new home in America. I hope you'll remember me when you see them and pray that God sends me as handsome a man as He sent you.

Love and prayers,
Charlotte

Poor Char. She was only biding her time until a handsome prince came to sweep her off her feet. To her, teaching was just a way of making a living. To Raine, it was a life's calling.

Feeling her throat tighten, she pushed thoughts of the children from her mind. God was leading her away from the Mission, and she would not allow herself to wallow in misery. Of course she would miss the children, but God had something better for her, didn't He? He would have something better for the children, too.

Of course He would, she assured herself as she powdered her nose. God was definitely leading her forward, and all she had to do was follow, no matter how unfamiliar the way seemed. The first step would be to find Paul. That in itself would be a glorious thing. She brushed her teeth with enthusiasm, picturing the moment. First he would stare at her in disbelief...then he would open his arms...

When she felt the ship lurch, she flew up to the top deck, not wanting to miss any of the action. After all, it was her first time out to sea. Watching with interest as the men worked to set the huge ship into motion, she could readily imagine Paul doing such work. She scanned the deck and was not surprised to see Ben working alongside his crew, clad in the clothes of a deckhand. He looked dashing.

Finally, a cheer went up as the *Capernaum* slowly maneuvered her way out of the harbor. The voyage was underway! "I'm coming, Paul!" she whispered. A quick prayer of thanksgiving flowed from her heart as the gulls dipped and swooped their farewells. *Hang on, love. I'm coming.*

∞

Ben was fuming. Angry with himself for giving in to his feelings, he was even angrier at Raine. *How can she look at me like that when she's engaged to Paul?* He paced up and down in his spacious cabin. *I never should have offered to let her come on this ship. I'll just stay away from her as much as possible, then get her to Boston quickly,* he vowed to himself.

He soon realized that it was not going to be easy to avoid the lovely Raine Thomas. Having made arrangements for her and the

177

six other paying passengers to take their meals with him and his officers, he knew he couldn't shun her without drawing censure from the rest of the company.

At dinner that night, he watched as she chatted away with the buxom woman next to her. What was her name? Oh, yes. Constance. Constance Rabinowicz.

He compared the two woman unconsciously. Raine in her traveling suit of navy blue, with that charming hat to set it off. Constance with her overly large hat and even larger bustle. Turning his attention back to Raine, he was mesmerized by the sound of her low voice. She glanced up then and their eyes locked.

"Who's the girl?" His first mate followed Ben's eyes.

"Miss Thomas is the fiancée of a friend."

"Oh?" Griff's eyebrows shot up. "He'd better marry her fast," he said mischievously, watching his captain out of the corner of his eye.

Ben glared at him. "Keep your observations to yourself, Griff."

∽

Ben stood at the railing a few evenings later. Bowing his head, he stood gazing into the dark waters for a long time. He was so weary. Weary in body, yes; but had he only admitted it to himself, most of the weariness was in his soul. He was weary of his constant fight against fear, the fear of surrender.

He was losing the battle. He had managed to stay away from Raine except when it was impossible to do so. Aware of the wistful look in her eyes, he knew she was puzzled by his behavior. Now with only a few days left before they arrived in New York, he had yielded to his longing to seek her out. Turning, he followed the path she'd taken toward her cabin.

His hand poised to knock on her cabin door, he stopped as he heard her singing. At first impressed with her melodic voice, soon he was caught up in the words she was singing.

"O the love that drew salvation's plan!
O the grace that brought it down to man!
O the mighty gulf that God did span at Calvary!

Mercy there was great, and grace was free;
Pardon there was multiplied to me;
There my burdened soul found liberty
At Calvary."

Slow tears began to course unheeded down his face. *God, how I long to know once again the peace that comes from accepting Your grace!* He had seen that same peace reflected so often in Raine's eyes. *But how can I?* his heart cried. *"Unto whom much is given, of him much shall be required."* The fragment of scripture that had been pounded into his mind as a child came back to hammer him once again. *God, I'm so afraid. I'm afraid of what You will require of me. . .*

Ben turned to go, to run from the familiar words of Raine's songs, but he could not run from the insistent, loving call of the Father. . .

∽

The sunny June days slipped by as the *Capernaum* steamed steadily toward New York. Raine had brought a couple of books with her, planning on catching up on her reading. However, that was not to be.

"Yoo hoo! Raine!"

She sighed, wishing not for the first time that Constance Rabinowicz had chosen another ship on which to immigrate to America. She didn't want to be unkind to the woman, but she did wish she could have just a few minutes of quiet to read. Maybe if she ignored her she would go away.

"Raine! Over here!" Constance increased her volume, further fortifying her presence by waving her handkerchief.

As if I were a cow being shooed into the barn, Raine thought. Grudgingly placing the marker in the volume of Tennyson, she rose. "I'm coming, Constance." She tried to wipe the frustration and annoyance from her face, but she couldn't wipe it from her heart. Constance seemed to want to spend every minute chatting with her, eating up the quiet, peaceful hours with her constant prattle.

She also had to resign herself to the fact that Ben was too busy to spend much time with her; he almost seemed to be avoiding her.

Perhaps he's just preoccupied, she thought. Disappointed that she hadn't had a chance to talk with him more, she hoped they would have more time together on the trip from New York to Boston.

That night at dinner, she felt his eyes on her as she finished the last of her plum pudding. Glancing at him, she was surprised that he didn't look away, but held her gaze before turning to answer a question from one of the men. *He looks more relaxed tonight,* she thought as she studied him. *Perhaps he's glad that we're almost to New York.* She looked down at her plate. In truth, she, too, was glad that this leg of her journey was almost over. She was not accustomed to so much leisure time, and Constance was grating on her nerves. Besides, she was anxious to begin her search for Paul.

"Excuse me, Miss Thomas. May I take your plate?" The cabin boy's voice intruded on her thoughts. Glancing about, she realized almost everyone else had left the table, even Constance. Raine had heaved a sigh of relief earlier when she heard the older woman accept an invitation to play bridge with two of the other passengers. An evening to herself at last!

She gathered her skirts and turned, only to come face-to-face with Ben. He smiled at her startled look. "Would you care to take a turn around the deck, Raine?"

She raised her eyebrows.

"It's a beautiful night," he coaxed, offering her his arm.

She slipped her arm through his, watching him surreptitiously as they walked up the stairs to the deck. His hair had become bleached even lighter and his skin was a golden tan from the days spent working with the crew. She liked how the deep blue uniform he wore set off the blue of his eyes.

The slight breeze toyed with the curls around her face as they reached the deck. Ben tucked her arm in closer. "Lovely night, isn't it?"

By their third trip around the deck, the crew began to glance at them with ill-concealed curiosity. Raine felt her stomach begin to twist into knots. Finally, she could stand it no longer.

"Ben, was there something specific you wished to talk to me about?" she asked. Tactfulness had never been one of her strong points. She bit her lip, then went on. "It seems that you've been avoiding me, and I thought since you sought me out tonight, maybe you needed to tell me something important." She finished in a rush, confused by the expression in his eyes.

"Ah Raine," he sighed.

∽

Ben led her gently into the shadows, away from curious eyes. Leaning on the railing, he gazed out into the blackness. *Why am I torturing myself?* he thought. *After all these years of waiting for the right woman, and then I fall in love with one who belongs to someone else.* It had been fine when all he had was a photograph, but now that she was here beside him, gazing at him so seriously with those big emerald eyes. . .

He didn't trust himself to look at her for fear he would take her in his arms, yet he was unwilling to let her go from his presence. He asked her the first question that popped into his head, hoping to keep her near him a little longer. "Tell me about your family, Raine."

She threw him an odd look, he noticed, but apparently she decided to humor him.

"My papa is a preacher," she began. "Papa is a strong man, and not always easy to get along with. But I'm sure Paul told you all about that," she added wryly. "Anyway, Papa always. . ."

"Tell me about you and Paul." Ben interrupted her narrative, suddenly curious about their relationship.

She smiled, a faraway look coming into her eyes. "Well, it's hard to know where to begin. Paul always understood me like no one else. He. . ."

I really don't want to hear this, he thought. About to interrupt her again, he froze as he heard her next words.

". . .Papa always said I was the willful one in the family, but Paul was just as bad, really. He always did take my side though. Once he even let Papa paddle him instead of me, even when I had been the one to. . ." Her sentence trailed off at the strange look on Ben's face.

An amazing thought had just occurred to him. *Please, God, let it be true!* Gripping her by the shoulders, he searched her face. "Raine." His voice sounded as if he hadn't used it in a hundred years. He cleared his throat. "Is Paul your brother?"

"Of course he's my brother!" she replied in amazement. "Surely you knew that?"

The look on his face answered her question. "I thought you were to be married," he said at last, hoping he didn't look as addled as he felt. "I knew Paul loved you. I just assumed. . . It never occurred to me. . ."

"I never dreamed you didn't know Paul and I are brother and sister, Ben. I'm sorry." Looking up at him now, she smiled, and he was certain that she must see the relief and joy on his face.

He grinned back at her, feeling ridiculously giddy. "This definitely sheds new light on the situation. I thought you were too beautiful for someone like that old scalawag brother of yours anyway."

"And just what is that supposed to mean?" Raine's voice was stern, but her eyes danced.

He merely smiled, letting her interpret his words as she would. "Come on, Raine, I'm starving. Let's go raid the galley."

Leaving her at the door of her cabin hours later, Ben touched her cheek gently. "Sleep well," he whispered.

⌒

She closed the door behind him, then whirled around the room a few times before sinking into the nearest chair. What a wonderful evening! Closing her eyes, she could picture again the look in Ben's eyes when he had learned that Paul was not her intended. Could it be that he felt the same way about her as she was beginning to feel about him? She had already admitted to herself that she was attracted to Ben, but had tried hard to dismiss thoughts of him from her mind because. . .because why? She had never really thought about it before.

Because you don't want to end up like your mother. The thought shocked her. *But Ben is not the least bit like Papa. . .or is he?* She had to admit she had never seen Ben under pressure. Would he fly off the handle and blame everything on someone else, as Papa often did? She had watched her mother take the brunt of Papa's anger over the years, usually over something that didn't even have anything to do with her. And then there was the way Papa was away from home so much. Was Ben married to his work as Papa had been? Sea captains probably had to be gone often.

Good grief, Raine, she scolded herself. *You act like he asked you to marry him or something. And I thought he was regretting that he had offered to escort me to Boston,* she thought with a smile. Realizing now that he had been staying away from her because of loyalty to Paul made her admire him all the more.

After their conversation, they both realized they were hungry, since neither of them had eaten much at supper. They had giggled like guilty school children as they snooped around the galley. Ben cut them each a huge slice of dried-apple pie that was still slightly warm.

"I hope Cook wasn't saving this for a special occasion," Raine whispered as they smuggled their loot back up on deck.

"This is the most special occasion I've had in a long time, Raine," Ben said, gazing deep into her eyes.

She had blushed and almost choked on her pie. Even now she could feel the heat flood her face as she thought of it.

"You're being silly, Raine Thomas," she scolded herself. Surely the evening didn't mean anything to him. Sighing, she wished for another piece of pie and a pair of sea blue eyes to go with it. Instead came a knock on the door.

"Are you still awake, Raine?"

Even if I wasn't, I would be now, Raine groused to herself as she swung the door open. "Constance! What a surprise!" She stood back to allow the other woman to enter. Constance plopped down in a chair, looking eager for a long chat.

"So, what are you planning to do once you arrive in America, Constance?" Raine asked politely as the other woman settled herself more comfortably.

Constance pleated the folds of her skirt thoughtfully. "You know, I've wondered that myself."

"Oh?"

"Yes. I really didn't have much choice in the matter, you see."

Raine didn't see, but she nodded anyway.

"My husband. . .well, my family didn't approve of me marrying him. Although he was Jewish by birth, he'd long ago stopped practicing Judaism. In fact, he even attended a Christian church. I believe he did it for business reasons only, but my family refused to have anything more to do with me. In their minds, I am dead. I was so lonely, but I found comfort in the church we attended. I believed that Christ is the Messiah. . ."

She shrugged. "Well, my husband and I never had what you'd call a close marriage, but I threw myself into charity work and filled my time that way. But then last year, my husband took up with some young thing and decided he didn't have any more use for me. He put me on this ship with a small fortune and wished me good luck in my new life." She turned her head in the pretense of brushing a speck of lint, but not before Raine saw the tears shimmering in her eyes.

"I'm very sorry to hear that, Constance." In truth, she felt like a heel. Had she been so wrapped up in her own little dream world that she'd become a snob? Surely she should have been able to see that the woman's overdone behavior sprang out of pain. *God, please forgive me,* she prayed silently.

Without meaning to, she yawned. "We need to get some sleep, Constance. But why don't you come to my cabin in the morning? My uncle John sent me some newspapers to read and maybe you could find some sort of work in there that you'd be able to do."

The smile on Constance's plump face erased a bit of Raine's regret.

She got ready for bed and slid between the covers, but hours later, she still hadn't been able to fall asleep, despite her tiredness. At last, she slipped from the narrow bed onto her knees, pouring out the evening's events to her heavenly Father.

Abruptly, Raine realized that she didn't know if Ben knew her Lord. *Oh Father,* she prayed earnestly, *please touch Ben. If he is not Yours, I pray that You would draw him to You. Please give me peace about my feelings toward him. . .*

The next day found Ben at his desk gazing vacantly at the dark porthole. Running his fingers through his hair, he leaned back with an exasperated sigh. *I have got to get this work done before we get to New York,* he thought.

He had been sitting here trying to work since early afternoon, but he was unable to get Raine off of his mind. Surely she was as innocent as she seemed. Her ready smile, the way her dark hair glinted in the sunlight. . .he shook his head. *You're never going to get anything done at this rate, old boy.* Finally he gave up and headed downstairs for supper.

Raine was already seated at the table. She flashed him a quick smile as he entered the room.

"Want to go for a walk after supper?" He leaned close enough that he knew she must feel his breath warm against her ear, and he didn't miss the quick blush that rose to her cheeks.

She nodded, her green eyes sparkling.

As he turned to take a seat, he saw Constance elbow her. "You and the Cap'n got somethin' goin'?"

Ben winced. As he began to eat, he had the feeling that the meal would never end. His impatience grew when Lloyd Ferris insisted on involving him in a conversation about Britain's recent agreement with China to limit the production of opium. It was a subject that normally interested Ben, but now the topic dragged on through the whole main course and dessert. From time to time, he cast apologetic glances in Raine's direction.

She smiled at him down the table. Finally free, Ben took her arm and once again escorted her up the stairs to the top deck. As if by mutual agreement, they walked to the same spot at the railing as the previous night. They stood gazing out over the soft waves for long moments, each wrapped in their own thoughts.

At last Raine turned. "I suppose I should finish the story I began telling you last night about Paul."

Ben smiled at her. "Maybe you should start at the beginning and tell me why Paul left home in the first place. He told me bits and pieces, but obviously I don't have the whole picture."

"Apparently not," she agreed. "Paul was always my best friend," she began thoughtfully. "He could always come up with something fun to do, and we often made up games that only the two of us knew how to play. One of our favorite games was to pretend we were spies. He made up all kinds of codes and ciphers, and we had to use them any time we wanted to send a message to each other."

The relief Ben felt was almost palpable. She was innocent, he was sure of it now. He silently blessed Paul for not involving her.

Raine's laugh was gentle, remembering. "We had so much fun. My friend Christina and her older brother Geoff Hathaway were our best friends, and sometimes we'd get them in on the game as well. We didn't really use the codes much after we all got older, but when Paul got in trouble. . ." Raine's words stopped as she recalled those painful days.

"Go on, Raine," he prompted gently.

"I told you before that my father is a preacher."

He nodded.

"Papa loved us deeply. He could be a lot of fun, but was very stern at times as well. He was the pastor of a good-sized church, and that kept him so busy, he was gone a lot of the time."

She was silent, remembering all the nights Papa's place at the supper table had been empty. "He is doing God's work," Raine's mother had said. Yet. . .

"It seems like it all started after Geoff found that old book of ciphers." She shook her head. "I never did know exactly what happened between Paul and Geoff, but their relationship was ruined. They argued. . . A few months later, Geoff died when the family's house burned down. It was horrible."

She closed her eyes for a moment. "Anyway, Paul started courting a beautiful girl named Lucinda right around that time. I was surprised, because he'd always been sweet on Christina. But Lucinda's family attended our church, and everyone seemed pleased with the match.

"Then quite abruptly, they stopped seeing each other. He would never tell me why." She sighed. "After that, Paul began spending more and more time with some boys he had gone to school with. They were a rough lot, and he began to pick up some of their ways. He spent a lot of time at the tavern. He wasn't bad though," she added hastily.

Ben gave her hand a reassuring squeeze and she continued. "My mother got sick about then. She just kept getting weaker and weaker, and then she died." Her voice broke. "Instead of our grief drawing us closer, Papa and Paul and I seemed to get further and further from each other. Papa was gone more than ever with church work, and when he was home he seemed. . .angry all the time. As though his grief had made him even more impatient and harsh than he had been before."

She sighed. "Meanwhile, Paul spent more and more time with those fellows from school. I hardly saw him. But then one evening he came home earlier than usual. He disappeared into his room, and wouldn't come out. Finally, he let me in. He wouldn't say anything, just kept staring out his bedroom window." Raine closed her eyes in pain.

Though Raine kept her face averted from him, Ben could see the tears flowing down her cheeks. "Lucinda was found to be with child, and she accused Paul of being the father." She nearly choked on the words.

He stared at her face. *Surely she didn't believe her brother was such a coward as to run away in the face of a lie like that,* he thought. There must be something she wasn't telling him.

"Why did Paul have to leave home if he was falsely accused?"

"Papa didn't believe him. After Paul left, when her baby was born, Lucinda confessed who the real father was. But Papa didn't care. I begged him to search for Paul and tell him—but Papa didn't seem to even hear me." Her deep hurt and sense of betrayal were mirrored in her eyes as she looked up at him.

"Ah." He nodded, feeling helpless in the face of her pain. Apparently to her mind, their father's lack of trust was an adequate explanation for Paul running scared. Not knowing what else to do, he drew her into his embrace. "I'm so sorry," he whispered soothingly. He let her cry, knowing that the pain had been sharpened again by the retelling of the story. *Fortunately, she doesn't know the half of it,* he thought.

She pulled away from him, swiping at her eyes with her fingers. "When Lucinda accused Paul, the whole church turned against my

Chapter 3

The arrival of the cargo ship the *Capernaum* was nothing exciting to the inhabitants of New York City, but it was one of the most thrilling experiences of Raine's life. As they sailed through the Narrows and into crowded New York Harbor, the sight of the famous "Lady of Liberty" brought tears to her eyes. She thought of Paul living in this welcoming land, and her hope of finding him alive and well was strengthened.

Passing the statue, the copper-clad towers and turreted brick of Ellis Island came into view on the left. Raine's heart went out to the swarms of immigrants crowding the decks of nearby ships. She had heard that sometimes the exhausted travelers had to wait as long as four days before a barge came to fetch them to the infamous island. It didn't seem fair that first- and second-class passengers were able to go right through customs, while their less fortunate brothers and sisters had to endure the endless examinations and inspections.

She turned her head as the *Capernaum* edged closely past a dilapidated sailing packet with the unlikely name of *Stella* gracing its bow. The mass of hopeful, fatigued faces tore at her heart. Where were all these people headed?

"Sad, isn't it?" Ben's quiet voice broke into her thoughts.

Raine nodded.

"Most of these ships are full of Polish and Russian Jews, fleeing from the pogroms."

Raine shook her head. Somehow, the suffering of other people always put one's own life into perspective. "We have a lot to be thankful for, don't we?"

Ben squeezed her hand. "That we do, Raine. That we do."

The *Capernaum* docked at Staten Island, awaiting the Ellis Island inspectors that would come aboard and conduct the medical examinations.

"How long does this usually take?" Raine asked.

"Well, it depends on how many passengers there are and how

thorough the exams are." He smiled at her sparkling eyes and glowing skin. "I don't think you have much to worry about."

"I'm afraid Constance is worried."

Ben gazed into the ship's saloon where the larger woman sat waiting. "She does look rather nervous." Even the feathers on her Chanticleer hat were quivering. He shook his head, not understanding why a woman would wear a hat shaped like a rooster.

"I'll go sit with her," Raine suggested.

"That's a good idea. I need to run up to my quarters for the manifest, anyway. The inspectors always want to see it." He took another peek at Constance's hat as he walked away. The look on his face made Raine smother a giggle.

She went to the other woman and asked gently, "Are you ill, Constance?" The older woman looked wretched.

"No, dear. Not physically at least."

Raine raised her eyebrows.

"All those people on that ship." Constance gestured with her arm. "To think of my people enduring such terrible things that they had to flee their own country. . ."

"Perhaps God has sent you to America for a purpose, Constance."

Constance looked startled. "I guess I'd never thought of that, Raine. I was too busy feeling sorry for myself. . .but I've got it so much better than most, don't I?"

"I found a verse in Isaiah just before we began this voyage. It says, 'I will bring the blind by a way that they knew not; I will lead them in paths that they have not known: I will make darkness light before them, and crooked things straight. These things will I do unto them, and not forsake them.' I've gained much strength from that promise." She patted Constance's hand. "I know He'll guide you, too, if you ask Him."

Constance blew her nose, reminding Raine of an elephant she had once seen at the circus. "I feel so much better, dear. You've helped me immeasurably."

Raine shook her head. "Not me, Constance. God."

The two women watched as the inspectors glanced at the ship's manifest. The uniformed men looked hassled, weariness etched on their brows. Handing the manifest back to Ben, they turned their attention to the medical reports.

Raine had easily passed the physical exam all passengers were required to take before they departed for America, but she still felt her heart beat a little faster as the men scrutinized the reports. She knew she didn't have anything to worry about; she had always been "healthy as a hog," as Papa would say.

"All right, line up over by the wall, please." The inspector's American accent sounded harsh, though his voice was pleasant.

Raine felt Constance stiffen as men made their way down the short line. The examination was mostly cursory for first-class passengers, since it was assumed none of them would be carrying disease.

She recalled Ben telling her of entire shiploads of people quarantined because of cholera, yellow fever, or typhoid. Victims of diphtheria or measles were often sent to the hospital on Ward's Island. She shivered. What a wretched welcome to America that would be.

"Open your mouth, please."

Raine obeyed and the man took a quick peek in her eyes as well, looking for the dreaded trachoma, she knew. He moved on to Constance. Raine watched the tail feathers on Constance's hat begin to dance. The poor woman looked like she would swoon any moment.

All went fine until the man heard the rattling in her chest. He raised his eyebrows. "Are you ill, madam?"

Constance glared at him. "No."

He frowned. "Stay there. I'll be back in a minute."

Raine's heart sank as she watched him stride over to confer with the other inspector. "What's wrong, Constance?" she whispered.

"It's nothing, dear." Constance took a long breath, as though she were forcing herself to appear calm. "My chest tightens up and I get short of breath when I get nervous. Always goes away in a few minutes."

Raine knew what the man would say the instant he turned around.

"We'll have to take you to Ellis for a more thorough examination, madam." He looked almost apologetic.

Raine closed her eyes, waiting to hear an explosion of tears. None came.

"Raine, will you come with me while I gather my things?" Constance's voice was calm.

Raine peered into the other woman's reddened eyes. Perhaps this was just the calm before the storm. Together they plodded down the stairs to Constance's cabin. Raine wracked her brain, trying to think of something to say.

"Well. I guess I will be going down some unfamiliar paths, just like that scripture said, won't I?"

"I'm so sorry, Constance."

The older woman snorted. "Don't be. You know, as I was standing there waiting for them to make their decision, I started thinking on what you said about God sending me here for a purpose. All of a sudden I pictured all those poor people crowded on those boats headed for the Island." She cocked her head. "Maybe God wants me to be with my kin, so to speak."

Raine was speechless.

"They think I've got tuberculosis, you know."

Raine nodded.

"But I don't."

Raine nodded again, for lack of anything better to do.

"So. I'll just go to that Island and find out what God has for me. You know, I've been so miserable the past year, that I forgot all about Jesus. I guess He just needed to get my attention again. And He used you to help me get back on track."

Would wonders never cease. "I'm glad you feel that way about it," Raine finally managed. "You will write to me and let me know what happens?"

"You can bank on it, Reverend Thomas. That was quite a sermon you preached to me. You'll always hold a special place in my heart."

Reverend? She only had a second to ponder that one before she was nearly smothered in a giant bear hug. When she could breathe again, she was surprised to find her cheeks damp with tears.

The last she saw of her friend was a large bustle and an even larger smile disappearing into a swarm of haggard immigrants. "God go with you," Raine whispered.

As they disembarked from the ship, her heart lifted as she thought about her heavenly Father. His heart so loving that He even knew when a sparrow fell. Without a doubt, His eye was on Constance Rabinowicz.

∽

Raine was charmed by the thick accents and the hustle and bustle of the city, as Ben escorted her to the famous Buckingham Hotel on Fifth Avenue where she would stay the night, as her uncle had directed. Once inside, she gazed around in awe. The shining marble floor of the lobby reflected the multicolored hues from the huge stained glass windows. Eight stories above her head, sunlight streamed through an enormous skylight. She had stepped into another world. Porters dashed in and out with baggage, lending a mood of excitement. Even the air seemed charged. She smiled. Maybe it was just being here, in America. It was, after all, the Land of Opportunity.

Her suite was beautiful. A fire crackled cheerily in the open fireplace, welcoming her into the bedchamber. She took a peek into the parlor, surprised to see another small room as well. A separate toilet room! Uncle John surely had spared no expense when he reserved this suite for her.

"I've got to get back to my crew, Raine," Ben said. "Shall we meet for supper at oh, six o'clock?"

"Six o'clock?" she moaned. "I think I'll starve by then!"

He chuckled. "I never knew a lady who had your appetite before. I'll be back before you know it."

Once he was gone, she pushed back the red damask drapes to watch his retreating figure from the vantage of her fifth-floor window. He was even handsome from the back.

She continued to stand at the window long after he had disappeared, smiling, fascinated by the endless activity on the street below her.

Her smile froze as she noticed a man staring up at the hotel, his eyes fixed on her face. Something about him seemed familiar. . . Slipping behind the heavy drapery, she peered out again, but the man had disappeared from view.

Surely he was merely admiring the hotel, she thought. *Why would someone in New York be interested in me?* Feeling slightly uncomfortable, she turned to unpack her small bag. She was suddenly glad that she would be leaving for Boston in a couple of days.

∞

Ben knocked on her door promptly at six o'clock.

Opening the door, Raine was taken aback as Ben presented her with a single yellow rose. "For you, milady," he said, bowing gallantly.

"Why, thank you, kind sir." Willing her heart to stop racing, she smiled up at him. "Shall we dine?"

"Indeed we shall." Ben escorted her to the hotel's dining room as if she were the queen of England. He seated her with a flourish. "Will you have the catfish or the pot roast? Or perhaps both? I know the sort of appetite you have."

She thumped him on the arm in mock indignation. In the end, she decided on the baked ham. It was cooked to perfection, but Raine found that despite her hunger, she was having a hard time keeping her attention on her supper. Ben's blue eyes were glowing with laughter, and his sun-lightened hair was set off by the dark suit he wore. She looked deep into his eyes as he smiled at her, suddenly eager to know everything about him. "Tell me about your childhood, Ben."

Instantly, the laughter slid from his eyes, replaced by an unreadable expression. "There's not much to tell, Raine," he said slowly.

"If you'd rather not. . ." she began, dismayed by his sudden change in mood.

"No," he said, pushing his pie around on his plate. "I want to tell you. I just. . .it's just hard to talk about, and I don't think you'll understand." Rising abruptly, he threw a tip on the table and offered Raine his arm. "Let's take a walk."

I must have ripped the bandage off of a festering wound, she realized as she glanced sideways at his expression. *At least he's willing to talk about it.* She breathed a quiet prayer for wisdom as they walked outside.

Ben led her to a small courtyard garden. Seating her on a bench, he paced back and forth in front of her. Finally sitting down, he ran his fingers through his hair, as though he were reluctant to begin his story.

"Ben." She placed a soothing hand on his cheek. "You can tell me."

Taking her hand, he held it tightly. "I'm an only child, and my parents were very strict with me. We went to church whenever the doors were open, and I was required to do quite a bit of Bible study and memorization, but. . ." He turned his face away from Raine, as though he didn't want her to see the pain etched there, but she could hear it in his voice as he continued. "There was no joy in our home. My parents were the most miserable people on earth, and they wanted me to be that way, too. They always quoted the scripture 'Unto whomsoever much is given, of him much shall be much required.'" He shook his head. "The way they interpreted it was that if a person was happy, or well off financially, then that person must not really be in God's will, because if you're doing God's will, Satan will be attacking you all of the time."

No longer able to keep the bitterness from his voice, he turned to Raine. "I wasn't allowed to be happy, Raine. If I so much as laughed out loud, they accused me of being influenced by the devil and in need of discipline. They felt that if I wasn't being buffeted by Satan, then they needed to do the buffeting—and they used a willow switch to do it. I suppose they did it because they loved me. They were trying to push me into God's Kingdom, after all."

Raine had never heard anything so sad in her life, nor such a mangling of scripture. Even though her own father had been short-tempered and frequently absent, he had never twisted God's love into the harsh condemnation Ben's parents had apparently believed in.

"That's not the worst part of it, I'm afraid." Ben bowed his head. "I learned to put on an act, to pretend to be what my parents wanted me to be. When I grew older, my father made me go to seminary. I even graduated." Looking up at her, he let the tears fall unheeded.

"But I'm a hypocrite, Raine. I feel nothing for God but bitterness and resentment—and yet I have a piece of paper that says I am a minister of the Gospel." He turned away from her, struggling to control his weeping.

Raine slipped her hand comfortingly into his.

"I left for Boston the day of graduation," he said in a hollow voice. "An acquaintance of my father's got me started in the shipping business. I worked my way up until eventually I owned my own line of ships. Whenever I get restless, I sail as the *Capernaum's* captain. I haven't seen my parents since the day I graduated from the seminary."

Pushing him away gently so she could see his face, Raine spoke with compassion. "Serving God doesn't have to be a drudgery, Ben. God is our Father. He loves us and wants us to have joy and peace."

"I know that in my mind, Raine, but I'm afraid," Ben whispered in despair. "I'm afraid that if I surrender to Him, He'll make me be like my father, or He'll ask me to do something that I just can't do."

"Total surrender is the only thing that will bring you the peace that you need, Ben," she stated quietly. "God will always give you the strength to do what He asks you to do."

He shook his head sadly. "I can't do it, Raine. I guess I'm a coward, but it just doesn't make sense to me." Seeing her stricken look, he put his hands on her shoulders. "I'm sorry. I shouldn't have burdened you with this."

She held his gaze steadily. "It will make sense to you one day, Ben Thackeray," she said, ignoring his apology. "One day, you will truly know peace."

∽

That night, she stayed on her knees for long hours before sleep finally claimed her. *I love him, Father,* she had cried, admitting out loud what her heart had known for weeks. *I want him to know You, to know Your peace. Please lead him to Christ, Father. Use me to minister Your love and joy to him. . . And please, Lord, bless Constance.*

Waking the next morning, her first thought was of a pair of sea blue eyes and a warm smile. She stretched luxuriously, letting the newness of the day soak into her soul. Arising at last, she brushed out her dark hair until it shone. She reflected on the previous evening as she braided her hair into an intricate crown. *I hope Ben doesn't feel embarrassed over last night,* she thought, anxious to see him.

She dabbed on a bit of her favorite lilac perfume and adjusted the locket around her neck, then glanced in the mirror one last time. Glowing green eyes looked back at her, and she was sure Ben would be able to see her heart in her eyes. She smiled. It was wonderful to be in love, but she knew she must not run ahead of God's will for her. He was the one leading her along these new paths, and she reminded herself to wait on His direction.

She and Ben had decided to meet in the ladies' parlor, then go to the breakfast room together. Scanning the room eagerly, she was disappointed that Ben had not yet arrived. She sat down to wait, enjoying the way the morning sunshine filled the airy room. An ornate chandelier hung from the ceiling, and large ferns graced the perimeter of the room. Fresh flowers spilled down over pedestals, their bright fragrance permeating the air. The carpet as well as the walls were done tastefully in white, French gray, and gold. Here and there an early-rising guest sat reading a newspaper or leisurely working on some fancy needlework.

Raine's stomach growled loudly, and she frowned at the huge grandfather clock. It wasn't like Ben to be late. Shrugging, she decided a trip to the necessary room was in order. Maybe by the time she came out he would be there.

A small commotion near the door attracted her attention as she rose from her chair. She glanced in that direction, feeling something akin to panic wash over her as she caught a glimpse of the man walking in behind the porter. It was the man she had seen yesterday.

Nature's call forgotten, she made a beeline for the breakfast room. Daring a quick glance back, she was startled to see the blond-haired man sauntering toward her. His scarred face seared itself into her memory. Something about it seemed familiar. . .

"Good morning, Beautiful." She whirled.

"Ben!"

"What's wrong, Raine? Do I look that bad in the morning?" he teased.

She glanced over her shoulder. The man was nowhere to be seen. "You look just fine," she said weakly as relief flooded through her. "Let's eat breakfast."

The day went smoothly as they prepared for the trip to Boston. Except for the dark circles under Ben's eyes, no mention of the previous night was made. Having realized her love for him, however, Raine found it hard not to let it show. She knew in her heart that she could never marry a man who did not love her Lord, yet she was sure that God had brought Ben into her life for a special purpose.

∞

Two days later, Raine stood on the deck of the *Capernaum* once again, hardly able to quell the thrill of excitement running through her. She glanced up at Ben. "How long do you think it will take us to find Paul?"

An expression flickered across his face that made her uneasy, but he responded cheerfully enough, "Well, he left us a pretty good clue to follow."

Raine smiled as she thought of Uncle John and Aunt Grace. It would be good to see them again. A sudden thought popped into her mind. "Where will you be staying, Ben?"

He frowned, staring over her shoulder into the distance. "I haven't decided yet."

His tone was so abrupt that Raine's heart sank. She turned back to gaze at the sea once again.

Surely he's not sorry that he promised to help me look for Paul, she thought. To her chagrin she felt tears begin to gather. *Maybe something came up and he doesn't know how to tell me. . .or maybe he just doesn't want to. . .*

"You don't have to help me find Paul," she muttered, staring blindly at the water. She felt his surprise as he pivoted to look at her.

Pulling her around to face him, he asked, "Why did you say that, Raine?"

"It just seems like you aren't very happy about it, so I thought maybe you were sorry that you had promised me you would help." Her voice was more petulant than she intended.

Ben winced. "I'm sorry it seemed that way, Raine. I really do want to help you find Paul. I just have a lot of things going on right now that need my attention."

Raine shrugged, feeling rather childish. "I shouldn't have even mentioned it."

Ben cupped her chin in his hand and smiled down at her. "We'll find him," he said finally. "Don't worry, Raine Ellen." Brushing her forehead with a soft kiss, he left to attend to his duties.

Raine had not missed the passion that had flared briefly in his eyes. She stood at the railing a while longer, daydreaming. What would it be like to be held in his strong arms, his lips meeting hers tenderly. . .

She wrinkled her brow as she remembered the cold look on his face earlier, but then she remembered again the tenderness in his voice when he said her name. Surely he cared for her. *"Don't worry, Raine Ellen,"* he had said.

Raine Ellen. She closed her eyes in sudden confusion. How did Ben know her middle name? Paul had not been in the habit of calling her Raine Ellen.

The disfigured face of the man in New York popped into her mind. Shaking her head as if to clear out the suddenly disturbing thoughts, she sank down onto a nearby coil of rope. *Father,* she cried, *please show me Your way. I want to trust Ben, and I need to find Paul, but. . .*

". . .I will bring the blind by a way that they knew not; I will lead them in paths they they have not known. . ." The scripture from Isaiah echoed in her mind, and with it came peace. "Thank You, Lord," she breathed. Praying quietly, she poured out her thoughts and feelings to her ever-loving Father.

Opening her eyes at last, she was surprised to see Ben standing in front of her, a look of interest on his serious face.

"I'm not interrupting you, am I?" he asked hesitantly.

She shook her head.

"I just wanted to make you aware that a storm is coming."

She glanced quickly to the north, surprised to see a roiling mass of dark clouds. She hadn't even noticed when the sky had become overcast.

"I don't think it will be too bad, but you need to get off the deck. Are you afraid?" he asked, holding her shoulders lightly.

Looking up into his eyes, Raine pondered his question. *Yes, I'm afraid that I shouldn't love you so much,* her heart cried. "No, I'm not afraid of the storm," she answered out loud, watching in fascination as his eyes slowly darkened.

"Don't look at me that way, Raine," he growled. Pulling her into his arms, he drew her to him. Raine could feel his heart thudding as her head rested against the warmth of his chest. Releasing her abruptly, he caressed her face with his eyes. "Go to your cabin, Raine." His command was gentle. "I'll have Sully check on you later."

Mesmerized by his touch, she obediently turned to go. Reaching her cabin, she walked over to the small porthole. *Surely Ben wouldn't lie to me.* A hint of his aftershave lingered to tease her senses as she stared unseeingly at the turbulent waters. *My heart trusts him, but my mind is not so sure,* she mused. She flung herself down on her bunk and began to pray.

Raine awoke to a sharp knock on the door. Blinking in confusion as she saw sunlight streaming through the porthole, she padded to the door.

"Good morning, sunshine!" Ben's blue eyes sparkled as they noticed her tousled hair. "I shouldn't have worried about you, Raine. You slept through the whole storm, didn't you?"

"I guess so." She was still groggy. Looking down self-consciously at her rumpled dress, she realized she must have fallen asleep while praying last night.

Ignoring her discomfort, Ben went on cheerily. "Well everything went fine, and we'll be in Boston tomorrow, right on schedule. Do you feel like eating breakfast?"

Raine stared at him for a moment. "I need a few minutes to get ready," she said finally.

"Good. I'll meet you in my quarters in ten minutes." Swiftly kissing her on the lips, he was gone.

In his quarters? Touching her lips, Raine backed into her cabin. She groaned as she caught a glimpse of herself in the mirror. Several deep brown curls had worked themselves loose and were hanging down her back. Her cheeks were still rosy with sleep, and her dress was hopelessly wrinkled.

Sighing as she began to undo her hair, she pondered Ben's kiss. *We need to discuss some things before we go any further,* she decided. *There are just too many things that don't seem to fit together.*

Peering through the open door that led to his quarters twenty minutes later, she saw that he had cleared his desk. A steaming teapot and a tray of crumpets sat waiting where a mound of papers usually resided. "I thought just the two of us could have breakfast together this morning." He grinned at her in delight as her stomach growled loudly. "Do you think we have enough food?"

She moved into the room, leaving the door open behind her. "If you were a gentleman, you would have ignored that."

He laughed, and her heart ached. She wanted so much to believe in him; she hated to wipe the happiness from his face by questioning him. . . Halfway through breakfast, though, she decided to plunge in. "Ben, how did you find me?"

"My heart led me to you, darlin'," he teased, then laughed as she blushed. "Actually, I was wondering when you would get around to asking me that."

"I guess I've been so caught up with what you told me about Paul that I haven't given much thought to how you found me in the first place," she confessed, relieved that he seemed so open about it.

"Well," Ben began, leaning back in his chair. "Paul served on several of my ships at various times. He was a top-notch sailor, and a great conversationalist to boot."

Raine smiled at this, fondly remembering the long talks she and Paul had often had.

"After a while," Ben continued, "Paul and I began to develop a real friendship. He often came to my quarters, and we would talk late into the night. You were one of his favorite topics of conversation," he added, smiling at her.

She wrinkled her nose, asking the question that had been bothering her for some time. "Then how could you have possibly missed the fact that we were brother and sister?"

For a long moment, Ben studied the bite of cheese he held on his fork. "I've asked myself the same question, Raine," he said at last. He shifted his gaze back to hers. "I have finally come to the conclusion that Paul purposely misled me."

"What?" Raine was incredulous. "Why would he do that?"

"I don't know. The only thing I could come up with was that maybe he was trying to protect you."

"Protect me from what?"

His index finger traced the wet ring his tea cup had made on the desktop. "I don't know," he admitted. "He told me his name was Paul Oliver."

"He didn't use his own name?" She shook her head slowly. "I suppose if he would have gone by Paul Thomas, you would have known right away that we were related. I guess I really don't know much about the person Paul was after he left home," she concluded sadly. "But I still can't figure out why he never wrote me any more letters after that one from Boston. The last letter I received from Paul was postmarked June 6, 1900."

"1900! I didn't even meet Paul until 1901, then the *Aramatnea* sank in 1903." Ben was astonished. "I looked for you for three years, so that means you haven't heard from Paul in. . .six years?"

Raine nodded. "That's why I was so shocked when you gave me the locket. I had given up hope. But how did you find me?" she asked, anxious to hear the rest of the story.

"I first met Paul on the *Galilee*. He was new to the crew, and I keep a pretty sharp watch on the men. I don't question them about their past, but I expect them to do an honest day's work for me." Ben explained. "Paul never talked much about his past, except you, and I didn't pry. Once in a while he would mention something that made me wonder what had happened, but I never asked."

He shook his head before continuing. "One day after we had become quite close friends, Paul showed me the locket. He didn't give it to me then, but told me that it contained a message for you. He made me promise that I would find you and give it to you if something ever happened to him."

"When was that?"

"It was before we set sail on the *Aramathea*. I don't know what prompted him to ask me at that time," Ben added thoughtfully.

"Am being pursued." The phrase from the message in the locket flitted through her mind. "Could Paul have been running from someone, and he was afraid that the person would harm me as well?" she wondered out loud. "Maybe that's what he meant by 'am being pursued'."

"I just don't know."

"Anyway, how in the world did Paul expect you to find me?"

Ben smiled at her over his glass. "He showed me your photograph, for one thing. I used to look at it every night while Paul and I were talking. After a while, I was pretty familiar with your features."

Raine looked down in embarrassment. She knew what photograph Ben was referring to. She had had it taken when she was eighteen, and had given it to Paul on his birthday.

That's how Ben knew my middle name, she realized with swift insight, remembering what she had written on the back of the large photograph. "To my one and only—Love, Raine Ellen." Raine had meant her one and only brother, but she could see how the inscription might be taken wrong.

She glanced up at Ben when he chuckled softly. "I memorized every line of your lovely face, Raine."

She involuntarily covered the birthmark on her temple, feeling her cheeks grow hot. This man had a way of making her feel things she wasn't accustomed to feeling.

"Other than the image of your face stamped on my memory, I didn't have much to go on. Paul had given me the address of your home in St. Albans of course—but when I went there, your father told me you were gone and refused to tell me anything more. He practically slammed the door in my face."

Raine shook her head. *Oh Papa, what a mess you've made.*

Ben took her hand. "I guess it was fate that I found you, then," he said lightly. "After I reached the dead end in St. Albans, I didn't know where else to look. I had pretty much given up hope of ever finding you—and then after all these years, I saw you on the wharf. Something about your face compelled me to look closer, and well, you know the rest."

Raine felt a thrill of excitement go through her as Ben explained how he had found her. "I don't believe in fate, Ben," she stated with conviction. "I believe that God allowed you to find me when the time was right."

He looked thoughtful. "That may be, Raine," he said slowly, gently pressing her hand to his lips.

⁂

El Paso County, Colorado

The rain pounded relentlessly, turning the thirsty prairie land of the Crooked P Ranch into one huge mud puddle. Unseasonable rains had begun two weeks earlier. The constant dripping showed no signs of letting up as Tom paced back and forth in frustration.

Finally dropping into his chair in disgust, he absently rubbed his fingertips over the still-sensitive scar on his cheek. *I'm going to go crazy if I can't get out of here soon,* he told himself. After keeping himself busy with all of the things he could think of to do inside, there was nothing left to do but wait for the rain to subside. *This must be how Noah felt,* he thought without humor.

The idea crossed his mind to go to the bunkhouse, but he decided he was in no mood for the never-ending jokes and loud disagreements that he was sure to find there. His eyes wandered to the bookcase. He sighed. "I've read every single one of those books at least twice," he complained to the empty room, knowing from experience that if he didn't find something to occupy his mind, his thoughts would become too painful. Heaving himself out of his chair, he walked to the window once again, swearing softly as the rain picked up its intensity.

As he turned away sharply, his eye fell on the large Bible lying on the bookshelf. Deliberately, he went to the kitchen and poured himself a fresh cup of coffee, then returned once again to the warm living room. Drawn like a magnet to the book that he had not opened in years, he took it down with reluctance, blowing the dust off the worn leather cover. He hated himself for trembling, but he could not help it as he turned to the inscription he knew was written on the first page. Though he knew it by heart, Tom read it again through eyes blurred with tears. Closing the Bible, he laid his head down and wept. *I don't know how to come back to You after all this time,* he cried in his heart. *God, help me. . .*

He raised his head, glancing down as he felt the heavy weight of the Bible in his lap. He must have fallen asleep. Rising, he placed the Bible back on the shelf. The rain pattered a gentle lullaby as he blew out the lamp.

Chapter 4

Raine woke with a start. Today the *Capernaum* would arrive in Boston! Rolling over, she reflected on what she had learned the day before. There were still so many unanswered questions. Why had she suddenly stopped hearing from Paul so long ago if he were alive and well? Why had he used an assumed name?

She had known right away why Paul had chosen to go by Paul Oliver; their mother's father, their beloved grandfather, had been named Oliver Cox. That much made sense to her. *But what did he want me to find in Boston? And what did the water erase?* She fingered the locket that hung around her neck, recalling one of their last conversations.

"I'll prove that I'm innocent, Raine," Paul vowed before he left. "Papa may have disowned me, but one day he'll have to eat his words. Then I'll never come back, even if he begs me to."

Raine was shocked at the bitterness in her brother's voice. "Paul—"

"Come with me, Ray," he pled.

She wavered, but in the end decided she had to stay. "Where would we go?" she asked, tears flowing down her face. "How would we support ourselves?" She shook her head. "No, you'll be better off on your own for now. But I'll find you after a little while, and then we'll be together again."

She hadn't known then she, too, would be leaving her father so soon, making her own way in the world. That had been so many years ago. "I'm finally coming, Paul," she whispered.

The *Capernaum* slipped silently into the harbor like a turtle sliding off a rock. Unable to stop herself, Raine scanned the crowded wharf. *Stop it, Raine,* she chided herself. *Paul doesn't even know that you're on this ship, much less in Boston.* She tried to ignore the thought that her brother might not even be alive. God had brought her here for a reason.

∽

"Good morning, Sunshine!" Ben greeted her as she walked through the door of his quarters. He always felt like his day had begun when she walked through the door. "Are you ready for the big search to begin?"

"More than ready!"

"I'll be done in a minute." He indicated some papers on his desk. "Then I'll be free to escort you to your uncle's house."

Raine smiled her thanks. Choosing a large leather chair, she sat down and closed her eyes. Ben could tell she was trying to quell her excitement and nervousness. He stood up and picked up her bags. "Are you ready to go?"

She was on her feet in an instant. "Lead on, kind sir!"

They bounced and jounced over the stone-paved streets for what seemed hours before Ben stopped the carriage in front of a large brick house on Joy Street. He heard Raine give a sigh of relief as she craned her neck to view the old house.

"It's beautiful," she breathed, taking in the well cared for lawns and sparkling flower beds. Ben saw a look of peace settle over her face as she turned to him. "Would you please come in and meet my family?" she asked. "I know they would like to meet you."

Ben squeezed her hand. "I would love to."

The huge front door flew open. "Raine!" A tall, slim woman rushed to the carriage.

"Aunt Grace!" Raine was out of the carriage and in her aunt's arms in a flash.

Pushing Raine away after a moment, Grace looked her niece up and down. "You're the picture of your mother," she cried, pulling Raine into her embrace once again.

"Ahem." Ben looked beyond Raine's aunt to see her uncle beaming at her. "Is it my turn yet?" he asked in a gravelly voice.

"Oh Uncle John! It's so good to see you!"

Finally released from her uncle's bear hug, Raine seemed to remember Ben, standing silently next to the carriage. Walking over to him, she shyly took his hand.

"Uncle John, Aunt Grace, this is Ben Thackeray." Raine's cheeks grew rosy at her family's knowing looks.

Her aunt and uncle welcomed Ben cordially. "Come into the house, both of you. We have cool lemonade waiting."

"I'm afraid I need to get back to my ship, but thank you anyway," Ben apologized. "Raine, may I speak with you a moment?"

Raine's aunt and uncle graciously excused themselves, leaving Ben and Raine alone. "I need to stay on the ship tonight, Raine. The crew is waiting for some last-minute instructions from me before I turn the ship over to the first mate and they take their leave. I'll be back to see you at the end of the week. That should give you some time to get settled in and. . ."

"But I'll miss you!" she blurted. She lowered her eyes in embarrassment, and he knew she missed the tenderness he couldn't hide at her impulsive words.

Lifting her chin, he saw a hint of tears shimmering in her dusky green eyes. "I'll miss you, too, love," he murmured, pulling her into his embrace. Feeling her soft lips tremble beneath his, he kissed her deeply, the scent of her warm skin making his blood pound. He put her from him then, breathing hard. "I don't know what you're doing to me," he whispered huskily.

She gazed up at him, her heart in her eyes.

"Don't look at me like that, Raine," he groaned, longing to crush her to him again.

She touched her fingertips to his lips. "I'll see you soon, Ben," she whispered.

He waved from the carriage, the light scent of lilacs still clinging to his senses. *If you had any sense, you'd marry that woman right now.*

⁂

Raine waved as Ben's carriage rolled away from her. *You are entirely too attached to that man,* she scolded herself as she watched him turn the horses. She stood rooted to the spot until he was out of sight. Entering into the dim coolness of the foyer, she braced herself for the barrage of questions that was sure to come.

"Raine! Who is Ben? Is he a captain of a ship? When did you. . ."

"Whoa, Grace." Uncle John chuckled. "Let's let the little gal get settled before we interrogate her."

Raine smiled at her uncle gratefully, enjoying his Americanized

209

accent. "We'll have a heart-to-heart talk later, Auntie Grace. I promise."

"I'm sorry, dear," her aunt apologized. "It's just that we're so glad to see you, and your Ben is so handsome, and. . ."

Uncle John winked at Raine. "Why don't you go and see about that lemonade while I help Raine with her things?" Giving his wife no time to reply, he started up the stairs. "Coming, Raine?"

Raine nodded. "We'll be down in a minute, Auntie," she called to her aunt who had already disappeared down the hallway.

∞

"So. Start at the beginning, Raine." They were all seated at the enormous oak table with tall glasses of lemonade.

"It's a long story," Raine warned them.

"We have plenty of time," Grace assured her. "Besides, we haven't seen you in years."

"Well, let's see," Raine began. "You two moved to America in. . ."

"1886."

"So that was while Mama was still living and. . ."

"We're so sorry we couldn't come for her funeral, Raine," Grace interrupted again. "I felt so bad being so far away at a time like that."

"I'm sure you would have been there if you could," Raine said soothingly. "We surely felt your prayers."

"How's that scalawag brother of yours?" Uncle John asked, as though he were trying to change the subject tactfully. "We haven't heard much news about him lately. 'Course we haven't heard much news at all."

Raine stared at them. Was it possible they didn't know about Paul? "Papa didn't tell you about him?" she asked cautiously.

"No." Grace looked puzzled. "The last we heard, he was sailing, and we assumed that he was happy and well. Oh dear, did something happen to him?"

Raine stared at her aunt. *Something is wrong here. . .* "How did you know Paul was a sailor?" she asked in a strained voice.

"Why, your papa told us in one of his letters a few years back. Raine, are you ill, dear?"

Raine was trembling. *How could Papa have known where Paul*

was? Could he have known all this time? Why didn't you tell me, Papa? Oh Paul... A wave of darkness rushed over her.

"She's so pale, John." Raine heard her aunt's hushed voice.

"Shh, she's coming to."

Raine sat up, feeling like a hive full of bees was buzzing in her head. Realizing she was no longer at the table, she looked questioningly at John.

"You fainted, honey. I carried you to the sofa."

How embarrassing. She had never fainted before in her life. Suddenly recalling the conversation that had prompted her shock, she buried her face in her hands.

Aunt Grace enfolded her in a firm embrace. "It's going to be all right, Raine. Go ahead and cry."

A dam broke inside of Raine at her aunt's motherly touch. Silent weeping gave way to great heaving sobs. It had been so long since she had felt another woman's comforting touch.

Finally collecting herself, she looked up at her aunt. "Thank you," she whispered.

"Do you feel like talking about it, dear, or do you just want to rest now?" Grace's concern was evident on her face.

"I'm fine now." Raine gave her a watery smile. "It was just such a shock."

"I'm afraid we don't understand what's going on here, Raine," her uncle said.

"I don't know if I understand either, Uncle John," Raine said wryly. "But I'll explain what I know."

She started at the beginning, describing the circumstances that led to Paul leaving home. Tears of anger stood in Grace's eyes as her niece recounted the story.

"I'd like to take that brother of mine over my knee," Raine heard her mutter at one point.

"After that," Raine concluded her story, "I received one letter from him that was postmarked in Boston, but that was all until Ben brought me the locket."

Grace sat up abruptly as Raine ended her story. "Boston!" She looked at her husband. "Remember that time I thought I saw him outside that—" She broke off and her forehead puckered.

"You thought you saw Paul?" Raine asked eagerly. "When?"

Grace shook her head. "It was some years ago. I was looking out the window of the carriage, on my way to the dressmaker's, and I saw a man come out of a tavern. He was. . .well, from the way he walked, he was obviously under the influence. But when I first looked at him, I thought I recognized him. He looked just like Paul—but it was so quick. I told the driver to stop and go back, but the man, whoever he was, had disappeared. When I got home, your uncle told me I must have been imagining things, and I put it out of my mind." She shook her head again. "So he did come here, just like your father told us. Why wouldn't he have come to see us at least once?"

"Father said. . . ? You knew. . . ?" Raine's head whirled with confusion. Suddenly it was all too much for her. "I think I need to get some rest," she said apologetically. "Maybe a good night's sleep will help me sort all of this out."

"I think that's a good idea, dear." Grace patted Raine's cheek softly. "We can talk more tomorrow. Why don't you just head upstairs, and I'll. . ."

"Wait, Grace." John put a large hand on each woman's shoulder. "I think we should pray before Raine goes upstairs."

Raine nodded gratefully. "I would like that very much, Uncle John." She dashed away a tear, and joined hands with her aunt and uncle.

"Dear Father," John began, "thank You for bringing Raine here safely. You are so good to us, Lord. Now I ask that You give us peace concerning Paul. Let Raine especially feel Your peace this evening, and allow her to have a restful night's sleep. Please minister to Paul wherever he is. Keep him safe, and draw him continually to You. . ."

Raine felt a sense of peace wash over her as she listened to her uncle's heartfelt prayer. "Yes, Father," she whispered.

"And touch the young man Ben wherever he is tonight," her uncle continued. "Let him feel Your love in a way he's never felt it before. Thank You for hearing us, Father. In Jesus' name, amen." John cleared his throat. "Now, off to bed with you, young lady!"

"Thank you, Uncle John." Halfway up the stairs, Raine couldn't resist turning around. "Why did you pray for Ben?" she asked curiously.

Uncle John winked. "Good night, Raine."

Raine didn't think she'd be able to rest at all, but sleep overtook her quickly, the words of her uncle's prayer ringing in her ears.

∽

"Rise and shine!" Raine's eyes flew open. The sun was streaming in through the window, and Aunt Grace was knocking on her door.

"Come in, Auntie," she called.

Grace perched on the side of Raine's bed. "How did you sleep, dear?"

"Very soundly." Raine grinned.

"Good!" Grace was pleased. "Come down and have breakfast with us before your uncle leaves for the office." Grace paused at the door. "After all, there's still some things we need to talk about," she said in mock sternness, giving Raine a pointed look.

"I know, I know. I'll tell you all about Ben. Now let me get ready for breakfast!" Raine shooed her aunt out the door. She was anxious to learn what her father had told her aunt and uncle, but the thought of Ben made her smile. She pictured his blue eyes and golden hair as she hurriedly dressed. The thought of his good-bye kiss yesterday did funny things to her insides. How could she miss him so much already?

"Well now, here's the world traveler!" Raine's uncle greeted her cheerily. "How did you like sailing, anyway? I didn't get a chance to ask you yesterday."

Raine considered the question. "Well, I wouldn't want to be at sea all the time, but I did enjoy the voyage for the most part."

"Especially with such a handsome man for a captain!" Grace noted.

"Grace!"

"It's all right, Uncle John. Auntie is dying to hear about Ben, so I'd better oblige her or we'll never hear the end of it."

John rolled his eyes good-naturedly. "I suppose."

Grace settled into a chair, pouring herself a cup of tea. "I'm ready." Raine related the story of how she'd met Ben and all that had happened since then, enjoying her aunt's eager expression.

"And?" Grace prompted when Raine stopped talking.

"And what?" Raine hedged, knowing what question was coming next.

"Do you love him?"

"Grace!" Uncle John scolded again.

Raine blushed and dropped her eyes, but not before her aunt saw the answer to her question.

"I knew it!" Grace said excitedly. "Does he love you, child?"

"I think so, Auntie." Raine answered truthfully. "We've never talked about it, but. . ."

"Does Captain Ben love our Lord?" Uncle John asked seriously.

Raine's face was troubled. "Not yet, Uncle John. But he wants to." Raine explained Ben's past to them, her eyes softening as she remembered the yearning that had been in Ben's voice.

"Well, wanting to know God is the best place to start," John said thoughtfully. "I'll be praying for him."

Raine smiled her gratitude at the two dear people across the table from her. "I love you two," she said quietly. "And now I need to know what my father told you."

"Show Ray the letters from Richard," Uncle John said to his wife. "Maybe they will help clear up some of the questions." He got up and gave Raine a peck on the cheek. "You're a special gal." Kissing his wife as well, he headed for the door.

Raine looked at her aunt eagerly. "Did you save all my father's letters?"

"I think so." Her aunt was digging in the desk drawer. "Yes, here they are." Raine grasped the packet of letters written by her father, her heart thudding at the possibility of what they might hold.

"Here, let me help you with the dishes, Aunt Grace," she offered, reluctantly laying the letters down as she realized her aunt was clearing the table.

"No, no, I'm fine. You just go on ahead upstairs. Take your time." Grace fairly pushed her niece from the kitchen.

Raine sat at the desk in her room, her hands trembling.

Breathing a quick prayer for strength, she slowly opened the first letter.

> *Dear Grace and John,*
> *Hope this letter finds you both well. We are all fine here. Paul*
> *and Raine are doing well in school, and Ellen is...*

Glancing at the date, Raine realized that this letter had been written long before Paul had left home. Laying it aside, she sorted the rest of the letters by date, then started reading with the ones dated the year Paul left.

The first letter she read contained nothing but chatty, newsy information about the church, the weather, and so on. The next was the same, and Raine laid it aside with a sense of disappointment. Scanning the third letter quickly, her brother's name caught her eye. Tucked in among some pleasantries, her father had written casually, *"Paul has left home to find work. He'll be gone for some time."* Left home to find work! Raine was appalled at her father's twisting of the truth. She hastily read the rest of the letter, but found no more reference to Paul. She put it down in growing anger.

The next three letters gave just passing mention of Paul, saying only that he would still be away for a while. Raine opened the next letter with a sigh of frustration, suddenly a sentence leapt out at her.

> *Paul is living in Boston when he's not at sea. Perhaps he will come*
> *and visit you, but I hear he's pretty busy.*

Raine clenched her teeth. How could he? How could Papa have known where Paul was and not told her? She looked at the date at the top of the letter. She was still living at home, she realized.

Scanning two or three more letters, she felt nauseated at the trivial manner her father spoke of her beloved brother. *"Paul is enjoying the life of a sailor"* and *"Paul is thriving in Boston."* And meanwhile Raine hadn't even known for certain if Paul was still alive.

Abruptly, a thought struck her. What if Papa had made all of this up? What if he really didn't know what Paul was doing all that time, but he wanted to make it sound like he did?

Hurriedly opening another letter, Raine froze as she read the first line.

Thank God, Paul survived the sinking of his ship, the Aramathea.

Raine read the words again, letting their meaning soak into her shocked brain. Her brother was alive! Putting her head down on the desk, she wept with thankfulness. Rejoicing at the news that she had waited so long to hear, it took her a few moments to react to the fact that her father must have known where Paul was all along. Her anger began to build. *If Papa knew that Paul had survived the sinking of the* Aramathea, *then he must know where he is now,* she reasoned.

Why didn't you tell me, Papa? Why did you let me wonder in agony all this time, not knowing if my brother was dead or alive? Then a new thought jolted her. *If Paul is alive, why hasn't he contacted me? If he wrote to Papa, why wouldn't he want me to know about it?* She shook her head as if to clear out the questions. Surely Paul would want her to know where he was, wouldn't he?

She stood up and stretched. *I can't make any sense of all this.* She skimmed the rest of the letters, surprised to see that there were no more references to Paul, except in the last letter which said only, *"Haven't heard from Paul in a while."*

She gathered the letters into a neat stack. *I guess I'll just have to wait until Ben can help me follow the directions in the locket,* she decided. It seemed forever since she had said good-bye to him in front of Uncle John's house.

❦

"How would you like to see some of the sights of our fair city tomorrow, Raine?" John smiled at his niece later that day.

Raine nodded with enthusiasm, her mouth full of banana bread. She would be fat and lazy if she stayed at Aunt Grace's much longer.

"First we'll go see Paul Revere's grave at the Old Granary Burial Ground. Then perhaps a drive down by the Charles River would be in order. After that we'll stop for tea at. . ."

"We don't want to wear her out the first week she's here, John."

"Don't worry about me, Auntie. I'm used to being busy."

Though she would not have admitted it, by the next afternoon Raine was more than happy to stop for tea. In one morning's time, she had learned more American history than in all her years of schooling. Her favorite place by far had been the Park Street Church where Uncle John regaled them with an account of the church's colorful past.

"They call this 'Brimstone Corner,'" he had said, indicating the site. "I guess that's because of all the fiery sermons preached here over the years." He chuckled. "Actually, I think it's because brimstone used for making gunpowder was stored in the church's basement during the War of 1812."

"And this church was the place where 'America the Beautiful' was first sung in public." Grace added proudly.

John nodded. "That's true. It's also the only church I know of that had a fountain in the pastor's study."

"What?" Raine lifted her eyebrows. This she had to hear.

"Yes ma'am. A few years ago, I think it was 1895 or so, a workman in the Tremont Street Subway accidentally stuck his pick into a huge water main. A geyser spurted upwards so forcefully that it broke the windows out of the pastor's study. The whole room was filled with mud."

"You're teasing me, Uncle John."

"No, I'm not! We were there for the evening service." He chuckled. "The reverend was not amused. He called the subway 'an infernal hole' and 'an unchristian outrage.'" Uncle John was clearly tickled.

"That poor man." Aunt Grace sighed. "We haven't seen him in years. I hope he has been able to overcome the shock."

Raine giggled.

They savored their tea, enjoying each other's company. Soon the afternoon found them strolling along on Pinckney Street. Almost ready to call it a day, the threesome had decided to stop and admire the lovely homes that lined the famous street.

"Look at this little tunnel!" Raine called to Grace. Peering through the wrought iron gate, she saw that the narrow passageway led under the house to a beautiful courtyard garden. Standing on tiptoe to see better, she felt the gate catch on her voluminous skirts. Still standing on tiptoe, she tried to extricate herself. She was afraid if she moved too much, the thin fabric would tear. And her favorite blue silk, too, she thought mournfully.

She glanced in her aunt's direction, but she and Uncle John were energetically discussing the architecture of the house. Besides, Uncle John would tease her unmercifully if he had to rescue her from a gate. *This is ridiculous,* she scolded herself. *I can't just stand here stuck on this gate forever. Besides, what if the owner wants to visit his garden? Excuse me, miss. Could I just swing you aside to get through my gate please?* She rolled her eyes.

"Raine!"

Prepared to yank her skirt loose, her hand froze. Had someone whispered her name?

"Raine Thomas!"

Her heart hammering, she surveyed the grounds. There, in the bushes. "Who are you?" she called.

The blond man stepped away from the shrubbery, his disfigured face in plain view. "Raine, I've been wanting—"

She heard the tear of fabric as she fled.

∽

After that a cloud of anxiety seemed to descend over Raine. Her anxiousness increased as the week wore on and she did not see Ben. Finally on Friday afternoon, a note was delivered to the house.

Dear Raine,
I'm finally free of my duties. May I come by tonight? Send a reply back with the messenger.

Yours,
Ben

Joyously, she scribbled a response. Handing the note back to the young messenger, she danced into the kitchen. "Auntie, Ben is coming tonight!"

Grace took in the sparkling eyes and glowing face of the

nger woman. "I'd better bake an extra pie, then," she said with a inkle in her eye. "You'd best get upstairs and get ready."

"Thank you, Aunt Grace." Raine pecked her aunt's heat-flushed eek. "What do you think I should wear?"

Her aunt rolled her eyes. "Good heavens, Raine. You act like you en't seen the man in a year! You look beautiful in anything. Now out of my kitchen!" she ordered with a smile.

Raine dutifully trotted up the stairs, only to return minutes later. "How does my hair look like this?"

Grace glanced up from her pie crust. "You look lovely, dear. I'm sure your Ben will be pleased. Now, if I'm to get these pies done. . ."

"I'm going, I'm going!" Raine backed out of her aunt's kitchen, almost knocking her uncle over. "Uncle John! I'm sorry. I didn't know you were standing there!"

"Apparently not," he agreed wryly. "You look especially glowing tonight. Are we going to be graced with the company of the dashing Captain Ben?" he teased.

Raine's cheeks grew hot. Were her feelings that transparent?

"He'll be here at six."

"Good, good!" Uncle John boomed. "I'd like to spend some time getting to know the man that stole my gal's heart." Noting the look of consternation on her face, he patted her hand. "Don't worry, honey. I won't embarrass you."

Raine gave him a weak smile. This evening might not go exactly as she had anticipated it. . .

The knock at the door at five minutes before six sent butterflies racing through Raine's stomach. *Stop being silly,* she scolded herself in vain. Opening the door, her heart leapt at the sight of Ben's tall form.

He touched her cheek with a gentle hand. "Hello, Raine," he said softly.

She couldn't take her eyes off of his face as he stepped through the door. "It seems like it's been so long since I've seen you. . . I'm so glad you could come," she whispered.

"So am—"

"Well, well!" Uncle John's voice preceded him into the foyer.

"Gracie, come greet our guest!"

The spell was broken. Raine giggled as she shrugged at b
watching him shift gears mentally.

"It's nice to see you again, Captain Ben!" Uncle John pump
Ben's hand with enthusiasm.

Though obviously taken aback at the zestful welcome, Ben g
Raine's uncle a broad smile. "Thank you for having me, sir."

"Now, none of that, young man. You must call us Grace an
John." Grace's manner put Ben at ease instantly. "We're not very for
mal at this house," she added.

Soon the men were settled in the parlor to await supper. Rain
disappeared into the kitchen with Grace, but couldn't resist peekin
in at Ben. Uncle John had launched into one of his favorite stories
delighted to tell it to someone who had never heard it before.

"I don't think those two will lack for things to talk about," she
said.

Grace smiled. "Your uncle would gab all night if I let him."

∞

By the time they sat down to the huge meal Grace had prepared, Ben
felt like he had known Raine's aunt and uncle all his life. Bowing his
head as John said the blessing, he was unprepared for the emotions
that assailed him. The biscuits had cooled before John finished praying, but Ben hardly noticed the length as he felt the joy and thankfulness emanating from the older man's words.

What would it have been like to grow up in a family like this?
Visions of his long-faced father droning out a mournful prayer filled
his thoughts. Shaken more than he cared to admit, he was quiet for
a few minutes before entering into the light banter going on around
the table. Soon he was regaling them with stories of his own.

As the supper was nearly over Ben began yet another story, this
one about his partner's aunt, who had a habit of sneaking around
Ben's office making sure that Ben was "conducting business in the
proper manner."

"Yes, that Vida Daniels is one lady to reckon with," Ben said,
leaning back comfortably in his chair.

"Daniels!" Raine's eyes flew wide with surprise. "But I thought she was—"

Ben grinned. "You thought she was what?"

"Younger," she said lamely. She dropped her eyes in embarrassment, obviously recalling the two elderly women who had been in Ben's office that morning, and then she giggled in spite of herself. Fascinated, he watched the flicker of expressions cross her face.

Grace gave John a pointed look and the two excused themselves. "I'm sure we'll be seeing you again, Ben," Grace said. "You're always welcome."

Ben thanked his hosts, then turned to Raine as they left the room.

She said softly, searching his face, "I've missed you this week."

"I missed you, too. It didn't seem the same on the *Capernaum* without you to brighten my day."

"I've been waiting for you to come so I could tell you my good news." Her eyes had taken on a glow. "You'll never guess."

He raised his eyebrows. "Does it have anything to do with a missing brother?"

"He's not missing anymore! At least, I don't think he is." Her brow clouded suddenly.

"I'm afraid I lost you there, Raine."

"Well, it seems that Papa knew where Paul was all along."

"Was?"

She frowned. "That's the problem. From what I gather, Paul survived the shipwreck, but Papa hasn't heard from him since."

An enormous wave of relief washed over him at her words. Taking her hand, he held it tightly. "Raine, you don't know how glad I am to hear that Paul is alive. You see," his voice broke, "as the captain of the *Aramathea* when it sank, all this time I've carried the weight of your brother's death, but now. . ." He swallowed the lump in his throat.

Raine stroked his hand with a gentle touch. "It wasn't your fault, Ben," she said quietly. "Even if Paul had died, it wouldn't have been your fault. I'm sure you did the best job you could." Her words felt like soothing balm on a burning wound. "We all make mistakes,

Ben," she said. Her sincerity was reflected in her eyes. "But what matters now is that Paul is alive—and we need to find him!"

Ben reached out and caught her chin in his hand, staring deep into her eyes. When he fell in love with her picture so long ago, he didn't realize that her lovely face was only a cover for her inner beauty.

She colored at his gentle touch but didn't look away. Tenderly lowering his mouth to hers, he felt her sigh. He pulled her tight against his chest, his heart pounding.

Stop now, he told himself. Pushing her gently away, he sank down into the kitchen chair. He didn't dare look at her, or he would take her in his arms again. "Go put on the teakettle or something, would you, woman?"

Raine smiled at his gruff tone. She knew as well as he did that neither one of them had wanted the moment to end.

Hours later, they sat in the deepening twilight, the porch swing creaking underneath them. "Let's read the message in the locket again now that we're finally in Boston," Ben suggested. "Tomorrow we can go find that address."

She reached for the locket she always kept around her neck, then paused. "There's something else I need to talk to you about."

His throat tightened at her serious tone. "Am I in trouble?"

"No, but I may be." Taking a deep breath, she told him about the man she had seen in New York and now again in Boston.

⌒

"Well, here we are!" Ben said the next morning as he drew the carriage to a halt in front of a large, two-story house on High Street.

Raine studied the old house as if it would speak and tell her where Paul was. Could it be possible that he lived here? She eyed the lacy curtains and well-tended herb garden dubiously.

"Are you ready to go in, Raine?" Ben asked.

She sighed. "I guess so. I just don't know what to expect. What if I find out something I don't want to know?"

Ben squeezed her hand as he helped her out of the carriage. "We'll cross that bridge when we come to it. I'll be right with you the whole time."

She tried to give him a brave smile as they walked up to the house, but she knew he must feel her trembling as they climbed up the wooden porch steps. *"The Lord is my shepherd,"* she told herself. *"I shall not want."*

"Do come in!" a bright voice called in response to Ben's knock.

Raine stared at Ben, frozen. He gave her a gentle push through the door.

"Who is it, please?" the voice asked.

Raine cautiously made her way into the cheery living room, stopping short as she saw an elderly woman in a wheelchair. Her snowy hair was caught up in an attractive bun, and a lacy shawl was draped over her thin shoulders. A smile lit her still-beautiful face as she held out her hands in welcome. "Come in, dear," she said kindly, her British accent warming her words. "How can I help you young people?"

Raine didn't know what she had expected to find, but this certainly wasn't it. Perhaps this wasn't the right address.

"I'm Raine Thomas," she said uncertainly.

"Oh!" The woman's wrinkled face lit up at once, her bright eyes sweeping up to Raine's right temple. "I knew you would come!"

Automatically, Raine put a protective hand over the birthmark. Why was this woman staring at her so intently?

Oblivious to Raine's bewildered expression, the woman examined her, then sat back with a satisfied expression on her face. "You're even more beautiful than Paul said you were." She beamed at Raine. "And who might this be?" she asked, smiling at Ben.

"I'm Ben Thackeray, ma'am. But I'm afraid we don't know who you are." He exchanged glances with Raine.

"Oh?" The woman raised her eyebrows.

"Yes ma'am. Paul sent me a message to come here, but I don't know why." Raine was starting to feel as confused as the elderly woman now looked.

"Well, I'm Violet Fornell," the woman said, as if that explained everything.

"Show her the note, Raine," Ben said.

After Violet read the water-stained note that Raine had decoded, they explained to her how it had come to Raine. Violet's look of puzzlement cleared slightly.

"So you see, Mrs. Fornell, we don't know exactly why Paul sent us here. We were assuming you would clear that up for us," Raine said.

Violet nodded, absently stroking a calico cat that slept in her lap. "How long has it been since you've seen your husband, dear?"

Raine blanched. "Paul is my brother, not my husband, Mrs. Fornell," she explained, glancing at Ben. His eyes seemed to harden into blue glaciers as he stared back at her.

"Oh dear! I can't imagine why Paul. . .but now that I look at you, I see you resemble him quite—"

"Did Paul ever actually say that Raine was his wife?" Ben interrupted.

Violet stared at him thoughtfully. "Well, I. . .no, I guess he didn't. Not in so many words. But I just assumed from the way he talked about her. . ." Her words trailed off as she looked from Ben to Raine.

"We're just as confused as you are, Mrs. Fornell," Raine said, still looking at Ben. "It seems that Paul led a number of people to believe that he and I were something other than brother and sister."

Avoiding Raine's eyes, Ben spoke to Violet. "When was the last time you saw Paul, Mrs. Fornell?"

"Please, call me Violet." She peered at him over her glasses. "I don't know what's going on here, but I can tell you all I know. I last saw Paul about three years ago after that ship of his sank, and. . ."

"You saw him after the *Aramathea* sank?" Raine's voice was eager.

"Why, yes. He lived here." Violet was clearly perplexed.

"But. . ." Raine tried to compose her thoughts.

"He didn't stay very long once he was well, but before he left, he gave me the key and told me to expect you, Raine."

"What do you mean, once he was well?" Raine's voice came out in a whisper.

"Well my dear! Your brother had quite a time of it when the ship sank. He had to be in bed for quite awhile until that nasty gash healed properly, you know." Violet looked from Raine's pale face to the look of disbelief on Ben's. "Surely you knew..."

Raine shook her head.

"Oh dear. I better start at the beginning," Violet sighed. "Paul came to board with me shortly after he arrived here from England, I believe. I got to know him...quite well. In fact, he is very dear to me." Violet dabbed at her eyes with a lacy handkerchief. "I always prayed for his protection when he was on a voyage, but that last time was very unusual."

"Unusual?" Raine moved a large fern so she could draw her chair close to Violet's. Ben stood, his arms folded, his face tense.

"Yes. I had been concerned for him for some time. His soul, you know."

Raine nodded. Yes, she knew too well.

"He was such a bitter, hurting young man." Violet stared out the window. "Yet at the same time I knew his heart was still tender."

"But the voyage?" Ben prompted.

"Ah yes, the voyage." Violet smiled a faraway smile. "To make a long story short, I begged him not to go. I just felt in my spirit that he was not to go; that there was danger awaiting him. The Lord and I are on pretty good terms, you see." Her face shone with that special glow that comes only from an intimate walk with one's Savior.

Raine nodded, sensing the presence of the Spirit in this woman.

"Anyway, Paul wouldn't hear of missing that voyage." Violet sighed and glanced at her visitors. "I couldn't stop him. But I prayed for him. Oh, how I prayed. One night, after Paul had been gone two weeks or so," Violet continued, "I was awakened in the middle of the night. I knew it was the time of crisis. I begged God for Paul's life, pleaded for his soul."

"What day was that, Violet?" Ben's face was pale.

"I believe it was the twenty-eighth of February, around two A.M."

Ben dropped to his knees in front of her chair. "That's the day she sank," he whispered.

Raine shook her head in wonder. "Thank You, God," she breathed. The room was silent then, the gentle Spirit of God whispering to three listening hearts as rain pattered softly on the windowpane.

Two cups of hot tea later, Violet was refreshed enough to finish her story. Raine gasped as Violet described Paul coming home late one night, his head and face swathed in bandages. *Oh Paul,* she groaned inwardly. *What happened that terrible night?*

"I made sure he rested properly. The poor boy was nearly starved." Violet said. "But as soon as he was well enough to get about on his own, he packed his bags." The elderly woman closed her eyes, obviously picturing the young man she loved as a son.

"The last thing Paul did before he left was to give me the key," Violet said quietly. "Hand me that box, dear." She indicated a polished brass box on the mantel. Opening it, she drew out a small key and reverently handed it to Raine.

Raine took the key with a trembling hand. "But what is it for?"

"I thought you would know what it was for, Raine." The older woman's face was troubled.

Raine handed the key to Ben, who examined it carefully, then slipped it into his pocket. He leaned over and kissed Violet's cheek. "We'll let you know as soon as we find out anything."

Violet nodded. "You do that."

Raine put her arms around the invalid's shoulders. "Thank you," she whispered.

Violet put an age-softened hand on Raine's cheek. "Our God is a great God, dear. Don't ever forget that."

Raine followed Ben out to the carriage, feeling a strange yearning. What would it take to be that close to God?

The ride home through the misting rain was silent, each wrapped in their own thoughts.

⟨∞⟩

Three days went by before Ben was free to visit Raine again. They were sitting on the porch swing, the cool summer breeze teasing them with the scent of roses.

"Would you pray for me, Raine?"

She glanced at him. "I've never stopped."

He took her hand, gently tracing the backs of her fingers. "I don't know what's wrong with me. I want to have a relationship with

Christ, but I can't seem to get past the fear."

She was silent, giving him time to give voice to his thoughts. At last he continued, his voice heavy. "Also, I think we'd better not see each other any more." There. He'd said it. He felt her shock as she pulled her hand away to stare at him.

"Why?"

This was much harder than he imagined. "Because. . .because I need some time to think."

"Oh." The pain in her beautiful eyes made his stomach hurt. But what else could he do? He couldn't go on not knowing. . .

Her soft voice interrupted his thoughts. "Can't you tell me what's wrong, Ben?"

He couldn't bring himself to look at her.

"Ben?" She felt him touch his arm tentatively and he turned to her then.

"How do I know that it's not true, Raine?"

"What's not true?" Her face clouded at the coldness in his voice.

"How do I know that you aren't really married to Paul, and you're not just playing a game with me?"

She simply stared at him, as though too stunned to speak. "I've told you the truth, Ben," she said quietly at last. "If you don't trust me, then I guess there's nothing left for us."

She stood, and he almost gave in as he caught a faint whiff of her freshly-washed hair. He reached for her, then turned away.

"Good-bye, Raine," he said over his shoulder.

He saw her raise her hand as if to touch him, and then she wrapped her arms around herself as if to ward of a sudden chill. He couldn't bear to look at her any longer, and he quickly strode away and climbed into the carriage. He turned the horses and never once looked back.

If he had, he would have seen the tears streaming down Raine's face as she stumbled into the house, not caring who saw her misery.

"Why, Raine! What's wrong, child?" Her aunt's sympathetic voice only caused the tears to flow faster. She poured out the story, Aunt Grace clucking and sighing at the appropriate times.

"Why don't men have more sense!" Grace was thoroughly

indignant by the time Raine had calmed down. "I have a mind to. . ."

"Now, now Gracie. I'm sure the boy will come to his senses." Uncle John had come into the room in time to hear Raine's tearful recounting of the evening. "Captain Ben won't be able to stay away for very long, if I know him."

"But why. . ."

"Raine, Ben loves you." John smiled at the look on his niece's face. "But men are funny sometimes. Loving you makes Ben vulnerable, and the way the situation looks to him, he thinks he's going to end up getting hurt. Just be patient, honey. He'll come around." Uncle John patted her hand. "A few prayers wouldn't hurt either."

Raine plodded upstairs, somehow feeling like a lost little girl. Her heart hurt as she recalled the look on Ben's face. *Ben, I love you so much. How could you ask me to pray for you—and then doubt me?*

A quiet voice seemed to interrupt her anguish, saying, *"And how could you doubt Me?"* Raine slipped to her knees. *Please forgive me, Father God,* she cried. *I love Ben so much, but I want Your will to be done in my life. Please lead me in Your path.*

⊘⊘

The next day a letter from Constance arrived, bringing a smile in the midst of Raine's pain.

> *Dear Raine,*
>
> *You would never believe it! I have decided to stay here on the island! There are so many suffering people coming through these gates. My heart especially goes out to my Orthodox brothers and sisters, who are almost starving to death by the time they reach Ellis. You see, they only eat kosher foods, and no one seems to take notice of their special needs.*
>
> *Some of the Jewish workers here and myself are thinking of creating some sort of organization to help the Jewish immigrants. Not only with food, but with anything they need to get them established here in America. And if I get the chance, I'm not going to be afraid to tell them about the Messiah.*
>
> *Anyway, God is good. Thank you so much, dear, for leading*

me back to Him. I trust this letter finds you well. Kiss that handsome Captain Thackeray for me.

Sincerely,
Constance Rabinowicz

P.S. I TOLD them I didn't have tuberculosis.

I would certainly kiss Ben if he would come back to me, Raine thought mournfully. The dull ache in her heart would not go away. Tired of sitting around the house the last few days, she finally asked Uncle John to drive her to Violet's house. *Maybe she thought of something else helpful,* Raine hoped. In any case, it would be delightful to spend some time with the cheery woman.

"I'll be back in an hour, Raine," Uncle John called as he dropped her off at Violet's door.

Violet was delighted to see Raine, tactfully refraining from asking about Ben when she noticed the sad look in Raine's emerald eyes.

"Would you mind pouring?" she asked instead, handing Raine the flowered teapot.

Thoroughly enjoying the older woman's company, Raine glanced at the clock in surprise when uncle John knocked on the door. Could an hour have passed so quickly?

"Come in and meet Violet," she suggested as she let him in.

Uncle John obligingly stepped into the sunny room, stopping short as he recognized the woman in the wheelchair. "Well—"

"Hello, John!" Violet interrupted. "This is a surprise!"

Raine looked from Violet to her uncle John. "You two know each other?"

Her uncle looked distinctly uncomfortable. "Yes. We knew each other back in London, Raine." He looked at Violet. "I had no idea you had moved here to Boston."

"I wasn't aware that you and Grace lived in Boston either, John." Violet's eyes were steady as she gazed at him.

"Yes, well." John cleared his throat nervously. "It was nice seeing you again. I'll be sure to tell Grace." He turned to Raine. "We'd better get going, Raine."

Raine wasn't quite sure what was going on, but there was no mistaking the undercurrent of tension. "I'll come visit again soon, Violet," she promised.

"I'll look forward to it, dear."

"What was that all about, Uncle John?" Raine asked as soon as they were out the door.

John didn't answer until they were out of sight of Violet's house. "I'm sorry if I seemed rude, Raine. It was quite a shock to see an old acquaintance from England after all this time," he said slowly. Raine looked at him questioningly, certain he was not telling her everything.

She was surprised to see a carriage in the drive as they pulled up to Uncle John's house.

"Well Raine, it looks like your captain is back!" John seemed glad for the diversion from his thoughts.

She stepped down from the carriage, her heart pounding. Walking slowly to the front door, she failed to see Ben as he stood in the shade of the old oak.

∞

Ben's mouth went dry as he saw her. She looked like a breath of spring, the plumes of her hat exactly matching the peacock blue of her dress. *I've been such a fool,* he thought. *God, please let her forgive me. . .*

"Raine!" She whirled, her eyes wide, and he approached her slowly, as one would approach a frightened animal. Finally standing in front of her, he searched her face. "Can you forgive me?" he asked in a low voice.

He watched the joy leap into her eyes. "Yes," she said simply.

"I've been miserable without you, Raine. I love you." He pulled her into his embrace. He felt her smile against his chest, and although he couldn't be sure, he thought he heard her whisper, "I love you too."

"I missed you so much." Suddenly remembering something, he dug into his pocket. He folded her gloved hand around the key. "I've been thinking a lot about what you said about trust. I don't know what this key belongs to, Raine, but I know that I can trust you with the key to my heart. I was wrong to doubt you."

She looked up at him, her eyes shining. "I . . ."

"Well, now. Here's the good captain!" Uncle John clapped Ben on the shoulder.

Raine sighed. Uncle John had a way of choosing the most inopportune moments. . .

After supper, Grace laid the small brass key on the table, studying it intently. "I don't know for sure, but I would guess that this key would open a safety deposit box," she ventured.

"Of course!" Ben was elated. All four of them had been mulling over the various unanswered questions regarding Paul, trying to figure out the significance of the key.

Raine's heart soared, then sank. "We could spend months trying to find the right bank." Everyone was silent *Have we come this far only to reach a dead end?* Raine wondered.

"I think we ought to pay a visit to Violet again," Ben announced suddenly. "Didn't she say that she had Paul run errands for her sometimes? Maybe she knows what bank he would have gone to."

∽

"Yes," Violet nodded. "Paul often went to the bank for me. I use the one down on First Street."

"Sounds like a good place to start," Ben said.

Violet reached for both of their hands. "God go with you," she said fervently. "Please let me know when you find my boy."

Raine felt tears prick the backs of her eyelids. "We will, Violet. We will."

∽

El Paso County, Colorado

The Crooked P ranch hands were working furiously. The rain had finally stopped and they had to make up for lost time. Tom worked alongside his men, readying ten head of cattle for the trip south to Santa Fe.

Laying aside the branding iron, Tom wiped the sweat from his face. Stuffing his bandanna into his pocket, he ambled over to the well where several of the hands were gathered. He dipped himself a cool drink from the full bucket that stood nearby, then sank wearily to the ground.

"Only 'bout a dozen of them ornery creatures left, boss." Simon nodded toward the holding pen.

Tom nodded, then entered the log ranch house, throwing his sweaty shirt on the floor. Passing the fireplace, his eye caught sight of the Bible on the shelf where he had left it that rainy day. His soul reached out for it, but his mind would not obey. Turning his head, he walked away.

Two days later, he pulled his bandanna up over his face. "Let's get going, boys!"

The excitement of a cattle drive always did wonders for him, and he'd been especially looking forward to this trip to Santa Fe. Maybe he could leave the torment of his past for a few days. What he wouldn't give. . .

Chapter 5

Raine drew a deep breath as the teller directed her and Ben into a small room. Ben couldn't believe how easy it had been to find the right bank. The teller had taken one look at the key, asked Raine her name, and that was that.

Now, he set the long metal box on the table with a thunk. "Take as much time as you need."

Raine fitted the key into the lock with shaking fingers. *Will she at last find the answers to all of her questions?* Ben wondered. She looked up at him, and he smiled encouragingly. He was sure that they had been followed to the bank, but now was not the time to tell her that.

He frowned, remembering the face of the red-haired man that had been behind them all morning. He was sure it was the same man he had seen that time outside his office back in London. The face had seemed familiar somehow, not only because he had seen the man that other time but as though he should have known the man's name, as though he'd known him from some other place and time. . . "Go ahead," he encouraged her. He found himself holding his breath, distracted from his thoughts, and, for the time being, he forgot about the red-haired man.

She opened the lid slowly. Peering over her shoulder, Ben was surprised to see that it contained only two envelopes. As she picked up the largest one first, he noticed that Paul's handwriting was very sloppy, as if he had written Raine's name in haste.

Taking a deep breath, she slid the contents out. She glanced at the inner envelope, then held it out to Ben so he could see the note scrawled across it. *"Raine, please get this into the hands of Ben Thackeray."* He almost grabbed it out of her hands.

He ripped it open, heaving a huge sigh of relief as he glimpsed the contents. He had hoped against hope that it would turn out to be something like this.

"What is it?"

He glanced up at her, regret momentarily covering the joy in his eyes. "I'm sorry, Raine. I'm not at liberty to share this information with you yet. There's something I need to do first."

Her eyes widened.

"But I can tell you one thing—this is wonderful news!" He caught her up suddenly and whirled her around in the air.

"Put me down," she pleaded with a giggle.

He did so at once, standing back to admire her. What a picture she was. Her hat had fallen off, revealing the gorgeous mass of dark curls. Her cheeks were pink from laughter, and her mouth. . . He pulled her to him, no longer able to resist. Her lips felt soft beneath his as they yielded to the hungry pressure of his own. "Ah Raine," he whispered. "What have you done to me?"

He released her after a long moment, watching as she picked up the envelope that still lay in the box. She stared at the date that Paul had penciled in under her name. *February 1, 1903.* This was right before the *Aramathea* set sail," she whispered.

She slid a single sheet of paper out of the envelope. Yellowed with age and dog-eared, it seemed to be some sort of legal document. She stared at it uncomprehendingly for a moment, then gasped as she realized what she was holding. How could it be?

Ben took the paper from her shaking hand. He scanned the few words it contained, then shrugged as he looked up at her.

She pointed to a line on the birth certificate that stated a women named Miriam was Paul's natural mother. "My mother's name was Ellen."

"Ah." Comprehension dawned on him as he reread it. "I'm sorry, Raine."

"So am I." Her lips were pressed together in a tight line. "I'm sure this is most of the reason Paul never came back, even to see me." Slipping it back into the envelope, she stooped to pick up a single sheet of paper that had fallen to the floor, then held it so they both could read it.

Dear Raine,
I have missed you so! Has Papa poisoned you against me so

234

much that you won't even answer one of my letters?

Ben saw her eyes fill with tears, and he knew her heart was breaking at the thought that Paul might think she had abandoned him.

Perhaps Papa has forbade you to have contact with me? I can only hope that you have not forgotten me completely. I'm sure you can see why I will never come home —not until Ben follows the directions I've left him and lets me know the results. I don't have time to write you everything that happened, but I trust that since you have gotten this far, that Ben has told you as much as he could I am in danger, and I fear that you would be in danger also if you were with me. But how I long for your sweet company!

The tears were flowing freely down her face as she read the last sentences out loud. "'Please, Raine. If you can't find it in your heart to write to me, at least pray for me. Please pray for me, little sister.'"

Ben gathered her into his arms, rocking her gently. He could tell that all the pent-up emotion of the last weeks flowed out with her tears, soaking the front of his shirt. "Shh, it's going to be fine," he murmured comfortingly. "I'm right here, Raine. . .I love you."

She laid her head on his shoulder.

∞

"So where do you go from here, Raine?" Uncle John had just finished reading Paul's letter.

"I don't know." She wrinkled her brow. "I just can't figure out why I haven't received any letters from Paul. Apparently he thinks I know where he is."

"Do you think he could still be here in Boston, Raine?"

"No, I don't think so, Aunt Grace. There was no date on the letter, but somehow I feel that it was written quite awhile ago." She smiled suddenly. "I do know that God has led me this far. It looks like a dead end, but I know He can work it out."

"Especially since *He* knows where Paul is, even though we don't," her uncle reminded her. "What does Ben think?"

235

"I guess he's as puzzled as I am," she admitted. "Although there was something in that other envelope he can't tell me about yet."

She bid her aunt and uncle good night and closed the door to her room with a sigh of relief. The events of the day paraded through her mind as she knelt down by the bed. She was horrified anew at the indisputable truth that the old document had brought to light.

Papa, how could you? her heart cried.

"I love you, Raine." Ben's words of love comforted her again as she remembered the warmth of his embrace. She buried her face in her pillow. *I need to talk to You, Father. I know You've led me this far, but I don't know where to go next. Please lead me. . .*

She awoke the next morning feeling refreshed and at peace, but no closer to knowing what to do next. The cool morning air beckoned to her irresistibly. Letting herself out the front door without a sound, she took a long walk. She breathed in the freshness of the beautiful morning, and somehow it gave her courage to face the dawning of the new day.

"Good morning," she sang cheerfully as she entered the kitchen door.

The look on her aunt's face made her heart stop. "What's wrong?" she whispered.

"Your father—" Grace handed her a telegram. "This just came, dear."

Raine read the short message, its words chilling her soul.

RICHARD THOMAS VERY ILL STOP PLEASE COME QUICKLY STOP PASSAGE BOOKED ON THE *Cornucopia* STOP AUGUST 15 *Stop*

The telegram was signed by Dr. Delfin, an old family friend.

"August 15th? That's tomorrow!" She was stunned. "I need to pack and. . ."

"Slow down there, Raine." Uncle John's hand on her shoulder was gentle. "You'll have plenty of time."

"Oh Uncle John. What if Papa dies before I get there?" She had discovered in the past few seconds how much she loved her father, despite her anger with him.

"We'll pray that God will keep him until you have a chance to see him, Raine." John's voice was firm. "God is able."

"I know, Uncle John. It's just that Papa and I have been at odds ever since Paul left, and I don't want him to die until we can make it right." She bowed her head. "I've been so angry with him," she whispered. "I keep asking God to help me forgive, but just when I think I have, I find myself bitter again."

"Forgiveness is a process," John reminded her. "As long as you want to forgive, and you keep working at it, it will come."

⁊

"I'm so sorry I can't go with you back to England, Raine." As they stood by the *Cornucopia* the next day, Ben felt as though a weight was about to settle on his shoulders. "I wish I wasn't obligated to stay in Boston for at least a few more weeks."

"I'll be fine, Ben. But I will miss you terribly." Her eyes filled with tears. "When will I see you again?"

He enfolded her in his arms. "Don't cry, honey. We'll be together again soon, I promise. In the meantime, I'll try to track down that brother of yours. I'd like to talk to him before I take care of that matter he left for me to do."

He kissed her tenderly, then gave her a gentle nudge toward the gangway. Pressing a small package into her hand, he looked deep into her eyes. "I love you, Raine."

She kissed him swiftly on his cheek, then turned to go.

He watched until the ship was no longer in sight. *I miss her already,* he thought, a strange sense of foreboding coming over him as he climbed into his carriage. *Don't be silly, old chap. Nothing is going to happen to her.* Nevertheless, he felt a heaviness that he couldn't seem to shake. The sinister face of the red-haired man popped into his mind and suddenly, finally, he was able to put a name with the face.

Dag. Dagmar Rennet. Ever since Ben had seen him, he had been trying to remember why his face seemed so familiar. Now he knew, and it chilled him to the bone. Why, oh why, hadn't he gone with her?

Then again, maybe it was himself that Dag was after. After all, Paul had left the other envelope for Ben, not Raine. The thought was not a pleasant one, but at least it was better him than Raine.

His mind occupied with matters besides his driving, he was surprised when he realized he was driving down High Street, where Paul used to live. *I'll visit Violet,* he decided, smiling at the thought of the cheery old woman.

Nearing her house, the tiny seed of an idea that he had been contemplating suddenly bloomed. Pulling the horses to an abrupt stop, he marched up to Violet's door and knocked with conviction. He entered when he heard Violet's welcome float from somewhere within.

"Good morning, Violet."

"Ben! What brings you here? Did you find Paul already?" Her voice was eager.

"No, I'm afraid not, Violet. But I was wondering..."

"Yes?"

"Could I stay here for a while?"

She was startled. "Well, I...I haven't had any boarders since Paul..."

"It wouldn't be for very long," he said persuasively. "Probably a month or two."

She looked him over. "You aren't in trouble with the law or anything, are you?"

He laughed. "No ma'am." He explained about Raine's abrupt departure for England.

She closed her eyes. "I hope Raine gets to see her father before he dies." She smiled at him suddenly. "You know, it does get lonely here sometimes. Do you play chess?"

❧

The weather during the voyage back to London was unseasonably stormy and cold, emphasizing the contrast between this voyage and her experience aboard the *Capernaum*. Raine stayed in her cabin, nibbling on bread in an effort to keep her stomach on an even keel. She spent much of her time in prayer, not knowing what to expect when she arrived at her father's home.

At last, after many long days, the skyline of London came into view through the thick fog. Raine stood on deck, pensively fingering the small key that hung around her neck with Paul's locket. She had discovered the tiny key when she had opened the package from Ben.

> *Dear Raine,*
> *This is just to remind you that you hold the key to my heart.*
> *Come back to me soon.*
>
> > *All my love,*
> > *Ben*

His words of love warmed her as the *Cornucopia* steamed into the harbor. Scanning the crowded wharf, Raine's heart leapt as she saw a dark-haired man standing near the front of the crowd.

Paul! Her mind screamed. Grasping her bag tightly, she kept her eyes glued on the man as the ship moved closer. Disappointment flooded over her as she saw that it wasn't her brother.

Sighing, she realized that her knuckles were turning white from the grip she had on her bag. Setting it down, she leaned against the railing. *Father, please calm my spirit,* she prayed.

There had been no mention in the telegram of anyone meeting Raine in London, so she made her way to the Mission.

Mr. Duncan thought he had seen the last of me, I'm sure, she thought in amusement. Walking slowly, she reflected on all that had happened since she left London.

Deep in thought, she was startled when a small group of children joyfully accosted her.

"Miss Thomas, Miss Thomas!"

"Did you come back to be our teacher?"

"Did you miss us?"

Raine gave each little one a hug. "I'm afraid I can only stay for a little while, children," she said regretfully. Their disappointed little faces tugged at her heart, making her realize how much she had missed teaching them.

"Charlotte!" Raine felt a rush of joy at seeing her old friend.

"Raine!" Charlotte gave her a huge hug. "Where did you come from?"

"I thought I'd just drop by and see you since I missed you so much."

Charlotte raised her eyebrows. "Mmm-hmm. Why are you really here? Oh dear, did things not work out with Captain Bert?"

"Ben. No actually, it's my father. Apparently he's very ill. Do you suppose Mr. Duncan would put up too much of a fuss if I spent the night here, just tonight?"

Charlotte shrugged. "You're my guest. If he doesn't like it, then that's his problem."

∽

Raine pushed open the door of her old room, weary beyond belief. It would feel wonderful to have a good night's sleep before facing the ordeal tomorrow. She set the candle on the old dresser, groaning as she saw the piles of boxes on top of the bed. Apparently this was now the storage room.

Finally snuggled under the dusty coverlet, she tried to sleep. What was Ben doing right now? She could picture him standing at the railing of the *Capernaum* and wished she were with him.

Forcing her thoughts away from Ben, she thought of her father. *God, please let him live until I can get there,* she prayed once again. *Please give me the grace to forgive him. I can't do it on my own. And take care of Ben and Paul, please Father,* she continued. *They both need Your love...*

The knock on the door startled her awake. "It's just me," she heard Charlotte whisper.

"Do you realize it's one o'clock in the morning?" Raine opened one eye to glare at her friend.

"I know. But I forgot to ask you if that man found you."

Raine made a very unladylike noise. "What are you talking about, Charlotte?"

"A few weeks after you left, a man came looking for you. He said he was your neighbor or something."

"My neighbor?" What neighbor? Surely this could have waited until morning.

"Well, I just thought it might be something important. I'll let you get back to your beauty sleep." Charlotte sounded hurt.

"Wait, Char." A faint alarm went off somewhere in the back of her mind. "What did he look like?"

"Well, he had blond hair, and his face was. . .well, it was very badly scarred."

Raine's throat constricted. "What did you tell him?" she whispered.

Charlotte shrugged. "Just that you had gone to America. Oh, and that you sailed on the *Capernaum*. He seemed very nice," she added defensively.

Raine closed her eyes. "What was his name?"

"I knew you would ask me that. Let's see, it was something like George or Gregory maybe. . .that was it! Gregory Havner. I think."

She didn't know anyone named Gregory Havner. "Did he say what he wanted?"

"No. . .maybe his name was Guthrie. Guthrie Havner? No, no! It was Geoffrey. Yes, I'm sure of it."

"Geoffrey?" The only Geoffrey she had ever know was Geoff Hathaway, her brother's old friend. But it couldn't be him. He was dead, killed in the fire that had destroyed his family's house. She pictured the disfigured face of the man who had called to her that day in Boston. Could it be. . . ? Even at the time, she had had to admit that there was something familiar about him. But it couldn't be Geoff.

"Was it Geoffrey Hathaway?"

"Yes! Yes! That was it!" Charlotte bounced up and down on the bed. "So you do know him."

"Yes," Raine said slowly. "Except he's—dead." She remembered again the man's scars. Could it be possible that he had lived. . . ? And why would he be trying to find her?

It was a very long time before she gave her body the sleep it was craving.

Chapter 6

Ben scanned the room that had been Paul's and was now his. *If I were Paul, where would I hide something important?* He had come to stay at Violet's house with the general idea of gleaning more information about Paul's disappearance, but now a plan was beginning to formulate in his mind.

"There must be something obvious that we're missing," he mused out loud. *God, please help me to. . .*

He stopped short, realizing what he was doing. He had gotten so accustomed to Raine praying about everything.

Could it be this easy? Could he have a relationship with God like Raine and her uncle had? They made it sound so natural, talking to God as if He were really interested. Remembering the peace and joy that lighted Raine's beautiful eyes, his yearning suddenly grew undeniable. Falling to his knees in the middle of Paul's room, he cried out, "Jesus, if You really do care, please show me the way to You. I can't live without peace any more. . ."

∽

Across the ocean, Raine sat bolt upright in bed. The urge to pray for Ben was so strong, she got out of bed and knelt down. Pleading first for his safety, she soon found herself praying that he would be able to surrender himself to God.

Finally feeling a peace come over her as the first glow of dawn peeked through the darkness, she got up and got dressed. Between the excitement of Charlotte's middle-of-the-night revelations and the prayers for Ben, she hadn't gotten much sleep. Oh well. She could rest on the train on the way to St. Albans.

Digging her Bible out of the small overnight bag, she settled by the still-dark window. The train didn't leave for several more hours, but her stomach felt tight already, just thinking about seeing her father. She leaned back in her chair to watch the slowly-rising sun, relaxing in spite of herself. Opening her Bible, she tensed as she heard a slight sound at her door. She stared in horrified fascination as the door knob turned. The door opened slowly, soundlessly. She froze, clutching her Bible to her chest.

The large, red-haired man looked startled to see her awake, then an ugly smile creased his face. "So—we finally meet, Raine Oliver."

She opened her mouth to scream, but he was too fast. Clamping a grimy hand over her mouth, he pulled her back against his chest. "Now, don't make a sound, or you'll never see the light of day again," he threatened quietly. "We're going to go for a ride, and I don't want to hear one noise out of you. Do you understand?"

She nodded.

The man loosened his grip a hair. "If you cooperate, you won't get hurt," he said, watching her intently.

She nodded again.

He opened his coat slightly, revealing a wicked-looking knife. "Now, you're going to walk down the stairs and get into my carriage."

Oh, I am, am I? She gritted her teeth.

He whipped her around to face him as he felt her body tense. "You'd better not try anything, do you understand?" He prodded her out the door, almost stepping on the hem of her dress as he followed her.

God, please let someone see us, she pleaded silently as she made her way down the stairs. She walked as slowly as possible, stalling for time.

Passing Mr. Duncan's study, her heart leapt as she saw a crack of light under the door. Pretending to stumble, she slammed against the door. *Come on, Mr. Duncan.* The man behind her jerked her up. He gave her a shove, cursing under his breath.

Raine glanced back at Mr. Duncan's door, her hopes dashed when it remained closed. Her captor hustled her into a windowless carriage. Jumping in after her, he motioned to the waiting driver. The carriage started with a jolt as the horses leapt forward.

She glared at the red-haired man, mildly surprised that he wasn't Geoff, or whoever was pretending to be Geoff. Maybe this big lug was in cahoots with scar-face Geoff. That must be it.

"What do you want with me?" she demanded.

"Well, now. Ain't we the feisty one!" He chuckled.

She turned her back to him. His breath alone could kill her before he even got to her with the knife, she thought grimly. She wished she could see where they were going. Judging from the many turns, she guessed that the driver was trying to disorient her.

The carriage stopped abruptly, almost throwing her to the floor. Before she realized what was happening, her captor whipped a scarf out of his pocket and tied it around her eyes. Fear threatened to overwhelm her as she was jerked from the carriage and forced to stumble along beside him.

The Lord is my shepherd, I shall not want." She felt her whole body begin to tremble violently, then the blackness closed in on her. She crumpled in a heap at her captor's feet.

⚭

She came to slowly, knowing that she was on a ship even before she opened her eyes. The slight rocking motion and the damp, musty smell of the hold had penetrated her mind, even in her unconscious state. Reaching up, she pulled the filthy blindfold off, realizing as she did so that she was not alone.

Her captor sat perched on a crate, his leering smile barely visible in the faint light. "Well, I guess yer not so brave after all, are ya. Sure are purty though."

She recoiled at his suggestive tone, shrinking back as he rose and came toward her.

He laughed, a horrible sound that sent chills down her spine. "I won't bother ya none, yet. We'll just see how ya feel about me after a day or two down here, Mrs. Oliver." He grinned nastily. "I'm sure you'll have plenty of company with all the rats and such."

She heard a key turn in the lock as he left, then the heavy thump of a dead bolt. Thankful at least that he had not tied her up, she moved to sit on top of a large box. Pulling her feet up securely underneath her, she pondered her situation. *What does this man want with me? He apparently thinks I'm someone else,* she thought, wondering why he seemed to think her last name was Oliver. Oliver. . . Oliver. . .that sounded so familiar. Suddenly she knew, and she groaned out loud. *Paul.* Paul had gone by the name Paul Oliver when he was sailing. And this man had called her Mrs. Oliver!

Apparently he, too, thought she and Paul were married. Unable to make any sense of the situation, she stood up to explore her prison. Feeling her way around, she discovered many boxes and barrels, but no way of escape.

Settling herself on a bale of something soft, she tried to devise a plan of escape, but the loud growling of her stomach kept distracting her. The scones she had eaten for supper last night were long gone. Her fear was fast turning into anger the longer she sat in the dark. Determined to find a way out, she jumped down from her perch.

"Ouch!" Her foot landed on something soft and warm that squeaked. She scrambled back up on top of the crates, her stomach threatening to expel its meager contents. At least he was truthful about the rats!

"Why didn't I beg you to come with me, Ben?" She groaned. "Now what am I going to do? I can't sit on this crate for the rest of my life."

Closing her eyes, she concentrated on Ben, remembering his smile, his touch. Her thoughts drifting, she gasped as she realized that her father would be expecting her today.

If he's still alive, her mind whispered. She pushed that thought aside, hoping instead that her disappearance would be noticed quickly. *Father God, please send someone soon!*

∞

Several days later, heavy footfalls paused at the door. Raine jumped up from where she had been lying. The door had been opened only twice since she had been put there, once for a loaf of bread to be tossed in, and once for a bucket of water to be carelessly pushed through.

Her heart beat faster as the heavy door flew open. Shielding her eyes from the sudden glare of a candle, she felt her mouth go dry. Her captor loomed over her, a heavy rope in his hand.

"Did ya have a nice stay, Mrs. Oliver?" The large man was clearly amused by the situation.

Raine glared at him and he chuckled. Suddenly, his hand snaked out and grasped her wrist in an iron grip. "I certainly hope that ya feel like talking to me, sweetheart," he growled, "because I'm not a very patient man. I've waited too long as it is."

Raine stared numbly at her hand as it turned white from the force of his grip on her wrist. Her lack of response infuriated him. Jerking her around, he tied her hands together roughly. He prodded her out of the hold, forcing her up the stairs and into a small, brightly lit cabin.

Seeing her captor's face clearly now, she shuddered at the evil gleam in his eye. She kept her eyes averted as he tied her in a chair. He gently ran his fingers through her dark hair, then began to pace in front of her.

"Where are they?" He demanded finally.

She stared at him. *Where is who?*

"Answer me, woman! Where are those papers?"

Papers? Father, please help me! She met her captor's frenzied look with a steady gaze.

"I don't know what papers you're talking about."

He roared an oath. "Don't play innocent with me. I followed you and your lover to the bank. I know what you went there for."

She jumped as his huge fist crashed into the wall next to her. The papers that had been in the safety deposit box of course. The ones she had never read.

Closing her eyes, she fully expected to feel the next blow on her face. After a moment, she cautiously opened her eyes. He stood in front of her, visibly trembling, but under control.

"Come now, sweetheart. I won't hurt you." His voice was unexpectedly calm. "Just give me the papers."

She eyed him warily. "I think you've got the wrong person," she said. "I don't have any papers. Truly. And my last name is Thomas, not Oliver."

"Oh? Then how d'ya explain this?"

She gasped as he whipped a large photograph from his pocket. The picture was tattered and water-stained, but there was no mistaking it.

It was the picture that Raine had given to Paul before he left home. But hadn't Paul given the picture to Ben? Surely Ben isn't involved in this... She pushed the ugly thought from her mind.

"Where did you get that?" she whispered.

He looked smug. "You don't need to know, sweetheart."

The endearment coming from this man's lips made her cringe.

"Shall I refresh your memory as to what is written on the back of this purty little photo?" he continued mockingly. " 'To Paul—my one and only. Love, Raine Ellen.' "

She sighed. How could this get so twisted? If only Paul could explain...

"So, where is your husband?" The question jolted Raine, even though she knew it was coming.

"I don't have a husband." She was shocked at how firm her voice sounded.

Her captor looked stunned for a moment, but recovered quickly. "You mean Paul is dead?" he asked, the nasty gleam coming back into his eye. "Don't play games with me, woman. Tell me where he is."

Raine looked him in the eye. "I don't know."

Red Hair kicked the leg of the chair, sending her to the floor, the chair on top of her. Letting loose a string of profanity like she'd never heard before, he untied her and bodily carried her back down to the hold. Forcing her inside, he slammed the door closed.

"You will tell me sooner or later, little woman, so you might as well make it sooner. I'm going to get those papers, wherever they are. And then I'm going to get Paul."

Hearing the bolt thump into place, she sank trembling to the floor. *God, help me.*

☙

"Well, Captain." John looked at his Bible thoughtfully. "You just keep reading this Book and keep asking Him to teach you His ways. He'll show you."

Ben couldn't believe the joy and peace that he had known since he finally surrendered all to the Lord. After puzzling over some scriptures for days, he had finally sought the wisdom of Raine's uncle.

"Thanks, John." Ben got up to leave, pausing at the door. "Have you heard from Raine yet?"

John shook his head, a troubled light in his eye. "No. I expected that she would have arrived in London two days ago. She said she would send a telegram when she arrived in St. Albans, apprising us of her father's condition. It's just not like her to go back on her word."

I knew I should have gone with her. Ben felt a heavy foreboding drop on him like a cloak.

"I don't like it, John," he said out loud, images of Dag filling his mind "I don't like it at all."

Raine's uncle nodded in agreement. "I know what you mean, son. I don't have a good feeling about it either. I think. . ." His voice trailed off at the look on Ben's face. "What is it, Captain?"

Ben swallowed hard. Surely it couldn't be, yet. . . "Do you think it's possible that the telegram from Raine's father was a hoax?"

John started visibly. "What are you getting at?"

"I'm afraid someone has been following her."

"Someone?"

Ben sighed. "It's a very long story, John, and I think Paul is right in the middle of it."

"Go on."

"I think it first began before Paul even left England. Have you heard how he and a friend of his found that old code book?"

"Raine alluded to it, yes."

"It seems that code book belonged to a group of spies. They were gathering information from an insider in the British government, passing message's on to sailors bound for Africa, who in turn passed them along to the native rebels in South Africa. Their reward was South African diamonds.

"Paul stumbled onto their activities, apparently totally by accident, when one of his innocent code messages was intercepted by a member of the circle of spies. Needless to say, the spies were not happy that Paul knew about them—they were about to take action against him, when their insider in the government betrayed them.

"The government did a massive sweep, and caught most of the spies—and they almost caught Paul as well, mistaking the innocent message the spies had intercepted as the genuine article. It was all kept very secret by the government, and Raine never even knew what was going on. But apparently, espionage was among the numerous other things Paul was accused of before he left St. Albans."

"What? And Raine knows nothing about that?"

"Not a clue." Ben gave a rueful grin. "I have to admit that for a while I thought she was in on it."

John stared at him. "You knew about the espionage all along?"

Ben shook his head. "I didn't know any of this when I hired Paul. But it didn't take long for rumors to start flying."

John nodded, his face an unreadable mask.

"By that time, I had gotten to know Paul myself. I just couldn't quite believe he could do anything so underhanded. I decided not to say anything and just keep an eye on the situation. Then, just as the *Aramathea* left Boston on her last trip, one of my sailors came to me with what he said was evidence that Paul was a spy. He showed me a message that Paul had written in code, and said he had a friend in St. Albans who had heard the whole story. He claimed he had seen Paul passing information to another sailor when we were in port."

"Did you believe him?"

Ben shifted in his chair. "I'll tell you, John, I didn't want to. And I didn't trust the fellow who told me the story. But there was something about Paul, something that made me think he wasn't quite telling me the truth. I kept hoping that somehow he could prove his innocence." He ran his fingers through his hair. "I had intended to confront him with the sailor's story, but I never got the chance."

John raised his eyebrows.

"The ship sank before I had a chance to speak with him."

John blew out his breath. "This would break Raine's heart, you know."

Ben nodded. "I just couldn't tell her, yet."

"Wise. Do you still suspect Paul?"

Ben sighed. "I have. . .found evidence that has convinced me that Paul was framed." As much as he wanted to, he just couldn't tell John yet about those papers in the safe deposit box. There was too much at stake. Soon he would have to act on the evidence the papers contained. If only he could find Paul first.

"What are you telling me, Captain?"

"I think that the man who framed Paul may have found out that Paul is still alive and is trailing Raine to see if she will lead him to Paul."

"But how. . ."

"I saw the man following us when we went to the bank that day," he admitted. He shook his head. "I only caught a glimpse of his face, and I thought he looked familiar, but. . .who would've thought? It was the same sailor who told me the story about Paul being a spy in the first place. I'd give anything to go back and confront the man, demand he tell me what he was up to—but I can't."

John's face was tight with anxiety. "Is this man dangerous?"

Ben shrugged. "I'd wager that anyone who can hold a grudge that long isn't playing a game."

John passed his hand over his face. "I'll get a telegram off to Raine's father. In the meantime, it sounds like we better do a whole lot of praying, Captain."

∞

Ben was waiting beside his carriage when John came home from the office the next day. John's demeanor gave the answer to his unspoken question.

"I know something has happened to her, John!" The horses jumped as he slammed his fist into the carriage door.

"Calm yourself, Ben," John said sharply. "Do you or do you not believe that God will care for Raine?"

Ben stared at the older man. "I know He can take care of her, John. It's just that I wish I were there to protect her, too."

"I know, son." Raine's uncle looked weary. "But God has seen fit to do otherwise. Besides, Raine's a pretty strong gal, as I'm sure you know."

Ben nodded ruefully, remembering the steady light in her eye as she had told him of her plans to travel to Boston alone.

"I'm not afraid, Ben." He could hear her voice like it was

yesterday. *God, please protect her, wherever she is. . .*

∽

Near Santa Fe, New Mexico

Tom stared unseeingly at the backs of the cattle. Lifting his Stetson, he let the hot, dusty wind ruffle his hair and dry the sweat from his brow.

It felt good to be on the trail again, free from the day-to-day routine of the ranch, free from the daily strain of—waiting. Waiting for what, he wasn't sure, but he could feel the expectancy growing daily. During the day he could push it aside, but in the quiet of the night, it pulled at him, robbing him of much-needed rest. At the same time, it brought with it the hope of change; renewal. What was it? Why was his heart reaching for it, yet holding back in fear?

Chapter 7

Richard Thomas stared at the telegram from his brother-in-law, trying to still the violent trembling of his hands.

RICHARD STOP HOPE YOU ARE
FEELING BETTER *Stop* PLEASE SEND
NEWS OF RAINE'S ARRIVAL *Stop* JOHN

The last sentence rang in his fevered mind. Devastated when she had not shown up, he had assumed his daughter had chosen not to come to him. "I can't die without seeing her." Burying his face in his hands, he wept bitter tears. *Please, God, give me a chance.*

Raine lifted her head at the slight noise, then laid it down again. *It's your imagination,* she told herself. Her brain felt fuzzy, as if a fog had rolled in and encompassed her thoughts. Weak from hunger, she floated in and out of wakefulness.

"Raine!"

She jerked her head up at the loud whisper. "Ben?" Had he really come? "I'm over here."

"Raine, you need to get up!" His voice was urgent.

She stared groggily at him as he tried to rouse her. "You're not Ben," she said slowly. Maybe he was an angel? She had always wondered what angels looked like.

"Raine—if you want to get out of here, you need to listen to me." His voice was insistent.

Her brain felt frozen. Concentrating on his words, she sat up with effort.

"Raine, I'm sorry, but I need to cut your hair. It's the only way we'll be able to pull this off."

A faint alarm went off somewhere in her hazy thoughts, but she couldn't figure out why. She squinted at him as he snipped her hair, trying to make sense of his features, but she couldn't think. . .couldn't concentrate. . . Why was she here. . . ? She seemed to recognize the man, but no name came to her thoughts, no name that made sense. . . Her thoughts were clouded with hunger and confusion.

Her rescuer pushed some garments into her hands, then turned his back. "Get into those clothes, Raine," he commanded. "Hurry."

She obediently stepped into the trousers, feeling an odd sense of detachment from the scene. He turned back around, sweeping her with a quick glance. "It'll have to do," he mumbled. Slapping a tattered cap on her head, he gathered her in his arms and bolted up the stairs. Her head bobbed against his shoulder as he made a dash across the open deck and out onto the crowded wharf. Slowing his pace abruptly, he put her on her feet.

"Raine—listen to me. You're going to be safe soon. But you need to walk. We'll draw too much attention if I have to carry you." His voice was pleading. "Can you do it?"

She looked into the man's eyes, gaining strength as the word *safe* penetrated her mind. She nodded.

∞

She opened her eyes. What time was it? Weakly, she pulled herself up in the bed.

Martha, the Mission's nurse sprang up from her chair by the window. "Raine! You're awake!"

"Why are you in my room?" Maybe one of the children was ill and they needed Raine to help. . .

"You've been, ah, sick, Raine," Martha's voice was hesitant. "You don't remember?"

Raine stared at the ceiling, trying to think. "I remember coming here from Boston, and. . ." From Boston! Instantly, everything came flooding back. She had been kidnapped, then someone had rescued her, and. . .

"How did I get back here to the Mission, Martha?" she asked. This was too strange.

"I think I'd better have Mr. Duncan speak with you, Raine."

Raine grimaced. One of the last people she wanted to see. . .

The nurse laughed at the look on Raine's face. "Don't worry. He'll be nice. He's been just as worried about you as the rest of us. Maybe more," she added, leaving Raine to puzzle over her remark.

Martha bustled back into the room a few minutes later, a steaming bowl of soup in her hands. Raine's mouth watered as the nurse placed the bowl in front of her. "Mr. Duncan will be up shortly, so you eat. You can freshen up when you're done."

Raine nodded, her mouth full. After a second bowl, she felt almost as good as new. As she set the bowl aside, Charlotte breezed through the door.

"Raine! You look terrible!" The sincerity in Charlotte's voice was disturbing.

"Thanks. It's nice to see you, too." Raine rolled her eyes, then gave her friend a gentle push. "Could you move, please? I want to get washed."

Martha shooed Charlotte out the door. "Plenty of time for you to talk to her later," she said with a smile. Martha turned to Raine. "Here's a washcloth and some soap. And a hairbrush and a mirror."

Raine washed her face. The warm water and fragrant soap had never felt so good. She picked up the hair brush and ran the brush through her hair, then froze as she realized how short it was. She picked up the mirror.

Was that really her? Her rich brown hair lay in waves, ending just below her chin. The looser style enhanced her high cheekbones and large eyes. Putting the mirror down, she stared at Martha.

"It'll grow back," the nurse promised.

Raine continued to stare, wide-eyed. "But why?"

"He had to do it, Raine. Otherwise you might not have escaped."

"He who? Who had to do it?"

"Good morning!"

Raine jumped at the sound of Mr. Duncan's voice.

"You're looking much better," he said.

She was taken aback by the kindness in his tone. He seemed so— nice. Almost fatherly. . .

"How are you feeling, Raine?"

"Pretty fair," she said cautiously. He had never called her Raine before, always Miss Thomas.

"Mr. Duncan, Martha said you could explain how I got here to the Mission after, well, you know." She almost felt sick as she thought of the dark, musty hold she had been forced to live in for. . .for how long?

"Yes, well." He cleared his throat, sniffing nervously. "How much do you remember?"

She wrinkled her brow. "I remember the man forcing me from my room and into the carriage. I guess I fainted, because when I came to, I was in the hold of some ship. I don't know how long I was there. My captor questioned me once. . ." Her voice trailed off as she pictured her captor's evil face.

She closed her eyes for a moment. "I don't remember much else, until a man came and found me. I thought it was Ben, but it wasn't. The man was familiar, but I was so—" She stopped short at the look on Mr. Duncan's face. "It was you, wasn't it?"

He studied the floor.

She was incredulous. Never in a million years would she have guessed that the frosty Mission administrator would come to her rescue.

"How did you find me?" she asked in amazement.

"I was in my office the morning you were abducted, Raine," he said. "I heard some scuffling on the stairs, along with a large thump on my door. At first I thought that some of the children were being mischievous," he admitted. "I was just going to yank the door open when I heard a man swearing. Realizing there might be some sort of trouble, I waited until I heard the front door open."

"But how did you. . ."

"I opened the door a crack, just in time to see him force you into the carriage." He clenched his teeth. "I slipped out the back door and managed to get Oscar saddled in time to see the carriage turn the corner."

Raine stared at him in amazement. His eyes were glowing, his face animated.

"I followed the rascals to their ship and watched them manhandle you down to the hold. They had two guards posted, so I didn't even try to get aboard. I hated to leave you there, but I was going to need some help to rescue you. I went back to the Mission and I, well, I learned how to pray." His voice grew humble. "I've always been a pompous old thing, thinking that God was lucky to have me in His service. But when I realized how helpless I was to do anything about this situation, well, I just had to get down on my knees. Before I could even begin to pray for you, I knew I had to ask Christ for His forgiveness."

Mr. Duncan straightened in his chair. "Anyway, I gathered the staff together and we prayed. We kept watch on the ship day and night, trying to find a time when the guard would be the least likely to be alert. We were getting concerned about you being down there for so long, Raine, but they had someone posted constantly. Finally, we heard them talking excitedly about a big party planned for the next evening."

Mr. Duncan's gaze swept over her short hair and still-pale cheeks. "I didn't know what kind of condition I would find you in, Raine. It was pretty risky to try it in broad daylight, but in the end, I think it worked out fine."

She nodded, astounded at the risk that had been taken on her behalf.

Mr. Duncan's eyes traveled to her hair again. "We figured it would be less noticeable if you were not quite so, ah, so. . .noticeably a woman," he ended lamely, his face turning red. "Anyway, you're small enough that we hoped that everyone would think you were a young boy. I'm sorry I had to cut your hair." His eyes dropped to his hands. "So, I guess that's all. God was with us."

Chapter 8

Ben groaned as Violet captured yet another one of his pawns. "I just can't keep my mind on the game today, Violet," he apologized.

She eyed the young man sitting across from her. "I know it's hard, son, but surely you'll hear from Raine or her father soon."

"I hope so." He stared absently at the chess board, running his fingers through his hair. "It's just so hard not knowing what's going on!"

"The Lord has His hand on that gal, Ben. She'll be fine."

Later that evening, Ben sighed as he punched his pillow into a more comfortable shape. He had been in bed for hours, tossing and turning. *Christ, I know that I gave my life to You, and that I'm supposed to trust You. But I don't understand how You could let something bad happen to Raine. She loves You! I thought I was starting to get to know You, but I guess I don't. . .*

Unable to deal with his troubling thoughts, Ben got up and lit the lamp. Shivering, he grabbed his robe out of the massive wardrobe at the end of the bed. Being as quiet as possible, he eased the wardrobe door closed—and caught his toe on the leg of the bed as he turned. Losing his balance, he crashed into the wardrobe, sending an avalanche of boxes and bags crashing to the floor.

He sat up ruefully, certain that he had awakened Violet. He was silent for a long minute, listening, but he heard nothing except the faithful bonging of the grandfather clock. His shoulder ached from its meeting with the heavy oak door.

He stood, surveying the mess he had created. Feeling rather like a naughty little boy, he peered into one of the boxes, laughing out loud as he pulled out a very fancy hat. Large and purple, it was covered with faded violets. Hastily putting the creation back in its box, he couldn't resist opening another box.

Another hat. This one was brown felt with a mink band. A matching mink muff lay in the bottom of the box. He carefully stacked the rest of the boxes, pushing them onto the top shelf of the wardrobe where it was apparent they had resided for quite some time. He brushed the dust off his hands, smiling as he imagined Violet wearing the wild purple hat. She must have been quite a fashionable lady in her day. He chuckled.

Closing the wardrobe firmly this time, he inched around the bed to avoid repeating the mishap. He glanced down as he heard the crunch of paper. Deciding that the yellowed paper must have fallen out of the wardrobe along with everything else, he stooped to pick it up.

He hadn't meant to read it, but as he glanced at the old letter, a sentence jumped out at him. His heart stopped. Sinking down on the side of the bed, he scanned the letter. Could it mean what he thought it did?

⌒

Raine stood in front of her father's house, feeling her mouth grow dry.

"You can do it," Charlotte said.

Raine glanced at her friend. "I guess I'm just not sure I want to, Char." Grasping her bag, she marched to the big red door, wishing for Ben's comforting presence. It was nice to have Charlotte along, but it just wasn't the same.

She knocked. Hearing no movement from within, she knocked again with more energy. The house remained silent. She tried the doorknob, surprised as it turned easily in her hand.

Slipping through the door, she was gagged by the stale, closed-up odor of the house. *Surely Papa hasn't. . .* She couldn't bring herself to finish the thought. She set her bag down and tiptoed through the darkened living room, Charlotte close behind.

Reaching the hallway, she heard a faint sound coming from the bedroom. She felt like an intruder as she peeked around the corner. There. In the bed by the window. Her heart began to pound as she spotted him. "Papa!" She ran to him, taking his thin hand in hers. He moved restlessly, but didn't respond.

Raine was shocked at the gray in his hair, the dark hollows under his eyes. "Oh Papa." She glanced around the room. Where was Dr. Delfin? She could tell someone had been here recently; her father's bed was neat and clean, a vase of fresh flowers was on the bedside table.

She settled herself in a chair next to her father, noticing that Charlotte had disappeared. She looked at the man lying in front of her. How he had changed! There were lines etched on his face that she had never seen before, lines of remorse and grief. She put her hand out, smoothing the graying hair off of his forehead. "I'm here, Papa," she whispered. "Please come back to me!" Exhausted, she let her head drop against the side of the bed.

She woke with a start as she sensed another's presence in the room. Recognizing Dr. Delfin, she sank back down in her chair. "I'm so glad you're here, Dr. Delfin. What's wrong with Papa?"

A smile lit the old doctor's face. "It's so good to see you, Raine," he said heartily. "We were concerned that something had happened to you."

"Yes, I was. . .delayed." Raine felt reluctant to add to his worries by telling of her abduction. "But how is Papa?"

She saw the shadows in the old doctor's eyes before he concealed them from her with a cheery smile. "I think you're going to be his best medicine, Raine."

"Doctor—"

"Ah Raine. I can't lie to you. I can't help your father—he's dying of a broken heart. That's my best diagnosis."

Raine bowed her head. "If only he'd told us," she whispered.

"Then you know?" The old doctor sounded relieved. "You know that Paul was your half-brother?"

She nodded. "Paul evidently came across a copy of his birth certificate. He left it for me in a safety deposit box in Boston."

He sighed. "Miriam was so young. She had a terrible time delivering Paul. She hung on for a couple of hours, but I just couldn't save her." Dr. Delfin closed his eyes, reliving the painful day. "Your father was crushed. He had planned on marrying her, you know."

Raine shook her head. "No. All I knew was that the name listed on Paul's birth certificate wasn't the name of my mother. I didn't know any of the details."

"Paul's grandmother, his mother's mother, helped your father care for him for a while. Then Richard met Ellen. She was willing to take Paul as her own."

Raine was silent, pondering the strength her mother must have had.

"It was a happy day when they added you to their family, Raine."

She smiled absently, her thoughts perplexed. "But why. . .why did they keep it all such a secret?"

Dr. Delfin shrugged. "It's not easy to admit failures, Raine. Especially to your children. And when he became a clergyman, your father felt even more pressure to keep his past sins a secret."

"But for Papa to accuse Paul of doing the same thing he had done. . ." Raine's sentence trailed off as she thought of her brother. What added pain it must have been to discover his father's sin, hidden all these years.

The doctor nodded, his face grave. "It was your father's own guilt that made him so furious with your brother. But he only made his guilt worse when he sent Paul away. All these years, for all that he's a man of God, he's let guilt eat at him, consuming him. I suspect he became a clergyman as a way to try to atone for his sins—but of course we can never create our own atonement. God's forgiveness is the only medicine that can cure him now."

∽

John waved the paper wildly in front of Ben's nose. "Praise God! She's safe!"

Ben snatched the telegram from his hand. Reading the brief message, he let out a huge sigh of relief. "Thank God," he murmured, longing to hold her in his arms, to reassure himself that she really was fine.

"It says she'll be writing soon to tell us everything. I can't wait to hear what happened." Noticing Ben's silence, John put a hand on the younger man's shoulder. "What is it, Ben?"

Ben stared at John, misery filling his eyes. "I doubted God," he whispered, dropping his gaze. "I questioned Him. I was angry that He would allow something to happen to Raine."

John's eyes softened. "Ah Ben," he sighed. "Everyone has questioned God at one time or another. We're human, and humans are weak sometimes. But He still loves you. Just because you failed doesn't mean it's all over."

Ben looked up hopefully as John smiled. "Just ask Him to forgive you, son. Then ask Him to help you do better next time. You're going to be just fine, Captain," John continued, "especially when that pretty little niece of mine gets back!" He chuckled at the look on Ben's face.

"I love her, John," Ben said seriously.

"I know you do, son. I know."

⌒

Raine tossed and turned on her makeshift bed. She strained to hear her father's breathing. Convinced he was resting comfortably, she lay back down on the cot she had set up next to his bed.

Morning dawned at last, and she felt his eyes on her face before she was even fully awake. "Good morning, Papa," she said softly.

He started. "I thought I was imagining things!" Slow tears trickled out of his eyes as she rushed to his side. "I thought I would never see you again in this world, Raine."

She smoothed his hair back with gentle fingers. "I'm here now, Papa," she assured him. "I'll take care of you." She longed to ask him about Paul, but that would have to wait until he was stronger. He closed his eyes then, a faint smile on his lips, and she sat by his bedside until he fell asleep.

Studying him, she was amazed at the changes that had overtaken him since the last time she had been home. Richard Thomas was just a shell of the handsome, robust man he had once been. Pondering this, she felt the last shreds of bitterness toward her father dissolve. Sorrow took its place, sorrow that a once-strong man of God had allowed himself to slip into so much sin and pain.

Why, Papa? she cried silently for the hundredth time. *We loved you. You didn't have to deceive us. We wouldn't have forsaken you even if we had known the truth.*

Dr. Delfin stopped by in the evening, thrilled to find his patient resting quietly. "Ah, I knew you would be the best medicine in the world, Raine. Now, if we could only find that brother of yours."

Oh no. "Papa doesn't know where Paul is?"

Dr. Delfin looked surprised. "Not to my knowledge. Do you know where he is?"

She shook her head, disappointment flooding through her. "I thought, well, I assumed that. . ."

"Your father lost contact with Paul just after he learned that Paul survived the shipwreck."

Raine frowned. "He knows as much as I do, then," she said, sighing. "I thought for sure Papa could tell me where Paul was."

Had she come this far only to be stymied again? She felt hot tears begin to gather, and she saw Charlotte and the doctor exchange glances over her head.

"Come on, Raine," Charlotte said. "Let's get a breath of fresh air."

She nodded, following Charlotte out the door. It did feel good to be out in the warm sunshine after being in Papa's dark little room for so long. She took several deep breaths of pine-scented air and swallowed the lump in her throat. "I don't know what's wrong with me, Char." She bent to pick a sprig of aster. "I should be happy that Papa's doing some better, and I am, but I was just so sure that he would tell me where Paul was."

"God's timing is perfect, Raine."

Raine lifted the tiny flowers to her nose, breathing in the delicate perfume. Charlotte was right of course. She should be used to unfamiliar paths by now. "Don't stop praying for me, friend."

Charlotte smiled. "Never. Now, let's go get something to eat. I know how grumpy you get when you're hungry."

"I can't help it that I've been blessed with a healthy appetite, can I?"

Charlotte rolled her eyes. "Healthy? Try hearty. Or hoggish. Or manly. Or. . ."

Raine laughed, in spite of her worry. "All right, all right. Lead the way to the pig trough."

☙

But disappointment still lay heavily on her that night as she tried to sleep. Her father had only awakened for brief periods throughout the evening, so she had no opportunity to question him about Paul. *Where are you, Paul? I thought I was so close.*

She pulled the covers up more snugly around her neck. *Father, I know You've led me thus far. Thank You for delivering me from my captor, and thank You for keeping Papa until I could see him one more time. Please continue to guide me to Paul.* Finally drifting to sleep, she dreamed sweet dreams of Ben. Waking in the morning, he filled her thoughts. If only he weren't so far away!

"Raine?" She jumped as she heard her father's weak voice.

"Coming, Papa!" She hurriedly brushed her hair, smoothing it back as she entered her father's room. "How are you this morning, Papa?"

"I was hoping I hadn't dreamt that you were here."

"I'm really here, Papa," she assured him again. "I came as soon as I got the telegram from Dr. Delfin, but I was delayed in London for a few days." Giving him no time to question her, she quickly asked, "Are you ready for breakfast this morning?"

Her father raised an eyebrow. "Did Dr. Delfin appoint you as my personal nurse?" he teased, showing the first hint of his old self that Raine had seen since she arrived.

"Yes, he did, as a matter of fact." She smiled at him. "So—will it be oatmeal or toast?"

After he had eaten, her father put his napkin down with a tired smile. "Thank you, Raine. That was delicious."

"Are you ready to rest, Papa? Here, I'll help you. . ."

He pushed her hand away. "I'm tired of resting."

She sat back on her heels, waiting as he shifted restlessly, avoiding her gaze.

"I think we need to talk, Raine," he said at last.

Her heart began to pound. Now that the time had come, she wasn't sure she could handle hearing everything. "Papa—"

"I need to do this, Raine." Her father looked her in the eye. "I need to make things right." Averting his eyes again, he stared at the wall. "I just don't know where to begin."

Raine put a gentle hand on his. "I love you, Papa," she said quietly. "No matter what you have to tell me, I love you."

Richard Thomas heaved, and then sobs forced themselves out of his mouth in great gasps. It was long moments before he could speak. "You don't know what I've done, Raine. I've been so miserable." Tears poured down his face. "I forced my own son away, condemning him for something he didn't do. In my heart I knew all along he didn't do it—and then when that girl finally admitted publicly that the father of her baby was someone else. I was wrong. . .so wrong. . ."

She let him cry, knowing that he had to deal with it in his own way. Richard finally pulled himself together. Reaching for his daughter's hand, he held on tightly as if to gain strength from her. "I accused Paul of the very thing I was guilty of," he whispered in agony. "I don't know how to tell you this, Raine, but. . ."

"I know, Papa."

"What?"

"I already know." She explained how Paul had left his birth certificate in the safety deposit box. "Dr. Delfin filled in the details for me, Papa. You don't have to talk about it any more."

Her father hung his head. "I thought you and Paul would never have to know, that it would somehow be easier that way. But I've never forgiven myself. I should have. . ."

"Papa—"

"There's more, Raine." Richard looked at his daughter intently now, seemingly determined to get everything out in the open. "I'm sure you've agonized over not hearing from your brother all this time. He wrote you many letters, Raine."

She gasped. "Then why. . . ?"

He closed his eyes in pain. "I was being eaten alive by guilt, Raine. When it appeared that Paul had committed the same sin that I had been hiding, it just compounded my own guilt and pain. I felt that I had been a failure as a father; that somehow my sin had been passed down to my son even without his knowledge. I'm afraid I took out all those frustrations on Paul."

"But—the letters?"

"I was so angry, Raine. I didn't want to ever see Paul again. Just the sight of him inflamed my guilt. I didn't even want you to have anything to do with him, so I read the letters myself—something inside me still cared enough about him to want to know where he was and how he was doing. But then I burned every letter." He buried his face in his hands. "You'll never know how sorry I am," he groaned.

"Oh Papa." *No wonder Paul thought I had turned my back on him,* Raine mourned.

Her father took a deep breath. "I still loved your brother deeply, even though I was furious with him. I couldn't bring myself to speak his name out loud—but I had to know if he was safe, if he was telling the truth in his letters to you. I. . .I had him followed."

Raine stared at her father, feeling befuddled. What was he saying?

He sighed. "I hired a man to trail Paul, Raine. He reported back to me Paul's whereabouts and so on."

"Then why don't you know where he is now?" She winced as she heard the sharpness in her own voice.

Her father shook his head, infinite weariness in his eyes. "I don't know, Raine. My man had reported to me that Paul was recovering well from his injuries after the shipwreck. Then apparently without warning, Paul left in the middle of the night. Langley hasn't been able to track him down."

The words echoed in Raine's mind, triggering an avalanche of questions. "Papa, do you think Paul knew he was being followed?"

Richard frowned. "I don't think. . .why?"

She described the message Paul had sent her in the locket. "'Am being pursued' was the first sentence," she explained. "He also mentioned something about that in the letter," she remembered thoughtfully. "Do you think. . .?"

Her father was still frowning. "I don't think so, Raine," he said slowly. "I'm sure he could have noticed Langley following him, but I don't think he would have been perceived as a threat." Richard pictured the scrawny little man he had chosen to trail Paul. "No, I don't think so."

The evil face of a red-haired man popped into Raine's mind. Suddenly, she knew who had been pursuing her brother, and it wasn't Langley. "I think you need to rest now, Papa," she said firmly. "I forgive you for everything you did—and I know the Lord will as soon as you ask Him. Why don't you just talk to Jesus for a little while, and then go to sleep. We'll talk more later."

Her father closed his eyes without a word, and Raine breathed a sigh of relief as she stepped out of the stuffy room. Her head ached with the events of the day, and her heart was heavy with thoughts of Paul. The thought of her brother being hunted by the man who had been her captor sent chills down her spine.

"So how's Papa doing?" Charlotte's voice interrupted her thoughts.

Raine smiled. "Much better, now that he has started to deal with the past. I think we'll leave tomorrow. Now that Papa has turned back to the Lord, he's as anxious for me to find Paul as I am." She looked thoughtful, then added, "But before we go, there is an item of business we need to take care of."

"We?"

"Yes, we. I need you for moral support. We need to do a bit of sleuthing, that's all."

⬯

"This is where Geoff and Christina's house stood before it burned," Raine whispered to Charlotte.

"So now where do we go?" Charlotte whispered back.

Raine shrugged. "Let's look around a little. It doesn't look like anyone even takes care of the place anymore."

It felt eerie to walk through the deserted grounds. How well she could remember all the fun they had had here. It wasn't that long ago, really, that she and Christina climbed these old apple trees to spy on their brothers, giggling wildly when they were caught. . .

"Raine, I think we need to go." Charlotte's loud whisper held a note of panic. "There's someone. . ."

Raine jumped as a man appeared as if from nowhere. Turning to flee, the sound of his voice froze her.

"Raine! Please. It's just me."

She turned slowly to meet the plea in his blue eyes. "Geoff?"

He nodded.

"You've been following me."

He nodded again.

"Why?" Her heartbeat was returning to normal.

"Because I wanted. . .needed to make things right." His disfigured face twisted into an odd sort of grimace. "I couldn't find Paul."

Out of the corner of her eye, Raine noticed Charlotte peeking out from behind the outhouse. "It seems that no one can find Paul, Geoff. But how. . . I mean, I thought. . ."

"You thought that I was dead."

She nodded.

"I thought I was dead, too. It was horrible." He passed a trembling hand over his eyes. "I'll spare you the details, but suffice it to say that the road to recovery was very, very long. But there is good that has come of it." She looked into his glowing eyes. "I have come to know Jesus Christ, Raine. I mean, really know Him."

She watched as the tears coursed down his face, feeling her heart respond to the intensity of his feelings. "I hurt Paul so badly," he choked. He turned away, trying to compose himself. "And I know that must have hurt you as well. Can you forgive me, Raine?"

She nodded, though she wasn't sure what she was forgiving.

Geoff fell silent for a long moment. "I need to confess something," he said finally.

Raine looked at him, her eyebrows raised, but Geoff could no longer meet her eyes. "It was me," he said in a low voice. "It was me that made all the trouble for Paul."

Raine shook her head, confused. "You didn't make the trouble, Geoff. It was Lucinda who told that lie—and of course you weren't the baby's real father. What are you talking about?"

Geoff hesitated, then took a deep breath. "I was angry with Paul, jealous, I guess. We'd always been so close, doing everything together, and then suddenly he seemed to have outgrown me. And I hated him for hurting Christina. I was so angry that when a man came to the house with a coded message Paul had written me, I said I didn't know anything about it. I told the man that Paul had stolen that old code book from me—though really he'd only borrowed it—and I said that I had no idea what he wanted it for. I told him that Paul had been acting very strangely. I didn't mean anything by it, I had no idea the sort of mess I was getting Paul into. I just was angry at him. I was pretty sure the man was some sort of policeman and I thought it would serve Paul right to get in a little trouble. I never dreamt. . ."

He fell silent again.

Raine stared at him, stunned by what he had told her. "I never knew. . ."

He nodded. "No one knew. Except for me. Pretty soon another man came to the house, asking about Paul. He showed me a message in code, but it wasn't written in Paul's handwriting. He asked me if I'd ever seen anything like it before. I wasn't really paying attention, I was impatient to be on my way to the hunt at the Presteigns', and without thinking, I said, yes, I've seen lots of messages like that. The man looked angry and asked me where I'd seen them. I said Paul had given them to me, which was the truth, of course, because he was always writing messages to me in code. The man asked where the messages were now. I had my horse saddled by then, and I just laughed and told him they were all back in my room. I swung up on the horse and rode past him." Geoff shuddered. "That night our house burned and I—" He touched his face. "Nothing was ever the same."

Raine could not speak. Finally, her voice trembling, she asked, "Why did everyone say you had died?"

Geoff shrugged. "I asked my family to spread the story I was dead. I'd been thinking about that man, the red-haired one I'd spoken to the day before our house burned. I knew he was no policeman, and I understood now that he thought I knew something about coded messages. I was afraid he'd come back."

Raine's face was very white. "Red-haired?"

Geoff nodded. "He had red hair. And a tattoo on his hand. I think he must have been a sailor."

∞

Raine waved until Mr. Duncan, Charlotte, and the Mission staff were mere specks on the wharf.

At last she was on board and headed back to Ben. Leaving Papa had been hard, but he had encouraged her to go.

"Find my boy, Raine," he had pled. "I need to make things right before I go to meet the Father."

"I'll find Paul if it takes the rest of my life, Papa," she pledged solemnly. She squeezed his hand. "Pray for me."

Tears glistened in the old man's eyes. "I will, Raine. I will."

She smiled as she gazed out across the waters of the Atlantic. She thought fondly of her father, thankful that they had had the chance to cry together and pray together. *It's like we have a whole new relationship,* she thought gratefully. *Now, if I could only find Paul.*

God was at work. Hadn't Mr. Duncan recommitted his life to the Lord because of that situation? And then there was the telegram she had received from Ben, telling of his surrender to Christ. It would be wonderful to be in his arms again, this time to share his new-found joy.

She had decided to surprise him, so she had not wired her plans to return to Boston. Her heart beat faster as she imagined their reunion.

So much had happened since that day she had waved good-bye to Ben in Boston. She couldn't wait to share the glad news about her father and hoped that Ben had some good news of his own about Paul. *And Aunt Grace will be so relieved that Papa is doing better,* she thought.

The salty spray misted her face, reminding her of all the times she and Ben had stood at the railing on the *Capernaum.* . . .their first tender words. . .their shared hopes and dreams. . .

∞

Near Santa Fe, New Mexico

It was time. Tom had awakened before dawn with a sense of urgency pounding in his breast. It was time to go home.

He roused the sleepy cowhands, prodding them into action while it was still dark. "What's the rush, boss?" Simon drawled.

Tom shrugged. "It's time."

It's time, it's time. . .the phrase seemed to keep beat with Trixie's galloping hooves. The sense of expectancy that Tom had come to know like his shadow crescendoed with every passing mile.

Chapter 9

Ben sat at a corner table in yet another tavern, trying to keep the disgust from showing on his face. Now that he knew Raine was safe, he was concentrating on finding Paul. Raine had told him about her aunt thinking she had seen Paul outside a tavern, and Ben had decided the taverns would be a good place to try and get some information on where Paul had gone. He brushed a fly from his face with a grimace. He never had been able to figure out what the attraction was to these hot, stuffy places. The women were coarse and loud, the atmosphere thick with smoke and schemes. But surely if Paul had been here someone would remember him.

After questioning the people in the tavern, though, he was no closer to finding Paul. He stood blinking in the sunlight, filling his lungs with fresh air. *I just can't go to another one of these places today,* he decided. *One more day won't matter.* Turning to untie the horses, his heart sank as he met the icy gaze of Raine's aunt Grace. She leaned out of her carriage, staring at him in horror as he left the tavern, but before he could call to her, her carriage moved forward with a lurch and rattled away from him.

He pulled his horses to a stop in front of Violet's house, hardly realizing what he was doing, stunned that Raine's aunt would think the worst of him, without giving him a chance to explain. He had to admit that it looked bad for him to be coming out of a tavern, especially since he had recently committed his life to the Lord. *But I didn't do anything wrong,* his heart protested.

Slumping despondently on the edge of the bed, he pondered the situation. *What should I do next? God, please lead me to the right place. I know someone has to remember Paul. I just know it.*

The next morning found him in the seafront district, standing in front of the Red Witch Tavern. Taking a deep breath of the salty air, he heaved the door open. Waiting a moment for his eyes to adjust, he took in the heavy smell of ale and the high-pitched laughter of the women. How he hated this! He ran his fingers through his hair as he leaned back in his chair, catching the eye of the blond-haired girl behind the counter.

She grabbed a glass off the shelf behind her with a practiced motion and hurried over to him. He placed his order for a glass of lemonade and she returned with it promptly. Ben nodded his gratitude, then spoke to her softly, asking her the same question he had asked all the others.

She froze. "Paul?" she whispered, her face white. "Yes, I know Paul."

Ben looked at her trembling lips and wide eyes. "Can we talk outside?" he asked, glancing around at the growing audience.

He opened the door for her, following as she walked stiffly outside.

"Are you all right, Miss. . . ?"

"Hathaway. Christina Hathaway," she supplied. "I'm fine. It's just that. . . I just. . ." She looked up at Ben, her heart in her eyes. "Do you know where Paul is?"

Christina. He remembered something Raine had told him about her childhood friends and understanding glimmered. "No, I don't know where Paul is, Christina," he said regretfully. "I was hoping you could help me find him." He introduced himself, giving her a thumbnail sketch of what he knew of Paul.

"Well, I saw him after the *Aramathea* went down," she said. "He came here to. . .to have a drink."

He came here to say good-bye, Ben surmised. "Did he say anything about where he was going?"

She considered the question. "Not really, I guess," she admitted. "But he always talked about a life-long dream that he had." She smiled wistfully. "He was going to take me with him."

∞

Raine stood on deck, her heart pounding as the familiar sight of the Boston harbor came into view. She could almost feel Ben's arms around her. . .

One of the first passengers to disembark, she waited impatiently, flagging down the first driver she saw. She gave him the address of her uncle's house and settled back in the seat. Glancing about as the carriage pulled away from the waterfront, her heart stopped as she caught a glimpse of a tall, blond man. Ben! She craned her neck, trying to get a closer look. His back was to Raine, but she could see that he was in earnest conversation with a young woman. It sure looked like Ben, but why would he be standing in front of a tavern, talking to someone who looked like she belonged behind the counter pouring drinks?

Raine decided her longing for him was causing her imagination to run away with her. Dismissing the incident, she decided to freshen up a bit. She powdered her nose and patted her short locks into place, smiling as she imagined her aunt's shocked reaction. True, her hair had grown out some, but the rich brown waves still hung well above her shoulders.

Aunt Grace reacted to Raine's new hairstyle better than she had expected, and she barely had time to dash a short note off to Ben before she was pressed into telling of her adventures in London.

Her aunt and uncle were horrified as she told of her abduction. Aunt Grace clucked over her like a mother hen. Uncle John sat silently, at last breathing a quiet "Praise God!" when she had finished bringing them up to date.

Raine sighed as her story drew to a close. "I had so hoped that Papa knew where he was, but. . .maybe Ben found something more," she said hopefully. "I sent him a note to let him know I'm back. Maybe he'll come tonight."

Grace looked uncomfortable. "Raine, I hate to give you bad news. . ."

"Now, Grace," John spoke sternly. "Let the young people work things out for themselves."

Raine looked from one to the other. "What is this all about?"

"Don't you worry about it, Raine. You just go on upstairs and freshen yourself. I'm sure Captain Ben will be coming as soon as he receives your note." John stared hard at his wife.

Upstairs, Raine closed the door to her room and sank down on the bed, relieved that her journey was over. It felt good to have a steady floor beneath her feet. She pondered what to wear when Ben saw her for the first time.

Shaking the folds out of her favorite navy blue dress, she hung it up in the spacious wardrobe. *Maybe I ought to wear the green one. . .* Her thoughts were interrupted by a knock at the door.

She opened the door to her aunt. "Which one do you like best?" she asked, indicating the two dresses.

Her aunt closed the door behind her silently, ignoring the question. She wore an agitated look on her face. "Raine," she whispered. "Your uncle would be very angry if he knew I was up here, but I feel I have to tell you."

Raine frowned as Grace bit her lip. "I don't know how to tell you this, Raine." Her eyes filled with tears. "I was at the dressmaker's shop the other day, you know, on Grape Street."

Raine nodded, wondering what could possibly be so upsetting to her aunt.

"Anyway, I decided to drive down the street to Eva's Bakery to get some of that wonderful rye bread she makes." Raine nodded again, her curiosity growing. "I was almost to Eva's, when I glanced across the street, and I saw Ben come out of a tavern!"

Raine's mind instantly flashed to the man she had seen standing outside the Red Witch Tavern. Surely there must be a reason. . .

"Are you sure it was Ben?"

Her aunt nodded. "I'm sorry, Raine."

"I'd like to be alone, please, Auntie," Raine said softly.

"Of course, dear. I'm so sorry."

Raine eased down onto the bed, her mind reeling. Could that have been Ben who was talking to the tavern girl at the wharf? The more she thought of it, the more sure she became that it had to have been him. She pictured again the way the man had leaned eagerly toward the fancily dressed woman, and her heart froze.

Picturing his face, his tender blue eyes, she just couldn't believe that he would betray her trust. *I'm sure he'll explain the situation to me,* she told herself firmly. *He loves me.*

Pushing aside the nagging doubts, she finally settled on the mint green dress. Brushing her short hair, she wondered what Ben's reaction would be when he saw her. She dabbed on some of her favorite lilac perfume.

By nine o'clock, Raine conceded to the fact that Ben wasn't coming. She thought she had heard someone at the door earlier, but decided she must have been mistaken since no one had called her. Still unwilling to believe the worst of the man she loved, she told herself that he must have had something come up that prevented him from coming to her.

She undressed slowly, laying her dress over the chair. Crawling into bed, she lay staring at the ceiling, feeling more exhausted than she ever had in her life. Her anticipation of seeing Ben and the ensuing disappointment had drained her. "I know you'll come to me tomorrow, my love," she murmured as sleep claimed her.

∞

Ben threw the rest of his luggage into the carriage, closing the door with a grim smile. Stooping down, he placed a kiss on the forehead of the elderly woman in the wheelchair. "Pray for me, Violet," he requested softly.

She nodded, a single tear escaping to run down her wrinkled cheek. "God go with you, Ben," she whispered. "Tell Paul I love him."

Ben stared straight ahead as the train chugged steadily westward. The ache in his heart throbbed louder than the train's engine, and the lonely whistle echoed his feelings. He still couldn't believe that Raine had refused to see him. He had assumed that her aunt would tell her about the tavern incident, but he had fully expected Raine to give him a chance to explain. *I love her, God,* he groaned inwardly. *I thought she loved me, too. Why didn't she trust me enough to let me explain?* Closing his eyes, he was finally lulled to sleep by the clacking of the rails; the pain in his heart dulled by slumber.

∞

"Raine!" The pounding on her door dragged her from a dreamless sleep. She jumped out of bed and grabbed her robe just as her uncle burst into the room.

"Hurry up, Raine!" John was frantic. "Get dressed! We've got to catch Ben before he leaves!"

Raine stared at her uncle, unmoving. He thrust her dress at her. "Hurry! I'll explain on the way." He turned, closing the door behind him.

Catch Ben before he leaves? She had no time to think before her uncle was pounding on her door again. "Raine! Let's go!"

She jerked open the door and flew down the stairs behind her uncle. He fairly pushed her into the carriage, slapping the startled horses with the reins. "We'll be there in a minute, Raine."

Jerking to a stop in front of the train station, he jumped out of the carriage. "Wait here. I'll be right back!" He tore across the crowded lobby, pushing his way to the front of the long ticket line.

She stared after him, dumbfounded, then watched her uncle heading back to the carriage, his shoulders slumping. "We're too late, Raine. I'm sorry."

"What are we too late for, Uncle John?"

"Don't be angry with your aunt, Raine. She did what she thought was best for you, but she's often a short-sighted woman." He sighed. "Ben came to see you last night, Raine. Your aunt told him you didn't want to see him."

"Oh no!" Raine cried. "Why? How could she?"

"I didn't find out about it until this morning. I drove over to Violet's house as soon as I realized what had happened, but she said he had already left for the train station."

"Left?" Raine's voice was strangled.

Her uncle nodded. "Violet said he had gotten some information on Paul, and he decided to follow the lead."

"Where? Where did he go?" Her heart felt like lead.

"I think you'll have to talk to Violet," John replied.

∞

At Violet's house, Raine shook her head in disbelief. "I can't believe what you're telling me, Violet."

"It's true, honey. I really am Paul's grandmother. I hadn't planned on telling anyone, but when John recognized me and Ben found that letter, I decided that it wasn't really all that secret anymore."

"But, how...?"

Violet smiled. "God must have brought Paul to me, Raine. I had started taking in boarders, and then one day, Paul showed up, asking for a room. He had been asking around for a place to stay, and someone had told him my name. By that time he had seen the birth certificate and had guessed the truth about the circumstances surrounding his birth. When he heard my last name, he recognized that it was the same as his mother's, and so he came to me, asking for a place to board." She sighed and her eyes grew misty. "I hadn't seen him since he was three years old, and even though he favors his father, he still carries a distinct resemblance to his mother. My dear, sweet Miriam."

Raine swallowed hard.

"Paul was afraid to ask and I didn't tell him who I was right away." Violet wiped at her eyes. "He was so precious to me! We came to be friends, and after a while I told him what he had already suspected."

"But why did he leave Boston, Violet?"

Violet's face was troubled. "I don't know, Raine. I've asked myself that a million times." She shook her head. "He just seemed like a different person after the ship sank."

"Different?"

"Yes, he seemed. . .skittish. He had some pretty nasty wounds, and at first I attributed his nervousness to the trauma of the shipwreck. But I don't know. It was almost as if he were expecting something bad to happen." Violet lowered her eyes. "I had saved up some money over the years, hoping to give it to Paul someday. He is my only grandchild, you know. I gave it to him after he came back from the *Aramathea* that last time."

Raine was touched by the love she saw in Violet's eyes. "I'm sure Paul was very grateful," she said softly. "But how does Ben fit into the picture?"

"Ben found a letter one night in Paul's old room. The letter was addressed to me, written by my daughter while she was still pregnant with Paul. Ben realized right away what it meant and confronted me with it." She smiled. "He was sure I knew where Paul was and that I was keeping it a secret from everyone."

Raine could see Ben in her mind's eye, trying to coax Violet to tell him where Paul was.

"But then where did Ben go if he didn't know where to look? He couldn't have just made a wild guess." Raine was puzzled.

"Oh my, no!" Violet was astonished. "He talked to someone who knew Paul. She gave him a couple places to start looking. Didn't you know that?"

She? Raine shook her head. *How could this have turned into such a mess?*

"...in Colorado Springs," Violet was saying.

"What?"

"I said, the young woman told Ben that she thought Paul might have gone to Colorado."

"Colorado!" In all her imaginings about Paul, she had never envisioned him going west. "Why in the world...so did Ben go to Colorado?"

Violet nodded. "That he did, Raine. He was looking pretty broken-hearted when he left. If I were you, I would get myself out there, too. I have a feeling that there are two men there who would give a pretty penny to see your face."

⌒

Ben stepped off the train, breathing in the cool mountain air. Exiting the Denver and Rio Grande depot, he gazed appreciatively at the welcoming city of Colorado Springs. Taking in another deep breath of the tangy, pine-scented air, he felt as if he were awakening from a long sleep. The pain that had weighted his heart and deadened his senses for days lifted slightly, allowing him a fresh view on life.

He checked into the Copper Mine Inn, then quickly returned to the outdoors, reveling in the brilliant blue sky and beautiful snow-capped mountains.

The sense of welcome that he had felt initially deepened until it almost felt like a homecoming. Shuffling his feet in the golden autumn leaves, he lifted his hat to feel the warmth of the sun on his head. *Thank You, Father,* he breathed.

The crisp autumn days slid swiftly by. Ben had inquired in all the businesses up and down Pikes Peak Avenue, even questioning some of the streetcar drivers. Nothing.

He made forays to the outlying ranches. Still nothing. Could Christina have been mistaken? Or was Paul refusing to be found? Grasping at straws, he secured a pack mule and spent several days combing the area as far as Cripple Creek. He was awed by the masses of golden-leafed aspens fluttering in the fall breeze and the hidden valleys filled with wildflowers. The Rocky Mountains themselves were beautiful beyond words, filled with crags, meadows, and canyons. But the search for Paul was at another dead end.

Ben had used every resource at his disposal, including an advertisment in the *Colorado Springs Gazette*. Even an afternoon spent poring over the records at the El Paso County courthouse turned up nothing but disappointment. He should just pack up and go back to London; at least he could do what Paul had asked him to do in his letter. But he wanted to see Paul first, make sure he was really the man Ben thought he was. He couldn't give up. Not yet.

The days slipped into weeks, then into a month. He prayed continually for wisdom and guidance, gradually feeling the now-familiar peace of God surround him. Though his heart still ached for Raine, he had begun to sense that God had brought him here for a specific purpose. Lying in bed at night, he would feel the undeniable tug on his heart.

He had grown uncomfortable with the thought of running the shipping business for the rest of his life. *But that's all I know how to do,* he reminded himself. *Well, except for. . .* He sat up abruptly. *Surely not! Surely You aren't calling me to be a. . .a pastor!* He could hardly think it. He lay back down slowly, his thoughts racing. *But I haven't known You for very long. Surely I'm not ready to. . .to lead others?*

It was true that there seemed to be a dearth of churches in the outlying areas. Where did the ranchers and country folk go to church? He would wager that they would feel too uncomfortable to attend the imposing churches he had noticed in town. *But why choose me, God? I don't know if I could do it.*

"*In all thy ways acknowledge Him, and He shall direct thy paths.*" The scripture rang in his mind with such clarity that he knew it would change his life forever.

∞

He awoke the next morning, a sense of wonder filling his heart. "Please lead me, Father," he prayed earnestly. "And please minister to Raine. I love her so, Father. I don't want to be without her for the rest of my life. Please bring her back to me!"

He sat in the hotel dining room, absently chewing his apple pie. He couldn't believe he was actually considering the possibility of staying in Colorado Springs, yet he could not deny the tugging at his heart that grew stronger day by day. *I'd have to go to London to sell my share of the business,* he mused. *While I'm there I'll see those papers of Paul's get into the right hands.* He grinned in spite of himself. *Father will never believe that I'm finally going to quit sailing.* He chuckled out loud, then sobered. *Am I? Am I willing to sell a thriving business to become a cowboy preacher?*

Chapter 10

God go with you!" The farewells of Raine's aunt and uncle rang in her ears. Settling herself into a seat by the window, she craned her neck. Yes, they were still there, waving furiously as the train huffed away from the station.

She waved back until the train rounded the first bend. Sitting back with a sigh, she closed her eyes, glad for the first real moment of quiet she had had in quite awhile. It seemed like she had done nothing but rush, rush, rush since Ben left two weeks ago. But now she was finally headed westward.

West! Never in a million years had she thought that her search for Paul would lead her to a place like Colorado. She pictured herself arriving at the depot in Colorado Springs to find it surrounded by Indians. Or maybe the cowboys made sure the Indians stayed in the mountains.

She shivered. What kind of place was she going to? Surely there would be some place for her to stay. She remembered the photographs of log cabins she had seen once. *I don't know if I'm ready for this,* she thought. But maybe Ben had already found Paul, and she wouldn't have to stay in that wild country at all. Not that she was scared, exactly. Just a bit anxious.

It's only for a little while, she told herself. Yet somehow, she had a feeling deep within her heart that it would be a long, long time before she saw Boston again. Aunt Grace evidently had the same feeling.

"It's all my fault," Grace had sobbed. "If I hadn't sent Ben away, you wouldn't be running off all alone to that forsaken place." She blew her nose loudly. "How are you even going to find Ben once you get there?"

"Now Gracie, God works in mysterious ways. If God is sending Raine to Colorado, He'll take care of her."

Good old Uncle John. Raine smiled fondly as she recalled his parting comment to her.

"You just trust the Lord, Raine. I've got a feeling He has something amazing waiting for you."

"I do, too, Uncle John. I do, too," she murmured now, watching the miles roll by. *What is it, Father?* she questioned silently.

Squirming around in an attempt to find a more comfortable position, her eye fell on the small package Christina had thrust into her hand just before she left. Following a hunch, Raine had taken a jaunt down to the waterfront the day before she was to leave for Colorado. Then it was just a matter of waiting before Christina slipped out of the door of the Red Witch tavern.

"So you're the woman I saw Ben talking to," Raine exclaimed after she and Christina had hugged each other.

Christina nodded. "God must have led him to me. Although he said he'd been searching in all the taverns, asking if anyone knew anything about Paul."

"And you were able to tell Ben where Paul is now?"

Christina's eyes clouded. "I haven't heard from Paul for over three years now. But he always dreamed of going west, to Colorado."

"And that's where I'm headed now." Raine shook her head. "I can't believe I have to go now, when I've just found you, Christina."

Her old friend nodded. "I know. It's so good to see you. I'd love for us to spend some time together."

"Why don't you go to Colorado with me? You could find a nice place to work out there. Maybe be a seamstress or something."

Despair filled Christina's eyes. "I would give anything to go, Raine. But I'm bound for three more months."

"Well, maybe we'll all be back by then. Christy—" Raine stopped. She looked at Christina thoughtfully, afraid to ask the question that hovered on her lips.

"You're wondering why Paul didn't take me with him." Christina sighed. "It's a long story, Raine, but suffice it to say that he did it to protect me."

Raine raised her eyebrows.

"I think Paul will have to be the one to explain it to you, Raine. I don't think I even know the whole story."

She could see that Christina had said all she was going to say. "You love him."

"Yes. I always have. You know that."

Raine nodded.

"Find him for me, Ray. He needs me."

Raine felt her throat get tight. "I'll do my best, Christy. Pray for me."

"Always." Christina bit her lip. "Would you give this to him when you find him?"

Raine reached out for the small package, asking no questions.

By the third day of her journey, Raine's anticipation had grown to a feverish pitch. How close was she to finding Paul? Maybe Ben had already found him, and they would both be waiting for her at the depot. No, that was silly. Neither of them even knew she was coming. Then, too, maybe Ben was still upset with her. She couldn't wait to set everything straight again. She pictured their reunion, her stomach fluttering at the thought of it. She finally took to getting off the train at every stop, pacing around the boarding area to relieve some of her pent-up energy.

She lay in her berth that night, lulled into drowsiness by the steady clacking of the train wheels. Tomorrow, tomorrow, tomorrow, they seemed to sing. Tomorrow—what would she find? She felt as if she were being drawn to Colorado by more than the strong engine of the train. Her heart was strangely pulled; there seemed to be almost a yearning. *Show me, Father. What would You have me to do?*

Sometime during the night, she awoke abruptly. Someone was having a whispered conversation outside her berth. She lay frozen, her heart pounding wildly.

"She doesn't know anything, I tell you!" She heard a man's loud whisper.

"Shut up! I'll take care of this," someone else growled softly.

"It's not time yet! We need to wait and see if Oliver. . ."

The men's voices trailed off as they moved away. She blew out her breath, her body alternating cold and hot with fear. She could never forget that voice. What was he doing on this train? Was it possible that he had trailed her all the way from London, waiting for a chance to. . .to. . . She couldn't finish the thought. *Oh*

God, please help me.

The day dawned bright and clear, cheering Raine after her sleepless night. Looking around, she could hardly believe that the whispered conversation had really taken place. Was it all a bad dream? The ugly voice floated back to her. She shook her head. It wasn't a dream. *Maybe they weren't talking about me,* she tried to convince herself. She smiled wryly, knowing she was fooling herself if she believed that.

~

She was unprepared for the feeling of homecoming that swept over her as she stepped off the platform in Colorado Springs. Drinking in the beauty of the land around her, her heart lifted in a song of praise. She had never seen country like this; it seemed that one could see for miles and miles in all directions—and there was not one cowboy or Indian in sight.

The snow-capped Rockies seemed to surround her, enfolding her in the wonder of their age-old beauty. Even the very air seemed to dance with life and expectancy, making her want to run and skip. She gathered her bags, letting the beauty and joy seep into her soul as she made her way down Pikes Peak Avenue. Waiting until the streetcar had gone past, she crossed the street to the telegraph office. Aunt Grace would never believe it, she thought with a smile. Colorado Springs was certainly no cow town.

She composed a short telegram, letting her aunt and uncle know she had arrived in one piece. The young clerk took the message, eyes widening slightly as he read her name. "If you're Raine Thomas, then I've got a telegram for you. Arrived yesterday."

She lifted her eyebrows in surprise, accepting the paper from the clerk.

RAINE STOP RECEIVED LETTER FROM BEN *Stop*
Copper Mine Inn *Stop* Love Violet

Her heart leapt. "Where is the Copper Mine Inn, please?"

The young man directed her to the inn, grinning and shaking

her head as she tried to pay him. She hurried down the street in the direction he had pointed her, nearly running through the hotel's doors. In a breathless voice, she asked the clerk about Ben.

"Yes ma'am. Ben Thackeray had a room here. But I'm afraid he left yesterday."

"Left?" Had she missed him again?

"Yes'm. Don't know where he went. Sure left in a hurry."

Raine felt suddenly weary. "Do you have a room available?"

She made sure the door was locked securely before she lay across the hard bed. It felt good to be away from the constant rocking motion of the train. *Where has Ben gone,* she wondered, so discouraged that tears pooled in her eyes. She tried to think where he could have headed. Maybe he found Paul, and they both left for Boston.

She sat straight up at the thought, then slumped back down against the headboard. *Surely someone would have gotten the message to me if that had happened.* As it was, the telegram from Violet didn't say anything about him leaving. Raine's thoughts chased each other in circles until she finally fell asleep, the yearning to be held once again in Ben's arms was her last conscious thought.

She awoke feeling refreshed. Though her heart ached for Ben, she still felt a sense of anticipation as she prepared for the day. After all, she had come here to find her brother as well as Ben, so she might as well give it her best shot. Opening her Bible, her fingers turned directly to the often-read passage in Isaiah. Once again she gained strength as she read the promise God had given her in London. . . *"I will bring the blind by a way that they have not known; I will lead them in paths that they knew not. . ."* "Thank You for leading me thus far, Father," she prayed. "Please continue to guide me. . ."

She set out in determination. She sought out every place she could think of where someone might know her brother. After days of asking, she was almost ready to concede defeat. *God, I thought You led me here,* she cried one evening. Her feet were aching from so much walking, and the small amount of savings she had brought with her was dwindling along with her hope.

"Here I am in a strange town all by myself, without Ben—or

Paul," she complained to the blank walls. "And with an evil man chasing me." True, she hadn't actually seen Red Hair since she escaped from him in London, but it had to have been him she heard that night on the train. She shuddered at the thoughts that were triggered in her mind just by recalling his voice. What were they talking about anyway? She was sure she had heard the name Oliver.

A new thought struck her. Could Paul still be living under an alias, even all this distance from Boston? Perhaps he was so afraid of being found, he wasn't using his own name at all. Maybe she had been going about this the wrong way.

She began making the rounds again the next day, this time describing Paul. Most people still shook their heads, but a few thought they might know someone who looked like the man she described. After a long discouraging day, she had met a rancher named Andrew, a shopkeeper named Bjorn, and two cowboys named Charlie, all of whom were very nice, but they weren't Paul.

Shoulders drooping, she let the tears fall freely. *I can't hear You anymore, Father. I thought I was trusting You, but I...* She was startled by a knock on the door. Hastily wiping away the tears, she opened the door.

The young clerk from the telegraph office shifted nervously from one foot to the other. "Ma'am? Sorry to bother you." He eyed her tear-streaked face. "I heard you was lookin' for your brother."

She nodded.

"Well, I might know somethin' about him."

Raine's heart leapt.

"I heard you explainin' what he looked like and, well, I think I've seen him before."

"You've seen Paul?" she whispered.

"I ain't for sure, ma'am. But I'm pretty good at noticin' things, and I noticed a man before that sounds like him."

"Why did you notice him? Is he a stranger?"

"Nah, he's not a stranger. He's a rancher that lives 'round here. I always notice him 'cause of that big ol' scar on his face."

Scar? Paul doesn't have a scar. . .or does he? Her mind flashed back to the first time she met Violet . . . *"I was scared to death when I saw him come limping in, his head and face all covered in bandages. . .'"* Violet had said.

"Where did you say this man lives?" she asked cautiously.

"Don't know, ma'am. I jest know he lives south of here. Comes in for supplies now and then."

A rancher that lived to the south. Not a very big clue, but the best so far. "Thank you so much." She smiled at the young man. "I'll let you know if I find him."

The next morning found her driving southward. Setting her jaw, she stared out intently over the backs of her rented team. The man at the livery stable had objected when she asked to rent the team and wagon.

"I'll take my business elsewhere, then," she said stubbornly, turning to go. The man relented, eyeing her dubiously as she clambered up onto the seat. *I must look more confident than I feel,* she chuckled. In reality, she had only driven a team of horses once or twice in her life. But nothing was going to stop her from finding Paul after coming this far.

She stopped at the first ranch south of Colorado Springs, receiving a warm welcome, but no sign of Paul. The young ranch wife waved wistfully as Raine started down the road. She waved back, wishing she had time to stay and visit. It would be nice to have a friend here.

The drive to the next ranch was interminable. Surely she hadn't misunderstood the directions. She frowned. It was hot enough out here to be the fourth of July. *September was never this hot in London,* she thought as she felt the perspiration run down between her shoulder blades. Patting the moisture off her face as she finally neared the next ranch, she was startled to be greeted by shouting children, dogs yipping joyously at their heels. Why weren't these children in school?

She smiled at the children as she climbed down stiffly. Those wagon seats sure weren't made for comfort. "Is your mama home?" she asked.

"Yes'm." The oldest girl spoke up politely. "I'll go fetch her for ya."

The younger children grouped around Raine. In a flash, she was back at the Mission, surrounded by her children.

"Are you the teacher, ma'am?" a small girl asked shyly.

"Naw, she's too pretty to be a teacher, Polly." The little girl's brother glared at her. "She's prob'ly a singer or somethin'."

Raine almost laughed out loud. "Well, I *am* a teacher, Polly," she said, smiling. "But I don't think I'm the one you're expecting." *That's why these children aren't in school at this time of year*, she thought, relieved. *They must be waiting for a new teacher.*

"Oh yes, Ma'am. You are the one. Mama said. . ."

"What did Mama say?" A young woman with twinkling gray eyes and a pleasant face joined the small group.

"Mama! This is the teacher!"

"Oh?" The woman looked from her young daughter's animated face to Raine's bewildered expression. "Won't you come in for a cool drink, Miss. . . ?"

"Thomas. Raine Thomas. Yes, I would like that." Raine found herself drawn to the young ranch family.

"I'm Emily Johnston." The woman introduced herself as she bustled around the kitchen, placing a plate of still-warm cookies on the table. "There. Help yourself." She sat down then, pushing her black hair back with a small hand. "Now, what was Polly jabbering about? She's my talker." She shook her head with a smile.

Raine responded immediately to Emily's warm smile. "I don't know, Emily. Your children greeted me when I pulled into the yard. Polly asked me if I was the teacher." She wrinkled her brow. "I *am* a teacher, but I'm not. . ."

Emily's eyes opened wide. "You really are a teacher?"

Raine nodded "Yes, but. . ."

"Do you love God?"

"Yes, but I. . ."

"Then you are the teacher."

"What?" Raine was shocked as Emily's eyes suddenly filled with tears.

"I've been praying and praying that God would send a teacher for my little ones. He must have sent you."

"But I'm not. . ."

"How did you know to come to our ranch?" Emily's eyes were sparkling with excitement now.

"Well, I. . ." Raine hated to disappoint the lovely woman in front of her, but. . . "Could you explain a little more of the situation to me?" she heard herself saying. What was she thinking? She couldn't just suddenly be "the teacher." What about Paul, not to mention Ben?

"Yes, yes of course. I was just so excited that you're finally here!" Emily smiled wistfully. "None of the children who live this far from town go to school, because there's not a school close enough for them to attend. We do our best with them at home, but I'm afraid it's not enough. We've all been praying that God would send a teacher to open a school close by, and here you are!"

What? Raine blinked. All this anticipation that she'd been feeling—could it be that God had a work for her to do in this beautiful country?

"I'll need to come back and talk to you about it some more, Emily," she found herself saying. "Could I come by next week?"

"Please do, Raine. I'll be waiting." Emily's face was as eager as little Polly's.

Raine waved as she turned to leave, the joy on the children's faces tugging at her heart. Shaken, she stopped the wagon as soon as she was out of sight of the Johnston ranch. A shiver of excitement quivered through her as the thought took hold. Could it be possible that God had brought her all the way to America to fulfill the call she knew He had placed on her life? She sat under the shade of a tree several minutes longer, considering the idea.

She had always sort of assumed that when she found Paul, they would both go back to England, and then. . .and then what? Paul and Christina would get married, and she would be alone. . .again. And what of Ben? Did he really love her? He had never mentioned marriage, though she had dreamed about the day she would become Mrs. Benjamin Luke Thackeray. But now. . .

Finally climbing back into the wagon, she realized that she had not even spoken with Emily about her real reason for coming to the ranch. Shrugging, she urged the horses on, making the rounds of a few more ranches before heading wearily back to town. If Paul was anywhere around here, she would find him. God would just have to take care of the rest.

By the time she pulled up in front of the livery stable, her backside ached so badly she wondered how she would walk the short distance back to the hotel. She handed the reins over to the stable hand, glaring at him as he flashed her a grin. She suppressed a groan as she crawled down from the wagon seat, silently thanking God the hotel wasn't too far.

The hot water soothed her aching muscles as she leaned back in the tub with a sigh. She hadn't found her brother, but maybe she had found something else. The small faces of Emily's children seemed to float in front of her eyes along with the steam. Her heart pulled her toward them, yet. . . *Paul! I have to find you. I can't just give up searching for you. Where are you?* Her heart was torn. *Lord Jesus, I feel Your presence, and I know You led me this far. But what do I do now?*

She crawled out of the tub and into bed, weary beyond belief. She felt like a dog chasing its own tail, her thoughts and prayers spinning in endless circles. Determined to continue the search for Paul, she tried pushing the faces of the children out of her mind. Finally falling into a fitful sleep, her dreams were filled with crying children, the faces of Emily's children mingling strangely with those of the children she had left behind at the Mission. She sat up in bed, suddenly wide awake, gripped with the conviction that God wanted her here in Colorado, teaching.

Dawn brightened the sky with changing hues of pink and yellow. Raine groaned and rolled over, putting the pillow over her head. She tried to tell herself that her experience in the night had been only a dream, but memories of other times that God had carefully led her flashed through her mind. She jumped up from the bed, nearly passing out from the sudden action.

She stomped over to the mirror and glared at her reflection, then she let her gaze roam to the large window. *It's not that I don't want to teach, but I thought You sent me here to find Paul, Father,* she argued weakly. Staring out the window several minutes longer, she received no more answer than the one she already knew in her heart.

Unable to deny it any longer, she blew out a long sigh. *I'll do it, Father,* she whispered.

⁂

El Paso County, Colorado

Trixie snorted joyfully as she trotted through the gates of the Crooked P Ranch. "I agree with you wholeheartedly, Trix." Her weary rider patted her neck affectionately. "It's been a long trip home."

Tom slid stiffly from the saddle, turning Trixie's reins over to the waiting cowhand. "Thanks, Pete." He let his eyes rove over the familiar landscape as he trudged to the ranch house. "Looks the same to me," he muttered, disappointed. Somehow, he had expected something to be different when he arrived home.

What is it that I keep expecting to happen? Am I going crazy? Pushing open the door with a sigh, the strange sense of urgency flooded over him again. Finally dropping to his knees, he cried out. "God, I can't stand it any longer. What would You have me to do?"

⁂

A few days later, Tom sat nursing a cup of coffee at a back table in the Lantern Hotel, his thoughts a million miles away. He had gained a measure of peace since his prayer the night he returned from Santa Fe, but there was still something gnawing at him. *God, what do I need to do? I can't live with this feeling hanging over me constantly. . .*

"Heard 'bout the new schoolmarm since ya been back, Cox?"

The booming voice jolted Tom from his reverie. He raised his eyebrows questioningly over the rim of his mug.

"Purty little thing. Wants to start a school for the rancher's children." The man shook his head as he slid into the chair across from Tom. "Good idea, I reckon, but it sure seems a waste of a good woman, if ya know what I mean."

Tom smiled across at his friend. "Yeah, I know what ya mean, Jackson," he said, gently mocking the older man's western drawl.

"Why don't you just get yourself a wife? Then you wouldn't have to worry yourself over every pretty new woman that comes to town."

"I'm tryin', I'm tryin'!" Jackson peered through his glasses at Tom. "Why don't you?" He asked pointedly.

Tom glanced away. "Been too busy," he muttered, even as a vision of beautiful blue eyes and golden curls grew in his mind. Pushing aside the painful memory, he stood. "Got to get back to work, Jackson. I've been gone too long."

Jackson nodded. "See ya, Cox. Watch out for that schoolmarm!"

Jackson's cackle followed Tom as he stepped out of the hotel door. Tom snorted. *Why would I be interested in a schoolmarm?* Striding into the general store, he picked up his supplies and headed back to the Crooked P, unaware of curious eyes watching his every move.

Chapter 11

London, England

Ben tapped his foot impatiently, glancing at his watch. "I can't believe how long this is taking," he complained to himself. Finally the door opened. "Mr. Rosen will see you now."

Ben sprang up in relief. Striding into the lawyer's office, he plunked the packet of papers down on the desk. "Here they are, Frank. What do I need to sign?"

The lawyer raised an eyebrow. "I still can't believe you're going through with this, Ben."

He shrugged. "I'm not going to change my mind, Frank. Just do what you need to do to make it legal."

Shaking his head, the young lawyer pulled out several forms. "You'll need to sign here. And here."

Ben sat back with a satisfied smile. Minutes later, he stood in front of the small house he had not seen in too many years. Tucking the papers into his breast pocket, he knocked firmly on the door.

"Hello, Father."

"Ben?" The older man threw the door open wide, his face lit with one of the only smiles Ben had ever seen there. He reached for his son eagerly as if to embrace him, then ended up patting him awkwardly on the shoulder. "Come in, come in!"

Ben stepped through the door. The house still smelled the same, a heavenly mixture of warm bread, freshly-washed clothes, and lavender sachets. Instantly he was ten years old again.

"Where's Mother?"

"I'll get her." His father started toward the kitchen, glancing back as if to make sure his son was still there. Ben took a deep breath, gathering his thoughts. Would she welcome him as his father had? He knew he must have hurt her by staying away so long. Perhaps she would refuse to see him.

He glanced up as she flew into the room. Her outstretched arms and radiant smile erased any doubts. Lifting her off her feet in an enormous hug, Ben felt tears spring into his eyes. "I've been wrong to stay away for so long," he began, looking from one parent to the other. "I've been bitter at you for the way I was raised." He sketched in the details of his life since they had parted ways, ending with a heartfelt plea. "Since I've accepted Christ as my Savior, I've realized that I need to ask your forgiveness for being angry and bitter against you. Will you forgive me?"

His father stared at him, tears flowing freely down his lined cheeks. "Ben—your mother and I are the ones who need to ask forgiveness. We have finally started to learn about the joy and peace that comes with a real relationship with Jesus Christ. Can you ever forgive us for leading you in the wrong way?"

❦

Ben pushed his plate away. "Mother, that was delicious. I can't eat another bite." His mother smiled, and Ben was struck once again by how much his parents had changed. He had accepted their offer for him to stay with them and had enjoyed the time immensely. But it was time to be heading back to where his heart told him he belonged.

"Father, Mother." They both looked up at his serious tone. "I have something to tell you. God has called me. . ." He described the yearning in his heart to serve as pastor to the hard-working ranchers near Colorado Springs. "Anyway, I sold my share of the shipping company." He paused, waiting for his words to sink in. "I want you to have half of the money."

❦

Ben had one more piece of business to take care of in London. When he accomplished his goal, the results were better than he had ever dared to hope. His heart was so light that he felt as though he could fly across the Atlantic. Now if only he could find Paul. . .

The next day found Ben on the deck of a ship, waving until his arm ached. The memory of his parents' faces as they stood arm in arm on the wharf was something he would treasure forever. There was a new sparkle in his mother's eye, and the look on his father's face could only be described as joyful.

What a blessing that they have truly come to know You, Father. Looking out across the calm waters of the Atlantic, his smile dissolved as he thought of a different time, a different ship. He remembered the way Raine's dusky green eyes had sparkled with laughter as they talked together on so many cool, moonlit evenings. He could almost feel her silky hair slipping through his fingers, the smell of her skin when he kissed her. . . *God, if there's any way, please give her back to me.*

Some days he could almost pretend that he had never given his heart away, but on days like this, the longing became unbearable. *I don't want to live my whole life without her, Lord Jesus. But I want to do Your will. If You mean for me to be alone, then I'm going to need Your strength. . .*

⌒

"Raine's not here?" Ben stared at Raine's uncle John in consternation.

"I'm sorry, son. We tried to catch you before you left, but we were too late."

Ben shook his head in disbelief. "I must have just missed her. I can't believe she's been in Colorado all this time while I've been in London. If I'd come back to Boston before I left for England, at least I would have known. But I was in such a hurry to take care of my shipping business and have it done, that I left straight from New York. What a mess!"

"I have a feeling everything's going to work out just fine, Captain Ben. You do still love her, don't you?"

"More than I thought possible. And all this time I thought she had believed the worst about me." He grinned ruefully. "Things sure can get twisted around, can't they?"

"That's for certain." John chuckled. "But I think things will untwist pretty quickly once you have that niece of mine in your arms again."

Ben felt the familiar longing press against his heart. "I hope so, John," he said softly. "I hope so."

Raine sighed as she went to the door of her small hotel room. Would she ever have a moment of peace? Reluctantly pulling the door open a crack, she opened it wider when she recognized the young telegraph clerk. "Hello, Clay."

He was fairly vibrating with excitement. "I've seen him again, Miss Thomas! The man with the scar!"

Raine's heart leapt. "Where?"

"He was right here in town. I seen him eatin' at the Lantern Hotel. Then he went to the store, then left town." Clay hopped from foot to foot. "I heard another man call him 'Cox.'"

"Cox?" Raine wrinkled her brow. "But my brother's name is. . ." Her voice trailed off. *Of course. Grandfather's name was Oliver Cox.* "Thank you, Clay!" She smiled at him. "I think you've been a great help to me today."

Alone once again, Raine mulled over the new clue. If this man were Paul, how could she find out for sure? She grabbed her hat. She would just go and see for herself.

Her heart sank as the woman at the Lantern Hotel shook her head. "I remember seeing a man that sounds like the one you're after, but I surely don't know his name." The motherly woman looked at Raine kindly. "Are you in trouble, child?"

"Trouble?" Raine shook her head. Suddenly, the color flooded to her cheeks as she realized what the woman meant. "Oh no, ma'am." She hastened to clear herself. "I'm looking for my brother."

Covering her flaming cheeks with her hands, Raine missed the look of compassion in the woman's eyes. "Well, the best of luck to you, child."

Raine turned to go. Almost to the door, she looked up just in time to avoid crashing into an enormous man. "I beg your pardon," she murmured, her eyes glued to the man's chest in embarrassment.

"Not at all, not at all, little lady," he boomed. "You're the new schoolmarm, aren't you?"

She jerked her gaze back up to the man's twinkling eyes. "Yes, I am. But how——?"

The man laughed. "Aw, I make it my business to know just about everything going on in this town. In fact, I couldn't help but hearing part of your conversation with Nancy here." He gestured to the woman Raine had just spoken to. "I reckon I could tell you a bit about the man you're looking for."

Raine stared at him. "You know Paul?" She whispered.

"I don't know about any Paul, but I do know the man you described to Nancy. Name's Tom Cox. Owns a ranch south of here. Why is it you're looking for Tom?"

He certainly isn't shy, she thought, amused. "Actually, I'm not certain that it's Tom I want to see, Mr. . . ?"

"Jackson. Just Jackson, no Mister. Why are you asking for Tom if you don't know if you want to see him?"

She sighed. "It's a long story, Mr.—Jackson."

Jackson took the hint and stopped probing. "Well, it was mighty fine to meet you. I've got to get going now, myself."

Raine put out a small hand. "Thank you for telling me about Tom," she said sincerely.

Jackson shook her hand until she was sure it would fall off. "Most welcome, ma'am. Most welcome."

Back in her room, Raine stood staring out her window, deep in thought. The growing twilight mimicked her thoughts—fuzzily outlined ideas, barely discernable theories swathed in shadows. *Tom Cox, Cox, Cox.* She had been unable to think of little else, the man's name beating a rhythm in her brain.

She lay down with a sigh, images of a dark-haired man with a scar merging with loving thoughts of a tall, golden-haired man. Restless, she tossed back and forth. "Ben, please come to me," she mumbled as her dreams became more real. "I need you. No one will believe me that Paul Thomas is my brother. . .Paul Thomas has a scar. . .Tom Cox, Paul T. . ."

She woke with a start, her dream still vivid in her mind. She knew suddenly without a doubt that Tom was short for Thomas and since Cox was their grandfather's name; it had to be Paul. She hugged the pillow to her chest, too excited to go back to sleep. *Surely I can find his ranch now that I know his name,* she reasoned.

Maybe Jackson will help me in the morning. Maybe he even knows where the ranch is. She made joyful plans, whiling away the long hours of the night. The only pain left to mar her joy was Ben's absence.

∞

"Well, I reckon I could spare some time to drive a pretty woman out to the Crooked P Ranch." Jackson was delighted with Raine's request. "And even if that ol' Tom Cox isn't your brother, I reckon he wouldn't complain any about having the new schoolmarm pay him a visit."

Raine smiled in embarrassment. Jackson was a nice enough man, but he was so—big. Everything about him was big, from his boots to his voice.

"I'm ready to go now, if you are," she said politely.

"Well, just climb right up here into the wagon seat then, little lady. We'll be out to the Crooked P before you know it." He clucked to the horses, waving his hat proudly at every man on the street. "They just wish they were so lucky to have the schoolmarm ride with one of them," he boomed to Raine.

Raine doubted that it really mattered to anyone who Jackson was driving around in his wagon. Nevertheless, she ducked her head slightly, cringing under the curious stares of everyone they passed. Soon they were out of town, and she let out a relieved sigh. "How far is it to Paul's—I mean Tom's ranch?"

"Little ways yet," was Jackson's cheerful reply. "Aren't those mountains about the prettiest sight you ever laid eyes on?"

Raine had to agree that the beauty of this country was breathtaking. At the moment, though, all her thoughts were focused on what awaited her at the Crooked P Ranch. Could it really be possible, after all these years? She could hardly imagine being in her brother's strong arms once again, seeing his precious face. . .and just wait until she wrote and told Papa! What a wonderful. . .

". . .and that over there is one of those pesky little prairie dogs." Raine's thoughts were jerked back to the present as Jackson waved a hand in her direction. "They dig those little burrows, then the horses step in them and break their leg. Yep, those prairie dogs sure are a nuisance. Kinda cute little critters though."

Raine looked around. Sure enough, there were little mounds of dirt dotting the prairie as far as the eye could see. Anxious prairie dogs stood up on tiny hind legs, prepared to dive for safety at the slightest hint of danger.

Jackson glanced at her. "You must be pretty excited to see Tom again," he said, his voice as near to quiet as he could manage.

Raine nodded, scanning the prairie as if she would see Paul suddenly materialize before her. "Yes, it's been a long time, Jackson." Her voice quivered as a sudden thought assailed her. "I just hope he wants to see me."

Jackson's voice dropped even lower. "Aw, Miss Thomas. Don't you worry. That old rascal has been pining away about something ever since I knew him. Never would tell me about it. I bet he's just dying to see you."

"I hope so," Raine said quietly.

⊙

Tom squinted at the small cloud of dust in the distance. *Must be Jess coming over to drive those stray calves of his home,* he decided. Swinging up on Trixie's broad back, Tom rode out to meet his neighbor. Drawing closer to the dusty cloud, he realized that it wasn't a lone rider as he had expected, but a wagon. He squinted at it, frowning as he recognized the driver. *Jackson! Why in the world is he coming out here in the middle of the day?* Usually only bad news could tear a rancher away from a hard day's work; visiting was reserved for evenings when the work was done.

Tom nudged Trixie into a gallop, his heart beating faster in spite of himself. Maybe someone had finally fallen into that dry well near the Baxter's. He knew it was going to happen one of these days. Or maybe it was Grandma Lydia. The dear old saint had been barely clinging to life for days now. . .

"I brought the schoolmarm out to meet ya, Tom!"

Tom barely heard Jackson's shout over the pounding of Trixie's hooves, but his heart slowed its frantic pace as he noticed Jackson's smile. Yanking Trixie to a halt, Tom stared at the woman sitting next to Jackson. Her face swam before his eyes as a loud rushing filled his ears. He shook his head in disbelief, then raised his eyes slowly to meet hers.

"Raine?"

She was out of the wagon almost before he could dismount. Throwing her arms around his neck, she wept until there were no more tears. "Oh Paul! It's really you! Thank God I finally found you!"

Paul let his sister cry, his own tears falling thick and fast onto her hair. Holding her tightly, he felt the last of the restlessness in his soul all but vanish. All the waiting, the longing; this was what his heart had needed. Pushing her away gently, he gazed lovingly at her face. She had grown into a beautiful woman since he had last seen her. He took in the short hair, the beautiful eyes filled with joy and yet somehow marked with sadness. "It's time for us to talk, little sister," he said huskily.

Raine nodded, too full of emotion to speak. Suddenly remembering Jackson, she turned to find that he had tactfully slipped away.

Paul helped Raine mount Trixie. Swinging up on the patient horse, Paul turned her toward the house. "Home, girl," he murmured.

Raine clasped her brother's waist tightly as they rode, laying her head on his strong back. *Thank You, Father.*

∞

"So—start at the beginning, Ray." Raine was ensconced in the only comfortable chair Paul owned. He sat on a stool at her feet, his face eager.

"Well, first of all, you have to understand that I didn't receive any of your letters, except one. That's partly why it took me so long to find you."

"What?" Paul jumped to his feet. "I must have written you a hundred letters since I first left home. I finally gave up writing about the time I came out here. I didn't dare. But how could you not. . ." His voice trailed off as understanding dawned. "It was Papa, wasn't it?" he asked flatly.

"I'm afraid so, Paul. All that time I couldn't understand why you didn't write me any letters, and Papa was destroying them all before

I could see them." Raine's smile was sad. "But he is sorry, Paul. He begged me to forgive him."

Paul shook his head. "I thought that he had poisoned you against me, and that's why you never answered any of my letters." He turned his head so that Raine could not see the tears shimmering in his eyes. "Back in Boston—and even here in Colorado—I checked my mailbox every week, hoping somehow that you still loved me and cared about me."

Raine slipped from her chair, gathering her brother into her arms like a small child. "I never stopped loving you, Paul. I thought I would die of loneliness when you left."

"Me, too," he whispered.

She wiped the tears from her face. "I'm never going to get through the whole story if we don't stop crying!" She laughed shakily.

Many minutes and many tears later, Paul sat looking at his sister in amazement. "You've grown into a strong woman, Raine Thomas," he said quietly. He frowned. "Tell me again about the man who abducted you."

Raine described the man once again, watching as her brother's face paled. "I can't believe he would go that far." Paul gritted his teeth. "I'm sure he's the same man who has been after me, Raine. His name is Dag."

"You know who he is?"

Paul nodded grimly. "I know all too well. He tried to kill me." Determined not to dwell on the subject, he made an effort to smile at Raine. "We can talk about that later. I know you have a few questions of your own that I need to answer."

She sensed his need to change the topic of conversation. "Yes, I have quite a few questions that need answering, as a matter of fact," she replied with mock sternness.

He flashed her a boyish grin. "It's not that bad is it?"

"You didn't make it very easy on me, big brother. What was the idea of telling everyone we were married?"

Paul smiled at the look of reproach on her face. "Seriously, I never dreamed it would make trouble for you. I didn't do it purposely at first." He shook his head, remembering.

Ben took a long look at the photograph. "So this is your girl," he said slowly. "She's beautiful."

Paul opened his mouth to correct Ben, then snapped it shut. For some reason, it didn't seem like a bad idea to let Ben assume that Raine was his fiancée. He didn't know Ben well then, and he wasn't sure he liked the look on Ben's face as he gazed at the photograph of Raine. Then somehow, the lie had mushroomed.

"I didn't always do the right thing at that point in my life, Raine." Paul hung his head. "After I let Ben believe that you and I were engaged, it got easier to lie about it. I didn't intend for it to turn into such a big thing, but I guess I'm a coward."

Raine stared at her brother in confusion. "But why?"

"I figured that if I let it slip to the other crew members that I was married, maybe they wouldn't be so rough on me." He looked at Raine pleadingly. "I didn't mean to cause you trouble. It's just that it was hard enough to stay away from the tavern, and when my fellow sailors thought I was married, they didn't pressure me so much about, well, the girls." Paul ended his sentence in embarrassment.

Raine's eyes softened. "I can understand that, Paul. But Violet. . ."

"That was another matter altogether," he admitted. "She just assumed. . .and I never bothered to correct her. I guess after what I'd been through, it just seemed like a nice change, me a respectable married man instead of. . ." He flushed.

"But you did know that Lucinda revealed the father's true identity after the child was born? Surely you heard. . ."

The look of relief on her brother's face was so profound, Raine knew he hadn't known until that moment.

"Oh Paul. All this time. . ."

"But Papa. . . ?"

"He was too guilty himself to be able to reconcile with you. I know that now. At the time, I thought you would come back as soon as you found out that you were absolved. I guess it just made it all the harder when I didn't hear from you. Oh Paul, I thought you were dead!" She finished with a sob, recalling those dark days. "Thank God He kept His hand on you all these years."

Paul nodded soberly. "I'll say amen to that." Then he paused. "Is that why you thought I stayed away? Because of Lucinda and the baby?"

She nodded. "Of course. Then when I found out your true identity, I assumed you were angry with Papa for hiding it from you. I didn't know anything about the espionage until Geoff told me."

"You know?" Paul stared at her. "Geoff—?"

Raine explained about her meeting with Geoff.

"So that's what happened." Paul shook his head. "I can't believe he's alive! Of course I forgive him—I know he had no idea what he was getting me into. I just wish the whole mess would end now."

"We've found each other. That's what counts. I promised Papa I'd bring you home to him."

Paul shook his head. "I can't. I can't go back to England. Why do you think I talk like an American now?"

It was true; she had noticed that he had wiped away all traces of a British accent. She shook her head.

"I'm not a free man, Raine." He set his jaw. "I won't be free until my name is cleared. I ran away to escape being hung along with those other fellows. That's why I never told anyone when I left for Colorado. Dag had found me in Boston, and I knew I had to get away. I even had all my mail sent to Denver, just in case he is still hunting me. It's a bit far to go to the post office, but I didn't want to lead anyone straight to my door."

She wanted to weep, but she pulled herself together.

"I hated to sneak away from Boston like that," Paul continued, "but I had to. That big galoot of a sailor was after me again, and I had to..."

Raine interrupted, "Is that who you meant when you said you were being pursued?"

"Yes. I'm so sorry you had to go through what you did. I never dreamed he would involve you, too."

"But what was he talking about, Paul? Why did he want those papers that you had put in the safe deposit box?"

"Because they proved his guilt and my innocence." Paul stared out the window. When he turned back to Raine, she was shocked at the pain revealed in his eyes. "It's another long story, Raine. The gist

303

of it is that I made a mess of things once again. And Christina. . ."

He fell silent.

"What happened, Paul?" Raine prompted gently.

He stood up, pacing in agitation. "One of the chaps that was accused of smuggling had gotten off from lack of evidence. He showed up on Ben's ship, as a crew member. I suspected that he was still up to no good—and he thought it was a big joke that I was still wanted for the crime for which he had escaped conviction. He kept threatening to notify the authorities in England, turn me in. But then I began to suspect that he was still up to his old tricks. While we were in port at Boston, I searched his cabin and I found papers hidden beneath his mattress. The papers were in code, but they were easy enough for me to decipher. They proved that I had never been involved in the espionage ring back in England—and they also proved Dag's guilt. I should have gone straight to Ben with the information, but I didn't. I wanted to be a hero. And then it was too late."

He sighed and fell silent for a moment before he continued. "I had spoken to an agent in New York. He promised me that if what I said was true, there would be hefty reward for my part in Dag's capture. I already had enough evidence to convict him of his part in the spy ring back in England, but I wanted proof that he was still up to his sneaky tricks. Anyway, I was going to go on one more voyage and see what I could catch him at, then be done with it. I would collect the reward, pay off Christina's agreement with her employer, and we'd head west together."

Raine nodded, totally absorbed as the pieces of the puzzle finally fell into place.

"I was going to whisk Christina away from that miserable hole she has to work in, and the two of us would start a new life together."

"But?"

"But it didn't work out that way. I was getting pretty cocky, and I think Dag started to become suspicious of me. Anyway, someone told Ben that I was involved in something underhanded. At the same time, Dag threatened to turn me into the English authorities, and I countered by telling him that I had information that proved my innocence and his guilt. That was my biggest mistake. I should have gone to Ben instead."

"Oh Paul."

"I could tell Ben wondered whether to trust me, but he didn't say anything, and I thought I would wait till the thing was over and done with and then I'd tell him."

So that's why Ben had seemed ambivalent toward Paul sometimes. "So Ben suspected the worst."

He shrugged. "I suppose so. After the *Aramathea* sank, I determined that no matter what, I would not be blamed for something I didn't do. I decided rather than risk going through what I had gone through before, I would just run away. Like I said, I'd been planning to go out west anyway, and I figured Ben would get the locket to you, so you'd know where I was. I hoped Ben would be able to clear my name for me, and then get word to me when it was safe to come back east. And I hoped you'd find me. . .maybe follow me."

Raine's heart felt as though it would break when she thought of Paul's loneliness and pain all these years, but she forced herself to say cheerfully, "Well, I did. It just took me a little longer than you'd thought, thanks to the seawater that destroyed most of your message in the locket."

Paul shook his head ruefully. "I thought I was being so clever. I knew I'd lost Christy. . .but I'd always hoped I hadn't lost you, too. I made plans to head west as soon as I returned."

"But where does Christina fit in?"

Paul's eyes took on a soft light. "Ah, Christina. We were so happy. We had big plans to come out west and live happily ever after on a huge ranch."

"What happened, Paul?" Raine felt her brother's pain as if it were her own. He closed his eyes. "She was so beautiful. I can still see her standing there waving to me as we left the harbor."

Paul turned wistfully from the railing, only to meet the blazing eyes of Dag.

"You're right about this being your last voyage, Oliver," Dag had whispered ominously. "I'll see to that."

Paul felt a quick chill of fear flutter through him, quickly replaced by anger. "Don't threaten me, Dag. Go do your job." Paul's voice was cool, but the look in the other sailor's eyes sent fear racing through him.

He watched Dag closely throughout the voyage, finding himself relaxing as each uneventful day slipped by. Then, waking to the shrill sound of the warning alarms and the frantic cries of passengers that fateful night, all thoughts of Dag disappeared.

He shook his head. "It all happened so fast, Ray. I gave the locket to Ben, with the message inside that would tell you to go see Violet and then look for me in Colorado, and then we began doing what we could to make sure everyone got into a lifeboat safely. I was helping a young woman with a baby into the lifeboat, when I felt a horrible sensation crawl up my spine. I whirled around, but it was too late."

Raine was stunned. "He pushed you off the ship?"

Paul nodded, his face haggard. "After he slashed my face with his dagger. I think he was aiming for my heart, but I ducked. . .anyway, while I was still reeling from the blow, he gave me a shove over the railing. I clung to him, tried to tell him it wouldn't do any good, since the papers that proved his guilt were safe in a bank, but it was useless of course. I felt myself drop, and the floats in my life preserver caught me under the chin when I hit the water. I was lucky not to have broken my neck. When I came to, I was too far away to get aboard any of the lifeboats." He brushed at the moisture forming in his eyes. "That was the first time I had called out to God in a long, long time."

Raine felt tears prick her own eyes. "How did you make it back to Boston?"

He smiled sadly. "I guess God didn't think it was my time to go yet. Another ship picked me up at dawn. I had pretty much decided I was going to die out there, but here I am."

"I can't believe all of this, Paul." Raine shook her head in amazement. "So then you went back to Violet's, and she nursed you back to health. Then what? Why didn't you let Ben know you had survived? And what about Christina? Why did you leave her?"

Paul shrugged. "I don't know. I was kind of confused, maybe from the blow I took on my head." He stared out the window again.

"I was feeling some better and decided to go see Christina. She stared at me like I was a ghost when I hobbled in."

Paul smiled as he remembered the look on her face. "She had heard about the ship and assumed I was dead when I was not brought back in with the other crew members. We decided to get married as soon as I was well.

"And, I was taking a walk a day or two later. Violet always got after me to get some fresh air."

Raine smiled, picturing the kindly old lady ordering her brother around.

"Anyway, I saw him, Raine."

"Who, Dag?"

"Yes. Maybe it was an accident that I ran into him, maybe he was checking to make sure I was really dead. Anyway, I knew he now knew that I had survived, and he was after me. I was sure that sooner or later he would try to kill me again. I was afraid he would even hurt Christina." His forehead wrinkled. "Actually, there were two men following me. I have no idea who the second man was, and I never saw him at the same time I saw Dag."

"He wasn't out to harm you, Paul." Raine smiled at his startled look. "Papa had a man trailing you."

Paul stared at his sister incredulously. "Why?"

"He still loves you, Paul. He is longing for your forgiveness."

Paul opened his mouth to speak, then snapped it shut, shaking his head in disbelief.

"Anyway, so you left Boston in the middle of the night to escape from Dag. Why didn't you take Christina with you?" Raine changed the subject tactfully, sensing that Paul was not yet ready to talk about their father.

"I panicked, Ray. I knew by then that Dag was serious about killing me, since he had already tried once. I left that night, intending to either sneak back to get Christina in a few days or send for her to come to me."

Raine winced at the pain written across her brother's face.

"By the time I arrived in Colorado, I had myself convinced that I was worthless. My name was muddied, my father accused me of something that he was guilty of, my sister hated me, and a man was trying to kill me. On top of all that, I was a liar and a drunk who had turned his back on God. I couldn't ask someone like Christina to share life with me."

Paul stared at his sister wistfully. "All these years, I've been hating myself for leaving her, hating myself for making such a mess of my life, trying to get up enough courage to contact her again and see if she still loves me. Finally, I decided that by now she has found someone else."

Raine dropped her gaze, feeling like an intruder as she witnessed the raw agony in her brother's eyes. "Do you remember the time I told you that Christina would wait for you until the end of the world?"

He raised his head to stare at his sister.

She smiled. "She's still waiting, Paul."

Chapter 12

Raine lay awake for hours, reliving the reunion with Paul. She had to smile as she recalled the look on his face when she had handed him the small package from Christina. He had not opened it, but held it in his hands lovingly. She guessed he would open it in private, and she didn't begrudge him that at all.

She sighed. There were still so many unanswered questions. Was Dag still tracking Paul? She was loathe to mention her suspicions to her brother, but she could not forget the whispered conversation she had heard on the train, nor the chill of fear it still sent down her spine whenever she thought of it. True, she had seen no sign of the red-haired sailor in the weeks she had been in Colorado, but. . .

Father, thank You for finally leading me to Paul! You are so good to me. Please show me how to minister to him, Lord. His soul is still so wounded. Give me wisdom, Father, and protect us from this evil man Dag. And Father, please bring Ben back to me!

Despite her joy of finding Paul, lonely tears escaped down Raine's cheeks as she ached for Ben's strong arms around her. *Please come back to me, my love. . .*

∞

"Crooked P Ranch sure is a busy place these days, I'll say." Jackson said when Ben asked him to drive him out to the ranch.

"Why do you say that, Jackson?" Ben asked absently, his mind on other matters.

"Well, first I took that pretty little schoolmarm out there a couple of days ago. Then just this morning I took a big ol' feller out there. Said he was an old friend of Tom's. Didn't look very friendly to me, but I reckon that's none of my business."

Ben glanced at Jackson. Something made him ask, "What did the man look like?"

"Big ol' feller, like I said. Hair as orange as carrots and a big tattoo on his hand."

Dag again. Ben found it hard to believe that the man would trail Raine all the way from London, but it had to be him. He blew out his breath.

"Jackson, I think we're going to run into some trouble at the Crooked P. Are you still game to drive me out there?"

The old rancher's eyes sparkled. He patted his hip. "Got my trusty pistol right here, Mr. Ben. Let's go."

Ben perched tensely on the edge of the wagon seat, thinking back over the past few weeks. Raine's aunt and uncle had received a letter from Raine the same day Violet had received one from Paul. Violet had smiled through her tears. "He finally wrote! Paul is alive!"

Ben had read Paul's and Raine's letters, filled with joy, wishing only that there had been a letter for him. . . . A jolt of the wagon brought Ben back to the present.

"Just one of them prairie dog holes," Jackson mumbled.

Ben stared at the rolling plains, praying for wisdom. "All right, this is our plan, Jackson. When we get about a mile away from the ranch house, we're going to have to abandon the wagon and go the rest of the way on foot."

Ben related the rest of the plan, fear threatening to cloud his good sense as he realized what they might be stepping into. He took a deep breath. "If you're a praying man, now's the time to pray, Jackson," he said grimly.

Grasping his pistol tightly, Ben closed his eyes for a moment, taking deep breaths. Abruptly, his eyes flew open. *"I will never leave thee, nor forsake thee."* The words of scripture came from nowhere, flooding through him like great calming waves. "Thank You, God," he whispered.

Jackson jerked the wagon to a halt behind a small rise. "Ranch house is just over that hill," he whispered. "Are you ready?"

Ben nodded. "This is it." The two men swung silently to the ground. Ben helped the older man tether the team, praying that the horses wouldn't whinny and give away their presence. The men parted ways with a grim handshake. "Remember, if we can just make it inside the house, we'll be able to pull this off. God go with you, Jackson."

Crawling quietly through the tall prairie grass, Ben's heart was pounding crazily. He and Jackson had decided to take separate routes to the ranch house in hopes that if one was seen, the other would still have a chance. *Please, Father, don't let us be too late.* He shook his head, refusing to imagine what was happening behind the closed door of the ranch house.

∞

Raine sat motionless, tears flowing steadily down her cheeks and soaking into the rag that was gagging her. She longed to cover her ears, but could not get her hands loose from the tightly tied knots. She winced as another cry sounded from the bedroom. *Father, please don't let him kill Paul! Please deliver us somehow!*

It had all happened in a flash. Raine awoke to Dag standing over her, a knife at her throat. He had forced her into the kitchen where Paul already sat, ashen-faced. Dag bound Raine to a chair, then gleefully waved the dog-eared photo of Raine in front of his captives. "I always knew this would lead me to you, Oliver. You thought everything was lost in the shipwreck, didn't you?"

Paul blanched.

"Well, it just so happens that your precious captain left this behind in his hurry to do his duty. All I had to do was wait until he led me to the beautiful lady in this photograph." Dag sneered at Raine. "And sure enough, she led me straight to you. It took awhile but that doesn't really matter much anymore, does it?"

Raine stared at the man's twisted face. His eyes blazed, and she realized then that it was madness she saw gleaming in his eyes. He had yielded so long to his obsession of hatred and revenge that he had become insane. Why else would he have pursued her and Paul so long and so far?

Whirling suddenly, Dag untied Paul without another word and led him into the bedroom. For twenty minutes now there had been curses and blows intermingled with unspeakable cries as Dag struck Paul repeatedly. She stared out the window helplessly, not even knowing how to pray. Surely God wouldn't let them die at the hands of this man, after bringing them this far.

She watched the midmorning sun shimmering on the plains. Watched as the ranch hands poured out of the bunkhouse and headed in the direction of the corrals, too far away to hear the commotion going on in the ranch house. How odd that everything seemed to be going on as normal, except inside this house. Her thoughts drifted as she tried not to think of what might happen next.

What was that? Raine's eye had caught a flash of movement just above the windowsill. She watched the spot intently, finally rewarded as she saw another swift flutter of. . .what was it? Cautiously thumping her feet once on the floor, she kept her eyes glued on the window.

∽

Ben knelt beneath the window, his blood pounding in his temples. Taking a deep breath, he started to rise when he heard a small thump.

Just do it, Thackeray, he commanded himself. Springing up, he started as he met Raine's frightened gaze. He collapsed under the window. *She's still alive! Thank You, God!* Even in his quick glance into the room, he knew that she was alone, at least for the moment. Standing up cautiously, he mouthed the words. "Where is he?"

Raine jerked her head toward the bedroom, her eyes now aglow with hope.

"I love you." Ben mouthed, rewarded as he saw her eyes soften in answer. Ducking back down, he flattened himself against the wall, inching his way around to the other side of the house. His heart leapt as he saw Jackson already there, listening intently with his head pressed against the wall.

"God is truly with us, Jackson," Ben said softly. He told him of finding Raine alone in the kitchen. "I think we can make it into the house through that door." He nodded toward the kitchen door. "Ol' Dag is swearing so loudly he won't hear us anyway." As if on cue, the big sailor let loose a stream of foul language, followed by several loud crashes.

Ben grimaced. "We'd better hurry!"

He peered cautiously through the kitchen window, relieved that Raine was still alone. Stealthily, the men slid through the door. Ben hurriedly cut the ropes that bound Raine. Jerking the filthy rag out of her mouth, he couldn't help himself and brushed a tender kiss across her swollen lips.

Taking a swift inventory of the minuscule kitchen, he pushed her toward the pantry. "Get in there and don't come out until I tell you it's safe," he whispered, giving her a longing glance.

∽

Raine sat silently amid the jars, cans, and bottles, praying as never before. *God, protect Ben and Jackson. Show them what to do. Protect Paul, please Father. Deliver us from this horrible man. . . Jesus, help us!* She covered her head involuntarily as a shot rang out. Hearing nothing more, she stood up carefully, but her still-numb legs betrayed her. Her knees buckled, and she sent a shower of jars to the floor as she tried to keep from falling. She stood clinging to the shelf, her heart in her mouth as she heard heavy footsteps approaching. She stifled a scream as the door jerked open, then suddenly she was in Ben's arms. Weak with relief, she clung to him tightly.

"Shh, it's all over now, kitten. You're safe," he murmured comfortingly.

"Don't ever leave me again, Ben," she sobbed, the emotions of the lonely weeks and months pouring out uncontrollably.

"I'm right here, honey." Ben smoothed her hair back tenderly. "I love you, Raine," he whispered.

Raine nodded her head against his chest, relishing the feeling of safety that came from being in his arms at last.

"Hey, little sister. Don't I get a hug too?" Raine jerked away from Ben at the sound of Paul's weak voice.

"Oh, Paul!" The tears flowed anew at the sight of her brother's battered face. "What did he do to you?"

"I've had worse." Paul tried to smile. "I just don't have Violet to cluck over me this time."

"Well, you have me," Raine said firmly. "If you think Violet was tough, you haven't seen anything yet."

"Yes ma'am." Paul rolled his eyes. "I assume you know what

you're getting yourself in for, Ben?"

"What?" Raine felt the blood rise to her cheeks. "What do you mean by that?"

Paul smiled. "I've got eyes in my head, Ray, even if they are a little swollen at the moment. When are you two going to tie the knot?"

Raine's cheeks grew even rosier. She glanced at Ben. "Well, I . . ." She jumped as someone behind her cleared his throat loudly.

"Guess I'll be getting back to town, now." Jackson grinned. "Looks like ya'll don't need me any more."

Ben smiled as he watched Jackson saunter away. "That man was sent by God for us today," he said seriously. "I wouldn't be surprised if He's got some big plans for him."

"Well, I know someone who has some big plans for you, Captain." Paul grinned at his sister. "Just get me a cold rag for my poor face, then go take care of Ben, Ray."

Raine obeyed her brother with a sparkle in her eye. After seeing him tucked in bed to her satisfaction, she turned to Ben shyly. Ben smiled down at her, then turned to Paul.

"I almost forgot! A lovely young lady in Boston asked me to deliver this to you." He flipped a letter onto Paul's bed, smiling at the eagerness on Paul's face. "And by the way—you're a free man now. The authorities took the information in those papers you left me and put it together with clues they'd received from other sources. They reached the conclusion that you were innocent of espionage." He grinned at the dazed look on Paul's face. "I said I'd pass this along to you."

Paul took the official-looking paper and nodded absently, but he was already opening the letter from Christina.

Ben smiled at Raine, offering her his arm. "Shall we leave him alone now?"

She returned his smile and nodded.

Once outside the kitchen door, Ben couldn't stand it any longer. Drawing Raine eagerly into his arms, he kissed her deeply.

She clung to him, heady with joy. "This is where I belong," she murmured, snuggling deeper into his arms.

Ben held her tenderly, his heart overflowing. "I love you, Raine Thomas."

"And I love you." She looked up at him, her eyes sparkling with joy. "I missed you so much, Ben. I prayed and prayed that God would bring you back to me."

Ben nodded. "I prayed the same thing. I was so hurt when I thought you didn't trust me. I came out here to find Paul, but instead, God found me."

Raine stared at his joyful face. "What do you mean, Ben? I thought you had already given your life to Christ in Boston."

"I did, Raine," he assured her. "It's just that I didn't know what God wanted me to do with the rest of my life." He hesitated. "I would love to ask you to be my wife, Raine, but I have to be honest with you. God has called me to stay here in Colorado and start a church for the ranchers."

Raine could only smile at him.

"Could you live here the rest of your life, Raine?" His voice was low.

Raine finally found her voice. "Ben," she whispered, "God has called me to stay here, too. I'm going to teach at the school for the rancher's children!"

Ben looked at her wonderingly. He took her face into his hands, staring tenderly into her beautiful eyes. "Then, will you spend the rest of your life with me, Raine, and be my wife?"

Raine's yes was joyful and full of promise, for she knew that God would continue to lead her along unfamiliar paths, making the crooked ways straight.

Amy Rognlie is an author and teacher, who, like the characters in her book, has traveled many unfamiliar and unexpected paths in the course of her life. She has seen God's faithfulness every step of the way, and wants her readers to know that no matter what circumstances look like, God is good. Amy and her family live in Central Texas, where she teaches language arts and Latin, writes Bible studies and Sunday School curriculum, and is involved in ministry in her local church and community.

COMING SOON

Journey of the Heart
by
DIANN MILLS

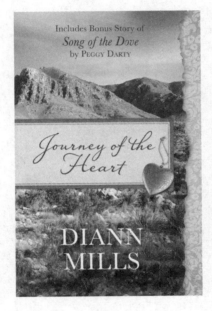

Available wherever Christian books are sold.